Scott Speer is a movie and music video director and a graduate of the University of Southern California's School of Cinematic Arts. He directed *Step Up Revolution* and has worked with Will.I.Am, Jordin Sparks, Paris Hilton, Ashley Tisdale and other Hollywood personalities. He is also the author of the Immortal City series. Scott lives in Los Angeles, California.

www.ImmortalCitySeries.com

BATTLE ANGEL

AN IMMORTAL CITY NOVEL

SCOTT SPEER

SCHOLASTIC

Scholastic Children's Books
An imprint of Scholastic Ltd
Euston House, 24 Eversholt Street
London, NW1 1DB, UK
Registered office: Westfield Road, Southam, Warwickshire, CV47 0RA
SCHOLASTIC and associated logos are trademarks and or registered
trademarks of Scholastic Inc.

First published in the US by Penguin Young Readers Group, Penguin Book Ltd., 2014
This edition published by Scholastic Ltd, 2014

Text copyright © Scott Speer, 2014

The right of Scott Speer to be identified as the author of this work has been asserted by him.

ISBN 978 1407 13314 0

A CIP catalogue record for this work is available from the British Library.

Printed in the UK by CPI Group (UK) Ltd, Croydon, CR0 4YY
Papers used by Scholastic are made from wood grown in sustainable forests.

This is a work of fiction. Names, characters, places, incidents and dialogues are products of
the author's imagination or are used fictitiously. Any resemblance to actual people, living
or dead, events or locales is entirely coincidental.

www.scholastic.co.uk

CHAPTER 1

There was everything to say, and there was nothing. But the silence that filled the moment was strangely peaceful, Maddy thought. The push and pull of the water against the pier pilings. Flagpoles making that familiar rope-on-metal clanging sound in the breeze. It could have been an altogether pleasant moment, if only she didn't have to say anything. But this moment couldn't last. Finally, Maddy knew it was time to speak. And what she was about to say would change everything.

She looked between the pairs of expectant eyes that looked back at her, the two stares that waited for her answer. The piercing blue eyes belonged to Jackson Godspeed, whose gaze was familiar yet still so thrilling to her. Though she had known Jacks for two years now, she really had never gotten used to the way that glance could pierce straight through her and see the real, vulnerable girl inside her. Jacks's gaze was perfect, *too* perfect, all blue fire and insufferable beauty. It was divine, something more than human. It was the gaze of a Guardian Angel. His eyes made her feel breathless, made her pulse go wild, and had always made her feel – in some way she couldn't quite understand – not quite good enough.

She turned to meet the other expectant gaze. These eyes were green, watchful and kind. They were newer to her, and yet, strangely, she felt somehow more at ease with them. This was Tom Cooper, who had come into her life at a time when she thought she was utterly alone in this world. Tom's gaze felt like patience and soft vanilla, like sinking into a warm bath at the end of a long day. It would never spark with the blue electricity of Jacks's, but maybe that was all right. Tom's eyes were human eyes, and being held in his gaze was the closest thing Maddy had ever felt to home.

She thought if there was some way to bottle this moment and live in it for ever, she would jump at the chance. To live in a constant state of about-to-answer, where neither Tom nor Jacks would know the truth, both hoping for the answer they heard in their heads, the answer each expected. In this moment, Maddy didn't have to break someone's heart. In this moment, there seemed to be a strange sense of balance. But it was a balance that could not last.

Maddy shook off her reverie and took in the two figures in front of her. The aircraft carrier holding the fighter jets floated behind them as both Jacks and Tom turned to face one another with jaws clenched, fists at the ready, as if looking to each other for Maddy's answer. Between them, Maddy formed the tip of a triangle, and she was the only thing that was keeping them from crashing into each other in anger and fury.

Time stretched out like a blade. There was Tom in his olive flight suit. A hero. A *human* hero. He looked handsome. Perfect, even. What more could she ask for? Then she looked at Jacks in his black battle armour, mechanical wings flexed and ready, gleaming in the sunshine. Jacks was no longer perfect. His journey with her – *because* of her – had altered him. Studying those sleek, man-made wings, Maddy knew the Jacks she had met at the diner was

2

gone for ever.

But couldn't the same be said about Maddy? Was it really just a coat she was wearing? A coat that she could take off in the end and still be the same girl underneath? Or had the training and the embrace of this new Angel's life changed her? Had she allowed herself to be altered, in the way that couldn't be undone? The answer dawned on her bitterly, just like when she thought about those mechanical wings. The answer was yes. Just like Jacks, Maddy Montgomery, waitress and high school student, was gone, too. They had both been affected, irreparably wounded, and now they bore the scars of their journeys. Some journeys change us for ever, and the idea filled Maddy with a sudden, welling sadness. There was no going back. There was only going forward now. It was time to choose, not just between mortal and Immortal, but also between two worlds.

She couldn't keep stalling. It was time to speak. The moment of about-to-answer had slipped away and was gone. Life was like that. A series of fleeting moments. Maddy faced the two guys who would do anything to protect her, who would fight for her. Maybe even die for her. She'd made her decision. It was the only decision she *could* make. With a sick feeling, she parted her lips and let a word fall out.

"Jacks." She said his name but couldn't look at him. "I can't go with you."

Her voice sounded very far away.

"I choose Tom."

CHAPTER 2

Had she really just said that? Whatever just happened, it was too late to take it back. Life can pivot on a single choice, a pinpoint of time, causing ripples of consequences to circle out endlessly. Now she watched the ripples of her decision engulf and transform everything they touched.

They reached Jacks's face first, warping it out of shape, twisting his Immortal features into an ugliness Maddy didn't want to look at, but couldn't bear not to. Jacks took an almost imperceptible step back, as if the decision were a physical weight that he had to strain against as it pushed him backward. Before the anger came and clouded over his face, Maddy caught the glimpse of another emotion as it flashed across his features. She saw it around the corners of his eyes, and it was impossible to miss. Helplessness. A glimmer of the Jacks whom she had left standing on the platform at Union Station, the Angel who had been on top of the library tower with the demon. It was the Jacks who had watched her go at the viewpoint. *Betrayal is worst for the betrayer*, Maddy thought.

The ripple wave struck Tom next. In Tom's eyes, Maddy saw someone plunging into the waters of baptism, as if a new life force surged around him. He looked reborn. If the ripple had knocked Jacks back, it seemed to buoy Tom, making him stronger, making him stand taller. Maddy looked away.

4

Why was it that she felt compelled to wallow in Jacks's gaze of helplessness, rather than soak in Tom's triumph? Why couldn't she focus on the elation in Tom's eyes? What was wrong with her? Was she afraid of what she would feel? Was she afraid she wouldn't be able to mirror his unbridled happiness? Maybe it was that meeting Tom's gaze would confirm something even worse: that she *was* happy. That she was just as happy as he was.

"Maddy, you're not one of them," Jacks said in that hoarse, bargaining tone, the one that she had heard him use on the train platform. "Listen to me. I have somewhere you can go. Where you'll be safe. With us."

Before she could answer, Tom did it for her.

"She made her choice. Have the decency to respect it." His voice rang with the confidence that comes with victory. "Not that I expect decency from an Angel."

Maddy saw muscles twitch inside Jacks's armour, but the Angel stayed put.

"You don't understand," Jacks said slowly, carefully, enunciating every syllable. "This is an army that cannot be defeated. At least, not like this." He pointed at the massive carrier. Up on the deck, the soldiers had their rifles trained on him, itchy fingers ready at the triggers.

"We're pretty good in a fight," Tom said, his jaw set.

"This isn't a just a 'fight.' This is an extermination. An enslavement."

"No one's making a slave out of me," Tom growled.

"They will. Before this is over, you will beg for your own death. Or, if you're a coward, which I have a feeling you are,

5

you'll beg for mercy and happily become a slave." Jacks's eyes narrowed.

In a flash Tom was on him, grabbing at Jacks's armour, thrusting his forearms against Jacks's chest. Jacks had his hands around Tom's throat before Maddy even saw them move. She heard a wet gurgle as the air was forced out of the pilot's throat.

"Get back! Get back!" shouted a soldier from the carrier deck.

Maddy screamed. "Jacks, no!" Yet even as the words came out of her mouth, she knew Tom wasn't in danger. Jacks could have killed Tom in the time it took the soldiers on the carrier to react. Even in his rage, he was choosing to restrain himself. *For me*, Maddy thought. *Because he cares about me.*

The soldier shouted again. "Get back or you will be fired upon!" Maddy watched Jackson eye the carrier, then slowly release his grip, leaving Tom gasping on his knees. Maddy took a step towards Tom, but he waved her back, almost violently.

"I'm fine," he sputtered, and stood.

Hate and anger radiated off Jackson. And something else as well, Maddy thought. Fear. Fear for her?

"The humans can't win," Jacks said, his expression hard. "Make the smart choice, Maddy."

"What about Uncle Kevin? What about Gwen?" Maddy's voice came out almost as a wail.

"Why don't you ask your president-elect?" Jacks shot back, then caught himself and softened. "Linden made their choice for them already, Maddy. It's too late for them to be helped. But it's not too late for you."

"*Everyone* can be helped."

"No! There is *no hope*!" Jacks's voice was raw, naked.

"There is *always* hope," Maddy cried. "And even when there's not, we still stand with each other, because that's what people do." Maddy looked to Tom, who had quietly lifted a hand to tell the soldiers to stand down. He returned her gaze. Resolute. Determined.

"Explain that logic to me," Jacks grumbled.

"It's not *logical*," Maddy said. "It's human."

"*You* are not human!" Jacks roared. "You are a Guardian Angel! You belong with us!"

"My place is by my uncle's side. By Kevin's side. By Tom's side. My place is beside anyone who isn't strong enough to protect themselves. My place is beside anyone I can help." Maddy was gasping for air. "That is the true purpose of the Angels."

Jacks shook his head. "Your human side . . ." he muttered to himself. Then he looked to Tom. "They turned their backs on us, Maddy," Jacks said. "We don't owe them that. *You* don't owe them that. We don't owe them anything."

"Spoken like a true Immortal. You've got quite a sense of duty, *Guardian*," Tom quipped.

Jacks ignored him and instead did something Maddy didn't expect. The anger in his face flickered away, leaving only that raw helplessness Maddy had glimpsed before. Jacks let the helplessness wash over him and fill out his features completely.

"Please, Maddy," Jacks said quietly. "Why don't you get it?"

He was whispering now.

"I can't lose you."

7

Even Tom's confidence seemed to waver for a moment. There the Battle Angel stood, guard down and emotionally naked. Jacks looked at Maddy, and Maddy felt herself being pulled into one of their moments, where the outside world just slipped away, leaving only the two of them. She could *not* let it happen. She set her feet, moved her shoulders back, and pushed the words out in breathy, raw bursts as a new tidal wave of emotion broke over her.

"I will always cherish what we had, Jackson, but I don't feel that way about you any more. Too much has changed. *You* have changed. And my place is here with Tom." She stood firm as a sudden sea gust blew her hair forward and whipped it around her face. "I love him," she whispered.

Jacks flinched and spoke through his teeth. "I will not come for you. Neither will any of the others. The demons will make sure you're torn apart. Limb by limb. Your wings will be ripped out of your back—"

"That's enough, Godspeed!" Tom barked. Maddy felt Jacks's words prickling her skin all over. *Torn. Ripped.*

Jacks yelled. "You are choosing death, Maddy!"

"Then I choose it!" Maddy choked, and the tears finally spilled over. She didn't bother to stop them. "This is my decision." She reached out to him and let her fingers rest on the armour covering his arm.

Jacks pulled his arm away as if she had burned him. Shocked, Maddy watched as something changed behind his eyes. An *uncoupling*. Just then, an image jumped into Maddy's head, of a train that uncouples from a car and leaves it behind on the track.

Before, whenever Jacks was angry with her or felt betrayed by her, his eyes had always burned with a kind of frustrated loyalty, a refusal to give up on her. But Maddy saw now that those fires had been snuffed out. She watched, helpless, as Jacks unlinked her from his life, and from his heart. It only took an instant, and it gutted her completely. Jacks's eyes were cold now and held nothing for her. She knew it just as sure as she knew anything.

She had done it. She had lost him.

"It's time for you to go now," Tom said, his tone even, or as even as it could be after Jacks's vice-like grip around his throat.

"Don't worry, I'm going," Jacks said. Maddy lifted her gaze to meet his, and for the first time, it wasn't waiting for her. "There's nothing for me here."

And without saying anything more, Jacks rocketed into the sky, robotic wings hissing through the air, and was gone.

Maddy felt a gentle warmth as Tom took her hands in his.

"Maddy? Will you look at me, please?" Maddy realized her face was still turned up to where Jacks had disappeared into the sky. She turned and met the green eyes that were waiting for her.

"Are you OK?" Tom asked. Maddy was done being strong. The fearless Guardian Godright was all used up, and only the vulnerable Maddy Montgomery was left.

"I'm so afraid, Tom," she said, her voice small. "If something happens to you—"

"I'll be fine." Tom smiled. "I've got you. That's all I need."

Maddy's smile was tight, and her throat was closing in. Her cheeks were hot and wet. The truth, Maddy thought. What was the truth, anyway? The truth was that no one knew what to expect.

Not even Jacks. Not even the Angels. So why did she *know* he was right? They couldn't win. What had Jacks called it? Not a fight, an *extermination*. An enslavement.

Just then, Maddy became aware that they were no longer alone. The dock had filled with sudden life as the carrier and the soldiers prepared to leave port. Families were saying goodbye to their loved ones, wishing farewell to fathers, mothers, brothers, sisters. Children. She wanted to know what was going through their heads. Did they feel hopeful? Were they scared? She wondered what Tom was thinking, too. In her mind, there was only the ringing of Jacks's words. *An extermination.*

Maddy put on her bravest face.

"Take care of yourself," she managed.

"I better." Tom grinned. "I have to get back to you."

He kissed her, and Maddy kissed him back, but it felt strange on her lips. Not like a kiss of love. A kiss of goodbye.

And before she could process the feeling, he was gone. She stood alone as Tom walked towards the gangplank, eventually disappearing into a small sea of officers and sailors. It was all Maddy could do to fight the awful feeling that she would never see him again. She closed her eyes and tried to push the thought away. She listened to the wind. To the clanging rope-on-metal sound of the flagpole. To the flap of the flag. She opened her eyes to find it was the American flag that was flying, the Stars and Stripes. She hadn't noticed until just then, but there it was, fluttering overhead on this near-perfect day. This, she realized, might be one of the last. Very soon, there might not be any more nice days for Angel City. Only time would tell what they were in for.

At least she had done it. She had to focus on that. She could hold on to that, couldn't she? She had come here today to tell Jacks it was all over, that it was Tom who had stolen her heart, whom she had fallen in love with. She had told Jacks she didn't love him any more. She had done it.

So what if it wasn't true?

CHAPTER 3

In the car, the tears came again. She still hated the feeling of the hot liquid spilling over her cheeks, the quiet *dap dap* as the tears found her jeans. Crying made her feel weak. But she couldn't do anything to stop it. Holding on to the wheel with one hand, she pulled her sleeve over her palm and wiped her face with the other. This, she thought, was a very human moment: driving and crying at the same time. She wondered how many trips people had taken in tears, having to balance those two things, steering with one hand and wiping with the other. It should be called *cryving*, Maddy thought. She should trademark it. She gave a crooked half-smile through her tears.

Maddy turned on to an on-ramp to send her gleaming Audi racing down to the freeway. But she was stopped at the entrance by a National Guard roadblock.

Two soldiers holding machine guns and wearing Kevlar helmets stood there in front of a Humvee.

"I'm sorry, miss, but by order of the governor we have closed off all freeways to all nonemergency vehicles. Any citizens who are still in the area are advised to seek shelter and await further instructions."

Maddy pulled her sunglasses off and tried to smile at the soldier. It was funny; she had always thought using the *Do you know who I am?* move to get something you want was a terrible abuse of Angel celebrity, but she needed to get back to Kevin.

And it worked; another soldier off to the side lit up in recognition.

"It's Maddy Montgomery!" the soldier said.

"I just got here," Maddy said. "I need to get back to Angel City. How could I know you'd be blocking the freeways?"

The first soldier looked unsure, but the second one, who was obviously an Angel fan, approached and intervened.

"Let her through, Ernesto," the second soldier said. Maddy tried to maintain the smile, even though on the inside she was crumbling with sadness and fear.

"I don't know . . ." the first soldier, Ernesto, said. But the second soldier was already moving the barricade.

Maddy shot him a *thank you* wave and stepped on the gas pedal before the soldier could change his mind. As she zipped down the on-ramp, she peered out the windshield at a sight she had never seen before. The Angel City Freeway was completely empty. It was eerie. And just another reminder that this was not a normal day. Because normal days were over. The massive five-lane freeway looked naked with no traffic, no honking drivers, no cars changing lanes without signaling first. Deserted, Maddy thought, just like the humans. And empty, just like she felt. There was a strange silence to driving down this empty open stretch, with only the hum of her car and the whistle of the wind to remind her she was alive. If she closed her eyes, she would be able to convince herself she wasn't driving at all. She could be running. Nowhere in particular, just running away.

She switched on the radio and heard nothing but a long, monotonous tone for several seconds before a voice broke in.

"This is not a test," an electronic female voice announced. "This is the Emergency Broadcast System. A state of emergency has been declared. All residents of Angel City and immediate areas are ordered to stay indoors at this time. A citywide curfew has been put in place—"

Maddy switched the station. The message continued. "I repeat, this is not a test. Emergency shelters are located at—"

Maddy switched the station again. Same thing. Every station was broadcasting it. When the message ended, it simply started over again. Something about that message made this whole situation even more real. Made it worse. She listened to the robotic voice play again and again. *This is not a test. This is not a test.* She glanced up at the sky, which was beginning to darken. The sunny day was growing dim as a grey blanket of clouds stretched over the city. Wind gusts shot past the Audi now, almost shrieking. What was going to happen? What kind of hell were they in for? Gradually Maddy began to recognize her all-too-familiar surroundings. She was headed towards the heart of Angel City – home. She pulled her fingers through her hair and wiped her puffy eyes. The exit for Angel Boulevard approached, and she pulled on to the off-ramp.

Angel City, Maddy thought darkly. It was both the place she had always dreamed of leaving and the place that seemed destined to keep her. Every time she had tried to escape it, something about it only drew her back in. She felt caught in its web of criss-crossing streets, the allure of its bright downtown lights. It was capital city to the Immortals, and the unrivalled symbol of Angels and their power around the world. More than a city, it was an idea. It was synonymous with wealth, celebrity, and power – the perfect icon to represent the lavish Angel lifestyle that most of the world envied and craved. Maddy swung down Highland, passing under glowing billboards showing famous Angels selling handbags, cars and perfume. On one of the billboards was her own face, smiling seductively and holding a bottle of Chanel perfume. Maddy felt her stomach turn. On any other day, she wouldn't have been able to bear looking at it, but now she couldn't look away. Someone had spray-painted *TRAITOR* over her face in an angry red scrawl.

She drove down the world-famous Angel Boulevard, past the tourist shops and the Walk of Angels. Angel Stars blurred by on the pavement. How many millions of people had come from all over the world to pose next to those stars and take pictures with them? She used to weave around those tourists on her way to school, wondering how anyone could care so much about a sidewalk. Now she had an Angel Star of her own; now her name was etched in gleaming gold in the ground. It still felt strange. *She was a famous Guardian Angel. The* most *famous Guardian Angel.* She shook her head, thinking of how much she had wanted to just leave two years ago. Would she ever get out of this city? Maybe the bigger question was, would she ever get Angel City out of *her?* She used to think so, but now she wasn't so sure. Just as the ground had been etched with her name, she felt the city had been etched on her, too. As permanently as a tattoo. The tourist shops were all closed up now. No plastic wings for sale. No T-shirts with slogans like SAVE ME! or PROTECTION. The metal doors were all rolled shut.

Maddy squinted as she looked down the street through her windshield. There was life up ahead, a crowd gathered around the Temple of Angels. The last thing Maddy wanted right now was to be recognized. She sank down in her seat as she approached, but she couldn't help but ease up on the gas and look as she passed. In spite of the danger that was close at hand, a grab bag of fans, thrill seekers, and stranded tourists had gathered outside the temple in a bizarre, circus-like display. Several people stood in a huddle, holding a candlelight vigil. Others danced. Still others fought. There were young Angel-crazy girls, Angel experts, and families. There was even a man wearing nothing but a white loincloth, Rollerblades and neon sunglasses. He had taped styrofoam wings to his back and rolled around the crowd while others tried not to stare at his loincloth. It seemed the die-hard Angel fans had already managed to splinter themselves into even smaller categories. One group appeared to be anti-Maddy, calling her a traitor to the Angels, while another equally sized group held up signs that glorified Maddy and praised her for being a "true" Angel. Maddy groaned. It was worse than she'd thought. She cut the wheel and swung up a side street to avoid the rest of it.

As she turned off Angel Boulevard, a familiar sign came into view. Although it was off, she could still make out the neon lettering against the fading paint. *Kevin's*. Her uncle's diner, where she had worked all through high school. And the place where she had met Jacks. It was dark inside now. No one sat in the booths; no food was being served. How could it have been just two years ago that she was a waitress there? It felt like another lifetime. She pulled past the diner and into the driveway of her uncle's house just past the restaurant. She looked up at the small, two-storey bungalow where she grew up. The simple, aging house stood bravely in the gusts of the oncoming weather. With all that had changed in her life, there had always been this dependable house. A companion. A friend. An island of consistency in the ever-changing sea of time. She cut the Audi's engine and stepped out.

There was Kevin, standing in the doorway, his face creased with concern. He wore old jeans and a worn, flannel shirt – his uniform.

"You're back," he said, and Maddy could tell he was trying not to appear like he had worried too much. He searched Maddy's face with his intelligent grey eyes. "And . . . Tom?"

"He's gone," Maddy said, trying to keep her voice steady. "The fleet is going to fight."

Kevin's face darkened. After a moment, he nodded.

"Jacks was there, too," Maddy added.

"What?" Kevin's tone took on a harshness. "What did he want?" Kevin's opinion of Jacks had been like a roller-coaster ride over the past two years. Of course, he didn't care for Angels on principle, and had downright hated them after what happened to his sister. He had done his best to give Jacks a chance when it became clear that he was in Maddy's life, like it or not. But now he had hardened his heart towards Immortals once again. Kevin was pro-Maddy until the bitter end. He would do his best to support her in whatever she wanted, despite his own reservations or opinions. It was the reason why Maddy loved Kevin so much.

"He offered me a choice," Maddy said quietly. "To go with him and the other Angels."

"I see. . . . Well, what did you say?"

Maddy bit her lip. How would Kevin feel about her decision? She might be the most famous Guardian Angel in the world, but she would always care about what Uncle Kevin thought of her and her actions. She just couldn't help it. Just like when she was a little girl, part of her always wanted his approval.

"I'm here, aren't I?" she said at last. Then she quickly added, "Tom asked me to wait for him."

Kevin paused, as if searching for the right thing to say. But when his response finally came, it was simple. And just what Maddy needed to hear.

"It's going to be OK," he said. "Tom is going to be OK. We all are."

"Do you really believe that?" Maddy asked softly.

"I have to, Mads." Kevin gave his most reassuring smile. "And so should you." Then he grinned even wider, the corners of his mouth wrinkling up in the way she knew so well. "Want some ginger tea?"

"OK." Maddy smiled. She wasn't going to argue with ginger tea. Kevin always made ginger tea for her when she was sick, or just feeling under the weather, with lemon and loads of honey.

Kevin headed into the kitchen, and Maddy walked into the little living room, with its secondhand furniture and the pictures of her as a kid. There were some new photos, too: pictures of Maddy from *Angels Weekly* and the newspaper, which Kevin had cut out and clumsily fit into frames. Maddy heard from the kitchen the familiar sounds of the gas stove snapping on, the whoosh of the flame, and the kettle being placed on the burner. As she listened to the heating water begin to murmur, she let herself lie back and sink into the couch. For this one small moment, there was suddenly nothing for her to do. After everything that had happened, she now found herself in a little pocket of calm. She sat quietly, just listening to her uncle make the tea. Her gaze settled on the new flat-screen TV, the only piece of furniture or technology in the house that had been manufactured after 1998. She grabbed the remote and turned it on.

"And the question on everyone's mind is," said a stoic-looking woman in a blue suit, "where are the Angels? Guardian Angels in the Immortal City have disappeared overnight, leaving everyone to wonder where they have gone, and whether they will be coming back." A graphic of an Immortal Ring appeared next to the women's head, cueing Maddy to play with her own. "The Angels have disappeared from the glittering Immortal City, and fans willing to brave security checkpoints and the possibility of being caught in a war zone have come to the Walk of Angels to participate in a candlelight vigil in hopes that the beautiful Immortals will return."

Maddy changed the channel to NBC News, where she was shocked to see Tara Reeves, the usually bubbly host of A!'s morning gossip show, standing in front of the camera. Tara had finally made the switch from entertainment reporter to news journalist, covering the Angel crisis and the mysterious sinkhole threatening to swallow Angel City. It must have been more than shocking for her normal A! audience to see her now, though: Tara had switched her look from glamorous red-carpet reporter to something more like an international war correspondent. She wore smartly cut khakis and a sensible button-up shirt, and had her hair drawn back in a ponytail. Of course, her make-up was still impeccable, her high-waisted trousers were Gucci, and she totally couldn't resist accessorizing with a Louis Vuitton field bag.

"I'm Tara Reeves, reporting live from Angel City for NBC News," she began in a breathless, urgent tone. "The question on everyone's lips as Angel City faces a possible threat is, *where are they?* All those beautiful mansions in the Hills empty. All those glamorous cars sitting in garages instead of cruising down the freeways. Security isn't letting anyone up near the houses, but authorities are confirming that no one is home. Where are the Angels of the Immortal City?" Tara walked her cameraman to a large crowd gathered at the Temple of Angels.

"Despite the Angels' disappearance," she announced with signature drama, "their true fans, as they call themselves, remain undaunted. They are determined to support their Angels, no matter what they do." The camera panned over the crowd Maddy had seen on her drive home. Some of the fans had SAVE ME T-shirts on, while others held up signs displaying Ted Linden's face crossed out with big red X's. They were chanting something, but it was hard to make out what.

"Their message?" Tara quipped as the camera scanned the scene. "*Bring back our Angels.* They stand in front of the Temple of Angels, the very same temple where the glamorous Commissioning takes place. The building stands silent now, no Immortals to be seen." The report switched to interviews with several of the fans in the crowd. The first was a teenage girl with her mother. The girl was wearing an oversize shirt bearing a name that made Maddy's stomach twist: *Emily Brightchurch*.

Emily was written in seductive pink cursive, right above a picture of her face. "There's no way the Angels won't come," the T-shirt girl was chirping. "They're just trying to teach us a lesson because humans were being mean to them. If you're out there watching, Jacks or Emily, or Chloe, or even Archangel Godspeed, please come back! We need you! OMG, we *love* you!" She shrieked until she was practically swooning.

The next interview was with a middle-aged man holding a sign depicting both an Angel and a UFO, with a big green question mark painted between the two. A conspiracy theorist, Maddy figured. "Where are the demons?" he asked. "Have we actually *seen* them besides on specially staged television broadcasts?" He was getting more and more worked up. "This whole 'war' is just a diversion to distract us from what's really going on in the government with Senator Linden. It's a cover-up. A conspiracy to turn America against the Angels, and people are swallowing it hook, line and sinker. Just like the supposed 'moon landing,' as if anyone believes that. Save the Angels!" Behind him, the group of Angel conspiracy theorists howled and cheered.

The image cut and Tara was back, spinning towards the camera with a dramatic flourish. "Also out of the spotlight is Maddy Montgomery." Maddy bolted upright on the couch. "Since her public announcement in support of the Immortals Bill, we have heard nothing from Angel City's newest Guardian. What are her thoughts on the impending demon attack? Has Jackson abandoned her to be with the Immortals, wherever they are? Will we ever see those famous Maddy Montgomery wings flying over Angel City again?" Footage of Maddy in flight, her luminous purple wings outstretched, hair cutting across her face, filled the screen, and she flipped the station.

On the Angel News Network, a grave-looking anchor was in the middle of a story. "There are even some global experts who say that despite so-called demon sightings, the sinkhole off the coast of Angel City will not develop further." The shot cut across the news desk to a bespectacled man in a sharp suit.

"The Angels are playing a game of chicken. A very, very sophisticated game of chicken. It's all about who blinks first. They'll come to our aid, but they want to teach the entire world a lesson first. It's not as if they would simply *abandon* us, would they?" He chuckled nervously, and Maddy felt bad for him.

She flipped and flipped again, only to land on more of the same. Every channel was reporting either on the attack or on the growing crowd in front of the Temple of Angels. A! seemed to be the only network that had given up running anything about the demon attack. In fact, it had switched to a rerun of Chloe's reality show, *Seventeen and Immortal*, to be followed by a marathon of old Angel Commissioning ceremonies.

"It's just more of the same," Kevin said as he entered the room and handed Maddy a mug.

"Thanks," Maddy said, and smiled at her uncle through the steam. "This is great." And it was. The warmth of the tea radiated through her chest as she drank. Kevin just shrugged, but Maddy could see the intensity in his face, and she could tell he wanted to say something to her. He looked down at his tea.

"We're all in this together, Mads," he said, finally looking up at her. "Even if the Angels really have left us, I'm still here. And so is Tom. And President Linden. He'll know what to do." Maddy smiled a little and wrapped her arm around him, pressing the side of her face against his chest. She could feel his heartbeat against her cheek. She felt Kevin's hands fumble for a hug, which was a bit awkward, but warm all the same. Suddenly Maddy felt herself being pulled back into thoughts of the pier, but she stopped herself before she could get started. There were more important things at hand, she told herself.

"I know there are a lot of people who don't think this is real," Maddy said. "But, Kevin, we need to assume the demons are coming." Maddy looked at her uncle.

"I know what you're trying to tell me," Kevin said. "And I'm not leaving. They've already closed down the freeways for emergency vehicles only. All the chaos earlier today blocked everything. No one's getting out now."

"I could make a call—" Maddy started to suggest. Kevin stopped her by putting a hand on her shoulder.

"When your mom and dad left you with me, I made them a promise. I promised that I would protect you, no matter what," Kevin said. "Nothing about that has changed." He looked at Maddy. "I know you, Maddy, and I know what kind of young woman, and Angel, you are. I know you aren't leaving like the rest of them. You'll stay here and fight. And I'm not going anywhere, either. We're going to get through this together, just like we always have. Even a Guardian needs someone to look after her."

Tears started to form in Maddy's eyes, and they hugged again. Kevin's eyes welled up a bit as well, but he quickly wiped them dry. He looked out the living room window. "Besides, who's going to be here to reopen the diner after everything's over if I'm out in Kansas somewhere with a bunch of refugees? No. I'm staying right here."

Maddy took a long, hot shower, willing the steaming water to wash away the day's events. When she was finished, she wrapped herself in a towel and walked into her old room, the one she grew up in. Kevin had more or less kept it the same way Maddy had it while in high school, but it looked much different now compared with her new glass condo. By contrast, this room was old and worn, yet somehow that was comforting. Maddy sat on her bed, which, as Kevin had promised, was neatly made. She couldn't help thinking it was a different person who used to live in this room. A different young girl, with different dreams, who was going to live a different life. Maddy felt like an impostor.

On the bedside table sat Tom's flight wings. She picked them up and felt the weight of them in her hands. Their heaviness always surprised her, considering how small they were. As she held the wings and sat in the quiet of her old room, the thoughts began to flood her mind. Thoughts she had tried to push away since leaving the dock, and there was no stopping them now. She replayed a string of decisions in her mind, as if going over them again would convince her that they were, in fact, the right ones.

Why had she chosen Tom? Because he needed something to fight for. He was going up against an enemy he could not possibly beat, and the least she could do was give him a reason to survive. Fear welled inside her as she pictured Tom aloft in a fiery sky, fighting for his life against supernatural creatures that couldn't be

24

killed by bullets or bombs. In a moment like that, Maddy thought, death might feel like a welcome escape. If the future he saw for them together could keep him alive, then so be it. Her love was the best weapon she could give him to use against the demon army. And so she had done what needed to be done, just like she always tried to do. It was her job as an Angel. Sacrifice. Tom was her Protection now.

But – what about Jacks? She let herself fall back in the bed and listened to it creak like it used to with her weight. Her eyes traced the familiar edges of the room. Did she love Jacks? Of course she did. She always would. But she would have to forget about Jacks. Not just for herself, but also for Tom. She had made a promise to Tom, and she intended to keep it. The only question was, could she?

Could she forget two years in which she and Jacks had been inseparable, in which Jacks had been a part of her? She knew exactly how they fit together, and could so vividly recall the way she would reach for his hand and lace her fingers with his, like it was the most natural thing in the world. She thought of the way he would bend his head and kiss her slowly, and could practically feel the pressure of his lips on hers. They had each other memorized. How could she just erase it all? An aching chill started in her throat and radiated through her body, and suddenly she was freezing. Shivering against her wet hair, she realized it wasn't the temperature in the room making her cold. It was the dawning of the idea that, from the very beginning, she knew this could never work out. She'd been a fool. She had known from their very first date, when Jacks had taken her flying over Angel City, and yet she had let herself be pulled into this whole misadventure, this emotional black hole. She willingly let herself be lulled into a dream because she so badly wanted it to be real.

It was this same blind desire that had driven her to train as a Guardian Angel, and to believe that she and Jacks could actually have a life together and be happy. She didn't want to see that she and Jacks were too different, that they came from different worlds and had different values. Just like she didn't want to see that Jacks's injuries were as severe as they were after his fight with the demon, or that he would withdraw from her as her own star rose. Just like she didn't want to see herself becoming swept up in the glamorous lifestyle of a Guardian – the money, the fame, the adoration – so she just closed her eyes to the world while it all washed over her, while she let herself be sucked into everything she used to hate about the Angels. Maddy thought back to the moment she received her rich, entitled Protections, the same moment she realized she had lost herself and become just another Angel. The memory turned her stomach. That wasn't who she was, but it was who Jacks was. She had wanted the dream of the two of them together so badly that she couldn't see that was all it was ever going to be: a dream, a fantasy. They were just too different to ever work. How often, Maddy wondered bitterly, do people really see things for what they are? How often do we instead just see a *version* of things – the version we want them to be? Here she was, two years later, and things were exactly the same as they'd been on that first night. And now she really had to face it: Maddy Montgomery and Jackson Godspeed just weren't meant to be.

She turned over and looked at the flight wings in her hand. If she somehow survived the demon attack, if she could help Tom and Kevin and everyone she loved to survive, then it didn't matter what happened to her afterward. If she and Tom could have a life together, wouldn't that be enough? Maddy's smile was slight, bittersweet. There's a strange sense of freedom and calm in letting go of your own desires and giving in to the path that fate has placed before you. She pictured her life up until this point as standing waist-deep in a swiftly moving river, straining and fighting against a relentless current but getting nowhere. Now she was finally letting go and was ready to let the current take her. There was something beautiful about it. Maybe the current would take her to the place she was always meant to go. Maybe everything was going to be OK. She felt a weight lift off her chest, one that she hadn't even realized was there until now.

Yet, deep inside her, the flame that still flickered for Jacks had to be snuffed out. She conjured up an image of Kevin in the claws of one of the demons, crying out for help – crying out for her – and white-hot anger raced through her veins. Even if she was the last thing standing between Kevin and an entire army of monsters, she would never abandon him. Jacks knew the kind of danger her uncle was in, the danger everyone was in, and yet he was content doing nothing. He was actually going to stand by and leave those weaker than him to their fate. Tom, on the other hand, was out there right now, preparing to go up against impossible odds without a second thought for himself. The anger came to a boil inside Maddy, replacing her blood with bitter water and filling her. Consuming her. She erased those pictures of the Jacks she loved, of the impeccable Angel she had memorized, and replaced them with the new Jacks. This was the Jacks in battle armour, worn to attack humans. That armour and those robotic wings were all that was left of him now. She let herself think through her next realization very slowly. If the Angels wouldn't help the humans against their enemy, then the *Angels were the enemy, too.*

She sat up and looked out her window to the Angel City sign that stood on the hill, still gleaming and white, like a beacon. How she hated that sign and everything it stood for. How she hated the city and everything it had done to her.

In a low voice, Maddy said aloud, "Non-action is complicity." She thought of the Emergency Broadcast on the radio. That broadcast was like her life now. This was *not* a test. This was really happening. The Angels were the enemy. The logic was irrefutable. And that could only mean one thing.

Jackson Godspeed was now her enemy, too.

CHAPTER 4

Nestled in between the trees in the Angel City Hills, the ostentatious glass cube building was perfectly under the radar. In Pittsburgh, Plymouth, or Podunkville, USA, it would have stuck out like a sore thumb. But here up off Mulholland it was just another display of Angel taste, wealth, exclusiveness and prestige. The front entrance was the site of what would likely be the last public Angel televised appearance for some time. Archangel William Holyoake had stepped out with Jackson and other Guardians at his side to state that the Guardians would not be taking part in the demon war. And all just before the first demon scouts had been sent into the Immortal City.

As Jackson dropped down from the sky, he entered the glass doorway and retracted his glowing wings, all in one smooth motion. The security guards positioned inside the cube saluted him, but Jacks didn't pay any attention to them as he walked – stomped, really – to the large elevator, which was housed in a marble column in the rear centre of the cube. The gleaming doors opened smoothly, and Jackson stepped into the plush car. Soothing music played from sleek speakers, and an enormous TV embedded in the back wall displayed footage of underwater tropical fish swimming calmly along a coral reef.

He didn't have to push a button. There was only one way the elevator could go. And that was down.

It took some time for the elevator to reach its destination. Not too long ago, Jacks had idly wondered how deep down the sanctuary actually was. Now he couldn't have cared less, and he didn't even notice the ride. After what Maddy had done to him on the pier, his mind – his whole body – had become a tempest of rage, sadness, and confusion.

The elevator dinged, the doors opened to reveal another world, and Jackson began walking, his footsteps echoing along the Italian marble floor. The secure Angel complex had been prepared as a haven for just the kind of emergency the demon attack posed. It had been dreamed up during the Cold War, when the threat of nuclear annihilation was a real concern, but this was no bare-bones underground bunker. Far from it. In true Angel fashion, no creature comfort was left uncared for.

Long, elegant passageways extended underground, illuminated by soft light coming from frosted windows along the way, which simulated sunlight filtering through to the lush plants. Jackson's footsteps echoed as they stepped along the marble floors. The Immortals' living quarters were furnished with huge flat-screen TVs, enormous claw-foot bathtubs, king-sized beds with feather pillows and balconies that looked out over artificial lakes. All the interior windows were outfitted with electric bulbs timed to simulate natural light from dawn through sunset, and the air was pure and fresh from outside. They had everything they needed for quite some time. Everything had been planned out immaculately.

It was called the sanctuary.

The complex was known only to a handful of non-Angels who had been forced to sign threatening-looking, ironclad agreements promising they would never say anything about it. Any slip of a word and an army of Angel lawyers would be suing the pants off them. Back when the sanctuary was being built, a construction worker blabbed his story, and the *National Enquirer* ran a story with the headline, "HOLE-Y COW! SECRET ANGEL UNDERGROUND LAIR!" The construction worker was sued into the next century, and the next week the tabloid took the very unorthodox step of totally taking back every part of the story, saying: "How sad we are to admit we had been fooled so easily." And so the legend of the sanctuary died.

But the legend was real. The sanctuary was quietly refurbished every few years so it remained up-to-date for the finicky Angels. There were the living quarters, which were lavish and suitable for those Angels who were only accustomed to the finer things in life. Along the passageways were rows of boutiques displaying the latest trends, fine jewellery shops, a half-dozen organic gourmet restaurants and a couple of fancy cafés. Everything the Immortal City had to offer, all kept safe and tucked away in the sanctuary. It was all perfectly planned and was the ideal place to ride out the demon attacks while still ensuring that the Angels kept their foothold in Angel City, no matter what happened upstairs.

The Angels had only been down there for a day, but they were already settling in nicely. The sanctuary was always prepped for their arrival and ongoing comfort, and now the time had finally come. As soon as the demons struck with the sinkhole, the Angels had simply disappeared from human sight, stealing away from their homes in the Angel City Hills and descending to their paradise below.

But the sanctuary wasn't only used for hiding. Somewhere along the way, the maze of passages led to the Council chambers. Once a year, the Angels convened in the sanctuary ballroom for an ultrasecret gala where they honoured the Council of Twelve, who had brought them into the Light. And sometimes the Archangels would have their most secretive meetings – or, depending on whom you asked, secret parties, complete with wild debauchery – down here. There were also darker rumours about darker things that had taken place in the sanctuary during the Troubles, but they were never substantiated.

"Godspeed," said Mitch, Jackson's closest friend, calling out to him as he passed.

Jackson kept walking.

"Godspeed!" Mitch caught up to him and put his hand on his best friend's shoulder.

Jackson stopped on a dime and spun around to Mitch.

"What?" Jacks growled.

"Whoa, bro, relax," Mitch said. "Your stepfather was looking for you."

"He can keep looking."

Mitch looked at Jackson. It didn't take a psych major to see something wasn't quite right. "What's going on?"

"Nothing," Jacks said. He continued down the hall again, and Mitch followed alongside him.

"Sorry, I should have known you'd be upset. You know, we're all worried. From a certain angle, it's pretty harsh that we're leaving the humans out in the cold like this."

Jacks looked at Mitch in disbelief.

"I mean, I understand why you're a little upset, bro. We've been protecting the humans for how many thousands of years?" Mitch said. "That's a long time. And now, just to turn away from them with the demons coming? Even if the humans *were* trying to ban Angel activities, we could've worked through that, at some point. But to leave them alone like this, and they don't even know what they're up against?"

Jacks gave him an incredulous glance. "Are you an Immortal or a human, Mitch? Think about it. Would they have supported *us*? No. They would have been glad to see us wiped out."

Mitch's expression betrayed his confusion. "What are you talking about? I thought you were mad because we're *not* helping the humans. You've always been pretty liberal in comparison with the National Angel Services, or NAS. We've talked about this for years."

Jacks snorted.

Mitch put his hand on Jacks's shoulder and stopped him again. "What happened? This isn't like you, Jacks," Mitch said. "I knew you were gone for a while today. A bunch of Angels saw you leave. No one said anything to Mark or anything, though." Mitch paused. "Did you go see her?"

Jackson ignored the question. "Don't you remember the Immortals Bill, Mitch? They were going to imprison us. Remember whose side you belong to. Don't be a human sympathizer." Jacks paused and steeled himself. "They deserve whatever they're going to get."

"You don't know what you're saying, man. You can't believe that.

Whatever's happened between you two, you still have to think about Maddy!"

The name was like a billowing red sheet waving in front of a speared bull. He shoved Mitch out of the way and stormed down the gilded passageway.

Jackson hadn't gotten far before a beautiful female assistant of the Council's dressed in a luminous modern robe stopped him.

"Jackson," she said calmly.

"What?" Jacks spun around angrily on the woman.

"You're wanted in the solarium."

Gabriel was unmistakable as he sat on a bench near the tree in the solarium, with his mass of lustrous white hair and seemingly ageless face illuminated by the artificial light. The sanctuary solarium had been built many years ago as one of its first features. Situated on the edge of the sanctuary, near the passage to the Council chambers, it was reserved exclusively for the Council and its closest circle. Jackson had never been inside.

Gabriel wore his normal golden robe, which seemed almost to glow as it touched his skin. Jackson's stepfather, Mark Godspeed, was there as well, standing just off to the side of the bench alongside a few advisers to the Council. Behind them, a small stone bridge crossed an indoor stream that ran through the solarium. All around, lush green and flowering plants were flourishing, making a small path circling the entire area. A butterfly flitted past. Above, a span of domed, frosted glass covered the whole scene. Behind the glass, huge electric bulbs shone with the warmth and light of the sun.

Gabriel, chief True Immortal of the Council of Twelve, leader of the Angels in the Great Awakening, founder of the NAS, looked at Jackson Godspeed and smiled.

"I know I've said it before, but the armour of the Battle Angel suits you well," Gabriel said, observing the young Angel in front of him. "Rest assured, Jackson, we will not forget your loyalty, your willingness to stand by us on the brink of the human-Angel war. Even though, thankfully, it did not come to pass."

"I would think of doing nothing else," Jackson said.

Once again Gabriel gave his ancient smile. Throughout the recent dramatic events, Jackson had found a kind of shelter with Gabriel. Far from being simply a figurehead, he was genuinely concerned about the welfare of the Angels on a daily basis, and it showed. He could have delegated everything, but he didn't. He felt he had a duty, and Jackson admired him for that.

"There is a reason we wanted to see you, Guardian Godspeed," Gabriel said. "Jackson, we've been discussing the possibility of helping the humans."

Jacks struggled to mask the shock that ran across his face.

Gabriel continued. "It is obviously quite difficult for us just to stand idly by. Even if the humans were planning to turn on us with the Immortals Bill. After all, we have ancient ties and lines of duty to humanity, stretching back far, far before we ever left Home and made ourselves known on Earth."

Mark nodded silently at Gabriel's side.

A flood of emotion crashed across Jackson's face, colouring it, as he thought of what might happen between him and Maddy if the Angels could rejoin the humans. It might not be too late after all. But the painful image of her in the arms of that ... *pilot* chased away his fresh-born hopes. Gabriel looked at Jackson and smiled once again.

"I can see you have some feelings on the subject, Jacks," Gabriel said. "Do you mind sharing them?"

Jacks hesitated a moment, looking to both Gabriel and Mark. He wondered what the right answer was. What did he *really* feel?

"It's hard to say, sir," Jacks said uncertainly.

"That's why we've been discussing this for so long here in the solarium. There's no easy answer. You're right to see that. Prudence in these matters is vital," Gabriel said. "That said, Jacks, after our debate, I still think we have no choice but to leave the humans to their own devices. Even if we'd not had problems with them and Linden, there is just too much at stake for us to compromise everything by entering the battle against the demons." Gabriel paused as if to let this monumental fact sink in.

"The fact of the matter is," he went on, "we did leave Home when I decided to bring us out of hiding. And for a good reason: We have a destiny here on Earth. We need always to keep our thoughts focused upon preserving the Angel line. We have no idea how large the force of the Dark Ones will be. It is quite doubtful, even with our highest standard of training and loyalty among the Battle Angel corps, that Angelkind could realistically weather an attack from a large number of demons. Too many would be lost. Too much blood would be spilled. While, if we stay here in the sanctuary, we will remain safe, and in the end Angel City will ultimately remain under our control. Just as it was meant to be. The demons are here for the humans, Jackson. Not us."

Mark cleared his throat and spoke up. "We've debated this a lot, Jacks. Even in the face of the anti-Angel Immortals Bill we have thought of helping the humans." The worry lines written in his forehead grew more pronounced as he spoke. "But there's nothing we can do."

"And the Book of Angels has spoken clearly on this matter," Gabriel said. "For centuries our scholars have deemed this to be a prophecy about humanity, not Angels. We just did not think it would come so soon for our human brothers and sisters." As he said this, Gabriel's ageless face took on a sad, faraway look, his mind likely drifting to thoughts of the countless human beings he'd protected and served throughout his epic lifetime.

"I as much as anyone know that there may be . . . temptations to help the humans in the coming conflict with the demons." Gabriel cast his kindly, Immortal gaze on Jackson.

"Archangel Godspeed has informed us of certain feelings you probably still have for the Madison Godright girl. This, too, is understandable, my son."

"That won't be a problem," Jacks said, unblinkingly and without pause. "I promise."

"You needn't put up a front for us, Jackson. We know you are prepared to do your duty. But we are not hard. We have loved, as well. Our entire order is, in fact, based on love. A love of righteousness and for the Protections we have sworn to save."

Gabriel turned partially and looked out past the foliage into the pathways of the solarium. "It is difficult, of course, to see all those Protections we have spent our lives Protecting now be put in such grave danger. But endangering ourselves just to help those who would have rendered illegal our one true purpose is worse than insane. It is against our principles. Our homes can be rebuilt. Communities will be reconstructed. All these things would pass on their own accord, as part of history, no matter how sweeping the destruction. But we Angels must endure," he said. "There is no other way."

He turned back to Jackson.

"For the mortals, there is a cycle of birth and death," said Gabriel. "This, sadly, may be their death. And their fate. According to some readings of the Book of Angels, this is exactly what is supposed to happen. Everything has its place, Jackson."

"I understand," Jacks said, his eyes fixed on Gabriel.

"Thank you, my son. This is a difficult time for all of us," Gabriel said. "No Angel wanted this; we have always wanted to protect humanity, and it won't be easy for any of us. I know it will perhaps be even more difficult for you than many. But I'm glad you understand."

The elder True Immortal now gave Jacks a bittersweet smile, but his eyes were dancing with light, still young in their Immortal age.

On their way out of the solarium, Jacks and Mark ran into Louis Kreuz, the brash and outspoken head of Guardian training. Kreuz wasn't wearing his normal full suit, but he did have on his broad pinstripe trousers and trademark suspenders strapped over his French-cuffed Brooks Brothers shirt.

"Godspeeds," he said, nodding, lighting a match for the Cuban cigar pressed between his lips. Surprisingly, Gabriel didn't mind his smoking in the solarium. "Haven't seen *you* in a bit, Jackson." His eyes seemed to study Jackson's face a little more closely than usual. "Been in to see the Big Cheese?" he said, nodding towards the Council chambers.

"Hi, Louis," Jacks said. He liked Kreuz – quite a bit, actually. Louis had supported him strongly throughout all his training. "Good to see you," he said awkwardly, still lost in thought after his meeting with Gabriel. "Sorry to be so short, but we're in a bit of a hurry."

Kreuz shot Jacks a strange glance as he and Mark walked away, then took a puff from his finally lit cigar and shook the match in his big fingers until the flame went out.

Jackson and Mark continued down the long sanctuary halls, dozens of Angels nodding at them as they walked along. The two Godspeeds together – Jacks still in his Battle Angel armour, Mark in his tailored suit – made an impressive duo.

"Jackson, I'm very proud of how you've been handling yourself through all this," Mark said. "You've shown yourself to be a true Angel and patriot for the Immortals."

They walked a few steps before Jackson responded.

"I've seen what can come of having . . . other loyalties," Jacks said.

"Believe me, we've had many long debates about whether there are circumstances under which we could help the humans," Mark said. "And it just isn't possible."

"Like I told Gabriel, Mark, I understand," he said.

"Good," Mark said as they entered an atrium. "And I'm sorry that he mentioned . . . Madison in there, Jacks. It's no secret among the Council that you two were quite serious. Gabriel pressed me hard, and I was honest with him about your feelings. As you know, it's always best to be absolutely honest with Gabriel and the Council."

"There's nothing to be said about it, Mark," Jackson said, cool and crisp. "I just want to carry out our duty."

"Good," Mark said. He clapped a hand on Jacks's shoulder. "Your mother has been wondering about you. Will you come say hello? Just for a second?"

The Godspeed quarters were large and suitably appointed for Angels of their standing, with Chloe having a whole section to herself since Jacks had his own place. Chloe was shopping with friends somewhere in the sanctuary when Jacks and Mark arrived, but Jackson's mother, Kris, was there to greet them. Mark drifted off into the master bedroom, leaving mother and son alone in the room.

"Jackson," she said. She came up and gave him a hug, then stepped back to look at him in his armour. "Look at you. Wow. How does it feel . . . ? The armour, I mean."

His mother's voice sounded as if it was coming from a thousand miles away. Jackson's mind was elsewhere. Outside in the sun. Standing on a pier.

"Jacks, are you OK?" Kris asked.

He turned away from her. "Of course. Nothing's wrong, Mom," Jackson said, trying to hide the pain in his voice. "It's wonderful to see you."

But his mother knew her son too well, and she placed a consoling hand on his armoured shoulder.

"Is it her?" Kris asked. "Up there, left to whatever the Dark Ones will do?" Jacks kept silent. He was tired of everyone prying into his personal life. Everyone seemed to have an opinion.

"You know, I lost your father, Jacks," she went on. "You can talk to me if you want to. I'm here."

"I know," Jacks said, nodding. "Of course I know." The thoughts, first of Maddy and then of his father, practically gutted him. But still, he wanted – he needed – to be strong.

Kris didn't press him, but her eyes reflected a silent compassion back to Jackson. Part of him wanted to open up to her, but that part was overruled by the part that was so hurt that it didn't want to let anything – or anyone – in.

"I'm sorry, Mom. I know I must seem a little . . . off. It's just that I haven't been getting very much sleep lately," Jacks said. "I really should go back to my rooms. I have some stuff to do for Gabriel."

"Jacks," Kris said, stopping him, slightly lowering her voice. "What's happening – up there – there is no way to feel good about it." "It doesn't have to feel good," Jacks said, anger bleeding in. "It just has to be right."

"But . . ." Here Kris paused, measuring her words. "How can you be sure of what is 'right'? Is what you're saying because you're sure that what we're doing really is right? Or are you saying it because of some anger you're holding on to?"

Jacks looked at her with an arched eyebrow. "What are you saying? Are you telling me you're pro-human or something?" He almost said "pro-*her*" but caught himself.

Kris's face quivered slightly upon hearing Jacks's words. "This isn't about being pro-Angel or pro-human, Jacks. What I'm trying to ask you isn't about politics. It's about you and your feelings," she said. Jacks and Kris both knew she didn't have to add "about Maddy" for him to understand what she meant. Kris continued, "Things will be changing drastically in the next few days, and I just want to say, don't forget who you are. What kind of Guardian you are."

Something inside Jacks cracked open, just slightly. A crack in his facade, which irritated him. "I don't know what I think, Mom," Jacks spat out. "And sometimes I wish people would just stop asking me. Because I don't have an answer."

"It's OK, honey," Kris said softly. "There are no easy answers here. No matter what Gabriel, or even your stepfather, might say. It's not so cut-and-dried."

Jacks let his mother's words touch him for a moment before suddenly making himself distant. Again, he remembered *her* at the pier, with the pilot. Her words, and how they knocked the wind out of him.

"I have to go now, Mom. I'll talk to you later."

"Jackson *God*speed!"

Taking a breath, Jacks stopped in the hallway on the way to his place. The Australian accent and layers of calculated, playful seduction in those two words meant it could only be one person.

"Are you really going to just walk by without saying hello?"

He slowly turned around to see Emily Brightchurch's famous red locks and beautiful face poking out from the partially opened door. The rest of her body was hidden inside her quarters.

"Come here!" she demanded.

42

"Now's not really a good time, Emily," he said. But she had already disappeared inside, leaving the door slightly cracked.

Her voice was muffled, but he could still hear her. "Jacks, don't be silly. Just give me a second to get ready."

Ever since she was a teenaged Immortal arriving in Angel City from Australia, Jackson knew that Emily Brightchurch had had her sights set on him. She had been a Vivian Holycross wannabe for a couple of years, mirroring the older, fashionable, and ultra-fabulous Angel's every move when she was with Jacks. When they broke up and Jacks got together with Maddy, she told all her friends that there was only one half-human, half-Angel standing in her way. From her provocative billboard-sized ads on the Halo Strip to her semi-scandalous everyday wardrobe choices, Emily played up every aspect of her sexpot personality.

And now that she and Jacks were alone in the close quarters of the sanctuary, there was no way she was letting him get away.

The door swung almost fully open, and Jacks could now hear the television chattering away from inside.

"All right, then, what are you waiting for?" Emily said.

Jacks came to the door, sighing. Emily was wearing just a towel.

"You know, they have robes, Emily," said Jacks.

"Do they?" she said innocently, showing way too much leg for her own good. The Aussie Angel seemed suspiciously not wet for having just stepped out of the shower. Was her idea of "getting ready" for Jacks taking her clothes off and just putting on a towel?

"I really should be . . ." Jacks couldn't finish his sentence.

Emily yanked him, unwillingly, into the room, and before he

43

knew it, the door was closed behind him.

She eyed him up and down, a devilish grin on her face, faking modesty by wrapping her towel a bit more tightly around her chest.

"You went outside, didn't you?" she asked.

"What?" Jackson said, taken aback.

"You don't have to pretend with *me*, Jacks. I won't tell anyone. I knew you were gone. I saw Mitch looking for you. Not too many places to hide down here."

Emily looked towards the glimmering frosted glass in her room, which had been designed to look like a window on to a sunshine-filled day outside, and not like what it essentially was – a decoration in an underground bunker.

"Do you ever think about how funny it is that we Angels go *down* for sanctuary?" she said. "Shouldn't we be going *up*?" She apparently got a laugh out of this, but Jacks was not in the mood for comedy.

"I hadn't really thought about it," Jacks said quietly.

"But, I guess, where would we go otherwise? Home?" she said. "Do you believe what they say about Home?"

"You mean that it's where the Angels came from? And someday we'll go back again? Supposedly, at least." The lore said that Gabriel had been the one to lead the Angels from Home to help humanity and that one day he would lead them back. It was his destiny.

Emily eyed Jackson as if he'd said something strange.

"I wouldn't even want to go there. Home," she said. "It would be boring. A lot more fun things to do down here."

Trying to ignore the implications behind her sexy stare, Jacks turned to leave. But before he could get the door open, Emily's voice stopped him again.

"What's it like?" she said. "Outside, I mean. What's going on out there? Have they started yet?"

For someone who had just recently cowered in his arms in fright at the sight of a demon flying by, Emily seemed to have recovered pretty well, Jacks thought. He remained quiet.

"Come *on*, Jacks," she said. "I know you were up top. I'm not going to tell anyone. I just want to know if it's started yet." What looked like a flash of excitement flitted across her eyes.

"No," he said. "It hasn't."

"Take me with you next time?" she said eagerly. "We can totally outfly the demons. I know it. You and me."

"There's not going to be a next time," Jacks said, a pall casting over his face. The finality of what had happened between him and Maddy was starting to slowly sink in. Not just the initial shock of it, but the true reality.

"Jacks, are you OK? What's the matter?" Emily said.

"Nothing," Jacks said, but his face had grown ashen, his lips thin and colourless.

Emily pursed her lips, as if she was able to see something else on his face. "Have you been to see . . . *her*?" Emily couldn't bring herself to say Maddy's name. "You just need to forget about her, Jacks. And think about your future. What's available to you right here, right now."

But Jackson's attention had turned inward, and even though Emily crossed her towel-clad legs an extra time in a desperate attempt to try to bring him back, it was clear that it wasn't enough.

"I've got to go," Jackson said broodingly, and turned away before she could do or say anything else.

"I'll see you later, right?" Emily asked.

She received no answer. Jackson had already left.

CHAPTER 5

Upstairs in her room, Maddy felt a strange impulse to take an old shoe box out from under the bed. She pulled off the tape from the lid, lifted it, and spread the box's contents out on the bed. Fanned across the comforter were ancient diaries, from way back in middle school, their covers marked with all kinds of stickers and cheerful marker graffiti.

Maddy smiled wistfully as she flipped through the pages, wrapped up in wonder at all the things that had seemed so important at the time: what boy Gwen was into at the moment, how embarrassed Maddy had felt when she tripped during an assembly, what they served and where she sat at lunch, whether she'd die before she ever kissed a boy. (*Really* kissed a boy, not just a peck like she'd done during the spin the bottle game in James Durgan's basement that one time.)

Looking at her diaries, she didn't know whether to laugh or cry – or both. When she'd had enough, she carefully put them back in the old box and slipped it under the bed, then sank down to sit on the floor with her back against the mattress edge.

Maddy started to shiver as she thought of the Darkness growing across the ocean, sprawling in the distance as it grew out of the sinkhole. The demons would cut down Tom and his fellow pilots without blinking. She could almost see the jets dissolving into blazing wreckage as the demons knocked them aside and advanced on humanity.

With a shudder, Maddy chased the bloody images from her mind. She couldn't think that way. She couldn't stand even another hour thinking that way, even if it might be true. She needed some kind of hope.

Spurred by this restless energy, Maddy knew she couldn't just sit in her uncle's house, waiting. For what, she could not say.

Non-action is complicity. Maddy forced herself to go outside, to do something. To get out of her own mind and feelings. *Anything* would be more productive than wallowing. On her way out the door, Kevin insisted on coming with her.

Aside from the occasional emergency siren, Angel City was eerily silent. Kevin and Maddy decided to check on the neighbours. Some had managed to evacuate via the chaotic freeways before the mandatory curfew was put into place, but others were left with no other choice but to hole up in their houses with as much food and water as possible, and hope for the best. Not everyone believed the demon sinkhole actually posed a threat, and some stubborn folks simply didn't want to leave their homes behind, but for the most part, and for most people, there was just no way out.

A hush of expectation hung over the city. The atmosphere was strangely calm, almost like a holiday, Maddy thought to herself. Except on a holiday, tactical fighter jets didn't scream in the sky on their hourly demon patrols.

After talking to some of their remaining neighbours, Maddy and Kevin reached the house at the end of the block, where the old woman they'd known for years still lived. They knocked on the door.

It cracked open and an old lady with a head of white hair peered suspiciously out the small opening. Two small dogs yipped at her feet.

"Mrs Dawkins?" Maddy said. "It's Maddy. Maddy Montgomery, from down the street."

"Who are you?" the woman said. "You're not going to make me leave my home!"

"I'm not here to take you out of your house, Mrs Dawkins. I'm Maddy. Remember? I used to help you pull weeds?"

The suspicious lines around the old woman's face softened. Just a bit.

"They'll have to pull my cold, dead body out of here before I leave my house and my babies behind!" The two lap dogs yipped even louder at this, as if agreeing with their batty owner. Behind Mrs Dawkins, coming from the living room, Maddy could hear the TV news loudly blaring updates about the demon attack.

"Well, please, just stay inside. If anything should happen . . ." Kevin said, then stopped himself. "Well, it's just best to stay inside. I'll check on you later to make sure you're OK."

Mrs Dawkins opened the door slightly more to look Kevin up and down. "Thank you," she said, then closed the door. The barking dogs and the loud TV faded as Maddy and Kevin walked down the street.

"Let's go back to the house," Maddy said. "I want to see if I can get in touch with the authorities. They're going to need me, Kevin. I just know it."

"I had a feeling you'd say something like that. I'm going to be worried about you, kiddo," Kevin said, squeezing her shoulder. Before they knew it, they were back at the house.

"I have no choice, Kevin," Maddy said. "I need to do something."

"I know. I know you do," he said. "It's just . . . it's so hard to watch you go out, to step right into something I can't even imagine. It's selfish of me, I know. But I always want to protect you."

Maddy felt strange as she and Kevin walked into the house. Her mind was racing, and she realized she hadn't eaten anything all day. This was no good; she needed to stay sharp. She was going to force herself to at least drink some juice.

Each step she took towards the kitchen seemed so real, so clear, yet somehow distant, as if she were floating above, watching someone else do it.

"Kevin, is there any apple juice left?" Maddy asked. Her tongue felt thick in her mouth, and the voice sounded far off. Her feet felt controlled by a puppeteer as she watched them stepping off the carpet and on to the scuffed linoleum of the old kitchen.

Kevin walked into the kitchen and passed in front of Maddy. Her eyes followed him slowly, and it almost seemed like there were blurry streams of light trailing him as he walked by.

He opened the fridge and looked inside. "We sure do have some apple juice. You want a big or little glass?"

"Little."

Kevin pulled a cup down from the cupboard and began filling it as Maddy cast her eyes towards the window and looked to the city. She thought of her Protections, almost all of whom had probably been able to leave the city. The most fortunate ones always were able to get out and save themselves first. Either way, she couldn't feel their frequencies any more. The Global Angel Commission, the organization in charge of handling "the Angel question," had banned Angel activities, and with the Angels now nowhere to be found, they knew no one was going to protect them now. Those who had the money to escape were taking no chances, fleeing however they could, whether by private jet, helicopter, or even hired boat. As usual, the people who couldn't afford those luxuries were left behind to protect themselves against the unknown.

Maddy just stood there as Kevin put the juice away, her hands held tensely against her chest, when suddenly something struck her like a thunderbolt. Nausea spread from her stomach through her limbs. She was definitely not OK.

"Kevin, I don't feel so good."

He turned around, and, seeing her ghostly face, he put the glass of juice down on the counter.

"Maddy? Maddy!"

Maddy felt the ground disappear underneath her. She was falling, falling into nothingness. There was no bottom. There would be no end. At once, a maelstrom of fire and smoke exploded before her eyes. And there was blood. She couldn't see it, but she knew she sensed the smell of blood. Out of the flames emerged two eyes, then almost what looked like limbs as she kept falling, each one on fire and boiling with dark smoke. A Dark One. The *thing* seemed to grin at her.

Maddy opened her mouth to scream, but as the fire consumed her, no sound escaped.

Suddenly she found herself back in the kitchen, staring at her uncle as he took her by the shoulders.

"Maddy!" Uncle Kevin shouted. "Are you OK?"

She was standing upright, safe there with Kevin. The Dark Angel, the fire, the smoke – all of it was gone. Then she realized what had happened. It had been a premonition. She shook like a leaf in a winter storm.

This had been her strongest premonition since the one of Jackson's death, right before she saved him.

"Was it . . . did you have one of . . . those things?" Kevin never really knew how to talk about her powers.

Before she could answer, the ground suddenly began to quake violently. China rattled in the cupboards as Kevin steadied himself against the counter. The glass of juice smashed to the floor, shattering. Just as he was standing up straight again, Kevin had to grip the counter tighter to stay steady as an even larger tremor rolled across the Angel City basin. The quake rumbled louder than thunder.

Suddenly, an air raid siren began howling in the distance, rising above the din of all the car alarms set off by the quakes.

Maddy kept her balance throughout the event, just staring, almost blankly, out the kitchen window in shock. The absolutely terrifying vision she'd had was still frozen in her mind: an almost abstract, grisly scene of destruction.

But what was happening now wasn't just a vision.

When she finally turned back to her uncle, her brownish-green eyes deepened into a grey sadness as she watched him struggle to keep upright against the force of another tremor shuddering the floor underneath their feet.

"It's starting."

CHAPTER 6

In the ocean below the navy surveillance helicopter, the demon sinkhole spun and boiled. The blue-green whirlpool of the massive, mile-wide sink appeared to extend downward infinitely. Its watery walls were steep, dropping into the darkest of pits, opening up a fissure to a demonic portal.

And no one knew what was waiting at the bottom.

US military helicopters, flying from a nearby aircraft carrier, took shifts monitoring the site, but were staying much higher than their first patrol crafts had. At the very beginning, when they hadn't understood the danger, at least three helicopters had been drawn into the orbit of the whirlpool and had been lost. They weren't making that mistake again.

"Hey, Chen. I'm beginning to wonder if these demons are ever going to come," Private Dee Jacobson said to the guy next to him. "How long have we been up here, anyway?"

"Too long," Private Chen said, yawning. He checked his watch. "And we got another three hours. And I'm hungry. You got anything to—?" Then his eyes grew large as he looked out the window at the swirling pit underneath the helicopter. "Jacobson, what's that?"

The crewmen looked out into the dangerous waters. Below, the sinkhole seemed to be shrinking before their very eyes, growing smaller and smaller with every passing moment. They watched with hope as the swirling waters seemed to fold in on themselves.

Jacobson leaned out the window. "Is it going away? Is it?" He laughed in relief. "It's going away! Chen, you see this?"

An enormous gust of air blew up towards the helicopter from the pit below as the sinkhole kept shrinking inexplicably.

"Hold on!" a shout came from the cockpit. The chopper shuddered and tilted sideways, violently, before the pilot steadied them again.

Jacobson radioed back to their carrier. "Giant Killer, we have action here at the sinkhole site," the crewman said. "It almost looks like, well, you're not going to believe this, but it looks like the sinkhole's disappearing!"

"*Go again, Charlie Niner Niner?*" the voice from the carrier responded in disbelief. Below, the water had become darker and darker, until almost black.

The crewmen hadn't noticed the change and were still laughing. But Chen was quiet as he looked once more out the window. "I have a bad feeling about this. . ."

The others followed his gaze and saw the problem. For several moments, all the crewmen on the helicopter held their breath. The water below became still. Silent. The pool had become smaller than ever. It all looked so harmless, except for the inky black spreading out from its centre like an oil spill.

Suddenly the pit began spiraling again. Faster, faster this time. The whirlpool started developing rapidly, expanding and expanding, and growing faster by the second.

"What the hell is that?" Jacobson screamed.

Crimson red tendrils began spiraling up from the bottom of the sinkhole into the churning black waters. More and more red frothed up to the top until the entire roiling waters spiralled into a giant, frothy sinkhole.

Of blood.

One lone demon emerged slowly from the bloody froth. It was enormous. Its black skin, rugged with scales, seemed to actually be *on fire*, a putrid mass of black flame and smoke roiling off its body. In fact, its skin most certainly *was* afire, shifting, moving, and searing with dark flames. Enormous spiny protrusions ran along its back, terrible and murderous. Multiple heads gnashing black teeth emerged from its chest, jaws snapping and snarling at the sun itself. The Dark One beat its scaly wings once, then twice, circling the sinkhole in a counterclockwise motion.

Then another demon emerged.

And another.

Soon, dozens rose up, all dripping fire, blood-red and blood-black, from the terrible waters.

"Dear God," Chen said.

"Get us out of here, now!" Jacobson shouted frantically to the pilot.

The military surveillance copter fought against the storm winds and rose higher and higher, away from the pit.

"*Charlie Niner Niner, achieve safe distance!*" the voice from back on the carrier yelled over the radio.

Suddenly, an F-18 shot across the sky, deafening as it roared overhead and began to circle back.

"*Boys, the cavalry has arrived. Proceed back to bearing zero-niner-*

twenty-four," a voice from the fighter jet said over the radio. "*We'll take it from here.*"

"Roger that, we are heading back," Chen said. "Gladly. You watch your six out here, Trav."

"Roger that. Getting a read on the enemy."

The helicopter moved towards the relative safety of the carrier and battleships, some miles away.

"Will you get a load of that," the copilot of the fighter jet said in disbelief and practical wonder as he looked at the sight below.

The demons were flying just above the surface, still in the shelter of the swirling pit, circling in the opposite direction of the roiling black and red froth.

"Looks like they're not coming out to play," the pilot said.

Suddenly, one demon rose up and skimmed just metres above the surface, advancing towards the fighter jet, which was trying to get a position on the hole.

"We have a bogey," the co-pilot said. He leaned down and took a picture of the demon below with his iPhone as the jet banked hard right.

"I'm not scared or nothin'," he said over the radio. "But that's one ugly sucker."

"Focus, man, focus," the pilot said.

"Got it," the copilot said. "OK, move in tighter. Let's see how he likes a taste of Uncle Sam's medicine."

"Moving in," the pilot said, speeding up until they were right behind the Dark Angel as it roared across the ocean surface.

Beeeeeeeeeep. The targeting screen turned red as it locked on to the demon's heat source.

"Missile lock! Missile lock! Let's smoke this demon right now!"

"Engaging," the pilot said, flipping up the trigger guard and pressing the missile button.

The missile fired – and flew right over the demon's shoulder.

"Damn!"

The Dark Angel spiralled its body around, shooting left. It looked only mildly irritated.

"Giant Killer, we need some backup firepower!" the copilot shouted.

The answering voice came from flight control over the radio: *"Roger. Incoming. Course set to niner-eight-four-niner."*

All at once, four surface-to-air missiles launched from a tactical battleship in the strike group with the aircraft carrier, leaving wispy jet trails as they flashed towards their target. At the same time the jet spiralled to follow the demon and launched another missile its way.

The Dark Angel only had a half second to look sideways, its expression almost curious. First the jet's rocket struck, and then, a split second later, the ship's missiles seared the sky and collided with the demon as it skimmed along the surface of the ocean. One shot after the other. *BOOMBOOMBOOM BOOMBOOM.*

The force of the explosions was visible in the orange fire below, which flared back in the tinted glass of the pilots' helmets.

"Target hit. Bull's-eye," the pilot confirmed.

"Did it work? Did it work?" The co-pilot's voice was calling frantically. The F-18 circled around, and from the billowing smoke of the explosion, not a demon was seen. Only a disturbance in the water where the flaming wreckage of the missile lay.

"Roger that," the pilot said coolly.

"Holy crap, it worked! We got the bastard! Giant Killer, we have downed our first Dark Angel," the copilot said. "Ha-*ha*!"

Screaming against the g-forces, the jet banked backward, away from where they had struck at the demon.

The navigator checked his green radar screen. "Giant Killer, looks like we have three bogies on radar. Hell's bells, this is going to be *fun*."

Suddenly, behind the jet, the demon that had been struck by the missiles emerged from the water. And it looked angry.

"*Pull up, pull up, pull up!*" the copilot screamed. "Bogey is back, bogey is ba—"

In what seemed like a mere blink of an eye, the Dark Angel was on the jet, colliding in a cataclysm of fire and fury against the wing. Jet fuel incinerated as the aircraft crumpled into destruction. The demon continued flying up even as the fiery wreckage of what once was a mighty fighter jet arced towards the ocean at 200 miles per hour. The flaming ball impacted the blue-green surface so immediately that it appeared as if it had hit concrete. It shattered instantly into a million pieces, taking the lives of the pilots along with it.

"*Do you read, over? Do you read, over? Dammit, Trav, answer me!*" the control tower called from the carrier.

But there was no answer.

From the sinkhole, even more demons began to rise, circling. They looked to Angel City.

Maddy's gaze was focused on a small fly on the inside of the kitchen window. The insect beat itself against the glass as if striving for the sun outside, launching itself again and again, its wings flapping more desperately now. Even though it was a few feet away, this fly seemed to take up every inch of Maddy's field of vision. Suddenly, the bright sun outside dimmed dramatically until it cast off the glow of a very red sunset. But it was still two in the afternoon, hours from dusk. The fly was now bathed in a blood-red light as it even more frantically tried to escape, too insignificant to realize it was trapped inside the glass. Maddy was transfixed.

The earth shook again, snapping her out of her reverie.

"Maddy!" Kevin shouted as a cupboard door swung open and a stack of plates was hurled towards her. He pushed Maddy out of the way as the plates smashed to pieces on the linoleum.

They were coming. She'd had the vision of the demon bearing down upon her, so strong that she was still reeling, only half-conscious to this world, the real one. That image of the Dark Angel was burned into her mind, still appearing before her in a slightly faded form, like the trace of bright light that followed everywhere she looked. A nauseating pit had been dug into her stomach, settling in with a hollow, sickly feeling.

Turning towards the window again, Maddy realized that her mind hadn't been playing tricks on her; the sky really had taken on a sunset-red hue. She had a bad feeling that this wasn't going to be the strangest thing she saw all day.

The earth shook again.

"Kevin! Listen to me! You have to stay inside like we planned," Maddy shouted, adrenaline rushing upon her.

"What? Where are you going?" Kevin asked.

"I have something to do," Maddy said.

"Maddy!" Kevin yelled as she dashed to the back door. Without another word, she was gone.

With bounding strides Maddy rounded the large oak she loved from her childhood to get to the front of the house. She peered into the distance and, with a sinking heart, saw activity across the darkening ocean horizon.

She could hear the distant rumble of fighter jet engines miles off, towards Santa Monica and the ocean, and could make out small specks in the distance. Whether they were demons or fighter jets, or both, she could not say.

She immediately tried to key into Tom's frequency, but in bitter disappointment she found she couldn't. Straining again to find Tom's frequency emanating from the carrier, she still felt blocked. She had just felt it minutes before. But now it was gone, and there was no way for her to know what was happening to him.

With so much confusion and fear bubbling up all at once in the city, her neural circuitry was getting overwhelmed, even though she was superb at frequencing, something Susan Archson, her favourite Angel professor at Guardian training, had taught her. Maddy had excelled in the course, and Susan had been really impressed with her talent. Maddy had had visions since she was just a little girl, but had never known what they were. When people in her proximity were going through extreme situations, Maddy had thought she was just different or weird, and she'd kept the disturbing premonitions to herself.

But now the entire city seemed to vibrate with terror and confusion, and she couldn't do a damn thing. It was flooding her all at once, and trying to focus on one frequency was impossible.

The overwhelming static from all the panic of the people in the city swamped her senses.

And yet she still would try to focus on Tom's, if she could.

In the distance there were the flashes of explosions. The distant rumble of booms rolled through the air from the ocean, indicating the first line of defence against the demons. But it was all too far away for Maddy to see what was really going on.

BOOM. BOOM. BOOM. The reports of the far-off bombs continued to roll in.

With hope rising in her chest, Maddy realized that she hadn't yet seen an actual demon. Maybe the humans could repel the Dark Angels after all. Maybe they could save themselves. If anyone could stop the demons, wouldn't it be the biggest and most capable military in the world?

Then, with bitter disappointment, Maddy saw one, then two burning black shapes in the distance. They were growing closer, closer as they streaked across the sky towards Angel City. Dark Ones. All the hope that had just been glimmering inside her crumpled up in an instant. They had already broken through!

She could see that the defences had slowed them down a bit, but clearly some demons had already made their way through the first line of defence along the coast. Maddy heard some terrified yells from the neighbours as they stumbled out of their homes and stared with wide eyes and gaping mouths at the reddening, darkening sky.

It was really happening.

Blood pounded in Maddy's ears as she flashed back to the night she saw her first demon in the high school lab. How much damage just that one had caused. She felt half here and half there, somehow still trapped in that terrifying world of blood and fire that had struck her vision. She shuddered as she realized that the real world and the world from her premonition were soon to collide.

Suddenly, as she still stood on the front lawn, her senses returned to the present. She noticed the neighbours outside again, their jaws dropped open, their feet rooted to the ground as they watched the Dark Angels move in across the darkening sky: small spots of fire and smoke growing closer.

Then, as if cued by an invisible conductor, they screamed.

"They're coming!" Maddy shouted at them. "Everyone, go! Get inside!"

Maddy's pitch must have been sharp enough to break their collective trance, because it only took a second for them to scramble indoors as quickly as they could.

Maddy heard the distant rumble of fighter jet engines off towards Santa Monica and the ocean, then the boom of an explosion. Then chaos closed in around the entirety of Angel City. She could make out small specks in the distance, and, for just a moment, she saw a flash in the sky – a missile aimed at a demon? Or could it have been a jet exploding? Or, Maddy couldn't help but think as a raw, hollow feeling dragged its nails across her stomach, could that have been . . . Tom?

She reeled under the sensation that passed as she thought that the flash and boom might have simply been *it*. Tom could be gone, ripped apart by the force of the explosion into pieces no one would never find. And to top everything off, try as she might, Maddy couldn't focus her frequency on Tom. He was either too far away and caught in the frequency static caused by the panic spreading across Angel City, or that *had* been a jet she'd seen explode, and it'd been *his* jet. The reason she couldn't track his frequency was because he was . . .

Maddy chased the word out of her head before it could enter. He couldn't do that. She wouldn't let him. He *had* to survive.

Kevin burst through the front door, breaking Maddy's reverie.

"Thank God you're still here!" he said. "It's all over the news, Maddy. Some of the demons have already broken through at the coast. They're headed straight towards Angel City, but, Maddy, get this – they're following the freeways."

Maddy didn't turn to face her uncle, and instead just kept looking up at the sky. Kevin took a few steps farther, out from under the eaves of the house, and followed her gaze up towards the evil brewing in the sky.

"Are you . . . ?" Kevin trailed off, visibly overwhelmed by the scene.

Maddy finally turned to Kevin. From the look on his face, she could tell he understood.

Her inner Angel had come out.

"Stay inside until you hear from me," Maddy said. "Or if we . . . can't reach each other, try to get out, any way you can. Maybe they'll reopen the evacuation routes. Just . . . stay safe, Uncle Kevin."

She looked up and their eyes locked. All their years spent sharing each other's lives passed between them in that moment.

"You be careful," Kevin said.

She gave him a faint smile – the biggest she could muster in the moment – and nodded. Slowly, as if reluctant, Kevin headed for the front door and, with an attempt at a cheerful wave, went inside.

Maddy turned back to the darkening sky. Inky clouds ran from behind the demons' tails, spreading blackness from the ocean, as fighter jets gave pursuit.

In the distance, a huge explosion of concrete and flame rocked the edge of downtown as a demon touched down on a freeway, pulverizing a large stretch into ash and fire instantly. As Maddy looked out across as much of Angel City as her front lawn perch would allow, it seemed to her that the demons weren't flying straight. It was just as Kevin had said – it looked like they were following the freeways.

BOOM.

Before she had a chance to think for even a microsecond longer, an enormous explosion erupted just blocks away, rocking the very ground Maddy stood on. The shock waves from the blast rippled through her body.

Gasping and stunned, Maddy sprinted into the middle of the street. Out towards the Walk of Angels, a snarled cloud of flame and smoke crept towards the skies above rooftops and palm trees. Car alarms blared all across the city, and emergency sirens began to wail.

Overhead, a sudden streak of black fire and flame passed, followed by the deafening roar of two F-16s, which appeared to be trying to get in position to fire on the Dark Angel. Something in Maddy's subconscious told her to duck, even though the jets were hundreds of feet in the air. They launched missiles as the beast passed over the hill, and soon the whole group disappeared over the ridge towards the Valley.

Still more demons appeared in the far-off sky, and the air raid siren began singing its howling song again. There was already a smattering of fires all across the city.

Chaos. Pure, hellish chaos.

Maddy dizzied under waves of panicked frequencies running through the city all at once. Using her every ounce of effort, she tried to isolate them, just like Susan had taught her in class. But it was too much. And there were too many. How would she be able to—

Suddenly, a vision. Maddy braced herself under the impact of grisly imagery and human misery. *It was close. The young woman was close. There was still time before she was lost.*

With a holler, Maddy leaned forward. Her wings rocketed out of her back faster than they ever had, creating a huge *whoosh* and ripping two surprisingly clean holes in the back of her shirt. Before they'd even reached their full span, Maddy took two big pumps and began rocketing west, soaring over buildings and swaying palms. In only a handful of seconds, Maddy shot north, skimming over the 101 freeway in the Cahuenga Pass up into the Angel City Hills, which was lined with lush trees on both sides. The freeway was almost empty, except for a few cars that had used the chaos to evade the checkpoints and were frantically fleeing the city.

Clenching her jaw, Maddy streamlined herself as much as she could and tried to put on speed. She had only seconds. Any miscalculation would be fatal.

In her peripheral vision she saw it: the Dark Angel. Careening towards the exact spot she was zeroed in on, streams of dark smoke pouring off its back as it flew at top speed.

Maddy dropped towards the freeway with a final burst of energy. Below, the concrete and painted white lines blurred with the speed.

Then, in one horrible, single instant, the demon tucked itself into a ball with nonchalant flexibility and violently smashed down to the freeway, just to the left of Maddy, who had almost reached the road. She had nearly gotten to her target – a young woman on a Vespa riding on the access road right next to the freeway who would never have known what hit her if it hadn't been for Maddy. At the exact moment the demon touched down, the middle of the freeway exploded in a fury of concrete and flame, and Maddy used everything she had to concentrate on one point and one point only.

And she screamed.

Suddenly everything – the flames and concrete and demon and girl and Vespa and smoke – *froze*. The demon was still wreaking havoc on the freeway, halfway into making a gigantic crater, but it was frozen there, in all its evilness, its limbs curled up against its body like a cannonball, flames leaping off its back in one cold, solid fan. The lethal slabs of concrete and countless particles of dust that had just shot up from the freeway were now suspended in mid-air.

Maddy had frozen time. Though it had been infinitely more difficult than the first time, when she'd made a save with the jet and Jeffrey Rosenberg over the Pacific. But now, to her astonishment, she could feel that the Dark Angel was somehow *battling her effort*. She tried to ignore it and zeroed in on the save.

Hurtling right towards Vespa Girl was a huge Volkswagen-sized chunk of concrete. The tendrils of the girl's brunette hair were flying back from under her helmet and frozen in position. A strange look of unknown fear was frozen on her face, but experience told Maddy that the girl's inner survival instincts were telling her something was wrong. Still, she had no clue she was about to be crushed to death.

Maddy calculated. She would have a second, maybe one and a half, to make the save before the time freeze spun out of her control.

With every milligram of concentration she had, Maddy shot down as the time freeze began to collapse in on itself. The Dark Angel fought strongly against her power, but with a final push, just as time was about to tick back on and the concrete mass was starting to budge from its hold, Maddy violently scooped the girl off the back of the Vespa.

She put everything she had into pulling the girl up, but she wasn't quite fast enough to totally get away.

The concrete hurled itself sideways, catching the back of Maddy's left Converse sneaker as she flew up with the girl in her arms, and smashed the Vespa into a thousand pieces of Italian metal and plastic. The slight impact to her foot sent Maddy spinning as she flew, and she tried to shield the girl as they whirled in the air and tumbled to the ground in a heap.

Maddy tried to cover both herself and the girl with her wings as a shower of dust and fine bits of concrete from the impact cascaded down upon them. Flames shot above the crater, sending a car veering across the freeway to avoid debris until it hit the median, tipped to its side, and slid about a hundred feet.

Vespa Girl started hyperventilating and struggling in Maddy's grasp; she still had no idea what just happened.

"Shh. Calm down! Calm down!" Maddy gasped, trying to catch her breath as well amid the cloud of dust. "It's OK. I'm an Angel. I just saved you. You're going to be fine."

As she said it, Maddy had to wonder: *Are they actually going to be fine?*

With a sinking feeling, she heard the demon's raspy, ragged breathing. Maddy looked out from under her wing and saw the thing climb out of the pit it had just made. It had been a while since she'd seen one of *them* this up close and personal, and it was more soul-shattering than she remembered. The Dark Angel's very shape seemed to be shifting and changing, and Maddy realized that its skin was nearly on fire. It was a black fire, shimmering and roiling along its body. This one seemed to have only one head, but enormous horns speared out of it, and a series of jagged spikes exploded out of its shoulders and back.

Emerging from the crater like a messenger from hell, the demon turned to Maddy and the girl. Its dark red eyes glinted, dead-like, with recognition. One could almost say it looked excited. The demon took a step forward and flicked a blackened tongue out of its mouth.

Still in Maddy's arms, Vespa Girl screamed.

Maddy felt stunned from the grazing blow of the concrete and the crash, but she still attempted to stand up to defend them – with what? Her bare hands? Or . . . ? She found herself a bit dizzy. But she had to do something. There was no way she could outfly the demon with the girl in her arms, so Maddy steeled herself for the Dark Angel's approach while the girl fell back into her embrace, weeping in fear.

Suddenly, the demon stopped, as if it had heard something. It cocked its head towards the distance, then turned its unthinkable face back to Maddy and the girl. In impotent rage, it roared.

It unfurled its scaly wings and launched into the air, leaving a trail of acrid smoke in its wake. Maddy watched as it bore a course back towards the south, towards the ocean whence it came. It had departed so suddenly, and without attacking Maddy and the girl, that it was almost as if someone – or some *thing* – had been controlling it.

"It's gone. It's gone," Maddy said, trying to calm the young woman in her arms. She stroked the girl's hair as if she were a child, although she was probably Maddy's age. "Shhh, shhhh. It's gone. I don't know why, but it's gone.

CHAPTER 7

The numbers in the gleaming elevator steadily climbed up and up. Instead of projecting an underwater scene, the TV wall on the back of the car was now set to an African savanna. Giraffes and lions ran around, silhouetted against a setting orange sun, and beautiful herons skimmed the surface of grassy wetlands. Jacks was impatient. Finally, the car hit level G with a ding.

He'd felt the earthquakes announcing the beginning of the demon attacks. All the Angels had – the quakes' echoes had been so strong they even permeated their luxurious underground shelter.

A security guard came running up to Jacks. Above, through a skylight, Jacks could see the sky was turning black-red.

"Mr Godspeed, you're not supposed to be up here. I'm under strict orders that you're to be downstairs with the rest of the Angels," the guard pleaded.

Without a word, Jacks pushed past the guard.

Most of the glass cube of the sanctuary was sheltered by leafy trees to make it nearly invisible, tucked far into a massive estate in the Angel City Hills. But a few gaps in the foliage gave a slight view on to Angel City.

Down the hill, outside the giant gleaming glass walls and ceiling, bedlam reigned.

Spires of black smoke rose up across the city, which was

enveloped in dwindling red light. Visible on the horizon were Dark Angels, spectacles of fire born from hell, laughing off the fighter jets that desperately criss-crossed the sky. Jacks looked out across the bleak expanse and saw that most of the freeways were on fire.

Jackson was surprised there weren't more demons, actually. He had thought the assault would have started as an immediate curtain of fire and destruction, but right now he only saw a couple dozen or so demons. An explosion rang out in the distance, sounding like it might have come from the Walk of Angels, but Jackson couldn't be sure without seeing it.

Although he tried his best to keep up a stern facade, Jackson Godspeed's face fell as he saw the city he knew and loved struggling to defend itself from these dark emissaries from hell.

He tried to detach. Make it seem like he was watching an action movie set in some far-off unknown, with a cast of characters he'd never met. People he had never cared about. His jaw stiffened.

Behind Jackson the elevator dinged, and the gleaming doors opened with a whir. Emily emerged.

"Jacks, I thought I might find you here," she said. The hapless security guard ran up to her, but the Aussie bombshell brushed him off easily. "What are you doing? Checking out the action?"

She crept up to Jackson's side, eyeing the sky. "Mark would freak out if he knew you're up here." Her eyes danced with danger. "You're such a rebel."

"Emily, please go back downstairs. Nobody asked you to come up here, did they?" Jacks said, his tone flat as he watched the destruction unfold.

71

"Why are *you* up here, Jackson? Do you feel bad for them or something?" Emily said, her eyes darting about to take in the threatening scene above.

"It looks like they're going back," Jacks said, his tone curious, as if he were commenting on a baseball game on TV instead of a full-scale attack raging just outside the window. But it was true – all the demons seemed to have turned, and were now flying back out towards the ocean. But it didn't look like they were being driven away. It looked as if somehow they were being *called* back.

"They're retreating?" Emily said, eyeing the dark shapes heading back to the ocean. A look of excitement crossed her eyes. "We've been down in the bloody sanctuary too long. Let's go out! We're good-enough flyers. It'll be fine."

Jackson thought back again to Emily pitching a fit when they first went down to the sanctuary, when a demon had seared across the sky before them, smashing into the Hills.

"I don't think you'd want that, Emily," he said.

"They're leaving! They're gone. You said so yourself," she said. "C'mon. It'll be fun. Don't you like to break the rules?" She winked at him.

"It's not about the rules, it's—"

"Fine. Suit yourself." Before Jacks knew it, Emily's wings had extended with a whoosh and she had flown past the guard in a flash. She was a streak across the sky. She was always the fastest in her class at agility training – not only a sexy model but also a kick-ass Angel who had some serious moves.

"Emily!" Jacks called. He shook his head. With a quick tilt down, his wings ripped out of his back, fully sprung. In moments he was soaring out over the Angel City basin, ripping across the sky, trying to catch up with Emily.

The wind whipping in his ears, Jackson neared Emily – or perhaps she just *let* him get near – and she giggled as she darted out of his grasp, her red hair streaming behind her. "Can't you keep up with me?" She laughed.

Then Jackson looked below. The Angel City basin was burning. As far as he could see, hundreds of fires had sprung up, and the freeways looked all but destroyed. The city he had known his whole life had received its first blow.

And it was devastating.

His throat plummeted into his stomach as he soared over the destruction. Looking out, he could see the demons were barely visible as they retreated to their ocean sinkhole.

"I'm going back," Jacks shouted at Emily, turning back.

"Why?" Emily shouted, oblivious to what was going on below them. "Don't you like stretching your wings?"

Jackson didn't answer, just turned and soared back to the hidden glass box on the hill. Biting her lip in disappointment that he had so quickly ended their game, Emily followed closely behind. By the time she landed, Jacks was standing at the sanctuary entrance, staring with faraway eyes at the Immortal City. Somehow, his mind was blank. His emotions were inaccessible. He didn't know what he felt. In this hollow space, his mind turned to his discussion with Gabriel. This was the tragic, inevitable fate of the humans.

During their talks, Jackson had been struck by how hard all this was for the True Immortal: Gabriel had spent his entire life – lifetime upon lifetime in human years – guarding mankind.

And then they had turned on the Angels. Jackson could relate to Gabriel's sadness, more than Gabriel might even know.

"They should've known a good thing when they had it and just let us alone," Emily said as she walked up to Jacks. "Now, without their Angels, who's going to save them? It's their own fault, Jackson. Not ours."

As if suddenly broken from a spell, Jacks turned away from the carnage outside the window.

"I know it's not our fault," he said. "I'm just curious about what's going on. And you're right. They brought it on themselves. We gave them a chance. We gave them multiple chances. But they disappointed us." His face twisted bitterly into a grimace, and he turned back towards the elevator, Emily still following close behind.

She wound her arm in his as they entered the elevator. He didn't take it away.

CHAPTER 8

On that crisp night, moonlight spilled down off the side of a cluster of classic tan stucco buildings in old Angel City. Aside from the occasional bold person wandering around after dark despite the citywide curfew and the chilling reports of random, isolated demon assaults during the first wave just one day earlier, the rest of the street remained dark and silent.

"Disappearances" would be a better way to put it, rather than isolated "attacks." No one ever survived to tell anyone what actually happened.

But everyone knew what was happening.

A terrified silence hung in the air over this city under siege, its freeways and only exits to the outside world destroyed. The city could do nothing but wait for the next attack.

Off in the distance, silhouetted against the clear moonlit sky, stood the spire of the Blessed Sacrament Catholic Church, a hold-out in what had been the hub of ultra-modern, glitzy Angel City. The church had been devoted to the worship of the Angels and all their products, perfect skin, and high-profile lifestyles. Now the noise and glamour had subsided, the lights extinguished by electricity rationing, and the cries of the paparazzi had been silenced. Only the spire broke the skyline, jutting into the night.

Nearby, a figure walked quickly along a pitch-black street lined with darkened palm trees whispering above in the wind. The footsteps were quick and furtive as the figure moved along the sidewalk, barely sounding. Head covered, the figure kept looking over the left shoulder, as if suspecting a tail. The shadowed person made a sharp turn into a doorway and disappeared from the street.

The door swung open, casting dim light on to the otherwise blacked-out sidewalk. The figure stopped, frozen.

A man was silhouetted inside the doorframe.

"Here," he said. He leaned forward to quickly usher the person in off the street. His face was lit by the weak indoor bulbs, and a glare glinted off the lenses of his glasses.

"David," said the figure from the street as she entered the room. Relief tinged with something else, something vague, coloured her words.

"I was afraid you might have trouble finding it," Detective Sylvester said. "We had to change locations so fast this morning. I was . . . worried." Sylvester quickly looked up and down the street before pushing the door closed behind him, plunging the outside back into utter darkness.

Inside, the woman from the street pulled the shawl off her head. It was Archangel Susan Archson, the professor who had encouraged Maddy so much in Guardian training. As she unfurled her hair, her beauty shone full force in the small hallway. Even in this time of crisis, she radiated the mature beauty and charisma for which older female Angels were famous.

The detective's breath caught for a moment. Sylvester's and Susan's eyes locked.

"It's good to see you," Sylvester said. His eyes flashed behind his glasses, and a slight glow of red appeared on his cheeks.

"It's only been since last night at the office," Susan said, smiling.

"Like I said," he said quietly, "I was worried."

He turned down the hallway.

"Down here," Sylvester said, leading her down a narrow aisle lined with small, unoccupied offices.

"What's happened, David?" Susan asked, leaning in close to the detective.

"What *didn't* happen, more like it," Sylvester said. Sylvester's eyes were heavy with dark rings underneath, and it looked like the last time he'd seen a good night's sleep was sometime in the previous decade.

"I wish you'd get some rest, David," Susan said, concern lining her smooth Angel face.

"I'll rest later," Sylvester said, trying to change the subject. "This morning your tech guy discovered that our private network had been compromised. Someone cracked the first-level encryption, and the National Angel Services would have known our exact location in an hour, two hours at most. We moved out in twenty-eight minutes and came here. A safe house." Sylvester gestured to the rest of the building.

Susan lifted an impressed eyebrow and smiled at Sylvester. Smiles were a rare, welcome sight in Angel City these days, and Sylvester savoured this one. "Good. But if we'd gone with my emergency plan, it would have taken twenty-*five* minutes," she said.

Sylvester paused as he reached a closed door. A thin ribbon of light shone from underneath into the otherwise dim hallway. All was quiet. He opened the door to reveal a hive of activity, which pulled him and Susan in immediately. The formerly unoccupied office – furnished with not much besides a couple of old printers collecting dust in the corner, an overturned rolling office chair, and papers scattered along the floor – had been quickly transformed into a headquarters of sorts. A handful of humans and Angels sat around a long table, fingers running lightning-fast over laptop keyboards. Another group stood clustered around a stack of documents they were examining, slurping coffee. They'd been at it since before dawn.

Hanging on the wall beside the desk Sylvester had claimed for himself was an enormous map of Angel City, presiding over everything. It was a touch of home for the detective, who had a similar map decorating the wall of his own apartment. Across the map were red circles that marked all the locations of the demon attacks during the first wave, as well as blue dots that represented the isolated attacks on individuals. Of course the detective had started to formulate a theory. But he had been keeping it to himself. For now.

This was the resistance. A ragtag group of humans and breakaway Angels dedicated to bringing the Immortals into the fight against the demons. Before it was too late.

Moving under cover of darkness, using every tool it had, the resistance had to evade detection by the Angel authorities as it attempted to grow its network of spies and finally turn the Angels to the group's side. The Angels were the only chance for Angel City's survival, if everyone was being honest.

With the city already reeling after the first attack, supplies were barely trickling into the metropolis, and an entire populace remained hidden inside. Random demon scouts were prowling the borders, disrupting attempts to bring in support from the outside and making the city truly feel under siege. Outside Angel City, the rest of the world watched in horrified anticipation for what was going to happen when the demons struck next.

And as if trying to remain underground from the Council and the Angel Disciplinary Council Agents wasn't enough, the resistance also had reason to believe its members could be specifically targeted by the demons because of their efforts. Just another reason for the group to be extra, extra careful.

Sylvester thought back to how all this had begun for him. Back in his apartment, he'd been tracking demon sightings and "events" across the globe as the demons amassed their army. A derailed train in England. A five-alarm fire in an apartment complex in Beijing. Innumerable tragedies, all seemingly unrelated, but eventually they all started to add up. He had been getting anonymous tips from a woman, who turned out to be Susan, and Sylvester had made it all the way to the inner sanctum of Gabriel and the Council of Twelve to plead his case. But the Council denied his request for action. It had been more concerned with the human-Angel war. The demon sinkhole arrived just days later, and Susan swooped in to talk Sylvester off his bar stool. So it was that she and Detective Sylvester – and one other – had formed the resistance.

Susan had been privately working against the Council for years, organizing an underground resistance within the ranks of the Angels. Hers was a protest of conscience against the way the Angels had drifted from their true purpose. Throughout all the recent discord, Susan had remained quiet. She became an Archangel and trained new Guardians, all the while waiting for the right moment to move against the Council. Her organization went deep, with spies across every branch of the NAS, so when the Angels had decided to sit out the demon war and leave the humans to their fate, she knew it was time. That was when she found David, her old friend.

Publicly moving against the NAS had put Susan's life in danger, and she had been denounced by the Angels at once. They'd started a smear campaign against her, trying to discredit her with all kinds of lies. But still she'd moved forward despite everything, with Detective Sylvester by her side. This was too important for her to waste time worrying about herself. The resistance was what mattered.

An operative sipping coffee looked up as Sylvester approached. He was Sylvester's ACPD partner, Sergeant Bill Garcia.

"Didn't we agree you'd go home and spend some time with your family, Bill?" said Sylvester.

"My wife and kids understand what's at stake," Garcia said. "I won't *have* a family if the demons win."

Sylvester's brow darkened.

"And you know we can't trust the ACPD," Garcia continued. "The Angels have informants everywhere. I've got enough vacation days to cover this time away – don't you worry."

Detective Sylvester nodded, and put his hand on Sergeant Garcia's shoulder. "Just make sure you get out of here and go see them at some point. They'll need you, too. When the time comes," he finished gravely.

Sylvester's gaze travelled to where the tech brainiacs had set up. They made up a large team of Angel and human communications experts working around the clock to try to trace Angel communications. They knew that even though the Angels had gone down to the sanctuary, the Angels were still communicating around the globe to Angels in other countries, as well as communicating on secure channels inside the sanctuary itself. By tracking these communications they would be able to judge the state of the Angel leadership and the loyalties of the Guardians. And it was vital to Sylvester and Archson's group to have advance notice if one of their spies was uncovered – that way, their operative would have at least the slightest chance to escape.

"Any progress?" Sylvester asked. One of the human code-breakers sipped from a twenty-ounce bottle of cola and just shook his head. With one big slurp, he emptied the bottle, tossed it into a wastebasket that was already overflowing with empty bottles of the same sugary drink.

Susan approached Sylvester's side. "Today's the day we're going to try to get supplies and weapons to those working for us. We have to be prepared for what will happen when the full demon attack hits, especially if the sanctuary is still controlled by the Angels."

"I'm not ready to give in just yet." Sylvester shuddered as he recalled the grisly sight that had met him and Garcia in the tunnel along the Angel City River, when he had finally known the demons would be coming. The decaying remains of dozens of missing homeless men, that massive mound of blood, flesh, and bone they'd discovered where the demons had been feeding underground, made up a macabre monument to cruelty.

"Let's really drill down today on establishing safe communications with President Linden and the military," Sylvester said. "I have a good feeling if we can bypass the ACPD and local officials and go straight to Linden's people we can avoid any leaks back to the Angels. Linden doesn't have many friends in the Council or Archangels in his camp."

"On it, boss," said the computer guy with the cola habit as he turned to another one of his computer terminals. The monitor was spitting out an endless series of green digits on a black Unix screen. "Just need to find the secure band for the government channels . . ."

Sylvester waved him off. "I don't even want to know how many laws you break doing it. Just do it so we're not found out."

"Got it," the tech said.

Susan gave the detective a little smile. She liked to joke that he was a natural manager, which always rankled him. He liked to think of himself as being the solo detective, the guy who works alone. He still wasn't totally comfortable with a whole team.

"What's the latest from the Thorn?" Sylvester asked.

The "Thorn" was the semi-tongue-in-cheek code name they'd given to the resistance agent working deep in the Angel organization, inside the sanctuary. Only Archangel Archson and Detective Sylvester knew the mole's real identity. While the senior leadership of the NAS and the Council knew that Susan had broken ranks and was rebelling – an offence punishable by dewinging and mortalization if she was caught – they didn't have any idea that one of their inner advisers was working to bring the Angels into the war against the demons. And the resistance wanted to keep it that way. Of course, the group had other sympathetic Angels planted in the sanctuary, as well, but the Thorn was the most valuable. And was also at the most risk if exposed.

"The Thorn reports there is no change in the Council now that Angel City is under siege. They knew the demons would advance as if totally unopposed," Susan said. "Just as we'd thought. The leadership is not going to change. Change will have to come from outside. Before it's too late. Our only hope is that we can somehow make the Angels come around. You know it and I know it, David."

Sylvester nodded contemplatively and studied the map across the room. He turned to Susan and spoke in a hushed tone.

"Let's go where we have some privacy," he said, leading her into one of the abandoned offices to the side. She gave him an inquisitive look as they entered the room.

"There's something I've been meaning to tell you," he said, closing the door behind him. "I think it's time."

Was it Detective Sylvester's imagination, or did a slight flush bloom in Susan's face? Her beautiful Archangel features shone even in the depressed darkness of the little office.

"What is it, David?" Susan said softly.

"I didn't want to share this until now, until I was more certain. But I've studied the attack patterns from yesterday, along with the series of disappearances we've heard of since then."

"I knew there was something, but I couldn't put my finger on it," Susan said. "What have you found?"

"This is more than just an assault of demons causing chaos and sowing death. This assault is *organized*. Methodical. They're being led by one among their ranks."

A look of understanding crossed Susan's face. "So maybe, if we can get to the one who is controlling them, we could stop them."

Sylvester nodded. "There has to be a way to get at the head demon. And we're going to find it. No matter what," Sylvester said. "But we'll need some Angels to go after it."

"You're right," Susan said. "We need the Angels now more than ever. Only our kind could find this head demon and exterminate him."

Now it was Sylvester's turn to flush. He was touched that Susan still considered him an Angel, that she didn't see his disgrace and dewinging as an indelible stain for ever.

"The Angels. We have to get them back, David. It's our duty," Susan said. "For years I taught these Guardians. I put everything into training them. I believed in it. Just as you did. And then I slowly started to see what was happening. I first started to doubt them when . . ." She paused and looked at Sylvester. "When they did what they did to you so many years ago. When they took your wings."

Sylvester blushed and coughed into his hand. "Thank you. For your . . . kindness."

"I could never be anything but kind to you, David," Susan said. She smiled lightly, placing her hand on the detective's arm. It was strange, the feeling of that touch through his wrinkled dress shirt. It almost startled him. The touch of an Angel could do miraculous things.

A knock on the door interrupted their private conversation.

"Archangel Archson? Tech has a question for you," a young

woman with glasses said, oblivious to the moment she'd just walked in on.

"I'll be right there." Susan was gone in a few moments, the elegant Archangel following the resistance volunteer into the buzzing hive of workers.

Sylvester followed and returned to his desk – and the map beside it. He sighed, pulling his glasses off and looking at the dust that had accrued on the lenses. He started wiping them with his shirt, then sat down at his desk and poured himself a steaming cup of joe from his seemingly bottomless thermos of coffee.

He put on his freshly cleaned glasses and looked out across the open work area that had just been set up this morning, at the wide-eyed kids just barely out of college, the veteran Angels, his ACPD partner, plus several dissidents and former Angel activists. All brought together by his and Susan's efforts, with their undercover mole helping inside the sanctuary. They were a motley crew if ever there was one.

What would they be able to stop from here? Anything?

But they had no choice. They had to keep going. Any alternative was too bleak to consider.

CHAPTER 9

M addy woke with an unuttered scream on her lips, her hands desperately clawing in front of her as if defending herself. It took her a moment to remember that she'd made her way back to Kevin's house to recover after her near-death save by the 101. She gasped for breath as she sat up, drawing her tangle of sheets around her shivering frame. Cold sweat clung to her goose-pimpled skin, collecting in a small stream along the small of her back.

She'd had the dream again.

For the past two days she'd been plagued by a recurring nightmare interrupting her sleep like clockwork throughout the night. She kept seeing the same, unblinking visage. Of death. On the blasphemous face of a Dark One on the 101 freeway, just like the one she'd saved the Vespa girl from. In the nightmare, the demon would emerge unscathed from a crater, its body shimmering black smoke and fire, and stare right at Maddy.

Then, instead of flying off, the demon would slowly stride towards her. With terror coursing through her veins even in sleep, Dream Maddy would try to escape. Her now-trained wings would pump once, then twice – and nothing. Her feet were somehow stuck to the ground. She couldn't take off. In desperation she would try to run. But her feet merely became even more glued to the earth, until her legs wouldn't move. She was paralysed. Then the sky would grow dark, far darker than it had been on the day of the first attack.

The nightmare demon would take its time as it walked towards her, its terrible gnarled limbs swinging with confidence. Its horns towered over its hideous face, and spikes rippled along its back as it loped. Its black-red eyes would flicker, and it was as if the demon felt a distinct pleasure as it came closer.

Dream Maddy's skin would then grow hotter and hotter as the Dark Angel drew itself closer. So hot it felt as if Maddy's skin were somehow melting from inside. And still the demon came.

Was it smiling now?

The blood-red orb of its eye would draw closer and closer until it seemed to encompass Maddy's entire field of vision. The sensation was unendurable as she would struggle, to no avail, to escape.

The Dark One would then lean down, closer and closer, and open its dread mouth. In her dream, Maddy knew then that she was going to die. The demon's stinking, sulphurous breath blistered her skin as it hissed her name.

"Maddy . . ."

At the end of the nightmare, Maddy would always open her mouth to scream, but no sound would come out. It was too late.

The dream was always the same, and always so much more vivid than any normal nightmare. This dream had the ultra-real quality she felt whenever she focused on someone's frequency or had one of her unbidden premonitions. It was a fevered hallucination in her slumbering brain, but somehow more real than reality itself. It never failed to shake her to her very core.

Pulling herself together, Maddy looked out the window and saw it was still pitch-dark outside, in the small hours of the night. The cold sweat had already begun to evaporate and her fast breathing had calmed down, but there was no chance she'd get back to sleep for a while. Stepping out of bed, Maddy shivered and pulled her oversize T-shirt down closer to her knees as she searched for her pyjama pants. She slipped them on, went to the window, and slowly opened the curtains.

There was the Angel City sign. It had been such an important marker for her during her childhood, giving her something to rail against while everyone else venerated the Angels. Then, when she met Jacks and later discovered her own half-Angel heritage, it took on two completely new meanings.

Now the sign was cloaked in darkness. Power was scarce in the Immortal City right now, and on war footing it made no sense to light the sign. As she drew her arms around her chest to keep warm, Maddy thought of how people across the city could no longer look to the hill and its gleaming beacon to orient themselves, or to give them a signpost, something to hope, dream, and wish on. Instead it was a void, reminding the entire city of how bleak their situation was becoming.

The sign was dark, and the Angels were silent.

Maddy's gaze crossed over the neighbourhoods below the phantom sign, which had also been plunged into eerie darkness. The power had failed again in the night, and she walked now to her bedside lamp and to test the switch. Nothing.

The Immortal City was now entirely dark, its flashy lights and beaming billboards of perfect Angels having receded into the shadows. Residents in the city moved quickly back and forth between darkened homes, fearfully looking up at the sky for the next demon attack, and Humvee units, spread way too thin, patrolled the streets to prevent looting and to help those in need.

The severity and quickness of the first wave of the demon attack two days earlier took most everyone by utter surprise. But now they knew what the demons were capable of, and they knew more were coming. Many more, an untold number. Each one capable of causing unimaginable havoc and bloodshed equal to a major natural disaster.

The city staggered under the constant threat of demons. Evacuation routes had been totally destroyed, the supplies had all but stopped coming in, and the demons kept waging random terrorist attacks. But the worst part was the waiting: why wouldn't the demons just get it over with?

Maddy walked in darkness to her desk and found the candle and matches she always kept ready. With a spark against the rough strip along the box, the match head flared and lit. She brought the flame to the wick of the candle, hot wax drips falling on to the desk as it caught. The flickering flame cast her face in a warm yellow-orange, the corners of the room still lingering in darkness.

The city would wake to another morning under siege. At this point they were waiting, helpless, for the next demon assault. Any plans the city had ever made for emergencies proved to be worse than useless under the stress of a demon invasion, and instructions that looked good on paper turned to chaos and panic as soon as an actual emergency occurred. And now those who remained barricaded themselves behind boarded-up windows. They stayed inside, rationing food and water, waiting for the inevitable main strike from the demon army just lying off the coast.

The demons knew what they were doing, in the most terrible way – they were trying to crush Angel City's spirit before they even fully invaded.

Maddy sighed and tried not to brood. The night was still long. No rays of dawn cut through the darkness outside.

But it had been two days, and she still hadn't heard from Tom. A brief message had arrived via navy messenger that he was alive after the first wave, and she knew the navy had been fighting isolated battles near the sinkhole itself these past few days, but communications were spotty. And she still couldn't focus on his frequency.

To top everything off, Maddy felt so useless just sitting here in Angel City. She'd never been trained for battle of any kind. But was she really just supposed to wait for the next full attack and hope she managed to grab on to a frequency of someone to save? Then she thought of Tom out there, willing to risk his life every day . . .

And then sometimes she would think of Jackson. Stupid, silly stuff, like the way he'd tickle her when they argued about something to get her to laugh. And then, just like that, a sea of sadness would wash over her, and she'd have to go do something else, anything else, before she got sucked down too deep. Having to worry about Tom was hard enough; to sit and ponder Jacks every day was too much for her heart to handle.

Maddy lay back down on her bed, but it seemed hopeless that sleep would come. She turned over on her side and scanned her bookshelf for something to read.

*

She woke up curled on the couch. Early morning light streamed in through the window. It couldn't have been later than 6:30. Mercifully, she'd fallen asleep reading in the living room after going downstairs. The flashlight she'd used to light her book had fallen to the floor, and the novel was open, face down on her chest.

The old cream-coloured phone was ringing. Groggy from sleep, Maddy had to reach and stumble to even find it where it was stuck under a stack of magazines on the lowest shelf of the side table by the couch. Because of cell phones, which had stopped working after the first assault, she couldn't even remember the last time she'd heard the landline ring.

"Hello?"

"Maddy?" said the voice on the other end. "You're there? You're really there?"

"Tom," she said in a rush of relief. "You're all right."

"I'm OK. I'm OK," Tom said. "I've been trying to get in touch with you for so long, Maddy."

Maddy let the relief bleed through her body. Tom was alive. He was right there.

"I . . . I can't tell you how much I've been thinking about you," Maddy said, her voice starting to break up with emotion. "Wanting just to hear your voice."

There was a moment of silence on his end of the line.

"I miss you, Maddy. I miss you so much. It means everything to me to hear you say that. Just to know that you're out there, safe . . ."

"Of course I am, Tom," Maddy said, still tingling with relief. "I'm here for you."

"Maddy . . . I don't know what's going to happen. There were casualties."

Tears streamed down Maddy's face as she held the phone to her ear. "Don't say that, Tom. I know exactly what's going to happen. You're going to beat back the demons and be safe. . ."

"And come back to you," Tom said.

"Yes," Maddy said. "And come back to me."

But even as she said it, Maddy knew that they were each just pretending to be strong for the other, that the Dark Angels were even more powerful than they could have ever imagined. They were a force of evil hell-bent on dominating humanity, and enslaving those it didn't kill.

Maddy heard an air raid siren blare in the background on Tom's end.

"Tom? What's going on?" she asked, gripped by fear. As the siren continued to sound, their connection became worse and worse. . .

"It's OK, I'm OK. It's just a drill," Tom shouted over the noise. The poor connection made his voice crackle. "But I do have to go now."

"OK. I'm just so happy to know you're all right," Maddy said, tears still dripping down her face as she tried to be strong. "And you'll stay that way, too. You're going to be back here safe. Really soon."

Tom spoke, but she could barely hear him.

"Maddy, I lo—"

The line went dead.

"Tom? Tom?" Maddy's voice sounded small and lonely, echoing into emptiness.

He was gone.

Maddy carefully placed the ancient phone back into its cradle. She felt detached from her body and found herself once again questioning her true feelings for Tom. How was it possible she didn't know by now? And how could she ever sort them out?

And how could she ever believe that she could forget about Jackson so quickly?

Angel City under siege, Jackson, Tom, the whirlwind surrounding her illegal save and her consequential loss of celebrity . . . it was all just too much.

Maddy's cheeks were still wet with tears when the landline rang again.

"Tom?" Maddy said, hopeful.

"Madison Montgomery Godright?" a stern voice asked on the other end.

Definitely not Tom. "Yes?" she said tentatively.

"Please hold for President Linden."

CHAPTER 10

The morning sun cut hard against the besieged metropolis. The early blazing rays illuminated a cityscape raging with fires and thick, black smoke filling the sky and reminding the citizens of the previous days' terror.

Maddy looked out at the city through the tinted bombproof windows of the armoured black sedan. The sun and its glare had been muted to a cold grey, and the air-conditioning was so intense that Maddy felt like she'd catch a cold as they drove. For a few blissful seconds, the demon war felt like a distant dream as she watched the palm trees pass outside. She was being escorted to a meeting with Ted Linden, president-elect of the United States and president of the Global Angel Commission, which, as of a few days earlier, was in charge of coordinating the international defence against the demons.

Four Marine Humvees armed to the teeth with turreted guns and grenade launchers flanked the sedan as it drove down the abandoned Angel Boulevard. They weren't taking any chances.

Maddy idly looked up at the billboards still glittering with images of the beautiful Guardians, which now seemed like ancient relics from another age. She couldn't help feeling a small pang as she saw Emily Brightchurch's face splayed across one of the most prominent ads on the boulevard. There was Emily, nearly naked in just her underwear, pouting at the camera, covering her chest for decency with one free arm.

In gigantic, dripping, terrifying red letters, a vandal had spray-painted NO HOPE.

Maddy turned away.

The man on security detail sitting in the passenger seat reached into his inner suit pocket and pulled out a piece of black cloth. A blindfold.

He leaned forward and gestured with it. "For safety."

Maddy nodded, took the blindfold, and lightly tied it around her head. Through a tiny gap she could still see a sliver of sunlight, which brought her some comfort. But then the man reached back and pulled the fabric even tighter until everything was blackness.

"Apologies, Ms Montgomery."

Soon she could feel the sedan pull in somewhere and park, and Maddy was led into what felt like a flat, open space. Gusts of wind whipped and rippled against her body.

"We're taking a chopper," the security guard said as he took her by the arm and guided her on to what she imagined was a Black Hawk helicopter.

Maddy could hear what sounded like two fighter jets tearing across the sky, so deafening that she knew they must be nearby.

"Is everything OK?" she asked, cocking her head to show concern.

"Don't worry, miss. Those birds are just here to provide air cover," a young soldier's voice said. "We're just fine."

Maddy wasn't sure the soldier sounded fully convinced himself, but she nodded from behind her blindfold anyway. She had seen all too clearly how easily the demons were able to cut through the military's air defences. With a chill, Maddy imagined what would happen if one of the Dark Ones decided to come for the helicopter. They wouldn't have a chance.

"It's risky flying in broad daylight," the suited man said, alerting Maddy to the fact that she wasn't the only one with danger on her mind. "But we haven't seen any demon scouts in over twenty-four hours, so intelligence thinks we have a window."

"Do you, uh, do you maybe, uh, know what they're waiting for, miss?" Maddy recognized the nervous voice of the young soldier. "Like, as an Angel you can tell?"

Maddy shook her head sadly. "I wish I could."

"They're overconfident," the suited man said, most likely trying to bolster everyone's morale. "We'll take advantage of this. You'll see. They're making a fatal error."

Maddy once again nodded in agreement, but her effort was pretty halfhearted. She *wanted* to believe they could somehow figure out a way to match the demons. . .

But if she was being honest, she couldn't think of how they possibly could.

A terrific whine sounded outside, and Maddy heard the steady thrum of the helicopter rotors as they began spinning and spinning. Gusts of warm wind blew in through the open door of the helicopter, sending her brown hair streaming everywhere. The helicopter shook with force, and then suddenly she felt it lift off the ground.

They were in the air for an hour, and Maddy had to wear the blindfold the entire time. It only took a few minutes of temporary blindness to make all her other senses that much stronger. Her hearing captured all the tiny details of human movement inside the helicopter and the mechanical din of the engine; her sense of touch tingled with the feel of the smooth metal under the seat contrasting with the rougher, detailed texture of her jeans. During the flight, the security guard offered Maddy a candy bar, but she declined – she felt the sugar might be so intense on her taste buds that she'd go into shock.

"Suit yourself," he said. "But you're missing out – it's got peanut butter."

Finally they arrived at their destination. The helicopter landed with a soft bump, and Maddy was escorted off. Outside, the air was hot and her mouth felt instantly dry. Maddy could tell they were somewhere in the desert.

"This way, miss," her escort said, leading her by the hand into a building. Inside it was instantly at least thirty degrees cooler, and Maddy had never been so grateful for air-conditioning in her life. As they walked she heard a hallway door open, then close after her once they'd crossed the threshold. The security guard seated her in a chair, then finally pulled off the blindfold. She opened her eyes and blinked twice, first to adjust to the light, then to make sure she wasn't dreaming. Sitting at his desk in front of her, in a nondescript room lit more by the glow of numerous computer screens than by the single window, was President Ted Linden.

"I'm sorry for all the theatrics," Linden said, motioning to the blindfold, which now lay crumpled on the desk in front of Maddy. "But my security detail insisted. They still aren't entirely sure where your loyalties lie." He searched Maddy's face with his eyes.

"But now that I see you here, I have no doubts. I only needed to look you in the eyes."

Ever since he'd dropped in unannounced to visit her at the diner, Maddy had a pretty good opinion of Linden, even if she didn't always agree with his methods. She had even publicly stated her support for the Immortals Bill once the human-Angel war seemed certain, before the demon menace raised its head. She felt in her gut that Linden was someone she could trust. Otherwise she would not have agreed to meet with him.

Maddy regarded him now. He looked like he had already aged a couple of years since she had seen him last, just a month or so ago. A wartime presidency aged a person, or at least that's what they said. But when that theory was coined, there had only been human-versus-human wars. A presidency during a demon war was something else entirely. Maddy stopped herself before she imagined what Linden would look like a year from now.

"I'm glad you came," he said. "It's nice to see you again, Madison."

"Likewise, sir," Maddy said, her eyes focusing sharply on him. This is what she had come for. It was her duty.

"What can I do to help?" she asked.

"I'll be blunt, since time is short," he said, standing up and looking out the interior window, on to what looked to Maddy like some kind of control room. "Our allies are shoring up defence of their own cities and countries, while also lending us all the forces they can spare. But even those outside forces can't get through the intermittent demon patrols on the borders of Angel City. It's not enough right now. You know that. I know that." Linden paused. "We still haven't determined why the demons are holding back right now. One theory is that they're testing our defences, evaluating the weaknesses so they can exploit them. Another theory, one that I don't like to believe, is that this is some kind of psychological warfare meant to wear us humans down, until we're so terrified that we just relent to them out of fear. Whatever the reason, once the demons do attack with their full forces – and believe me, they will – our allies in the rest of the world will know that the aid we're getting isn't enough."

Maddy nodded silently. At least he wasn't pulling any punches, unlike the newscasters and pundits, who kept trying to soften the inevitable.

"Maddy, when you and I first met in your uncle's diner, I felt I could trust you," he said. "The Angels and I have had our fair share of differences. I'm the first to say it. But I also know that not all of the Angels support the NAS and the Protection for Pay programme. With the Immortals Bill, I wanted to create an atmosphere where the dissident Angels could feel safe stepping forward, out of the shadows. But I'll admit, the push-back was stronger than I'd anticipated."

"Sir, with all due respect," Maddy said, "did you really expect the Immortals to be happy that you were going to throw them in jail just for using their supernatural powers?"

"Desperate times call for desperate measures, Maddy. If you're honest with yourself, you'll admit the Angels would have never reformed without outside pressure."

"Maybe it was too much pressure," Maddy said. "Sir," she quickly added, remembering who she was talking to.

President Linden smiled. "Being a leader is about making hard decisions. And it was my decision that that much leverage was needed. My goal was never to put the Angels behind bars. My goal was to get them to fulfil their original duties on Earth. Which do *not* include Protection for Pay. Their purpose is higher than that. There was a time when they believed in something higher, and it's something I know they can believe in again."

"Some say humans have no right to mess with Angel affairs," said Maddy.

"They gave up that privilege the day they came out of hiding, Maddy. The day they began the Great Awakening and started the whole ball rolling on Protection for Pay."

He walked away from the window now and stood in front of her, his hands thrust into the pockets of his suit pants. Maddy hadn't realized how tall Linden was, taller than she remembered, and lanky, too. He cut a striking figure, even in this moment of crisis. Maybe *especially* in this moment of crisis.

"Maddy, I need you to go to the Angels. Personally."

Maddy couldn't believe what she'd just heard. She had been ready to jump into battle, to do whatever needed to be done for her city and her country. But to go to the *Angels*? After everything they'd said, everything they'd done? After everything *Jacks* had said and done?

"They'll never agree to help," Maddy said. "Why should they?"

"World history is full of allies who were once enemies but who came together to fight a common enemy who was even worse. Just look at the Soviet Union and America, at Stalin and FDR during World War Two."

"But that's just it – the Immortals don't view the demons as a common enemy right now. The Angels believe the demons are here to claim humanity only," Maddy said. "And right now, I'm thinking they might be right. Only human stuff – I mean, sir, human targets – have been hit in the attacks so far."

"The Angels are in hiding," Linden said. "Why would they be hiding if the demons were only after us?"

"I don't know, sir," Maddy said. "But it doesn't matter. Because even if the Angels were somehow convinced that the demons were a common enemy, the Council would never see me. Never. I'm nothing but a traitor to them. And even *if*, on the slight chance they would see me, I don't even know where to find them. Only those in the most inner circles are brought to the Council chambers."

"I don't want you to put yourself in danger," Linden said.

"It's not about danger, sir," said Maddy. "I'd put myself in any kind of danger if it meant protecting Angel City and its people. But I simply can't do what you're asking. It's impossible." Maddy had hoped he'd have some other use for her, but now she saw that the trip had been in vain. "I'm sorry to disappoint you."

Linden was quiet for a moment, studying Maddy.

"But there is one way, isn't there? There is one who would see you. One who has strong sway among the Angels," Linden said. "Our sources tell us he has become an Angel forces leader almost overnight."

Jacks.

The name came across her mind in a flash. The very name she had been trying so hard to forget, even though it was constantly running through her consciousness like a mantra. What President

Linden was asking of her . . . was impossible. After what she'd done to Jackson at the pier . . . The pain would be too much for him.

"You mean Jackson," Maddy said.

Linden's gaze deepened. "He's our best chance, Maddy. The others are too entrenched in their Angel ways, too blinded by popular opinion. Their loyalty is unquestioned. But his relationship with you . . . that's a completely different story."

"I'm sorry, Mr President. I can't do what you're asking. You don't know what he's like now. He's the most loyal and obedient I've ever seen him. It's like he's a different Angel. I don't even know if he'll" – emotion swelled inside her, forcing her to linger on the sentence for a moment – "want to see me. There are just some things about the situation that you don't know. And, like I said, we don't even know where they're hiding."

The president's jaw grew tense. "Our sources say the Angels are still close to Angel City. Maddy, we don't have another option. Under normal circumstances, I'd tell you to go with your gut. But we need you to at least *try* this." The circles underneath his eyes seemed to deepen as he paused. "Maddy. You do understand that this may be our last chance? The Dark Angels will not give us another opening like this."

Maddy nodded slowly. She knew that what he was saying was true in theory. But to go to Jackson? To reopen that fresh wound that both of them shared? It was perhaps the last thing on the planet she wanted to do.

But as she looked at President Linden, she felt a deep respect. She wanted to do what he asked, to help in any way she could. Even if it meant enduring the pain of seeing Jacks, and having to witness the pain it would cause him. She let out a heavy breath as she prepared to give him her answer.

"All I can promise is that I'll try."

"That's all we can expect from you, Maddy. Thank you. The Angels have cut off all channels of communication with every government in the world," Linden said. "They're not answering any calls, any pleas. They've really just disappeared. You, and your bond with Jackson, truly are our only hope of getting to them."

"But the phone lines are down, cell service, too. How am I even supposed to get in touch . . ."

Linden's eyes twinkled. "We're the American government, Maddy. We can fix that for you. That's the least of your worries."

And once again, like a sickness that comes in waves, Maddy's mind cast back to the fury and agony written all over every inch of Jackson's face as she chose Tom.

"Just don't invest too much hope in this," Maddy said, "because I have a feeling you're going to be disappointed."

CHAPTER 11

Jackson Godspeed wandered the quieter precincts of the sanctuary, lost in thought as his slow footsteps echoed down the empty hallway. The main portion of the complex was laid out like three wheels, one on top of the other, each one larger than the first, with numerous spoke-like passageways coming out from a central hub that connected them all. Jackson was now in the outermost ring, where he was sure he could be alone.

The hallway was dimly lit with soft lighting gleaming along the dark marble floors. He paused at one of the openings off the hall, where a small artificial stream ran along a short path, soothing as it babbled. Every so often, he saw a rainbow trout swim up and glisten in the current. But the serene scene still could not calm Jackson's relentless train of thought.

The images he witnessed during the first demon attacks remained burned in his mind. To watch his native city endure an assault like that, and for him to do nothing about it, had affected him deeply. And, of course, he also couldn't help wondering about Maddy, as painful as it was to even think her name.

Jacks let out a deep breath and made his way back to the centre of the sanctuary. He needed to *do* something besides wander around the outskirts, if only to get his mind off things.

He hadn't gotten far when he ran into Louis Kreuz walking with an assistant weighed down with files.

"Godspeed!" Louis said. Kreuz's meaty paw overwhelmed Jacks's fingers as the two shook hands. "Been out in the boonies?" Kreuz motioned towards the outer rings of the sanctuary.

Jackson was caught off guard. He hadn't expected to run into the brash head Guardian trainer, and for a moment he felt like he was back in training, being chewed out by Kreuz for some small mistake.

"Just clearing my head, sir," Jacks said.

"You don't have to call me 'sir' any more, Godspeed," Kreuz said, grinning. "It's just Louis these days, now that you're a Battle Angel." Jackson didn't return Louis's smile. "Seems like maybe you didn't get too much cleared up out there. Thinking about . . . ?" Louis pointed up, towards the surface, towards Angel City, where the humans were awaiting their fate.

"I don't know any more, sir – I mean, Louis," Jackson said.

"The humans *did* leave us hanging out to dry, you gotta admit," Kreuz said. "We had our backsides hanging out there in the wind with Linden and that bill."

Jackson thought he saw a strange sparkle in Louis's eyes as he spoke.

Jacks just nodded and didn't respond. He'd retreated once again into his thoughts.

"Well, if you're lucky, you'll run into Gabriel. He's just down there," Kreuz said. He pulled out an unlit cigar and chomped his teeth on it. "He just walked me out of another meeting. He likes getting air and visiting with the rest of the Angels. You know, he's got high hopes for you."

Kreuz was one of the few Angels with whom Gabriel consulted

regularly. Louis had been so instrumental over the years, training generation after generation and churning out groomed Guardian after groomed Guardian, that it only made sense that he'd remain a confidant during this current crisis.

"Well, take care of yourself, Godspeed," Kreuz said. He motioned for his assistant, who had busied himself on the sidelines while he and Jackson talked, and the two of them proceeded down the hall together.

"You, too, Louis," Jackson called after them.

Jackson rounded the quieter passageways and headed into the main section of the sanctuary. Up ahead he heard a low hum. In the hub of the sanctuary was a tree circled by a round marble fountain encircled by a bench. Just off the fountain was a piazza lined with various high-end stores, as well as restaurants and open seating.

Up ahead, Jackson saw Gabriel talking with a small group of Angels. Gabriel was easy to spot – he always gave off a kind of glow. The Immortals weren't used to seeing so much of Gabriel, but it only made sense that he'd venture out into the public more often now that they were all banded together in the sanctuary.

The True Immortal wore a more casual robe than usual, sleek and contemporary in its cut. Catching Jackson's eye, he excused himself from his conversation and approached the young Battle Angel with a smile and a clap on the shoulder.

"Good to see you, Jackson," Gabriel said.

"Thank you, sir. It's great to see you as well," Jacks said.

Gabriel smiled, and Jackson thought about how distant and mysterious Gabriel had seemed to him when he was growing up.

He was *the* leader of the Council. *The* Angel who had taken them out of hiding and formed the National Angel Services. He was a living legend, practically out of a myth. But now that they'd been meeting semi-regularly in the solarium, Jackson felt he was starting to get to know the real Angel, the *true* Immortal behind the figurehead.

"I've just left the company of your old friend Louis Kreuz. We've been discussing the human situation again."

Colour leapt into Jackson's face.

"Jackson, you shouldn't be angry at them," Gabriel said. "It's in their nature to err. And we can just no longer protect them from their own selves any more."

"I'm not angry," Jacks said. But even though he didn't even know what he really felt, he knew in his heart that he'd just lied to Gabriel. He just knew he didn't feel right, and that he was just trying to focus on the human-Angel situation without bringing *her* into it.

"Yes, well, that kind of . . . energy can be used for much more productive things," Gabriel said. "For the future, Jacks. Our future."

"I understand," Jacks said.

"Jacks, I was wondering if you might stop by again this afternoon. I'd like to discuss something with you," Gabriel said with a gentle smile.

"Of course, sir," Jacks said.

"Wonderful. I'll see you soon," Gabriel said. He put his hand on Jackson's shoulder and walked off, presumably back to the Council chambers. Jacks just watched him go.

"Jacks!" Before Jacks could react, Emily was up on him, kissing him on both cheeks. "What are you doing here? Rubbing elbows with Gabriel, I see? Sit down!"

A couple of younger Angels sat at a bistro table with Emily, their Immortal Marks displayed provocatively in their low-cut designer shirts. Emily's protégés, no doubt.

"I have to get going. . ." Jacks tried to protest, but Emily wouldn't take no for an answer. She grabbed his arm and tugged him to sit down.

"What were you two talking about?" Emily said, her eyes lighting up.

"Nothing."

"Well, even if it was something, I wouldn't want you to tell me if it was confidential," Emily said, as if she wanted to look out for Jackson.

Normally Jacks would have tried his best to keep respectful distance from a girl like Emily, just as he had with Vivian when she'd been obsessed with getting back together with him. But now, for some reason, Jacks was letting Emily do her thing. She did sometimes make him forget about Maddy for a while, but sometimes she made him think about her even more. This time, however, even though nothing had happened between them, she was making him think of her less.

"When are we going flying again, Jacks?" she said. Her Angel friends looked Jackson up and down with moony eyes as they poked at their green juices with their straws. They had surely heard about Jacks and Emily's recent flight after the first demon attack.

"We're shopping for new bags," Emily explained, without

giving Jacks time to answer. "Well, I am, for sure. Ashley doesn't know if she wants one or not. But I haven't been able to find one yet. The selection here in the sanctuary is just, like, OK. We're just taking a juice break."

Above, Angel City was preparing to face its destiny with a demon enemy, and down here, Emily was going on about green juice.

"The kale in it kind of tastes weird, but you get used to it. Plus, it's supposed to be great for your skin. You should totally try it."

"Cool." Jacks just nodded. He couldn't be less interested in kale juice if he tried.

"Gosh, Jacks, you always sound so serious!" Emily teased.

The girls whispered something between each other and started giggling, their laughter echoing down the sanctuary halls. Emily leaned in and put her hand over Jacks's as she talked, and Jacks was surprised when he didn't pull away. She noticed and gave him a smile.

"You're in with Gabriel. How long do you think we'll be down here?" Emily asked.

"As long as it takes, I guess."

"It's not so bad as long as you're down here," Emily said, and her friends started giggling again.

Jacks looked at his watch, still a bit thrown by how he responded to Emily's touch. "I should really go. I have somewhere to be, and I can't be late," he said.

The table grew a bit more serious. The girls didn't ask where he was going. They didn't have to. They knew he had to go meet Gabriel, and one didn't really joke about Gabriel. Jackson stood to leave, and Emily didn't stop him. The True Immortal, founder of the NAS, leader of the Angels, was waiting.

There was talk that Gabriel was grooming Jackson for something special. A wild rumour had even started that one day in the future, Jackson would be named the first Born Immortal on the Council.

Jacks was aware of the talk floating around the sanctuary, but he didn't pay too much attention to it. It was true he was now a Battle Angel and had volunteered to lead the Angels against the humans. And he had spent more time with Gabriel these past few days than he ever had before. But really, Jacks just enjoyed hearing him talk about the days before the Great Awakening and tell the ancient tales of the Guardians and of the last Age of Demons, when the Angels had emerged victorious. Gabriel had also known Jacks's real father pretty well. Sometimes they talked about him, too. A lot of the younger Immortals weren't so interested in these old stories, but Jacks found them fascinating. And more than anything, he really treasured the anecdotes about his father.

Gabriel was a steady North Star amid so many changes throughout the years. And he was especially dependable now, even though the end of the demon war would bring about a radically different Earth for the Angels. In contrast, Jacks was just a young Guardian, still discovering what kind of life he would live.

Far, far above the Council chambers, skylights rigged with an ingenious system of mirrors and reflections spilled shafts of light from the surface down to the vast rooms underneath. The Council chambers and halls never ceased to impress Jackson. Regular Angels only saw these sacred places maybe once in their lives.

Maybe. And Jackson was fortunate to have been invited in several times already.

Gabriel greeted him and they walked from the solarium into the main hall just outside the Council chambers, which were lined with Grecian columns like a beautiful chapel. The main hall itself was an enormous span of arches, with walls adorned with a jaw-dropping marble frieze, which, at its centre, depicted the most famous image of Home. In it, Guardian Angels wearing ancient garb stood in a circle around a flame. The rest of the frieze told the story of the Angels in intricate detail, from their very beginnings, through the Demon Struggles for control of Home, and all the way up to the Great Awakening. Gabriel had been a witness to all this history, first-hand, not just through sculpture and song.

"You know, you remind me so much of your father, Jackson," Gabriel said to Jacks as they strolled along the hallowed halls. He turned to Jackson, his seemingly ageless features warm and kind. He donned a simple white robe, lined with golden hand-spun embroidery.

"I'm honoured to hear you say so, sir," Jackson said. "From what I understand, he was a tremendous Guardian."

"Indeed," Gabriel said.

Jackson knew that Gabriel thought it was important that a warrior and leader have both physical courage and moral courage, and, most essentially, loyalty. Gabriel would often bring these topics up with Jacks, discussing both human philosophers and ancient Angel philosophers like Luxiticus, a brilliant thinker who was totally unknown to the humans.

"Loyalty," Gabriel said. "It's something the humans lack. We have been saving them for millennia, and now they turn on us at a moment's notice with no provocation. Like ungrateful children." Gabriel shook his head sadly. "Humanity is self-destructive, which is why we first came out of the shadows. I and the others who became the Council were tired of watching mankind kill one another, day after day, year after year. Brothers turning on each other in bloodlust. We tried to save them secretly, and then we tried to save them in public after the Great Awakening. But humanity cannot be saved from itself. We've tried for too long. And now it's our time to stop and let destiny take its course.

"Mankind is perpetually at war. They are as restless as they are violent. We Angels represent their better nature. We are their ideal. We are perfect. Even you, with your new wings, are perfect."

Jacks felt confused. He couldn't stop thinking about what he saw on the outside, and he had a hard time reconciling those awful images with the logic of Gabriel's argument.

"But . . . can we really blame humans for being less than perfect?" Jacks said.

Gabriel raised an eyebrow. "I wouldn't call five thousand years of war 'less than perfect'. I'd call it something far, far worse. Jackson, I know you must still have sentimental attachments to the human world. But you mustn't let those get in the way of your duty, which, first and foremost, is always to the Angels. In my lifetime I've had to face difficult decisions, many of which nearly broke my heart. But I've always known I was performing my fated duty, not for myself, but for the good of Angels everywhere. And that's made all the heartbreak worthwhile. You, too, have that opportunity now. We all do."

Jackson nodded. Gabriel was right.

"They have abandoned you, Jackson." He paused to study Jackson's face. "I know it's hard, but sometimes the truth hurts. *She* has abandoned you."

Jacks turned away, his lips curling in bitterness.

"That's another issue," Jacks said. "I can't let things get personal."

"You're right, son. It was wrong of me to bring that up," Gabriel said. "I apologize. I just want to make sure we're clear. You may face temptations, but you must strike them down." Gabriel turned and looked to the inscriptions underneath the depictions of ancient battles. "I don't know how I appear to you, Jackson. But you and I are made of exactly the same thing. I can feel it. And I want to protect you, as if you were a son."

"I understand," Jackson said. "And thank you."

"None of this means we don't have compassion for the humans. I will always have compassion for them, even though they turned on us. As a young Angel, I, too, once struggled with the love of a human," Gabriel said.

Jacks's eyes opened in shock. *Gabriel? In love with a* human?

"Shocking, I know. This was before our Home had become fully hidden from humanity, when human civilization was just emerging. A young woman, more beautiful than anyone – human or Angel – I had ever seen," Gabriel said. "She was enchanting. And she enchanted me. I knew there was no way it could work, that we could never really be together. But I trusted her anyway. And in the end, she let me down."

Gabriel's eyes came back into focus as he left behind memories of his ancient love and returned to the present.

"Even though they are simply humans, Jackson, they are

dangerous. Don't ever let them have you forget that."

They'd circled back to the main atrium in front of the inner Council chambers. Gabriel stopped and looked right at Jackson.

"Jackson, you know how much I have enjoyed getting to know you," he said.

"I'm humbled to hear you say that," Jacks said.

"But there's another reason I asked you to come see me today, in private," Gabriel said. "I've already discussed this with Archangel Godspeed, and he believes you might be ready."

"Sir?"

"Even here, deep in the sanctuary, there are Angels I cannot trust," Gabriel said. "Those who would work against us, for whatever reasons they foolishly believe."

"I . . . have heard some rumours."

"Those rumours are, perhaps, sadly true. Not even the NAS is clean. I need someone I can trust, someone who'll remain close to me, to help me find the rotten apples in the ranks. I know your mettle and your convictions, Jackson, which is why I'm asking for your help. These are trying times, and we need to fish out the traitors together. When I do call upon you, I will be entrusting you with the most important tasks." Gabriel looked at Jackson. "If you'll accept, naturally."

"Of course I will, sir," Jacks said without hesitation. He immediately thought of how having some kind of higher duty here could help him move on and get over all the pain he'd endured these past few days. As he moved on, he could help Gabriel and the Angels become stronger.

"It makes me happy to hear it, Jackson," Gabriel said, smiling.

"Now, if you'll excuse me, it's time for the afternoon session with the Council."

With a short word of goodbye, Gabriel was escorted by an assistant into the inner Council chambers.

Jacks's mind was swimming as he was led back to the sanctuary by another Council assistant. Maybe Jacks really was being groomed by Gabriel, and all that talk amounted to more than just rumours. Gabriel was bringing him in as a confidante. For Jacks to go from an injured, washed-up Guardian to working as a personal aide to the True Immortal responsible for bringing the Angels into the modern age . . .

He was so caught in this tumble of thoughts that he almost didn't feel his phone vibrating in his pocket.

He had a text message.

And it was from Maddy.

"Hey."

CHAPTER 12

Just like every other establishment in town, the old dive bar on the far side of Angel Boulevard had been closed for the four days the curfews and checkpoints had been in place. The owner, who doubled as the bartender, had ignored the evacuation warning and was now trapped in Angel City with the rest of the civilians. But where would he have gone, anyway? Angel City was his home, and this bar was his life.

Tonight, just as he'd done the previous four nights, he crept down to the bar, which was conveniently located below his apartment, to check in and make sure everything was safe and sound. He opened the door as slowly and quietly as possible, looked in on the dark and empty space, and sighed. Closed again. He wished the demons would just come in and get it over with.

Well, almost closed.

The bar was officially closed to the public, but he did have a few especially loyal customers who had permission to call him at home and request a nightcap at their favourite dive. Two such customers were Detective Sylvester and a mysterious, beautiful older woman who gave the bartender an Angel vibe, but he couldn't be totally sure she was Immortal. He knew better than to ask too many questions. But they were allowed in whenever they felt like it – Detective Sylvester had really helped him out during the vice squad crackdowns of '94, so the bartender owed him, and was a man of his word.

His special customers were in tonight, and they'd brought along a short, stout man in a snazzy suit who looked strangely familiar. The windows had been blacked out to prevent anyone from seeing any activity, and inside a single candle burned atop a table in the back.

The bartender wiped the layer of dust off the tabletop and nodded to the group.

"Whisky rocks, Jim," Sylvester said.

"I'll have the same," Susan Archson said.

"Just a Seven-UP for me," said the third man. "And go easy on the fizz – I gotta drive back." Sylvester was glad to see that even in this dark hour Louis Kreuz still had his sense of humor. He was a remarkable Angel who had held the Guardian training programme together for nearly a century through sheer force of will and a stand-up personality. His style was old school – he hailed from Central Europe and had been around since the Golden Age of Angel City – but it was still more than effective. Sylvester saw him as an essential part of Angel culture, and a colourful symbol of the Immortals' past and present in Angel City.

And he was also the resistance's mole working inside the sanctuary. The Thorn.

Kreuz liked the code name. It tickled his particular sense of humour.

The fact that Louis was working with Sylvester and Susan, that he'd been instrumental to the resistance's founding, was monumental. But it also made Angel life incredibly dangerous for him. Every day he stayed in the lion's den that was the sanctuary was another day he could be found out, which is why he took every precaution possible. He used only backup burner phones with untraceable SIM cards, so he could send coded texts to Susan and Sylvester for them to decode on the other end. He had a special "dead-drop" system, where he would leave documents for an unknown agent to pick up and deliver to the resistance. And if all else failed, his assistant, also a resistance member, had a sure-fire contingency plan should anyone ever come looking for him in the middle of those nights when he had to steal away from the sanctuary to attend a clandestine meeting.

"Any problem getting out tonight?" Sylvester asked.

"Nope, not a one. The boys have the system down pretty good," Louis said. He looked at David and Susan. "All right. Let's get started. You first."

"We've established lines of communications with Linden and the top officials of the Global Angel Commission," Archangel Archson said.

"Good. Don't talk to anyone even remotely associated with Angel City. Get as close to Linden as you can," Louis said. "I don't even know if I trust all his Cabinet members. If Gabriel has infiltrated any part of the GAC, he's not letting on one bit. At least not to me."

"What about David's fear that the demons have somehow evolved?" Susan asked. "Some of the information we got from the field shows sightings of demons that are larger, more advanced than any of the Dark Angels the Immortals faced in ancient times.

118

And they were so methodical, so . . . deliberate and organized. Are the Angels saying anything about that?"

"Are you talking about some kind of . . . super demon?" Kreuz asked.

"If only," Sylvester said darkly. "I have a theory. Some *thing* is controlling them. A leader. They're sending out scouts, finding our weaknesses. Wearing down the human psyche. They're making sure that Angel City will be that much easier to conquer. Normal demons wouldn't do that on their own. No. There is a leader among the Dark Ones. If we can find it . . . we could end this. We've just got to be one step ahead of them. *We* need to find *its* patterns, *its* weaknesses. That's our key to finding the leader, and the leader is our key to defeating these demons. We cut the head off the leader, we cut the head off the entire army."

"So . . . you're saying we wouldn't like to meet this head demon in a dark alley," Louis mused. "As far as head demon, or super demons, if the NAS experts monitoring the demons know anything about it, they ain't saying. Seems like they mostly just want to lie low, keep the sanctuary in one piece, and dodge any cross fire."

"It seems like just yesterday I was tracking that lone demon Angel killer . . ." Sylvester said. "Now we've got an entire army to hunt."

"Look on the bright side," Louis said. "At least property prices are finally going to go down. Even if it is going to be a hell of a lot hotter with all these demons around." He couldn't help laughing at his own joke – classic Kreuz, Sylvester thought.

"If David's right about the head demon, we're going to need all the support and Immortal firepower we can get to root it out.

Before it's too late," Susan said. "You've got to help us get to the Angels, Louis."

"Something is definitely going on with the NAS and the Council," said Louis. "They're getting nervous. Maybe they know the resistance is growing. Gabriel has tapped the Godspeed kid to be his boy."

"Jackson?" Sylvester said.

Louis nodded. "I don't know how much Godspeed Junior knows. But our other spies tell me he's spending a lot of time over in the chambers and with Gabriel in his little solarium. I know they ain't just playing checkers."

"We just need you and the others to stay in place," Susan said. "And for everyone's sake, be safe, Louis."

"Don't worry. I ain't going nowhere. We're too close," he said. "And from what I understand, you can't get a good steak or a decent Cuban up here in Angel City any more, anyway." He chuckled, gnawing on the tip of his unlit cigar, imported directly – and illegally – from Havana. "What about Maddy?" Louis asked. He'd always taken a particular interest in her, and, truth be told, he'd had a soft spot for all the Godrights since Sylvester could remember.

"Apparently she's spoken with Linden. We don't know details yet. We're waiting to talk to the big man himself."

Kreuz drained his 7UP and set the glass down on the table.

"I don't like it," he said. "I've got a bad feeling. There're too many loose ends. We're running out of time. It's going to be too little, too late."

"Maybe. But we're not in a position yet to strike," Susan said. "We just need a little more time."

"I hope we got it," Kreuz said.

"I suppose we'll find out," Sylvester said. "We just need to get to the head demon. We've got to make it happen, any way we can."

Susan's handbag started ringing. She plucked out her phone and looked at the caller ID. "One of Linden's people. Excuse me, gentlemen," she said, standing up to take the call at the other end of the bar.

The bartender, who had been busying himself by the bar, purposefully out of earshot, saw that the meeting was winding down. Their glasses had been drained. Kreuz was stretching. He went over to pick up the empties and wipe down the table.

"Just put it on my tab," David said.

"The Seven-UP's on the house," the bartender said.

Kreuz popped a final handful of peanuts into his mouth from the battered plastic bowl in front of him. "Funny, they got lobster in the sanctuary. But you can't find no peanuts. Talk about a lack of planning."

Sylvester felt Kreuz's eyes on his shaky hands as he handed the bartender his empty glass.

"You all right, David?" Kreuz asked.

Louis, of course, knew all about what had happened to Sylvester after he lost his wings and was disbarred from the Angels. He knew he was a first-rate ACPD policeman, but that he'd grown a reputation for having a bad case of nerves, which was why he had been quietly relegated to desk work for years. It wasn't until the famous Angel serial killer case that he'd had the chance to prove himself a hero in more ways than one.

"Of course," Sylvester said. "I'm just a little short on sleep, is all." He tried to smile but couldn't manage to look Louis directly in the eyes. Sylvester's daily fear was that his nerves would come back and overtake him. He dreaded that black overpowering sense of anxiety. What was going on now – the resistance, the war – was too important. He couldn't afford not to be at the top of his game.

"You know you can talk to me . . . whenever you need to," Louis said. Like all the Guardians, Sylvester had gone through Angel training under Kreuz's watch. He had been a brilliant Guardian student – just as brilliant as Susan, who eventually became an Archangel. Everyone knew that Louis really cared about his "kids," which he liked to think of them as.

"Sometimes I still think of it," Sylvester admitted.

"The child? That was a long time ago, David."

"You know I've never been able to let it go," Sylvester said.

"We're going to need you here with us, David," Kreuz said. "The Angels. You're one of us, and we're going to need leaders after this is all over. And you're proving yourself to be a born leader."

Sylvester opened his mouth to object, but Louis cut him off.

"Besides, there's more than one reason to move on from that," Kreuz said. "If not for your sake, then for somebody else's." He looked over at Susan, who was speaking quietly into her phone in the corner.

"What do you mean?" Sylvester asked, following his gaze.

"I've seen the way she looks at you," Louis said.

Sylvester was caught off guard, turning red. Susan was a beautiful, talented Archangel, and he was just a washed-up has-been Angel, a police detective, somebody trying to do a little good to make up for the wrong he still felt he had done. But still, he took a moment to think back to the way he'd felt when Susan reached out for his arm back in the office. . .

"You're imagining things, Louis," he said.

"Some detective! Ha!" Louis smiled. "Well, time I got home before the sanctuary sends out a search party. That would be mighty uncomfortable for me. See you in a while, Sylvester. And tell Susan I said 'so long'."

"Will do, Louis," said Sylvester. "And remember: take care of yourself."

CHAPTER 13

Maddy had agreed to meet Jackson at his place up in Empyrean Canyon. She figured that, after breaking his heart at the pier, the least she could do was meet him on his territory.

She arrived early, only to find Jackson's house and property eerily empty, totally dark. She didn't have to worry about curfew; she had a special pass from Linden that allowed her to travel freely to the exclusive Empyrean Canyon, to the house she knew so well. It pained her to look into the darkened windows, thinking about how much time she'd spent inside with Jacks; she'd even helped him pick the house out when he moved out of his parents'. But that felt like such a long time ago, back before everything started to unravel.

Not so many days had passed since the Angels had left their homes, but already things looked a bit shabbier. Lawns were yellowing, dried palm fronds lay scattered in driveways, and debris cluttered meticulously maintained driveways. But despite all the emptiness, she knew Jackson was somewhere nearby. She had felt his frequency.

And so Maddy waited nervously, her confidence waning with every minute. She'd felt fully confident on her way over, reassuring herself that she was there not as an ex-girlfriend, but as an emissary from President Ted Linden himself, to plead for the help of the Angels.

Their personal problems had nothing to do with it, and she hoped that Jacks could somehow see it that way, too. This was about more than just the two of them.

But as soon as she found herself standing at Jacks's front door, all that confidence just vanished into the dark night. Then she saw him.

Maddy had expected Jackson to fly in, but instead, there he was, emerging from the woods towards the back of his house.

Jacks hit a button on the side of the garage and the lights blazed on, revealing the roundabout driveway with the fountain at its centre. The fountain water was still and thick with a layer of green muck that had collected over the past few days.

For a few moments, Maddy held on to the slenderest reed of hope. Maybe Jacks had changed his mind. Maybe he thought that joining the humans in the fight was the right thing to do.

But as soon as he came into the garage light and saw the look on his face, she understood she'd made a huge error in judgement.

"What do you want, Maddy?" Jacks said. "And why didn't you bring Flyboy with you?"

This was not off to a good start.

"Jacks, don't start on . . ." Maddy said.

"What do you want me to do, then?" he said. His pale blue eyes flared in the glint of moonlight. He still didn't even know why he'd agree to meet with her. All the anger he'd been trying to suppress started to well up. "I don't get you, Maddy. Is this some weak attempt at patching things up?"

"This isn't about us, Jackson," Maddy said.

"No? Then what is it about?" Jacks said. "It better be important.

I would be in very serious trouble if they knew where I was right now. And especially big trouble if they knew who I was with."

Maddy had never seen Jacks so cold. So distant. He was purposefully keeping her away, at more than arm's length. How was she ever going to get through to him?

On top of everything, his aggression was making it impossible for her to remember what she had planned on saying.

"Jacks," she started, "you once loved a half-human half-Angel girl."

"I did. And I thought she loved me, too. But I was wrong," Jacks said.

"Don't say that," said Maddy. His words landed like a punch to her gut. But she had to keep telling herself that she wasn't here to make herself feel better. She was here for humankind. Maddy took a breath to calm herself before looking back into his eyes.

"Humanity doesn't deserve this," Maddy said. "And you know it."

Jacks turned and looked out on the darkened city. "Humans are self-destructive, Maddy. They can't be saved from themselves. Loyalty is not a component of human nature." He eyed Maddy coldly. "The demons are just doing your job more efficiently."

"Listen to yourself, Jacks," Maddy said, a cold emptiness gripping her heart. "This isn't you."

For a moment, she thought she saw a crack of doubt enter Jackson's face. He looked into Maddy's eyes, and Maddy could see it. Something she'd said had touched him. But as soon as it was there, it flickered away as if it had never been.

"Maybe you don't know me any more, Maddy," Jacks said.

"You sound like one of the Council's PR people," Maddy said.

Jackson's lip curled. "The Council and Gabriel were the ones who pardoned me. The NAS was going to take my wings after I saved you, Maddy, but they saw something in me and gave me another chance. They're the good guys."

"The good guys, Jacks?" Maddy shook her head. It was hopeless, just as she had known it would be.

At least now she could tell Linden she tried. That she had done her best. It had been a foolish, last-ditch plan, but she had still harboured a shred of hope that it could have worked out differently. Remembering that hope, she spoke up again.

"What have they done to you, Jackson? I barely recognize you." Maddy looked at the angry Angel in front of her. How could he be so brainwashed? This couldn't just be the result of her choice on the pier. . .

"They haven't done anything to me," Jacks said. "I'm just staying with my kind. There is a future for Angels, and I'm going to be part of it."

"A future? With the *demons*? Where are the Angels, Jacks?" She was feeling more frightened than devastated as she continued to listen to this Jackson impostor.

"I'm not here to discuss *our* plans, Maddy," Jackson said, face slightly flushing. "You chose not to be with us, remember? I came here to hear you out. To see if maybe you'd changed your mind and decided to listen to the Angel in you. And I did hear you. It's clear you haven't changed anything."

"I'm sorry to bother you, Jacks," Maddy said as diplomatically as possible. "I'm going to go now."

Jackson whirled towards her, his eyes blazing under the bright light shining down from the four-car garage.

"I don't know why I even agreed to meet you. You made your choice," Jacks said angrily. "It's humiliating for me to even be here." His voice cracked with emotion as he turned away. "I don't even know why I'm doing this to myself."

"Jacks—" Seeing him in front of her, suffering, made Maddy's voice turn tender. Despite his hardness now, her heart went out to him, the Angel she loved.

Almost unconsciously, she moved towards him, like she had done a thousand times before. And he turned to her.

Before she knew what had happened, their hands had found each other. As their fingers intertwined, Maddy felt as if her body had been jolted by a spark, just like it had in the diner the very first time they met.

Surprise struck both their faces as they moved towards each other. Jackson took Maddy in his arms and Maddy was right there with him, and their faces, which had tried to be so brave, were now so close, almost kissing, and she could feel his gentle breath. . .

Maddy suddenly pulled away.

"Maddy. It's not too late," Jacks breathed. He held her in his arms to keep her close, to make sure she felt the energy and attraction coursing through them.

"Jacks, I can't do this," she whispered.

Jacks's face fell, and he let go of Maddy. He took a few steps away and turned his back to her, not saying a word. When he did speak again, his voice was flat and distant.

"I'm glad you called. I needed to pick up some stuff from the house," Jackson said.

"You don't have to try to keep up appearances for me, Jackson. We know each other."

"We thought we did. But you're with . . . him now. Turns out I didn't know you at all."

"Jacks, how could you be so cruel?" Maddy cried out. "You don't know anything about it."

"I know *everything* about it."

"Jacks . . ."

"Maddy, please leave."

"Ja—"

"*Please.*"

He didn't have to ask twice. Holding her hand up to her face as if to hide her sadness, Maddy quickly got into her car and turned on the ignition. As she spun around the fountain to exit the grounds, her headlights hit on Jackson for a moment. He stood there in the cold, artificial light, sheet white, his face stony like some kind of vengeful god of old.

CHAPTER 14

Maddy sent Linden's team a report. *"No go."* She didn't explain further. They'd know what it meant.

The visit had gone just as she'd expected, only it had affected her much more than she had imagined.

The encounter with Jackson had left her rattled. Their unexpected burst of passion showed that their anger wasn't enough to keep them apart, but now she regretted ever agreeing to go. Jackson was so *different*, so in line with the Council, more than he had ever been before. And he was so cold.

Until, of course, that spark had flared between them.

She thought of Tom getting ready to face the demons yet again and felt raw. And guilty. All it had taken was just one moment to nearly betray her promise to Tom, to almost kiss Jackson, like some Angelstruck girl stuck in a dream. And after everything they'd said to each other . . .

Maddy barely slept that night and woke up early the next day, her mind spinning like an overworked hamster wheel. She went to the diner, which was still closed to the public. She made some tea and slumped down in one of the booths.

She looked over the quiet diner. Even though it was closed, Kevin had come in every day to give the place a good dusting and sweep. Always the optimist, Kevin had told her: "Need to be ready to open once the demons are gone."

Kevin had insisted on staying in Angel City even though Maddy could have easily gotten him out. He wasn't ready to abandon ship yet, and, if Maddy was honest, he wasn't ready to leave *her* behind, either. She had finally gotten him to agree to move to one of the bomb shelters set up all the way past Fairfax Avenue. But both of them knew that if the battle began, those shelters might not offer much protection.

Maddy looked out across the diner. She could have probably walked around blindfolded, carrying three hamburger specials, and still not spill a fry or a drop of milk shake. How many mornings, afternoons and evenings had she spent there? Funny, she used to always want to get out of that waitress uniform, out of Angel City altogether, and now she longed for those days again. In a few days' time, would there even *be* an Angel City?

A voice broke her reverie, startling her.

"Maddy. It's been too long."

Detective Sylvester, in the same old overcoat he'd worn when she first met him in at ACHS. Standing next to him was someone else she knew well. Someone she wouldn't have expected to see in a million years.

"Professor Archson?" Maddy said, a smile brightening her face.

The Archangel smiled back at Maddy. "I thought I told you to call me Susan, Madison."

"Sorry to burst in on you," Detective Sylvester said. "I know the place is closed, but I took the liberty of picking the lock.

I hope you don't mind if we share a table with you for a few minutes."

Maddy's eyes flipped from Sylvester to her former professor. Susan saw the look in Maddy's eyes, and the confusion.

"I'm not with the Angels, Maddy," she said. "It's been a long time coming. We've had an insurgent element within the NAS for years now. I've been helping as co-leader the entire time. We've just been waiting for the right moment to surface."

"You're a rebel?" Maddy asked, breathless. "And you and Detective Sylvester . . . know each other?"

"We go back," Susan said. "To Guardian training. We were the same Commissioning class. We were Guardians together."

"Maddy, we need you," Sylvester said.

"I've already told Linden – I can't do anything with the Angels. Jacks was my only chance. And he wasn't much of one," Maddy said. "The Angels aren't going to help."

"We're not giving up on that, Maddy," Susan said. "David – I mean, Detective Sylvester – thinks that something is controlling the demons."

Maddy thought back to the Vespa girl on the 101. "I saw a demon in the first wave. . . It was about to attack me, but then, it's like he heard something, and suddenly he left. Just like that. And he seemed . . . angry about it."

Sylvester nodded. "We've heard similar stories all over the city. They pulled back. As if by design. As if they were getting orders." He coughed into his hand. "This is more dangerous than we could have even imagined. The chaos of a demon army could be enough to topple the city. But with their forces of darkness organized and focused . . ." He trailed off. "But if we could somehow get to this leader, if we could cut the head off the body of the army, it could make all the difference. But humans alone wouldn't be able to do that. We need Battle Angels. Battle Angels willing to risk it all."

"How are we supposed to find this . . . head demon?" Maddy asked.

"There's no way to get at the head demon before they attack. But once they start moving in, that's when we think it will be exposed. That we can figure out how to identify and exterminate it. Before it's too late."

"But this isn't about the Angels," Susan said. "This is about you."

Maddy eyed them two cautiously. "What do you mean?"

Sylvester and Susan shared a look, as if each was daring the other to be the one to deliver the news. Finally the detective answered.

"We're speaking for Linden now," Detective Sylvester said.

"What?" *Linden?* Maddy's head whirled. Susan and the detective were working with the president?

"Linden is done with talking with the Angels," Susan said.

Maddy cast a questioning look to Sylvester and Susan.

"Maddy. We need your help. In the war," Sylvester said.

"But . . . what can I do? Don't get me wrong, I want to help. More than anything," Maddy said. "But I'm not a Battle Angel. I was barely even a Guardian."

"You have something that's more important than any Battle Angel. You have expertise," Susan said.

"Expertise?" Maddy said.

"You have actual first-hand experience with demons," Sylvester said. "That's more than any of Linden's four-star generals can say. He – and we – need your experience more than you can imagine."

"But that was just one demon at a time. This is . . . we don't know how many," Maddy said.

"You've seen them up close and personal," Susan said. "You know what they're about. But there's something they need even more. Linden's team knows you have a certain power."

Premonition.

Maddy didn't say it out loud. She didn't need to. Her eyes darted to Susan.

"You don't have to tell them how it works," Sylvester said. "But they are asking you to help them. On the front lines."

"But what exactly would I do? I'm not trained for anything like the *military*."

"The generals and colonels are positive you can give us a strategic edge," Sylvester continued. "That you can warn the military forces before . . . something happens. So they can get ready to defend and then counterattack."

"But what if it doesn't work?" The prospect of having such a huge responsibility all of a sudden got her heart thumping in her chest.

"Maddy, you're nearly the best I've ever seen," said Susan. "Your frequencing is incredible. Your premonition ability may be the best among all active Angels. You can help us hold them off while we try to hunt the leader."

"There are more demons than you can possibly imagine. Their numbers are beyond counting," Sylvester said. "They have been waiting for centuries, quietly causing chaos around the globe when they needed to feed, but otherwise remaining in the shadows. Building their numbers. Stocking their army. All for this opportunity. We can't let them win. We need you, Maddy."

She looked at their pleading faces and knew what she had to do.

"When do I start?"

CHAPTER 15

The sanctuary's artificial sun had already set by the time Jacks made his way back to his quarters. The corridors were strangely quiet, the only sounds being the classical music that was piped in through skilfully hidden speakers, and Jackson's own footsteps. This was nothing compared with the noise in his head, however.

Meeting Maddy had sent him in a tailspin, and he wondered why he'd ever agreed to see her in the first place. As if anything good could have come of it. He knew that a small part of him thought that maybe Maddy had changed her mind, was going to come running to him, beg for his forgiveness, want to join the Angels. But he knew now that was only wishful thinking. She had rejected him and the Angels twice already. Why would things change now? This was his stubborn Maddy, not just some fickle Angelstruck girl.

Jackson wasn't going to tell Gabriel about Maddy. If Jacks had just listened, really listened, to what the elder Angel had been telling him about the difference between Angel loyalty and human "loyalty," he wouldn't be in this whirlpool of sadness to begin with.

Rounding the corner towards his rooms, Jackson passed a small garden studded with slender trees and a series of reflecting ponds surrounded by grass and flowers.

Suddenly, from the garden shadows, he heard a voice.

"Hello, Jackson."

Jacks wheeled around. He thought he recognized the voice.

And deep in his mind, he associated it with danger.

Glass glinted, catching a ray of light as the speaker leaned forward.

"Will you come and sit with an old friend, just for a minute?"

Jacks felt a shock as a small shaft of light gave the face a brief moment of clarity.

"Detective Sylvester?"

"Shhh," Sylvester said. "I'm not exactly welcome here."

Leery, Jacks kept his distance. "They say you're with the anti-Angel group."

"They say a lot of things. Some of them are false, some of them are true. You'll have to decide which is which. Will you listen to me, just for one moment?"

"If anyone sees us . . ."

"No one will bother us. I've arranged for that." Sylvester said this with such confidence that Jackson was taken aback. Was the detective here to do more than just talk?

"How did you get in here?"

"We have friends everywhere, Jackson. There are many who do not want to just stand by while humanity is crushed by the demons. Even some in the sanctuary."

Jacks stared hard at the detective. He had seen him recently during the Angel bombing crisis, but that seemed like a lifetime ago.

"The humans made their own choices," Jacks said. "Now they must face the consequences."

"That may be true. But many in human history have made

mistakes only to learn from them later. That's what being human is. They're not perfect, Jacks, but they still deserve the opportunity to survive."

"Five thousand years of war is a little less than perfect, Detective Sylvester."

"You sound a lot like someone else I once knew."

Jacks looked away. "It's right there in the Book of Angels," Jackson said.

"Scholars and Archangels have been struggling for centuries to fully explain the Book of Angels," Sylvester said. "Those who think they understand fully its prophecies are worse than fools – they are dangerous."

"Gabriel is one of your fools, then," Jackson said. "But trust me, if there's one among us who knows the truth, it's him."

Sylvester stared into the reflecting pools, silently, considering Jackson's words.

"Why are you here, Detective Sylvester?" Jacks went on. "If anyone finds you . . ."

"I know the danger. Which is why this isn't purely a social call." Sylvester leaned in and pushed his glasses down the ridge of his nose, intensifying his stare. "We need your help, Jackson."

"I'm sorry you wasted your time by coming all the way down here. Mad . . . *she* already tried to talk me into joining your side, and bringing the other Angels with me. Like I have that kind of power, anyway. I'm a soldier, not a general."

"You have more influence than you think, Jackson."

"Even if that was true, I wouldn't be using it against the Angels."

"Not against the Angels. *For* the humans. For Earth." Sylvester took a breath, pausing before his next words. "Maddy's going out there. She's doing it alone."

"Don't say her name around here," Jacks growled. "She can do whatever she wants. She's made her choices. And I've made mine."

Sylvester regarded the Angel in front of him.

"You've changed, Jacks."

"You're not the first to tell me that," Jacks said. "But I'm not the one who's changed. The world has changed. There's a war afoot, and it's my duty to help the Angels be on the winning side."

"You may need to think about your larger duty."

"I am an Angel, and the Council has decided that this is my duty."

"The Council does not represent the voices of all Angels," Sylvester said. "You know that. You can decide what you want to do."

Jacks thought about Sylvester's tortured history as a Guardian, about his illegal save and his failure to save that young girl, the one person who had seemed to matter to him. And then he'd lost his wings and was banished from the Angel community. How could Sylvester know anything about Jackson's duty?

"And you're one to lecture me about duty?" Jackson said. "After what happened to you?"

"Wow. I would have thought you were above low blows, Jackson."

Jacks was silent. He was not about to apologize.

"The demons control through chaos, Jackson. They dissolve all faith through anarchy and disorder."

What was he talking about? Jacks hadn't heard anything about this. . . .

"What do you mean?"

"There's a head demon out there. Organizing them. Strategizing. This is different behavior, something new, and much more dangerous."

"A head demon? Controlling them? But there has always been a war between Angels and demons, and there's never been any rationale for their violence. They're indiscriminate. They are the embodiment of complete, mindless evil."

"It's different this time. I know it in my bones. If we can get to the leader, this whole thing could stop. Think how many lives could be saved, Jackson. But there's no question here. We need the Angels' help."

Jackson turned away, his face shrouded in bleakness. "I'm sorry to hear that. But humanity was ready to imprison us, to fight us. And now they want our help?"

"You know it was more complicated than that, Jackson. It was about Protection for Pay – it was about the system."

For a moment, Jacks looked as if he might give in. But then his face turned grim again.

"It's too late."

"It's never too late," said Sylvester.

"It is this time."

Detective Sylvester quietly slipped away, disappearing down whatever secret passage he had used to come in. Jacks knew he should probably report the intrusion immediately, but instead he just stood there, still as a statue in the garden. His strong hands turned into fists, his fingernails digging into his palms until they turned white.

He turned to meet his own face in the fountain's reflection. The ripples distorted his perfect Angelic features, crumpling and distorting his face into a picture of rage and unalloyed pain.

With another flex of his fist he swiped at his image in the water, sending up a mighty splash, and headed towards the main hallway.

"Hi, handsome," said Emily Brightchurch, smiling. She had snuck up behind him in the hallway, looping her arm through his. Her make-up was perfect, with lips glossed the perfect shade to complement her blazing-red locks. "What are you up to?"

Jackson murmured something noncommittal. Why was he always keeping her at such a distance? She was a pretty girl, he thought. She might try too hard, but he couldn't blame her for that. And she did seem to like him a lot.

"Can I show you my new dress?" Emily asked, as if the bright idea had just hit her. "You can tell me if it looks good on me or not?"

As if in a daze, Jacks agreed, and the next thing he knew, Emily was leading him to her quarters. He sat down on the sleek couch while she scooped up a shopping bag and brought it with her into her walk-in closet.

"Won't be more than a second," she said, her eyes smoky as she cooed at Jacks.

Emily left the closet door slightly open, and then pretended not to notice that the mirror on the other side gave Jacks a full view of her changing. She shimmied into a tight black dress, then made her grand re-entrance into the living room. She pinned her hair up and strutted back to Jacks.

"Well? What do you think?" Emily asked.

"You look great," Jacks said.

She turned around, and Jacks saw that the back of the dress was unzipped.

"Can you get it for me?" Emily asked with doe eyes.

She leaned up against Jacks. He started to pull up the zipper, but before he'd made it even a centimetre, she turned around and pressed her body against his. In an instant their mouths were at each other, and they were kissing. Emily exhaled heavily and grabbed the back of Jackson's head to pull him even closer.

The moment took hold of them both – Emily by design, Jacks by surprise – and for a brief moment Jacks let himself give in, surrendered all his pain and doubt to this girl in his arms. He grabbed her waist and pulled her closer. She nodded and bit his lip as they kissed.

Suddenly, it hit Jacks what he was doing. "Emily . . ." he said, pulling away and ending their kiss. Emily rubbed her mouth with the back of her hand and smiled at Jacks.

"It's OK, Jacks. We can take it slow," she said. "I don't want you to get the wrong idea about what kind of girl I am."

"I—" Jacks tried to speak, but felt too overwhelmed. Had he really just made out with Emily? After he'd already decided so long ago that he didn't feel anything for her?

"I should go," Jacks mumbled.

Emily smiled at him and gave him a peck on the cheek.

Jacks just nodded and slipped out the door, wondering what he had just gotten himself into.

CHAPTER 16

The Pacific waves pushed west towards what seemed like infinity under the bright sun. The whitecaps on the swells appeared like flourishes of sugary frosting cresting in lines across the horizon towards Angel City. Maddy relished the sight as she gazed out the thick glass of the helicopter.

"Five minutes to landing," a voice crackled in her earpiece.

They were moving Maddy to the ocean front line, to fight. She had volunteered; they needed her. She leaned into the window again, her eyes scanning the distance for the sign of the aircraft carrier.

Maddy suddenly realized that the last time she'd seen the ocean from this height was when she'd saved her Protection, Jeffrey Rosenberg and, illegally, his assistant. Maddy could still conjure the bloody vision of Rosenberg's demise, could feel the gravitational pull of the plummeting jet once again, the adrenaline, the split second she had to make the decision to save the cowering assistant, who was certainly going to die without her help. Her muscles ached as she remembered the incredible effort it had taken to freeze time long enough to make the double save. And then she remembered the aftermath. Her illegal save sparked the passing of the Immortals Bill, drawing support from Tom and fury from Jackson.

The memory made her heart quicken for Jackson, but she

stuffed the feelings down. Maddy didn't have time for them now. She was with Tom. And it would stay that way.

Finally, Maddy saw the aircraft carrier, so far away it looked almost like a toy boat bobbing in a bathtub. But as they drew closer, it became more and more massive, a giant among giants. It was a steel juggernaut against the waves, and humanity's last best hope to stem the coming tide of Dark Angels. Her heart beat faster in her chest.

Maddy saw there was a line of carriers and warships extending out in both directions into the distance, along the great blue ocean swells. The entire fleet had been mobilized. She knew the Chinese and the Russians were sending reinforcements, but there was no telling if they'd show up in time.

The helicopter drew over the deck of the carrier, and Maddy clutched on to a stabilizing strap as they descended. They touched down on the deck, the helicopter shuddering sharply as it made contact.

A sailor in a dress uniform ducked under the whirlwind of the spinning rotors and reached in to help Maddy out of the chopper. He grabbed her bag and gave a hand signal to the pilot, who then raised the helicopter slowly up off the deck. Maddy tucked her hair under her hoodie to keep it from whipping her face.

Clutching her elbow with one hand, the sailor led her off the deck, up some stairs, and into the relative silence of the bridge room. Along the way she was met with the gawking stares of sailors and military personnel, and it took all her strength to keep her head held high.

The captain was waiting on the bridge. He was about fifty-five, in good shape, with clear, sharp eyes. His khaki uniform was impeccably pressed and his boots reflected the bright, warm sunshine spilling through the bridge window.

The sailor snapped his heels together and saluted.

"Captain Blake – Madison Montgomery Godright, *sir*!"

"Ahem," the private said, lightly elbowing Maddy and looking at her sidelong.

Maddy got the hint, and, blushing, she brought her hand up in a salute before being waved off by the captain.

"No need for formalities here, Ms Montgomery." He had a lilting Southern accent that immediately put Maddy at ease. "You are dismissed." He nodded to the sailor flanking Maddy, who promptly saluted and left them.

"I know all about your reputation, young lady. Well, at least through my daughter. So when I got the call from the big guy saying we were bringing you on board to coordinate our forces on the front line, I was a little surprised," Captain Blake said. "I'm not so sure about this, but if they say it will help, hell, I'm open to trying. Anything to stop these demon bastards."

"I don't want to make any promises, Captain," Maddy admitted. "But I'm going to try. That's all I can do."

"Sounds like you have some courage, then," the captain said. "You're going to need it."

Maddy nodded.

Captain Blake motioned to the sailor standing just outside the door.

"This petty officer will show you to your quarters," he said. "Any questions?"

Privately, Maddy had about a million and one. But they could wait.

"No, sir," Maddy said, saluting again.

The captain smiled. "You know, technically I should probably be saluting you." He brought his hand to his temple and gave a quick salute. Maddy blushed again and went off with the waiting officer.

Because she was both a guest and an officer, Maddy had been given her own cabin. And after seeing the enlisted seamen's quarters, she was more than grateful – the sailors were stacked like sardines in a giant room, bunks running everywhere. Maddy slung her bag up on the unoccupied top bunk, a great luxury on a warship.

Just then, she heard a knock at the door, and a familiar voice spoke.

"Maddy?"

Tom.

Before she knew it, she was wrapped up in his embrace, blissfully pressed up against him.

"You're all right," she half-whispered, her voice quavering with relief.

"I made a promise, didn't I?"

She could hear the steady rhythm of his heartbeat through the cloth of his uniform as he reached his hand down to lightly stroke her hair.

"It's hard to believe you're actually here," he said. "Maddy, I've been thinking about you—" His voice peaked with emotion as he struggled to maintain control.

"Shh," she said. "We'll have time to talk about that later."

"I'm sorry. I'm a little all over the place," he said. "We lost some men in the first attack. All of them good, some of them friends."

"Tom, I'm so sorry. . . ."

"I don't know how long we can last, Maddy," Tom said. A darkness she'd never heard before had crept into his voice.

"Don't say that," Maddy said, straightening and looking him in the eyes.

Even though it'd only been a few days, something had changed in Tom. His eyes were a deeper shade, heavier, as if they had seen something they should have never, ever seen. His face looked gaunt, and Maddy wondered when he'd slept last.

Tom turned to her and met her worried gaze.

"You're right," he said. "And what am I even saying? With you here, now we have an advantage. We'll see them coming before they even know it."

"And don't forget I have the navy's top pilot standing right in front of me," Maddy said. "Don't tell me all those awards were for nothing."

Tom laughed, and it warmed Maddy's heart – which really needed some warming. She herself had huge doubts about their ability to hold out at all against the demons, but if staying optimistic kept Tom in good spirits and kept her from slipping too far into despair, then a hopeful attitude won out, hands down.

"I . . . love you, Maddy." His eyes were wide as he said it, and Maddy had never seen him look so . . . vulnerable.

She leaned in and kissed him lightly. Tom pulled her in closer and their lips were pressing harder now, more insistent. Maddy felt light-headed.

"Someone might see us," she said.

"I don't care," he said. They continued kissing, both swept away in the moment. Finally they lips separated and Maddy leaned her face against his chest.

"Maddy . . . you're crying," Tom said.

Maddy quickly wiped the tears away. "I'm sorry."

"Don't be."

Tom looked down at her, a wisp of a smile on his handsome face.

"Let's get you out of these civilian clothes and into something a little more . . . special."

"*Special?*" Maddy asked.

"Just follow me."

Maddy looked at herself in the full-length mirror, unsure. From the waitress uniform to designer dresses to Guardian robes and now . . . *this*?

Tom smiled appreciatively. "Fits like a glove."

The customized flight suit had been created especially for her. Instead of the normal olive-green coveralls, hers was a rich dark blue, to distinguish her from the rest of the flight crew and pilots. Special Kevlar-lined slits in the back allowed her wings to extend and retract seamlessly, and sealed when they weren't extended. Stitched on her right shoulder was an American flag insignia; on the left was a Global Angel Commission patch.

And the finishing touch: Tom's brass flight wings.

"You really do look great," Tom said.

"You think so? It feels comfortable, I guess. But still. You've had so much training you've *earned* the right to wear a flight suit. Don't I look like a fraud?"

"Maddy, you've had training from *me*, remember?" Tom said. "And according to you, I'm the best. That means you're *almost* the best!"

Maddy was happy to see him joking around.

"Now your pilot wings truly fit you, *Lieutenant Commander*," he said.

"I still can't believe they gave me that title."

"What were they supposed to call you? Miss?" Tom said. "Hell no. You're helping command forces, Maddy. And you know something? You outrank me now. You could order me around! That's actually kind of kinky. . ."

"Lieutenant, you're being impertinent!" It felt good to laugh a little; it'd been too long.

"You know, the other guys here are going to want your autograph," Tom said. "I might get jealous."

"Don't worry about the other guys," Maddy said playfully.

But suddenly Tom looked uneasy. Had she said something wrong?

"What is it?" she asked.

"It's . . . nothing," he said, his face turning hard towards the ocean.

The other guys. His friends. He was thinking about the men who'd perished in the attacks. Tom looked back at her, his face softening again. "Have I told you how glad I am that you're here?"

"Just a few times."

"Well, I'll say it again, then."

*

Tom was walking Maddy back to her cabin when they passed a wounded sailor, who was being rolled out of the sick bay on a stretcher. Half of his body was wrapped in bandages, and his left arm had been amputated.

Tom saluted the sailor, who returned the gesture with a meaningful stare. The haunted expression in his one uncovered eye said it all. Maddy could tell he'd seen something terrible, something that had frightened him beyond repair.

But Maddy saw something else in his eyes as he passed. It was recognition. And a tiny shred of hope.

CHAPTER 17

The atmosphere in the solarium was uncommonly pleasant, although Jacks didn't know why that would be the case. Everything was controlled and kept consistent, from temperature and airflow to flora and fauna. Nevertheless, something about today was . . . nicer.

Gabriel and Jacks strolled along a path lined with short cherry trees on the far eastern corner of the indoor gardens. Normally a few of Gabriel's sleekly clad assistants would be waiting in quiet corners for any orders, but today he had sent them out. There was something he wanted to discuss with Jacks. Alone.

Jacks had shown up determined to focus on the politics at hand, but he was still perturbed by what had happened with Emily. How had he let himself go that far? He'd just come back from that disturbing conversation with Sylvester, and then there was Emily, ready to pounce. That's what happens when you let your guard down, thought Jacks as he cleared his thoughts and turned his full attention to Gabriel. They crossed the stone bridge and stopped at a bench. Gabriel's face took on a cold, serious expression.

He reached inside his robe and pulled out a manila envelope, which he placed in the space between him and Jackson.

"Jackson, as you know, I fought alongside your birth father in the first era of the Troubles. During that time, atrocities were committed on both sides. Too much Angel blood was shed. I don't ever want that to happen again.

"However, ever since the Troubles, I have sworn that although difficult decisions must be made, if a small amount of blood must be spilled to save thousands, then that blood must be shed. For the greater good, for Angelkind. I need you to understand why that must be. And know that no decision is to be taken lightly."

Jackson nodded silently, thinking of the centuries Gabriel had lived through, shielding the Angels the best he knew how. What must that be like? What might it do to someone to experience so much bloodshed?

Gabriel tapped the envelope lightly with his fingers. "Open it."

Jacks reached down with a feeling of foreboding. He unfastened the brass brad, flipped open the flap, reached inside, and pulled out a glossy photo.

Panic and shock zipped up Jackson's spine and into his skull. It was a photo of Detective Sylvester.

With Louis Kreuz.

Kreuz was a traitor.

"I'm assuming you know both of those men, Jackson?"

"Yes, sir." Jackson hadn't told Gabriel about Sylvester's surprise visit, but Gabriel knew the two had worked together in the past.

"That photo was taken just a few days ago," Gabriel said. "Are you aware that Detective Sylvester is running an anti-Angel organization here in the city?"

"I've heard some things."

"So then you might be wondering what one of our most esteemed Angels, the head of our Guardian training programme,

152

would be doing with him. Outside the sanctuary. Wouldn't that strike you as a bit curious, Jackson?"

Jacks nodded. "It would, sir."

"This is a serious breach. Imagine, trusting someone with the most important information, and learning he's been a traitor the whole time. Right under our noses.

"Already, he's posed a serious threat to each and every one of us. Our security has been compromised from the inside out. He needs to be stopped before anything else happens. This is a war we are fighting here. And we must be victorious."

Gabriel looked at Jackson carefully.

"And after we stop him . . . we stop the detective. You understand what I'm asking of you?"

"Yes, sir," Jacks said. His stomach tightened, blood flowing with endorphins. "I understand."

"Good. I know this may be difficult for you," Gabriel said, putting a gentle hand on Jackson's shoulder. "But we must do our duty."

Jacks met his gaze and nodded, his eyes unblinking.

CHAPTER 18

D etective Sylvester sat with his hands clasped and resting on the worn, wooden pew in front of him. His eyes drifted around the darkened sanctuary of the Blessed Sacrament Catholic Church from behind his wire-rimmed glasses. He was the only parishioner in the empty cathedral at this hour. A few candles flickered near the altar, casting light up into the vaulted arches. A soft yellow-orange glow danced along the stained-glass windows that faced the pitch-black city beyond.

Sylvester was trying to pray. It had been a while, and he felt a block in his heart as he sat there. But he continued. He needed to. He didn't know what else to do.

Louis Kreuz had gone missing just hours before. He'd missed the nightly drop, and while Louis was many things, he wasn't forgetful. And he wasn't sloppy. The entire resistance was waiting with bated breath for any information, but so far nothing had come through.

And Sylvester had a bad feeling.

Despite the warm light from the candles, a chill hung in the air of the spacious cathedral. The detective coughed lightly, sending an echoing boom through the chamber.

Again and again Sylvester wondered what he could have done differently to prevent this. The detective racked his brain trying to think of what safety measure they'd overlooked, what contingency plan they'd botched, until he was washed over with echoes of the guilt he felt over the girl he was too late to save those many years ago.

And the worst part of all was that Sylvester knew it was useless. He'd never find the answer.

Yet now he was moved by a different feeling as he sat in the pews he knew so well. Somehow, he needed to get square with his God, and in a hurry.

He needed absolution.

He clasped his hands together tightly as he bowed his head.

Just then, the old door of the church opened with a creak, and a gust of wind sent the candles at the altar flickering. The priest had left long ago and wouldn't be coming back this night. A strange feeling came across the detective's entire body as he sat there kneeling. Was it anticipation? Or dread? The detective cast his eyes back to the church door.

A dark silhouette stood in the threshold. The door closed with an echoing boom, and Sylvester knew they were alone together.

"I thought I might find you here," the voice said.

"It's *you*?" Sylvester said.

"Yes. It's me."

CHAPTER 19

M addy stood on the deck and watched the dawn light creep up from the East, back towards Angel City. Purple clouds splashed with pink shimmered along the horizon, and streams of golden light stretched up into the sky.

Looking down to the water, Maddy felt dizzy. Hundreds of feet below, the dark Pacific foamed as it churned along the side of the massive ship.

She couldn't sleep. It was the nightmare again, more vivid than ever this time, and with one major, disturbing change. Instead of the 101, the dream took place on the aircraft carrier. Her legs were paralysed as an enormous Dark Angel, twice as large as the one she had actually seen, towered over her, its eyes smouldering with the purest hatred. Was this Sylvester's head demon? Tom was in the dream, too, but every time she reached for him, he seemed to drift farther away. And though she didn't see him, she could feel Jacks's presence, too. Right when the demon was about to close in on her, she'd woken up with a silent scream. She'd banged her head on the bunk above her as she'd bolted upright, gasping for air.

Now on the carrier deck, Maddy heard footsteps. She turned around to find a pleasant surprise.

"Up with the roosters?" Tom asked. Maddy smiled.

"I wanted to see the sunrise," she lied, not wanting to get into her grisly nightmare.

Tom stood behind her and tentatively placed his arms around her waist.

"It's OK," she told him.

Why was he being so cautious? Maddy knew she had to do something to reassure him, so that, for just a moment, they could pretend it was just a normal day, that they were just a happy couple, sharing the first morning light together. Maddy leaned back into Tom's strong frame and let him hold her even tighter. She turned and nuzzled against his chest, lightly pursing her lips to make a silent kiss against his upper arm. Together they stood in near silence, the only sounds their breathing and the crashing waves below.

So why did Maddy feel afraid?

She felt fear, but she also felt comforted. Maybe she really had made the right choice.

"I should get ready," Maddy said. "They'll need me soon."

Maddy stood on the deck in her customized flight suit, a breeze running through her hair. It was time to start her job. There was a briefing at 0700 hours in the combat control room, and she was determined to be fresh, sharp and attentive.

Inside the control room were dozens of suspended computer screens glowing with green maps, each one marked at its centre with the demon sinkhole. Maddy saw tiny digital crescents representing aircraft carriers and warships moving across the screens in real time.

"All right, all right, settle down," Captain Blake said as the pilots noisily made their way inside. He assigned Maddy to a seat right beside him, which once again made her feel like a bit of a fraud.

The captain cleared his throat. "We have business to get to. We've been at war six days, and we've not made much progress. So I'll cut to the chase. We're running blind right now. We don't know when the demons are going to strike next. Each and every aircraft that has been sent out to monitor the situation has been destroyed. Now the demons are patrolling a two-mile wide radius, taking down all our high-flying drones. So we're relying on satellites, but the demons have caught on to that, too, and have found a way to interfere with our signals. We can't get a clear picture. But we know one thing's for damn sure: the sinkhole's growing. And seismic activity in the area has spiked in the last twenty-four hours. The boys in scientific intelligence predict we'll be seeing some action within twelve to twenty-four hours."

A buzz erupted in the room as the pilots reacted to the news.

"Settle down, settle down," the captain said. "Now. We can't be caught by surprise like last time. We need to strike *before* the enemy does. And that's where Lieutenant Commander Madison Montgomery Godright comes in. She's been hand-selected by President Linden to help our frontline forces get the upper hand."

Groans and grim expressions cropped up around the room. Maddy's face flushed and she tried to keep a brave face as the pilots turned to look at her.

"Now, I know a lot of you may have some personal opinions about the Immortals, especially right now. But today I am ordering you to check those opinions at the door. And I want you to remember that Lieutenant Commander Montgomery Godright is on our side, always has been. So put aside any prejudices and let her help us. We have to trust her. She might be our best hope."

He turned to Maddy, gesturing for her to stand up.

"You can take it from here, Lieutenant Commander."

"I, um . . ." Maddy scanned the eyes in the room, most of which eyed her back with distrust. She felt panicked, and was reminded of how she felt the first time she went to a red-carpet Angel event. All those expectant faces, not all of them friendly. Finally she spotted Tom, nodding reassuringly and mouthing, "*You can do it.*"

She took a breath, thinking about what Susan Archson had taught her about concentration and staying in the present moment whenever she felt nervous. Maddy looked around the room and met each mistrustful gaze with pure grace.

"I know a lot of you are wondering, *What can this girl teach us?* And you'd be right. I can't teach you much. You've had years of military training, and I'm just an Angel. Well, a half-Angel, anyway. And to many of you I'm probably just a kid." She paused to let her words sink in. "But I know about your recent losses. The friends who died fighting in the first wave."

And of course, just when she needed to stay focused the most, she thought of Jackson, the Angel she'd just lost.

"I know what it's like to lose someone you care about," Maddy continued, avoiding Tom's conflicted gaze. Did he know whom she was talking about? "I get it. You want revenge. But that's what the demons *want* you to feel. So they can feed on your anger. They're counting on you to make mistakes in your grief. And if we make too many mistakes, they'll win. They want to sow chaos, evil and hatred, to make their job even easier.

"We can't let that happen. We all bear the pain of losing someone. But we can't let that get to us. Because by that point, they'll have already won.

"I know I'm not one of you, not really. I don't know how to fly an F-Eighteen. I don't know the difference between one missile and the next. But, like the captain said, I can tell when the demons are coming, and where they'll be coming from. I don't know the strategies and attack methods – that's what all of you are here for. But I can help the forces coordinate so that we can attack them before they have a chance to attack us. All I want is to help." Maddy paused and scanned the room, making sure to meet each pilot's gaze and show that she was sincere. "And I hope you'll let me."

As Maddy sat down, she was met with a room full of approving nods, and a smiling Tom giving her a thumbs-up. Well, at least she hadn't crashed and burned.

After the briefing, Tom and Maddy made their way belowdecks. Maddy felt the rush of adrenaline dissipating in her body after having faced, and survived, the group of skeptical pilots.

"You did great, Maddy," Tom said. "You won them over."

Maddy tried to smile confidently.

But she still felt uneasy. Everyone had so much faith in her, more than she had in herself. What if she *didn't* see the demons before they came? What if this was all part of a big joke, dressing her up in this flight suit, giving her an important title, and then all of a sudden the demons attacked and she hadn't even had a clue?

Maddy knew she was just caught in a spiral of negative thinking and she should focus only on the task at hand. But still, she couldn't shake it.

As if he sensed that she doubted herself, Tom said, "Maddy, you have nothing to worry about. You're amazing. And we're all so grateful for your help. Don't you realize what it means to have that extra edge of time? It's crucial. It's the difference between life and . . . between winning and losing."

She nodded unconvincingly, her steps slowing as they neared the end of the narrow hallway of the ship where her cabin was.

Suddenly, as they reached her cabin door, she felt something in her stomach. It wasn't exactly a premonition. But what was it? It stayed there, lodged in her belly. Her uneasiness grew, as the carrier lurched slightly sideways in the waves.

An unexpected flash crossed her mind. An image, like a garbled message. A dark wing blotting out the sun.

"What is it?" Tom said, studying Maddy's face, which had lost its colour and turned a pale, waxy hue.

"They're coming," Maddy said, breathless.

Suddenly the Klaxon of an alarm began ringing across the carrier.

Maddy cursed under her breath. What good was she?

"I'm too late!" she shouted over the alarm, desperate. She started running down the hall, then stopped and looked back at Tom.

Tom put his hand to his lips and pressed it towards Maddy. With tears in her eyes she grabbed the kiss and put it to her heart. Sailors were scrambling on all sides of them, and just like that they both disappeared into the chaos of the forces getting ready, Maddy running to the bridge and Tom sprinting to the pilot ready room.

Maddy bounded up the metal stairs, her feet clanging as she swung her body around a corner, gripping on to the metal railing and taking them three steps at a time.

It was madness in the control room when she arrived. People shouting coordinates, running around, radios squawking.

"Where the hell have you been?" Captain Blake yelled. "You were supposed to see this coming!"

"I – I did!" Maddy spat out.

"But not in time. We're caught with our pants down. We'll be lucky if we can get one bird up in the air before they reach us!"

"I—" Maddy started.

"Just stay out of the way!" the captain angrily said as he reached for his radio and intercom microphone. "That's the least you can do."

The captain began screaming orders over the intercom, his officers dashing around madly. Up on the deck, Maddy saw Tom emerge from below. He ran towards his jet, holding his white helmet with one hand and fastening his flight suit with the other. Spouts of steam poured out of hydraulic lifts across the chaotic deck.

Maddy looked to the horizon but could see nothing. Yet the radar clearly showed a battle line moving towards them. It was only a matter of a minute or two.

How could she have failed so miserably already? Why did they ever send her here in the first place? Maddy wasn't a soldier, no matter what the others said. And now she'd maybe made things even worse, because people thought they could count on her. Turned out they could only count on her to make a mess of things, she thought to herself miserably.

A deafening roar erupted as an F-18 fired off the deck of the aircraft carrier.

"At least we have one jet up," the captain said. He grabbed the mic. "Get out there and raise some hell."

Suddenly the line of demons on the radar shifted rapidly.

On the radio, one of the battleships started shouting. *"They've come around on us! They're flanking us from the south! Mayday! Mayday!"*

"What the hell happened?" one of the radiomen yelled at Maddy. *"This is it! This is it!"*

Drops of sweat formed on Maddy's forehead as she looked out towards the horizon. Why couldn't she get a read on them? With the first wave of demons, she'd been almost clubbed to the ground with her premonition. Had they figured out some way to avoid her?

A panicked voice crackled through the radio from a jet's transmission. *"Tower, we have bogies everywhere – everywhere! I can't even count them. They're all over my radar."*

"Hold. Hold. *Hold!*" the captain yelled. "Wait until you have a clean shot and we have a lock." Maddy could tell the captain was trying to keep his voice calm. Everyone on the bridge was frozen in anticipation, just waiting, motionless, for a full formation of demons, ready to destroy them all.

Suddenly the black line of demons appeared on the horizon, emerging from wispy clouds. So close. Dark silhouettes against the sky, the demons rushed inevitably towards the carrier and the rest of the ships.

Maddy felt sick.

The demon shapes made sharp black silhouettes against the bright sky, moving with menace towards them, gathering speed as they approached. A cold-sweat sheen broke out on the radarman's forehead.

"They're everywhere!"

The shadowed wings were almost there, blocking out the very sun. Searing towards them with dread certainty. This was the moment everyone had been fearing. The Darkness was coming.

"Prepare to open fire on the enemy," the captain said.

"*We have missile lock,*" the pilot of the jet said. "*Engaging, in three, two—*"

Maddy jolted straight up, as if electrified.

With all her strength, Maddy shoved the captain out of the way and grabbed the microphone from his hands.

"*Hold your fire – that's a direct order!*" she screamed.

Maddy slid down on to the floor, tears streaming down her face, utterly overwhelmed with what she had seen. The stunned captain was picking himself off the floor, staring at Maddy in utter disbelief and rage.

"You just have to trust me," she said through sobs.

The captain looked to the horizon as the demons drew nearer and nearer. In the tussle, the microphone had toppled over and slid to the other side of the floor. It was too late, anyway. He watched the messengers of death emerging from the clouds. He crossed himself. This was the end.

Maddy wiped the tears away from her cheeks and looked out the window.

She recognized the sleek white angles of the wings. These were no demons.

They were Angels.

And leading the charge was Jackson Godspeed.

"Jacks," Maddy said under her breath, still gasping on the floor. Suddenly she woke from her stunned state. "They're Angels. Angels! They're here to help, not to attack!"

The captain took one look at her face and decided to trust her.

Panicked sailors on the deck of the carrier scrambled for their guns as the Angels neared the ship.

"Hold your fire! Goddammit, lower your weapons!" the captain screamed.

Jackson was at the head of the formation. He landed first, his folding cybernetic wings distinctly larger than the other Angels' and glistening metallic blue under the morning sun. In one hand he held a large, glowing sword, the same kind of sword Maddy had seen when the Angels had descended on the library tower rooftop and battled with the demon. Jacks held up the sword in a sign of non-aggression as more Battle Angels slowly began to drop gracefully down on to the deck behind him, each of them with a sword. Mitch was among them, as were Steven Churchson and even Vivian Holycross's boyfriend, Julien Santé.

Maddy descended the stairs, and Jackson looked up at her.

Maddy hadn't even noticed that Tom had landed until, just then, he climbed out of the cockpit of his jet, pulling his oxygen mask off. Stunned, he looked at Jackson and the Angels, then up at Maddy.

Maddy's knees shook as she walked down the bridge stairs, wavering under the emotional weight of everything that was happening.

Jacks had come.

Of course he had.

CHAPTER 20

Maddy dizzied under the shock of Jackson's arrival. Just moments before, the entire battle group had been steeling themselves for the arrival of the demons, and now everyone stood silently, in awe at the sight of upward of forty Battle Angels on the aircraft carrier. A distinct glow glinted off the swords each Angel held, the perfect Immortals looking formidable in their black battle armour. Jackson turned his pale blue eyes up to Maddy.

Maddy had thought that the dark wing she saw for a split second in her premonition had belonged to a demon, but of course she should have known. It'd been Jackson's new wing in shadow against the sun.

Maddy took a few steps down towards the flight deck, where Jacks and the other Angels had landed, but she had to stop for a moment, holding herself up by the railing. Her head spun.

He had come to save Maddy. Just as he always had.

Tom jumped out of the open cockpit, tossing his helmet to a crewman nearby.

Making it the rest of the way down to the deck, Maddy approached Jacks. But Tom beat her to it, putting himself right between Maddy and Jackson.

"What are you doing here?" Tom said bitterly. "Haven't you done enough damage? Go back to whatever hole your kind is hiding in and leave us to our fate."

"I'm not here to talk to you, Tom," Jackson said, trying to stem his anger.

"This is just some kind of Angel trick," Tom said. He stepped up close to Jackson and looked him in the eyes. The Angel and the man faced each other eye-to-eye. A little thrill seemed to run down Jackson's body. "Isn't that right, Godspeed? What are you going to do this time?"

"Tom!" Maddy pulled at his arm, trying to get between the two of them. "Calm down!"

"I didn't come to fight you. I came to help," Jacks said, his nostrils flaring. Maddy still tried, unsuccessfully, to separate them. "But I will if I have to. Fight you, I mean. With pleasure."

"And I'll be glad to dirty my hands with some Angel blood!" Tom said.

"Please!" Maddy shouted, pushing them both away from each other. Captain Blake intervened and helped pull Tom back, and Mitch approached to stand next to Jackson, putting a hand on his shoulder.

"They said they're here to help!" Maddy said.

"If you even knew the danger these Angels put themselves in by coming here, you'd be a little more welcoming," Jacks said.

"Ensign, get the lieutenant downstairs and cool him off!" the captain shouted to a sailor. He turned to Jacks. "And you, Godspeed's the name, right? You have thirty seconds to explain what you and your people are doing on my flight deck without prior authorization."

Mitch stepped up. "I can do that, sir," he said, winking at

Jackson. "We're here to kill some demons."

The crewmen showed the Angels to their temporary living quarters. As everyone began to clear from the deck, Jacks caught up with Maddy in one of the hallways just one level down. Maddy had been trying her best to avoid his gaze ever since the Angels had arrived.

"I need to talk to you," Jacks said, catching her by the wrist.

"Oh, Jacks . . ." Maddy said, looking over her shoulder for Tom. "I don't know."

"Maddy, come on," he said.

"I made a promise, Jacks," Maddy said.

"A promise to *him*," Jacks said. "But what about the promises to me?"

"I've kept all the promises I've made to you, Jacks. Don't be unfair." Maddy stared intently at him. "I'm not just some waitress any more, Jacks," she said.

"And I'm not just some red-carpet Angel," he said.

"What do you want from me?"

"I'm not here to change your mind. But I needed to come. I realized, *this* is my real duty. Detective Sylvester helped show me," Jacks said. "And . . . Gabriel," he added cryptically. "You may find it hard to believe that this isn't just about me trying to get you back," he went on. "But I feel it somehow. It's somehow different."

Maddy could tell Jacks was serious.

He put his hand up to Maddy's cheek and lightly brushed it. She allowed it to rest there for a moment before turning away.

"Tom might see us," Maddy said.

"Seriously?" Jackson said. "You were my girlfriend for how long, Maddy?"

"I don't want any more problems," Maddy said. "Jacks. It's . . . it's too late for this." Maddy burned with guilt. "If this isn't about . . . you and me, then why are you and Tom *still* fighting?"

"I can't . . . help it," said Jacks. "Even just seeing him near you, I start to feel crazy." The Battle Angel sighed. "But I know this is bigger than either of us, Maddy."

"I know," Maddy said, somehow not able to look Jackson in the face. She was afraid of what would happen to her, inside, if she did. She thought of Tom's warm embrace around her, and the promise she'd made to him.

"After you saw me, Detective Sylvester found a way to come see me in the underground sanctuary." A darkness cast over Jacks's face. "To persuade me to join the humans."

"*Sylvester* convinced you?" Maddy asked. "And what's a sanctuary?"

"There's a lot you need to get caught up on," Jacks said. "And he didn't convince me right then. Although, he did help widen the crack of doubt I first felt when you and I met at my house. I was so angry when you met me." He paused, and Maddy remained silent. "I was almost blind with rage. But our abandoning humanity, no matter how right it may be for the Angels, it didn't feel right to me. Deep down, if I admitted it, I had doubts all along.

"In the end, to be honest, I did come because of you," Jackson went on. "But not why you're thinking. Gabriel wanted me to do something. . ." The Angel's expression turned inward for a moment. "I almost did it. I was so close. But then I thought about you, Mads. Your face came up. And I was ashamed.

"I realized how far I'd gone. Towards hate. Because of hurt. Or whatever it was. And I knew I couldn't do what Gabriel had asked. He wanted me to take another Angel's life." Jacks paused, and Maddy looked at him with deep concern. "And not only that. But I knew I needed to help the humans. And protect you. Even if you were with . . . him. That it was the right thing to do. That it was my real duty. No matter what Gabriel and the Council would think. How much they would damn me and defame me to the rest of the Immortals.

"I remembered something my mom said to me: to not forget what kind of Guardian I was. And I had," Jacks said, his voice colouring with emotion. "So I approached those other Angels I thought might want to come with me. Guardians I knew who would follow me. And others came, too, those I didn't even ask. They believed in me. It was a strange feeling, after so much doubt and anger about you turning me down and turning away from the Angels. To have these other Guardians believe in me, to want to follow me." His gaze drifted back to the coastline. "We left before the Council even knew what was happening. I had to do it; no matter how much I may agree with Gabriel on other issues, this isn't one of them. And these Angels came with me."

Maddy looked softly into the Angel's eyes as he finished telling the story of how he had become a traitor in the eyes of Gabriel and the others. How difficult it must have been for Jacks to make that decision and bring these Angels to humanity's side.

"Sylvester has a theory that something is controlling the demons," Jacks said. "That there is a leader moving them beyond

170

chaos and destruction into something more calculating and planned. And much more dangerous."

"He told me about it," said Maddy. "But what can we do?"

"It just makes it that much harder," said Jacks. "We won't be able to predict their moves. They're not just going to be moving in to kill. If Sylvester's right, they have some other plans, too."

Maddy looked at him with questioning eyes.

"Like . . . what?"

"I'm sure we'll find out," Jacks said grimly. "We need to flush the head demon out into the open. But how we will do that, I don't know. We might have to wait until they're actually attacking. And then we can make our move."

"But how would you ever find . . . *it*?" Maddy thought back to the chilling vision from her nightmare this morning, of the Dark Angel that was larger and more terrifying than any she'd ever seen.

"I don't know yet," Jacks admitted, looking down the hallway. "But if we can find it and kill it, we could end this whole thing. It might be our only hope. But we will have to hold them off long enough."

Maddy thought about how hopeless it all sounded. But what other plan did they have? They'd have to pin everything on Sylvester's theory and try their best to hunt down the head demon. She nodded at Jacks, then looked up the stairs to the bridge, where the captain was commanding the carrier.

"The military won't need me any more," Maddy said. "Not with you and the rest here. They don't know it yet. But you can see when the demons will attack better than I can."

Jacks regarded her. "Seriously?" he said. "Maddy, no one has advance premonition vision like you do. Your instructors have told you that."

"I thought Susan was just saying that to make me feel better," Maddy said.

"No. You're our best chance of seeing them before they fully attack," Jacks said.

"What if this . . . leader is somehow blocking me?" asked Maddy. "My frequencing, I mean. During the first wave I had a vision, but it was only just seconds before. And afterward, almost all I got was static when I tried to focus in on frequencies. What if I don't see it in time?" Maddy motioned to the door that led into the living quarters. "They're all counting on me. Their lives are dependent on it."

"Susan said you're the most talented she's seen," Jacks said. "If you're somehow getting blocked, you'll find a way around it. I have faith in you."

Maddy just nodded. She was going to have to start having some faith in herself, too, she thought.

"I brought something," Jacks said. "Something for you."

Maddy eyed the Angel as he reached for a slim package wrapped in cloth.

"We were able to get this before we left," Jackson said.

"What is it?"

He unrolled the fine textile before her. Suddenly her eyes were lit with the glittering of a gold-hilted sword blazing under the light. It was just like the swords all the other Angels had brought with them.

"Take it," Jackson said. "It's yours."

Maddy eyed the weapon nervously – she'd never even held a sword before. But she was also inexplicably mesmerized by it, and beheld it with a great sense of wonder.

"Jacks, I never got any Battle Angel training. I don't even know how—"

"Just take it." Reaching forward, he placed the weapon in her tentative grasp. She felt its weight in her hands; it was heavier than it looked. Jackson watched her.

"When the time comes, it won't feel heavy at all," he said.

She examined one side of the blade. Fine engravings had been etched along the dark grey steel, which dazzled under the light.

"Turn it over," Jacks said.

The golden hilt was engraved with the name GODRIGHT.

Maddy gasped, as if she'd seen a ghost. As she held the sword, she swore she could feel a strange presence.

"Why does it have my name?"

"It was your father's, Maddy. And his father's before him. And his before him. This sword goes back generations upon generations. Forged by the finest Angel craftsmen of the ancient times. A Divine Sword to smite evil in the world. The evil of demons. They were made for all the Angel families. For so long now they've mostly been used as mere showpieces, beautiful antiques, with the Dark Angels in hiding for so long. But now they are back. And now this sword is yours."

Maddy could feel the history coursing through the steel, straight into her. She had the uncanny feeling she'd held the sword before, that it was part of her and had been missing her – that they'd been missing each other. They shouldn't have been parted, but now they were reunited. Suddenly, she realized her Divine Ring and the sword were both glowing. Together, and in harmony.

"Are you OK?" Jacks asked. There were tears in Maddy's eyes as she held her father's sword in her grip. He put a hand on her shoulder, but she moved, letting it slip off.

"Jacks . . . thank you," Maddy said. "After everything I put you through, I—"

"No regrets," Jacks said.

Before he knew it, he was hugging her – he was just so used to it. They both tensed up, and Maddy shifted away, neither of them entirely sure how to act around each other, now that she was with Tom. Maddy wanted to make sure she wasn't mean to Jacks, but she also wanted to be fair to Tom. She couldn't even really tell what she was feeling; the emotions were coming on so fast and so strong. She just wanted to hold it together and, most of all, not make things worse than they already were.

After a moment Maddy spoke.

"Where did you get it?" she asked, breaking the silence.

"Archangel Archson. She and Sylvester were able to find it and get it out. Don't ask me how."

"And how does it . . . work?" Maddy held the sword up higher. Immediately she could again feel its power flowing into her. The light reflecting off it was a brilliant golden hue.

"The evil and chaos of the demons can overwhelm an Angel fast. Their dark powers are often too strong. These Divine Swords were forged as equalizers. The Righteous Blade, they sometimes call it." Jackson quickly pulled his sword from the sheath on his back. It made a smooth *whoosh* as he drew it in a flash. He sliced the dazzling blade deftly back and forth in the air in front of him before turning it over to examine it. Maddy noticed that GODSPEED was written distinctly on the hilt in gold, although the edges of the letters had slightly rounded with age. "When wielded by an Angel, a Divine Sword can slay a demon. The Dark Ones will fear them. And then they will fear us. For as long as we last, at least."

"Jacks . . ." Maddy said. But she knew it was no good to try to sugarcoat their situation. Jacks was right. Even with the help of the Angels, they were all facing the end. What could forty Battle Angels do against an army? This was just how they would be facing their end. Everyone either hiding in a hole or coming out into the daylight to do what was right.

"I've betrayed the NAS, the Council, my stepfather," Jackson said.

"It isn't the first time," she reminded him, her mind casting back to when Jacks saved her after Ethan McKinley's party, sparking the whole train of events that led to the Angel hunt and showdown on the library tower. Where she'd saved *him* from his demon.

"But this is different, Maddy," Jacks said. "I can feel it. It's like I've taken a step forward in the dark, and my foot hasn't landed yet. It just keeps going and going. And I don't know when I will find solid ground. Or if I ever will."

Maddy knew the exact feeling he was describing. It was the feeling she had during the premonition of the first demon attack, when she'd just kept falling, down into the abyss. It was absolutely terrifying.

Suddenly, a voice broke up her reverie. "What are you doing,

Godspeed?" It was Tom.

He stood at the end of the hallway, hands on his hips.

"Tom, don't—" Maddy rushed to step between them.

"Just giving Maddy something she should have had a long time ago," Jacks said. He walked away without another word, and Tom watched him go.

Maddy glared at Tom. She didn't need to say anything. And soon the pilot was left there, standing by himself.

The captain paced like a tiger in the bridge's combat control room, binoculars hanging around his neck.

"Sorry about our earlier greeting, Godspeed. But there are protocols. I'm sure you understand," Blake said, spinning around to face Jackson, who'd just joined the captain and a few of the Battle Angels in the combat control room. "Glad to have you and your Angels on board." He reached forward and firmly shook hands with Jacks, who stood there solidly alongside Mitch.

On the captain's side was his crew of elite fighter pilots, including Tom, who hung back slightly in the crowd. Maddy, in her flight suit, her hair drawn back into a ponytail, stood off to the side between the two groups. The pilots eyed the Angels warily. They had already been through battles. They were not going to be impressed just because some fancy Angels in black armour showed up.

But as for the Battle Angels, their presence – and intimidating appearance – was not to be taken lightly. Some of the most prestigious Guardians had joined Jacks, as well as a few of the most hardened Angel Disciplinary Council members. Emily

Brightchurch was notably absent. The Angels looked squarely back at the pilots. They knew the consequences of leaving the sanctuary. There was no turning back for them.

"How do we know we can trust them?" said Tom, breaking the tense silence, saying what all the pilots were thinking. The air grew thick with unspoken accusations. Mitch started to step forward but held back when Jacks put up a hand.

The captain's response was quick and to the point.

"Lieutenant Cooper, I know you have some strong opinions here. Some personal scores in the game," Captain Blake said. "Son, personal grievances have no place in battle. This is war."

"Sir, yes, sir," Tom said begrudgingly, saluting. "But, sir, if I may, this isn't personal. I'm thinking of our men. Sir." He looked at Jackson out of the corner of his eye.

"You're being borderline insubordinate, Lieutenant," Captain Blake said, narrowing his eyes at Tom. "However, Lieutenant, just to amuse you and answer your question: there is no way of knowing whether we can trust the Angels." Maddy watched Jacks take a long look at the line of stern-faced humans opposite him. "But we have no choice, do we? After what happened during the first wave, we're lucky to still be on our feet. To be able to fight for our lives. And that's what's important. Not yesterday's battles. But today's."

"Sir, where were they during the first wave, when Gonzo, Smitty and Jamison got taken out?" an irate pilot asked. An angry murmur of voices among the pilots backed him up.

"That'll be enough, Spader! What did I just—"

"Captain, may I speak?" said Jackson, stepping out of his line.

Blake's expression was severe, but he nodded at the Angel. "Thank you, sir. I just want to say that Spader is right. They're all right. We should have been there. But we weren't. We can't bring your friends back. But we can fight now. And we will fight. Together. Humans and Angels."

Maddy had never seen this side of Jackson before. It was a part of him she hadn't even known had existed. A strange, foreign feeling swirled inside her.

"Now, let's stop fighting and start planning," Jackson said. "While we still have time."

Maddy looked nervously towards the pilots. She saw a few heads nodding.

The captain spoke up again.

"That's right. And when they attack again you can be guaranteed we will be hammering the demons from every angle, with our fighter jets in the air and with missiles and artillery from the ships. My boys want revenge," the captain said. "We only made a few dents the first time around, but at least we slowed the bastards down a little bit."

"That's what we'll need. There's going to be too many demons for us to take them all on at once," Jacks said. "But if you can keep them off balance and slowed down, we can come in range and strike gradually. And we've got this on our side." Jackson drew his sword and held it in front of the captain and pilots. "It looks old-fashioned, but it's the only thing that can put fear in the heart of a Dark Angel."

In a flash, Mitch pulled his sword out, too. He smiled at the navy officers gaping at the blade. "Mine's almost crying out for demon blood, it's been so long. I think my great-great-great-great-uncle was the last to get to use it. It's about time a Steeples Guardian got to cut into some Dark Angels."

"With Lieutenant Commander Montgomery Godright helping out on the preparation side, we can coordinate our defence," Captain Blake said.

Maddy allowed herself a small internal smile, glancing over at Jacks, and as if Blake's words were a rehearsed cue, she stepped up to the luminous green screens displaying the radar position of all the ships and carriers in their battle group, along with the location and size of the sinkhole.

"The demons are ten miles away from us," she said. "I can't guarantee how much time I can give you – these demons are doing everything they can to block my vision. But I can give you some time, enough to coordinate our strike with the Battle Angels. You're going to need to cooperate as much as possible if we want this to work."

Maddy pointedly looked first at Tom, then at Jacks. The pilots and Angels looked at each other and nodded.

"This briefing is over," Captain Blake said. "Go get some chow and some rest. Boys, you show the Angels where the mess is and start introducing each other. You're going to be relying on one another soon enough."

Slowly, cautiously, the Angels and the pilots began talking to each other, shaking hands, speaking quietly as they left the briefing. The captain had ordered them to, and an order's an order.

Only Tom and Jackson stayed at a sizable distance. They eyed each other from across the room.

Sighing deeply, Maddy slipped away down the side stairs from the briefing room, away from them both.

Maddy was in her cabin later when she heard a light rapping on the door.

"Come in," she said warily.

It was Tom. He opened the door slowly, and she met his gaze with a look of soft disappointment.

"I'm sorry," Tom said, putting on his best puppy-dog face. "It's just that after all we've been through – we humans, I mean. And after what *he* put you through. Then he just shows up here like nothing happened. You know how I can get, Maddy."

"Jackson being here doesn't change anything between *us*, Tom," Maddy said. "And you're kind of being a jerk."

Tom sighed. "I'm sorry. It's just . . . difficult for me. Do you want to take a walk and get some air?" Tom asked. "I promise I'll be good," he tried to joke. He put his hand out and reached for hers. She let him grasp her pinkie and ring finger as they walked up to the deck.

The fresh air felt good in her lungs. Crisp and clarifying. They looked out at the ocean for a while, not saying anything.

"You know," Tom said, "I can't tell you how many sunsets I've seen here on the deck of the carrier. Looking out to wherever we may be at the time. Thinking if maybe someone out there was looking back at me. Someone special."

Tom reached over and squeezed her hand and smiled. "Who knew it was going to be an Angel who ended up here with me?" He paused and his smile turned a little slyer. "I mean, of course, being an Angel, she was spoiled and high maintenance and all that. . ."

Maddy mock-pushed him, laughing. "I could have you court-martialled, you know."

"As long as they lock us in the brig together, I'm fine with that," Tom responded with another laugh.

Silence fell over them again as the expansive orange-black sunset filled the horizon behind them as they stood on the deck of the carrier. They let the evening wind whip them. Maddy had her oversize navy-issued crewneck sweatshirt on, and Tom wore his trademark leather jacket even though he wasn't supposed to wear it on deck.

Suddenly, Maddy saw a familiar figure, silhouetted against the last of the sunset, walking on the deck, heading straight towards them.

"Oh no . . ." she said.

Maddy could see the muscles tensing in Tom's face as Jacks approached. He reached them, stopping a little too close to Tom for Maddy's comfort.

"I just want you to know this isn't about Maddy any more," Jacks said to Tom. "It's about something that's bigger than all of us."

"I agree with you, one hundred percent," Tom said. "By the way, I liked your performance with the captain today. If only I thought we could really count on you and the Angels when the chips are down. Instead of just when it's convenient and makes for a good photo op."

"You should be grateful—"

"Grateful that you're doing something that is obviously your duty? If you think the demons would have just stopped at destroying humans without turning to the Angels next, you're a fool."

"Stop!" Maddy pressed against Tom.

"Funny, you don't strike me as a scholar of the Book of Angels," Jacks said.

"Stop!"

Maddy stamped her foot down on the deck. Hard.

"Stop it!" she yelled. "We don't have time for this!"

Maddy's eyes were wild, nostrils flared as her steely gaze moved back and forth between Tom and Jacks.

"Maddy!" Jacks said.

She merely stared forward in response.

"What is it?" Tom asked.

But it was clear that Jacks knew what Maddy knew. The colour drained from his cheeks, but his face remained firm. His eyes looked to the sky.

Maddy began to draw back to her senses, slowly. "The demons. They're almost here."

CHAPTER 21

A bead of sweat had formed on Maddy's forehead. It tickled, just a bit. It struck her as almost funny that she would even notice something so small at such an intense moment as this. She swiped away the sweat drop.

Lieutenant Tom Cooper and Jackson Godspeed looked at her. In a brief moment of gallows humour, Maddy realized they'd stopped fighting for once.

"You're sure?" Tom said.

"I think so," Maddy replied.

"That doesn't sound so sure," the pilot said.

Maddy looked at him, then at Jacks, who nodded at her.

"OK," Maddy said, taking in a deep breath. "I'm sure."

"Go, go!" Tom cried.

Tom smashed the safety glass of an alarm panel and pounded the button. A Klaxon began ringing across the sky, along the short, narrow hallways, out into the mess hall – all throughout the carrier. Every soul on the ship bolted up straight for a moment as he or she realized what was happening. There was an extended moment of silence as if each of them drew in a breath, and then a burst of hurried chaos as the entire ship sprang directly into action.

*

Maddy ran up the stairs on the aircraft carrier's island into the combat control room, leaping up the steps.

"What do we have, Lieutenant Commander?" The captain was already there, gulping coffee from a paper cup. He was eyeballing the large vertical radar screen in the middle of the room. His face was cast in a ghostly green shade from the glow of the enormous screen. "No activity yet."

"Good. That means you can get your forces up," Maddy said. "But we don't have much time. They're planning on going" – she pointed to a spot on the map near one of the battleships – "*here* first." She'd seen the big warship clearly in her brief vision.

"OK, that's south," the captain said. He turned to his radioman. "Get the admiral on the radio. If Montgomery's right we're going to be engaging the enemy very soon. We're going to need to throw everything we've got at them, and more."

"*Move, move, move!*"

"*Look alive, people! This is not a drill!*" a voice yelled on the intercom. "*This is real!*"

Jacks and Tom approached and were now standing next to Maddy and the captain. Jackson's commanders, including Mitch Steeple and Steven Churchson, quickly followed suit, in gear and ready for action.

Jackson turned to Maddy. "Lieutenant Commander?"

She blushed. "The demons are headed here." She pointed at a space maybe three miles from the main line of carriers and battleships on the screen. "If the jets are coming from the east, then you can surprise them from the south." She looked around nervously at the military crew and the Battle Angels. "If that would work, I mean."

"Straight out of the Naval Academy, Montgomery," the captain said appreciatively with a nod.

Jackson looked at his Battle Angels. "OK, you heard her. That's where they're headed. Let's do this."

Black clouds were amassing in the distance, hovering near the sinkhole. Maddy knew that just beyond the clouds, the Dark Angels manoeuvred in demonic darkness.

Looking down from the bridge, Maddy watched as first one, then another, then another fighter jet screamed off the flight deck of the carrier in a deafening roar of jet exhaust and g-forces. Finally Tom's jet took off. He looked up through the bridge window at Maddy and smiled at her, just like when he had left the first day on the carrier. His F-18 started to rumble like the beginning of an earthquake and then was off before Maddy could even blink, the steam catapult sending it flying at 165 miles per hour.

The Battle Angels had already departed, soaring low along the water and swinging out wide of where Maddy had seen the Dark Angels arriving in her vision.

Anxiously, she looked out with a pair of binoculars the captain had given her. Then she saw the clouds starting to shift, and she knew the demons were moving. The jets were headed directly towards them.

Missiles began launching off the wings of the jets in the distance, screaming through the sky and exploding against the line of demons. And then she saw it, Jackson and his Angels emerging from a cloud bank that flanked the Dark Angel army.

*

Jackson flew up and over the fray. The Battle Angels had surprised the demons; the trick had worked with Maddy's help. He almost laughed at how foolishly the demons had practically sauntered into their trap. The Dark Angels had gone straight for the navy fighters, and then the Battle Angels had emerged from the darkness on their side, swinging Divine steel that sparkled gold in the filtering sunlight. They'd slaughtered at least three demons in short order.

But now the Dark Angels were regrouping.

Boom. Another missile exploded into a Dark Angel, stunning it for a moment. The mushrooming orange missile fire co-mingled with the demon's own shimmering black fire-skin, and its very form seemed to tremble and turn to static. Jacks flung himself overhead towards the demon, unsheathing his Divine Sword as he lunged. He steadied himself and in an instant had the blade pointed right at the Dark Angel's ugly head.

The demon screeched as the blade pierced into its skull, and a brief white light flashed off the sword as Jacks dispatched the Dark Angel. Before the attack, Jackson hadn't known the swords could do *that*. But he wasn't complaining.

Jacks gave a thumbs-up to the pilot, who was already circling around to target another cluster of demons. But before he even dropped his hand, a demon sheared off the back tail of the fighter jet like a bolt of dark lightning, sending it plunging towards the ocean in flames.

Cursing, Jackson started racing to make the save. But suddenly he could smell *it*. He had to roll backward and bank directly left as another demon appeared from the clouds to pursue him. Unless he had ejected, the pilot was lost.

The demon was fast. Jackson was giving it everything he had to try to lose the tail, but this Dark One wouldn't budge. It was slowly gaining on him. Jacks remembered Sylvester's theory, about the demons evolving, about their leader and their plan. Jacks started to sweat. Then he realized there were *two* demons right on his tail.

Suddenly, the roar of a fighter jet reminded him he wasn't alone.

The jet was on the demons' tail, trying to get a missile lock on them.

"Come here, you ugly suckers . . ." the pilot murmured, but it was too difficult to fire a missile with Jacks so near. "Too close! Switching to guns."

Pop-pop-pop-pop-pop – the rapid machine-gun fire tore into the line of Dark Angels, slowing them down just enough.

Jackson's wings suddenly dropped a shadow over the demons. He had managed to flip all the way up and backward as the storm of bullets hit the demons. His Divine Sword felt like it was being moved by its own righteous energy as it bore down on first one demon, then the other. Flashes of white lit the sky.

All along the battle line ahead of the battleships and aircraft carriers, fighter jets screamed back and forth across the sky. Bombs exploded, battleships unleashed everything they had, and the air was thick with smoke, demons, and Angels. This was real.

Suddenly Jacks looked farther up towards the clouds growing in the sky and saw a Guardian struggling with two demons mid-air. Was it Steven Churchson?

Jacks shot up as fast as he could, swinging his blade wildly at the pair of demons in hopes of somehow pulling them off Steven. The blade caught one of the Dark Ones on the leg, lopping off its limb above the scaly knee. Jackson's suicide rush was enough to startle the demons for a moment, and they let go of their hold on Steven, retreating to higher sky. Jacks swooped down and grabbed the Angel. Instantly, he could feel the warm blood pouring off his body. He didn't have time to check if he was breathing.

Jacks flew out to the nearest ship, dropping quickly to the deck, where he carefully laid the Angel down. But he feared it was too late. Steven's face was ghostly pale, marred with blood and angry wounds. Jacks could now see that his torso was torn and bleeding from the demons' claws. One arm hung uselessly at his side, forced into a direction it should never have gone, hanging only by a few tendons. Steven's wings had been mangled, his body armour shredded, and blood gushed from his exposed chest.

Steven couldn't speak. His eyes roamed helplessly as Jackson stood above him. Then, in a slow yet sudden motion, he gripped Jackson's arm with his good hand. Jacks was surprised by how much strength Steven had left in what he was sure were his final moments. Jacks put his hand on the Angel's cheek in a gesture of comfort.

"Everything's OK."

But the gesture was in vain. Steven was dead.

Jacks didn't have much time to contemplate the gravity of this loss. Looking up, he saw Mitch, flying with at least three black demons in pursuit. If he didn't want his best friend to end up like Steven, he needed to get moving.

*

"*They're all over me!*" the panicked voice screamed on the radio.

Cursing, Tom looked out the cockpit of his F-18 down below the clouds. They'd been fighting tooth and nail for the past fifteen minutes, and the demons just kept coming. He strained to get a good look through the chaos, and then saw Spader's jet flying through the sky at a blistering speed, trying to outrun the soldiers of evil. It was as if a swarm of locusts had descended upon him.

"They're too close, Spader! I don't have a clear shot!" Tom shouted over his radio.

Suddenly, in his peripheral vision, Tom saw a streak emerge and then smash into the middle of the flock of demons. The blur resolved into a female Angel wielding a Divine Sword. The surprised demons roared and dispersed, dive-bombing away from the attacking Angel and leaving Spader's jet clear to escape.

"*Damn, that was close!*" Spader's voice hollered through the radio as Tom watched him pull the jet up and shoot straight into the darkening clouds. Tom made sure Spader was clear before he checked his bearings again.

"Ah, hell," Tom said.

To his right, down towards the emerald and blue ocean, Tom could see the demons regrouping and were now turning on the Battle Angel who had saved Spader.

"I'm going in." Tilting his control stick down, Tom screamed the jet towards the skirmish, spiraling in between two Dark Angels darting for the battle lines.

The Angel was flying as fast as she could, a multi-headed demon right on her tail. It looked as if the demon was gaining.

With a quick bank, Tom dove to the left rear of the Dark Angel, before it had a chance to turn around and see what was coming.

The missile lock overlay in his helmet screen went red. "Bingo. Game over."

The rocket tore off the side of the F-18's wing with a *whoosh*, searing the sky with its trail. It crashed into the demon with a tremendous explosion. Stunned and writhing as it was engulfed in the fiery payload, the demon tumbled through the air, trying to get its bearings.

It would be enough time.

With incredible agility the Battle Angel had somersaulted around, changing direction mid-air above the ocean. Her sharp wings were set, the black body armour sleek against the light of the disappearing sun. Now, leaning in as resolutely as she could, she flew with the point of the Divine Sword leading the way. Tom saw the blade glint as it spiked into the dazed demon's main, noxious head. The beast screamed and a burst of light exploded out of the sword, blinding Tom for a moment. When the pilot's vision recovered, he saw the dead Dark Angel, falling like a rag doll lifelessly into the rolling waves below, dying flames sputtering off its body.

The Battle Angel had already disappeared in pursuit of more demons. There were just so many to fight.

Once the jets had been launched and the demons met, chaos had emerged in the skies above the blue Pacific. Maddy's premonitions weren't going to be helping any more. The attack was on.

Maddy felt worse than useless. She felt helpless. Her frequencing had become one enormous jumble of panic, fear and adrenaline. She couldn't focus on any of the fighters, even though they were just a couple of miles away.

She paced back and forth in the control room next to the captain, listening intently to the radio conversations, watching the radar screens and the clear plastic board tracking the locations of aircraft that almost resembled a game board. She would scan the horizon, trying to make sense of everything that was going on, then she would go back to pacing again.

Whenever Tom's voice came over the radio, Maddy would stop and strain to listen.

"Stop fidgeting, Montgomery. You're making me nervous!" Captain Blake said.

They had lost only one jet, but some of the other aircraft carriers in the battle line had suffered far worse.

Things were looking grim on the horizon. Too many demons kept coming. The dark clouds were growing closer and closer in spite of the gritty air and sea stands the Battle Angels and humans were making. One of the great battles of history was unfolding. Unfortunately, the good guys were losing.

Then something strange started happening. Maddy felt her intuition kicking in, felt it loosening. She noticed it first as she looked to the darkening sea and the battle raging in the distance.

"They're leaving," she said.

"What?" Captain Blake said, pulling at his binoculars. "Well, I'll be damned."

"Are they retreating?"

"Giant Killer, you're not going to believe this, but the demons are headed back," a pilot said. The radar screen showed the knotted, dark masses of green shapes moving westward again, towards the sinkhole.

Celebrations erupted on the bridge of the ship.

Only Maddy and Captain Blake remained serious, their expressions locked in thought.

"Why?" the captain asked. "It doesn't make sense. They were almost through."

Maddy thought about what Sylvester had said. About someone controlling them. About a strategy.

"They were testing us," Maddy said. "It's like they knew the Angels were here with us. They wanted to see what kinds of defences we had. Did you see how many they had behind their front line? Just waiting? They could have broken through. Easy."

"Testing us?" the captain murmured. "More like they're toying with us. Like a cat with an injured mouse."

One by one, Angels started to land on the deck, several of them wounded.

"See where all our boys are. Let's get them back, stat, and see where we're at."

Maddy strained to see Jackson and Tom come in. The sun had dropped very low in the sky, and neither of them were anywhere in sight.

"Captain Blake, all our remaining jets are inbound," the radioman informed his commander.

"All right, get 'em all home safe now."

A voice on the radio suddenly crackled in the control room.

"Giant Killer, I am in pursuit of a retreating demon that has separated from the main group."

Tom?

"Return to the carrier. I repeat, return to the carrier."

"Negative, I think I got this one."

The captain snatched the radio out of the sailor's hand. "Return to the carrier, Lieutenant Cooper. That's a direct order!"

"Giant Killer, engine number one is down!" the voice said.

"Which jet is that?" Maddy asked.

"Cooper, come in, over. Cooper, come in, over."

"Engine number two down! Entire fuselage is on fire, Giant Killer!"

Maddy turned, eyes wild, to the crewmen in the room. "What's going on?"

All the crewmen focused on their radios, ignoring Maddy, who was growing more and more frantic.

Blake grabbed the microphone off the flight control deck table. "Ditch the aircraft, Cooper! Eject!"

"Copy that," the voice said before it suddenly broke off into a terrible squeal of static.

"Did he make it? Did he make it?" one of the crewmen asked.

The radarman looked at the screen. "We do not have a location on Cooper. Repeat, do not have Cooper's location, Captain."

"How incompetent can you people be!" the captain growled.

Maddy grabbed the nearest crewman. "Tell me what's happening!"

"Miss, we need you to calm down," he said, guiding her to a chair.

"We have lost all contact with the aircraft," the crewman at the radio announced.

He reached forward out the clear board and grasped the

miniature plane that represented Tom's jet. Slowly, mournfully, he turned the jet over, signifying it was lost. The room was silent. Maddy stood stock-still and quiet, her breathing coming quick, her eyes wide and wild.

"Did Cooper eject, Goddammit?" the captain asked.

"Sir, we don't know."

A soft cry escaped Maddy's lips.

"Well, you better find out," the captain said. "And quick. The navy's lost too many good men already, and there's no way in hell we're ready to mourn our best one."

The smouldering wreckage of Tom's jet floated on the water, rolling with the waves. The aircraft had broken into hundreds of pieces, splintered into clusters of multimillionaire-dollar junk, smouldering flotsam in the ocean. Flames burned in the oil slick on top of the water, a strange sight to see. Their flickering fire lit the sea, giving it an eerie orange glow against a backdrop of endless black water and twilight sky as night approached. A chunk of the jet's stealth steel skin bobbed in the current. Through the char of the fire, some stencilled words were visible: FIRST LIEUTENANT THOMAS COOPER. The only identifying piece from the shattered plane.

A tangled white parachute drifted on top of the water some distance away. Tom's unconscious body floated face down next to it, caught in the ropes. Lifeless.

Suddenly, with a gasp, the pilot came to consciousness. He rolled over on to his back and immediately started ripping his helmet off. Tom's chest heaved as he choked, his body grappling with the water in his lungs. He kept coughing and coughing, the seawater burning as it streamed out of his throat and nostrils, until finally he felt he could breathe. Tom began extricating himself from the parachute ropes, which could drag a man down to the depths with surprising force. It would be far better to die in an explosion than to drown slowly, Tom thought grimly. At least an explosion would be instant. Drowning, you would have far too long to suffer as the water slowly entered your lungs, searing through your body with unbearable pain, bringing on the darkness, excruciatingly inevitable. Finally, the pilot broke free of the knotted parachute and started swimming, strong strokes, away from the dangerous snare. He sparked the waterproof flare attached to his vest. It burned bright white in the dwindling light as he held it up.

His head. It felt as if a hammer were raining on it in steady blows. And it felt strangely warm. Reaching up, he felt a huge swell, and blood pouring out. He must have been struck on his head during the ejection. Blood kept streaming down his face and neck, turning the water crimson.

Using his flare to light the sea, Tom scanned the waters for telltale signs of a shark: a dorsal fin knifing through the waves, an eerie black shadow rising from below to strike. The sharks would smell his blood soon enough, and then they would come to feed. He unsheathed the knife he kept inside his flight suit and saw the blade's jagged edge shine in the reflection of the flames. The sharks wouldn't get an easy meal out of him. He would take some with him if it came to that.

Pulling back his life vest, Tom checked the emergency locator transponder. Where a steady blue flash should have been transmitting, it was blank. Dark. Broken. Tom cursed under his breath. Night was falling. How would his men find him?

Tom listened for a rescue helicopter, dying to hear the steady thrum of its rotor blades across the sea. The sound of safety.

But none came.

From the corner of his eye, Tom saw some movement, causing him to twist around quickly with a startle, expecting to meet a shark. But it was merely a gull skimming across the water, unworried, heading to its next destination as darkness fell.

He chuckled at the absurdity of his response, blood still streaming down his face from his head wound. It hurt to laugh, and he began choking again.

The currents drew him away from the plane's wreckage and out into the pitch-black sea. He rolled with each swell that passed, his only light the flare. And the flare would not last for ever. He had fifteen minutes, maybe.

He struggled to stay awake. It was suicide to give into the darkness out here in these waters. He needed to keep conscious. He knew he had a concussion, and if he went out now, it could be hours until he awoke again. By then it would certainly be too late, with his emergency transponder not working. And with the demons liable to attack again at any moment.

He splashed his face with the cool seawater. And then he even took to slapping himself.

But the darkness was so warm, so inviting. *Why not just close your eyes? Just for a moment.* He knew he shouldn't; they always told you not to when you hit your head. But just for one teensy second, he told himself, then you could wake up again. How could it hurt?

Just a little nap. The warm darkness rushed into his field of vision, until all was black again.

A luminous image of Maddy's face rose in the front of his mind, but soon it turned to wisps, then nothing. Tom opened his eyes – or was he still dreaming? – and looked down into the depths below. A calm, blue-green light shone. An enormous whale, peaceful and silent in the deep, slowly drifted underneath him. A leviathan. Tom wanted to follow it. He knew it had something to tell him. It had something to say that was more important than anything up here, on the Earth's surface. He thought he could hear beautiful music emanating up from below. There were voices, too. Were they calling him? They sounded as if they'd been waiting for him.

He could just follow the voices . . . just slip right down to the depths. It'd be so easy. Effortless, even. Why not?

The same blue glow crept back behind the black walls of his eyelids again. Opening his eyes, Tom saw two wings. Wings spread wide, the moon just behind them as the seawater lapped and splashed.

"Maddy . . ." Tom moaned. "I'm sorry. I promised I'd . . ."

"Be quiet. . . . Don't move," a voice said. "You're badly hurt."

He closed his eyes again, and he felt a pair of arms wrapping around him.

And then he succumbed to the darkness once again.

CHAPTER 22

The flight deck of the aircraft carrier had transformed into a tri-age area for casualties of the demon attack. Bandaged-up navy enlistees were being led around by their arms to the sick bay and an Angel doctor tended to the stunned and battered Immortals. They had never before met such an enemy – such sheer evil and tenacity. It had been breathtaking in the most horrible way. Although medics were yelling and crewmen were shouting to each other over the radio, the air over the flight deck was filled with a deep, hollow hush. A solemn reflection over what they had just faced. And what was yet to come.

Things were looking grimmer and grimmer. Once again, the demons hadn't even hit them with a full attack before they moved back for reasons still unknown. During the first wave, it had seemed that their goal, aside from causing general terror and inflicting death, was to stop anyone from leaving Angel City. But this time, it almost seemed as if the Dark Angels were testing them – both the humans and Jackson's Battle Angels alike. More than ever Maddy was convinced there really was a head demon, and that it was clever, persistent and patient. She knew the demons wouldn't hold back next time. Almost everyone knew that.

There was an unspoken feeling, a reverence for those already lost and those who would still be lost. The final battle would be a great sacrifice for both humans and Angels – and they would ultimately be defeated.

There was almost something noble in the inevitable.

The first thing Tom saw was Maddy's face, peering over him.

"Shhh . . ." Maddy ran a comforting hand through his hair.

Tom tried to sit up, but as soon as he did, he fell back on the pillow, dizzy, his head throbbing terribly. Glancing to the side, he saw he was in the sick bay of the aircraft carrier. He put his hand to his head and felt a large bandage.

"How . . . ?" Tom asked, his thoughts still muddled. Slowly, he pieced the past several hours together. He had seen the wings. And now he was waking up here, with Maddy. He tried to sit up again, but a shooting pain winced through his entire body.

He managed a weak smile. "Ow. Won't try that again."

Maddy gave a light smile back.

Tom looked up at her. "You saved me?"

Maddy shook her head.

"I tried, Tom, but we couldn't find you," she said. "As soon as they said you went down they had to stop me from just leaving right there and then, totally blind into the night. I could see you were in danger, but you kept moving in and out of consciousness and I'd lose your frequency. Never long enough for me to find you. But we waited to see if we could get a read on your location. The transponder was gone. We started looking for you. But it was so dark. It seemed impossible." Maddy's face quavered with emotion as she recalled the failed search.

"Then who . . . ?"

Maddy gnawed on her lip slightly. "Jackson found you, Tom. He brought you here. He saved you."

"*Him?*" Tom's face was cast over with shock.

Maddy was silent.

Tom tried to sit up again, with more success this time. But he still groaned in pain as he moved.

"No . . ."

The darkness took him again.

After some searching, Jackson found Maddy leaning against the railing along the rear deck of the ship.

His approach was quiet, but Maddy still turned around at the sound of his footsteps. She broke her expression of deep thought with a faint smile, but in a moment it was gone and she turned back to look out to the sea. She had seen so many injured fighters, both Immortal and human. And she had seen Tom.

"Hi," said Jacks gently.

"Hi."

"How is he?"

"Sleeping again," Maddy said.

"He'll be all right," Jacks said. "He's stubborn. Like you."

"I just wanted to . . . thank you," Maddy said. "I don't know when Tom will be able to himself, and—"

Jacks interrupted her. "You don't need to get into it," he said. "I was just doing my duty."

"How are your Angels?" Maddy asked.

"We lost five, and four are injured," Jacks said. "That leaves thirty-one of us. We're going to do our best."

"Five," Maddy said almost under her breath, shaking her head. And it wasn't even a full attack.

"We need to slow the demons down, even more than we already have. I'd like to give Linden time to set up defences across the country. The longer we keep them from totally overrunning Angel City, the better chance he has of slowing them before they take over the next city. And the more chance Detective Sylvester has of finding out how to get to the head demon." He looked back towards the land. "Angel City won't last long. But the resistance can. There has to be a way to stop the demons before they take everything."

"It doesn't have to be this way," Maddy said. "Sylvester and Susan said that if we could find and kill the head demon, we could stop the assault. Without their leader, their forces would fall apart." Maddy looked out across the sea again and thought of all the people still left in the city. Including her uncle Kevin. They needed hope, now more than ever. "We need to find it, Jacks. For the city. For everyone."

Jacks nodded. "It would. I do believe what Sylvester says, Maddy," Jackson said. "But we need to find out how to get to it first. And we won't know if there's enough time. I'm sending a couple of my Angels to Linden right now, even though we really can't spare anyone. If we fail, Sylvester and Archson, along with those Angels, will have to keep the resistance alive as the demons move forward. Maybe they can figure out how to get at the leader of the demons in time to save other cities, other nations, before the Darkness falls on everyone."

"You're *not* going to fail," Maddy said. "We're going to find the leader. And we're going to bring it down, Jacks."

Jacks looked at her, a brave smile on his worried face. "You're right, Maddy. We have to find it. It's our only hope," he said. "But, Maddy, there are just so many of them. So, so many. For every one demon we were getting, there were four more coming to take its place. The harder we fought . . ." He just shook his head, chasing away his pessimism.

Maddy recalled her recurring nightmare. More and more Dark Angels were plaguing her dream; now there were dozens tormenting her.

"We're going to do it," Maddy said. "We have to. Even if . . . we don't make it. We have to stop them."

Jacks squeezed her hand in his and looked out towards the boundless ocean, which held the awaiting army of Dark Ones.

"No matter what happens, we'll take as many of them with us as we can," Jacks said.

CHAPTER 23

Gasping, as if emerging from underwater, Maddy sat up in her bed. She was covering her ears with her hands and rocked back and forth. The demons. They'd been screaming. Everywhere. There'd been no escape.

It was dark all around, and she struggled to remember where she was. The T-shirt she wore to sleep was drenched in cold sweat. Slowly, gradually, the details came back to her: she was on the Ford-class aircraft carrier USS *Abraham Lincoln*, in the Pacific Ocean, in her cabin.

Maddy's heart kept pounding, and the sweat from the terror of her dream did not dry.

Because she realized it was no dream. It did not fade with waking.

It was a vision.

The light clicked on, revealing Maddy's face, gaunt and haunted. As quickly as she could, she stumbled into a pair of sweats and a jacket so she wouldn't freeze up on deck.

"Lieutenant Commander." A seaman up above saluted as she walked by. But Maddy didn't pay any attention. She was focused on one thing and one thing only.

She looked out towards the sinkhole, and then spun around and gazed into the distance, back towards the shore and Angel City.

"Binoculars!" she shouted to no one in particular, but soon somebody on deck was handing her a pair. She took them and looked towards the Santa Monica beach.

The dark sky above Angel City appeared to be trembling, and veins of fire spread across the clouds.

"No . . . no . . . no!" she yelled in frustration.

Her vision was as gut-wrenching as she'd feared.

The demons weren't going to be attacking from the sky. They would completely bypass the Battle Angels and the navy's defences.

It would be a land invasion. The demons were marching up from the sea. The sight she conjured was beyond the most grotesque nightmare: a relentless demon army marching across the seabed, with only one bloody goal in mind.

The Angels had so little time.

Both the entire flight team and the Battle Angels were assembled in record time. They stood on the flight deck of the aircraft carrier in the predawn hour. Captain Blake had dusted off his old flight jacket for the occasion. He took in a lungful of the sea air before turning and speaking pointedly to the assembled troops.

"If Lieutenant Commander Montgomery is right, this takes away any kind of relative advantage we might get from our air-strike capability," the captain said. "They're going to fight this the old-fashioned way, on the ground. Our only hope is that Godspeed and his Battle Angels can get to Angel City and set up defences as they arrive. Force them into the air, give us a chance to catch them off guard."

Grim faces stared back at Blake on the aircraft carrier deck.

After a quick recovery, Tom had managed to get out of the sick bay, and he now stood off to the side with a bandage on his head and his flight suit under his arm. In the distant east, they could see the earliest glimpses of dawn. But black clouds swirled in against the usual golds and purples, and no sunrise would be seen that day.

"It's been an honour, Godspeed," one of the pilots said, nodding to the Angels.

They were under no illusion about what lay ahead of them. Or the likelihood of any of them surviving the onslaught. The Angels and pilots began shaking hands, and then some even began embracing. They'd formed a kind of brotherhood in these dark hours.

"Let's at least give 'em hell, boys," the captain said.

Just then, an awe-conjuring noise spread across the flight deck, causing everyone to look up into the still-dark sky. Birds. Thousands and thousands of them. They were all flying away. North, to safety.

No one dared say a word about the inauspicious sign.

As if to distract from the inevitable, Jacks lifted a hand and gathered his corps of Battle Angels near the edge of the flight deck. Angel City stood in the distance behind him, visible across the sea over the black outline of his shoulder in the battle armour. The sprawling Immortal City, gripped by fear and held under siege, lay in wait. There were only a few miles between the front line and a city that would be in flames.

Jackson began to speak.

"It is time to fight," Jacks said, looking each of them in the eye. "This is a fight we knew we would have to face the moment we decided to leave the sanctuary. All of you know the odds, and you've known them since the moment we left our safe haven. And you still came. That says something." The Angels nodded, moved by Jackson's words. He went on, his voice filled to the brim with conviction. "We will fight for those we've already lost, those Angels who've already made the ultimate sacrifice. And we will fight for the humans, our sworn Protections. All of them, not just those who have the means to pay us. We will defend as we were supposed to defend. We are Guardian Angels."

Jacks's proud gaze passed over his brave fleet.

"This is much bigger than any one of us," he said.

He looked out and met eyes with Maddy.

"For years, we were supposed to be heroes. They took our pictures, put us on TV, worshipped us.

"Well, today we get to be heroes. Not for the cameras. Not for the fans. Not for the money. Not for the NAS. But to carry out our solemn duty as Guardian Angels. This is the way it has always been. And it is the way it should have stayed up to this day.

"This is our duty. This is our fate," Jackson said. "Some of us – all of us – may die, but if some of humanity survives, we will give them something to say about Angels for millennia to come. That we perished protecting mankind. There is no greater destiny for an Angel. And I will be proud to lead you all."

Jacks didn't even know where these words were coming from; they just flowed out like water. Looking at his audience, he saw determined faces, some with tears welling in their eyes, yet all of them with jaws still clenched in fortitude. When he saw Maddy wipe away a tear that had rolled down her cheek, he nodded solemnly and made his way to her through the crowd.

Each Angel put down his or her sword and bowed to Jackson in respect.

Maddy could tell that Jacks's speech was more than just words. Something had happened to Jackson. He had become a real leader. He was no longer just the perfectly gorgeous visage on the cover of magazines and billboards, the most exemplary face of the glamorous Angels. He had become an actual leader. A figure of authority, power, and knowledge that the Angels could turn to. Whom they could follow. Whom they *would* follow, even if it meant their own deaths.

To Maddy it seemed as if entire lifetimes had passed. The boy who had picked her up in his Ferrari, who was a little vain and foolishly angry that he couldn't make her forgive him by simply smiling at her, had now become something different. Something more. Maddy realized that the things she had loved best about Jackson had come to bloom fully. He had become a true Guardian of the Godspeed class, just as his ancestors had been, and their ancestors before them, all the way back to before the recorded time of the Book of Angels.

He was claiming his destiny, even if it would mean his death. He stood before her now, looking more serious than she'd ever seen him.

"If I don't come back—" he started.

"Jacks, don't talk like that," Maddy pleaded. "You *will* come back."

"Maddy, it's OK. You know what we're facing here." Jacks put his hand on hers. "When I'm – if I'm not here, find Sylvester. He and Susan will be able to help you, get you to safety."

"I'm not going to abandon Angel City, Jacks."

"Sometimes it's not about what you want. Everyone needs you, Maddy. You can help coordinate the resistance if Angel City falls. We will do our best to slow the demons down—"

"I'm not saying goodbye."

"—so you can keep working," Jacks went on, clearly unable to face this difficult moment with Maddy head-on. "Linden will be waiting for you out east. The demons can only move so fast. You might be able to come up with a solution. Maybe find the bastard that's controlling these things. The resistance can survive."

"You're going to find the leader, Jacks. We already talked about this," Maddy said, but even she could hear the note of desperation in her voice. "You're going to make it."

"Well, if there's one thing I know, Maddy, it's that you're going to make it. You *need* to make it. You're a symbol, Maddy. What you stand for is larger than yourself. You need to survive. Me? I was just another spoiled Angel, and then I became something worse than that: a has-been. Bitter about everything I didn't have, ungrateful for the things I did. I pushed you away because I was angry and sad and didn't know what else to do. For some reason I've been given a second chance, and I want to make the most of it."

"What if I don't want to be a symbol, Jacks? What if I want to fight? I'm a Battle Angel—"

"I've already talked to Linden. It's a precondition for our help. Your safety. There's no getting around it."

"No! I'm *going* to fight," Maddy said. "I have to! You can't just force me to run away, Jacks. You can't always protect me."

"I can try," Jacks said. "I am here on this earth to be a hero, and

I've only just recently realized that, up until now, I've failed at that. But today I get to be one. It's an honour. And you are going to play a larger part. You have to survive, Maddy. You *will* survive."

Jacks leaned down and kissed her. His lips were light against hers, but he let them linger there for a moment. And Maddy let them linger, too. She had no choice in the matter; it was as if all of her soul and all of her body were possessed by Jackson's presence.

"Think of me," he said.

"I will," she whispered.

Jacks took her hand and put it against her heart. "I'm here with you."

Maddy was silent as the Angel walked along the flight deck to his destiny.

Jackson had almost reached the rest of his squadron of Angels when he heard a voice speaking from behind him.

"Godspeed."

Jacks turned around. It was Tom, still with a large bandage on his head from the crash.

"I just wanted to say . . . thank you," Tom said. "For finding me out there." He motioned to the expansive ocean. "But mostly just for coming. You and your Angels. You've given the people some hope." He motioned towards Angel City, which, from their vantage on the carrier, seemed close enough almost to touch.

Jackson didn't say anything. He knew how hard this was for Tom after everything that had happened. Silence hung between them as they studied each other. The pilot in his flight suit, the Angel in his black battle regalia. Tom and Jacks had never been able to be in the same room longer than five minutes without shouting at each other. Now they had a moment to size each other up in thoughtful silence.

"She loves you, you know," Tom said.

Jacks stayed quiet for a moment, looking down at the flight deck. Then he met eyes with Tom. "Take good care of her."

"What?" Tom said.

Jackson just turned and started walking towards the stairs to the hangar, where the rest of the Immortals were waiting. The ocean wind whipped his hair as he walked away.

"Godspeed!" Tom shouted after him. "What's that supposed to mean?" But he received no reply.

From the side of the flight deck, three military policemen and ensigns materialized and approached Tom. The pilot looked at them, annoyed.

"What is it?" Tom said.

"Sir, we've just received direct orders from President Linden that you and Lieutenant Commander Montgomery are to be transported as soon as possible to safety at a secure location east of Angel City, where you'll be further assisting the resistance. Your demon expertise is far more valuable than your tactical skill in this battle. You are recovering from a concussion, and are under mandatory break from flying. In your state—"

"My *state* is that I'm ready to kick some demon ass. You can't ground me! I'm fine! I need to be up in the air. That's where I'll be able to protect Maddy best. This is a *war*. I've trained my whole life for this." He rounded on the MP. "We're going directly to Blake. When he hears about this—"

"Sir, Captain Blake has already signed off on it. The call came from President Linden himself. There are no options, Lieutenant. You have to leave. You have forty-five minutes to get your things ready. You'll be fully briefed on the helicopter. We are under strict orders to bring both you and Lieutenant Commander Montgomery directly to the president."

Godspeed.

Angrily, Tom looked up to find Jackson, but he was no longer on the flight deck. The Angel was already gone.

CHAPTER 24

The flames waved, quivering like a moving wall. They began at the beach and snarled above the rooftops, snapping and crackling in the masked daylight, starting to move away from the ocean and into Angel City.

There had been no warning. No jets flying over, no air raid sirens. The demons were coming by land this time. They would be infesting the city, block by block. They would be methodical. No one would escape.

The steady *crack-crack* of gunfire came from the front line of resistance: a ragtag group of locals, combined with a squadron of US soldiers who had been stationed in nearby Venice Beach. They were armed with rifles, shotguns, pistols. Anything they could get together.

The tony beachfront properties of Santa Monica had been transformed into a snarl of barbed wire and sandbagged machine-gun nests. A makeshift barricade had been erected with the barbed wire and boards. Snipers were set up in smashed-open windows of multimillion-dollar beach homes, mortars placed in driveways next to the latest BMWs imported directly from Munich. All along this front line of defence, soldiers and citizen militia volunteers alike had been stationed and put into position. They stood shoulder to shoulder, ready to make a stand against the demons.

From far above in the dim darkness, the entire coastline as far as Jackson could see glowed red and flashed with explosions and gunfire. From the water, like lanterns of doom, he could see the dull black-red smouldering of the demons underwater as they advanced up out of the ocean and on to the beach. As they stepped ashore with their foul, unthinkable claws, they were met with the rapid fire of the machine-gun nests.

This was the Immortal City's last, desperate stand. Each block would be paid for in blood both human and Immortal.

Jackson soared above with his formation of renegade Battle Angels just behind, regarding the spectacle with wonder. It was quiet up there, somehow, as the Battle Angels flew wing-to-wing in their black armour in the darkness. But it didn't stay quiet for long.

Jacks pulled his sword out from behind his shoulder. He turned and looked to the Angels aloft behind him, soaring on the cool ocean breeze. Farther out, he could hear the navy's air support drawing closer. He nodded to Mitch.

"Now!" Jackson shouted, spiraling straight down.

With a great collective war cry, the Angels all drew their Divine Swords and began plunging one by one through the thin clouds into the hell that awaited them on the land below.

The demon army just kept coming. Like some unending nightmare you could never wake from, the beasts kept emerging from the water.

Now on solid ground, Jackson and his Angels fought them hand to hand in the streets. Smashing back and forth between buildings, the Angels wanted to slow the demons, hoping to coax the leader out, exposing itself, as they advanced. They would only have so much time to try to strike at this heart of the demon army. But who knew when that time or opportunity would present itself? Jacks had to trust the resistance to keep trying to track their patterns and home in on a source. Otherwise all – everything – could be lost.

In the air, the military's support was negligible – unless the demons were somehow forced into the open, the jets and bombers couldn't get a clear shot. They were strafing and bombing the open beach when the demons were emerging, but all it did was slow them, not stop them. The beautiful Santa Monica beach was becoming pocked with huge bomb craters as the demons moved forward, unleashing themselves on the city.

The battle lines were being pushed back towards Angel City already. How long until they had to make a final stand, Jackson did not know. But he knew it couldn't be too much longer.

CHAPTER 25

Tom scornfully looked out on to the flight deck at the helicopter waiting to take him away from his duty. The crew was just waiting for Maddy to show up with her bag, and then he'd be whisked away. He was a pilot in the US Navy, and this was his country's darkest hour. He felt sick.

He'd been under guard since they notified him of Linden's decision to take him and Maddy to safety, away from the battle. Tom knew that Jackson had cut this deal with the president, and just thinking about it made him nearly blind with rage. He was supposed to be fighting, not running away. Even if he was supposed to be running away with Maddy . . .

The officer in charge looked at his watch.

"Williams, will you go hurry Lieutenant Commander Montgomery? We were supposed to depart three minutes ago."

The petty officer saluted and went belowdecks to the living quarters. Tom looked up at the red tinge starting to appear on the horizon near Angel City.

Five minutes later, the officer returned, his face as white as a sheet.

"She's gone," he reported. "We can't find her anywhere. She left this." The crewman handed Tom a letter.

The pilot's blood went cold.

Numbly, silently, Tom opened it. He could have predicted what it would say, but he never would have guessed how short it would be.

I'm sorry. – M

In shock, the pilot let the paper slip out of his hand and watched it drift slowly down to his feet. Everyone was silent. Tom just stared at the paper resting between his feet.

Suddenly he made a quick move to break past the crewmen waiting to escort him off the carrier, but they quickly cut him off and grabbed his arms, stopping his progress.

"No! No! *No!*" Tom struggled, his teeth grinding, spit running off his lip as he used every ounce of strength to escape.

"Lieutenant, calm down! Calm down or we'll have to restrain you!"

Tom swung at one of the MPs, and before he knew it, three of them had him pinned to the ground.

"I'm sorry, sir, but this is an executive order. It doesn't matter where the lieutenant commander is – we can't wait for her. We have no time. She will have to meet you there."

One of the MPs held him as the other bound his wrists together with a plastic tie.

"This is just until we get you there. It's our ass if we lose you," he said. "I apologize, sir."

"Maddy . . ." His eyes were hollow as the MPs led him on to the helicopter.

The crewmen on board gave a thumbs-up, and the helicopter began rising off the flight deck.

Tom rested his head against the window and looked blankly

out the scuffed glass from inside the chopper. His face was pale, like a spectre of himself. Powerful gusts from the rotors of the helicopter and the crosswind off the ocean whipped his flight suit back and forth, but he didn't even blink.

They began their journey to safety. Without Maddy.

"Lieutenant, I'm sorry we had to use force back there," an MP said. "But orders are orders. You understand, don't you?"

Tom didn't reply. He just kept staring out the window.

Suddenly, he thought he caught a glimpse of a purple glow amid the clouds below. *Maddy's wings?* He shifted to get a better look.

On second glance, he saw nothing. His eyes were just playing tricks on him.

In the distance, towards Angel City, Tom could see the battle unfolding. The demons were flying around to avoid heavy fire, and flashes of artillery and bombs lit the darkened, cloud-canopied sky. He could see that the battle was moving farther into Angel City proper. The Dark Angels had broken through the frontline defences along the beach. Along the normally glamorous, palm-lined Wilshire Boulevard, tanks were firing as demons assaulted the military positions. Their rounds flew through the alleys between the shiny, glass-skinned Angel office buildings. It was bedlam. Destruction was moving slowly towards the heart of Angel City. Judgement had come for the Immortal City. Tom watched helplessly as the helicopter took him farther and farther away. Farther from the battle, and from Maddy.

Just then, Tom saw a battalion of Battle Angels moving forward in the sky against a contingent of demons. They all seemed to be moving as one chaotic group of good versus evil towards the centre of Angel City. Jackson Godspeed would be there.

And Tom knew that's where Maddy would be going, too.

He realized that it didn't matter that where Jackson was she would be going, too. He realized that he loved her more than anyone he'd ever loved before, far deeper than any other he'd ever known. He would do anything to keep her alive. Even give his life for her, if it came to that.

Tom continued to watch out the window but kept his guards in his peripheral vision. They were engrossed in the spectacle outside, the ongoing battle, not paying attention to him.

Tom hadn't endured months of Special Forces training for nothing. In one clean movement he leaned forward and jumped, swinging his bound arms out in front of him.

The MP didn't have time to think before Tom's elbow was bloodying his face, before Tom managed to pull his pistol out of the holster and train it on the other MPs. They put their hands up. He had them.

"Hell," one of the MPs said, spitting on the ground.

"Cut this," Tom said to the MP with the bloody nose motioning to the plastic wrist ties on his wrists. He trained the barrel of the pistol on the MP's temple. "Just don't make a quick movement with the knife. I'm allergic to knives. I'm liable to sneeze and I might pull a trigger."

Within a few seconds, the wide-eyed MP had sawed through the plastic ties with the blade, and Tom's wrists were free. He took the knife from the MP and disarmed the rest of the crewmen.

Still keeping a pistol trained on the guards in the back, he moved towards the cockpit, where the pilot remained oblivious to the quick turn of events.

Through the cockpit's glass, Tom could clearly see flashes of explosions continuing to light the horizon towards Angel City.

Tom tapped the pilot on the shoulder. He turned around, annoyed.

"What?" he asked in a grunt, but soon came up short.

Tom's gun barrel met his gaze.

"I'm sorry. But we have an unscheduled stop."

CHAPTER 26

Demons had begun to hurl themselves like live bombs into the Immortal City. They dropped down and curled up into balls of black fire and smoke, exploding violence and bedlam in the buildings and streets below. Fires blazed all across the Immortal City, roaring up from buildings into the dark night.

"Press harder!" Jacks shouted to his fellow Angels. A demon-bomb soared across the sky, and, launching himself with amazing precision, Jackson flew straight up and swung his sword at the exact right moment. A blinding light flashed off the blade as it cleaved the demon into two neat halves.

Mitch spotted another demon, this one flying lower, heading past their defences to the palm-lined Halo Strip. He gave a cry and hurled himself towards the beast, setting his wings hard behind him as the dark wind ripped along their sharp feathers. Intersecting the Dark Angel from the side, Mitch smashed it against the enormous billboard of a beautiful Immortal that hung over Sunset Boulevard. As Mitch and the demon ripped through the advertisement and hurtled down towards the concrete below, they struggled in mid-air, smashing each other by turns into the luxury apartment building at their backs. Mitch launched himself against the demon, and they crashed into the atrium of the building across the street, where they grappled in the middle of the once-glittering Halo

Strip. The demon managed to trip Mitch and fling him down to the ground, but Mitch used his wings to jump back up immediately while also drawing his sword.

Mitch drove the sword's point into the heaving chest of the Dark One. The Divine Sword flashed brilliantly. The demon squealed and then was silent as it flopped, dead to the ground.

"And stay out of my city!" he spat at the demon corpse at his feet.

Suddenly Mitch felt a blinding pain in the back of his head as the clenched claw of another demon clubbed him. He dropped to his knees and spun around as fast he could, but the demon had the advantage. It was bigger and somehow more menacing than any Mitch had seen yet.

Mitch managed to stand up, but he couldn't defend his right side in time. He groaned in agony as the demon's burning claw reached out and clutched his right arm, the one holding the sword. The Divine Sword dropped to the ground with a clatter as the claw began crushing through the battle armour, which was melting under the flames. In disbelief, Mitch looked into the demon's hellish face, which was framed by huge horns and two smaller heads on either side. The whole thing appeared to be shifting and shimmering, as if its actual skin was on fire. The beast drew its other powerful arm back to grab at Mitch. And rip him apart.

Clatter-crash. The unmistakable sound of someone smashing a window out, the glass shattering to the ground below. The demon still grasped for Mitch.

Chuk-chuk-chuk-chuk-chuk-chuk-chuk.

The report of a heavy-caliber machine gun rose over Mitch's

scream. The bullets blasted into the demon, knocking it first one way, then the other. A team of citizen soldiers had levelled the machine gun in the second floor of what remained of an exclusive Angel hotel. Floor-to-ceiling windows had been smashed out, and the muzzle fire lit up the night as they continued to shoot at the demon.

Stunned by the burst of machine-gun fire, the demon dropped Mitch to the ground as it swatted at the bullets. Even before he hit the ground, Mitch was rolling to his right, ignoring the excruciating pain in his arm, and he picked up his Divine Sword. He launched himself directly up from the ground, aiming the blade at the belly of the demon. Noxious vapors spewed forth as Mitch pressed the sword in to the hilt, skewering the demon's gut. The Divine Sword sent a blast of light into the night as the demon quivered to its grisly death on the end of Mitch's blade.

Mitch turned to the civilians in the bombed-out building across the street and nodded in appreciation. Then he was off, and the ragtag army began reloading for the next Dark Angel who would cross their path.

They would not have to wait long.

Five of Jacks's Battle Angels had already fallen to the enemy. They'd been taking demons with them as they went out, sending them back to hell with a final slice of the Divine Sword. But there were just so many of them. They could only hope to hold out a little while longer.

The forces were getting pushed back into Angel City too quickly, and Jacks knew they were going to have to make a full stand before his ranks of Battle Angels got too thin. The demons were ruthless and efficient. Jackson wondered if they'd see the head demon before long, the leader who seemed to be so relentlessly leading the Dark Ones. Jacks grimly imagined the head demon personally making an appearance to gloat over its victory.

"Jacks!" an Angel voice shouted from somewhere behind him.

In desperation Jackson saw that the Angel was looking at a scene worse than anything he could have ever imagined.

Moving rapidly towards them from the heart of Angel City was a thick, dark cloud, teeming with demons. An entire battalion had somehow flanked them and was getting ready to ambush. Jackson cursed bitterly.

The battle was going to be over before it had even truly begun. It was now the end, and they would be torn apart with no mercy. At least they would go out fighting.

"To me! Prepare to close ranks!" Jackson screamed. The patch of destroyed, smouldering asphalt before them seemed as good a place as any to make their last stand. Gritting his teeth, Jacks started drawing his fellow Battle Angels around him, looking to the phalanxes of demons advancing on the ground, and then the numbers forming in the sky behind them. Through some kind of trick the Dark Ones had been able to get around to their other side. How, though?

Then, out of the blackness of the demon battalion, with a wave of rising joy, Jacks saw white glinting on the underside of wings. White glints kept flooding the sky, and suddenly Jackson and the Immortals beside him knew that the cloud formation in the sky was not made up of demons after all.

Miraculously, the rest of the Angels had arrived.

Jacks and his Battle Angels gave loud whoops of joy as they took in the sight of their brothers, sisters and friends on the wing, Divine Swords in hand.

Jackson strained to see who was heading up the charge. To his great, wonderful disbelief, he saw that Archangel Mark Godspeed was leading the formation.

Confused by this sight of more and more Angels materializing as if from thin air, the demons faltered. They began to pull back slightly from this section of the city and streamed out into the streets.

A few eager Angels began to give chase but were stopped short by furious demons guarding the rear.

The Angels could tell this wasn't a real retreat, but that the demons were regrouping their forces. Either way, it would still give the Angels a chance to do some gathering of their own.

Mark landed right in front of Jacks. His face was set and determined, and he, like the Immortals behind him, wore the armour of a Battle Angel.

Jackson's stepfather stepped forward. Dozens upon dozens of Battle Angels landed softly behind him, some of them on buildings – mostly to keep a safe perimeter, but also because there was no longer room for them on the ground. The Angel fleet also stretched out into the streets, parks, and alleyways, and on the rooftops: a full battalion.

No such numbers of Battle Angels had been assembled since the days of old.

"Mark," Jackson said, still in disbelief.

"We've come, Jackson," his stepfather said with tears in his eyes.

"How?" Jackson was stunned.

"Because of you, Jackson. And your example," Mark said, motioning to the full battalion. "You are a true Angel. What you did, coming out here against the odds, not for fame, but for the principles behind being an Angel. You were the spark that lit the explosion."

Jacks looked out at all the faces of the Angels, most of whom he'd known all his life. He was overpowered with gratitude, emotion and wonder.

"These are your Battle Angels now, Jackson," Mark said. "Lead them. It is your destiny."

Jackson silently nodded, his face tense and set, his pale blue eyes as sharp as they'd ever been. He looked at the array of Angels in front of him, above him, everywhere. They were ready to lay down their lives for the city, and they were awaiting his command. He walked a few paces back and forth, then opened his mouth and shouted.

"Angels!"

They raised their swords and called out a response that echoed throughout Angel City. It was the call of hope for those who had been hopeless up until now. Hope shimmered across the rooftops and the city.

Jacks now found himself wondering whether, someday, young Guardians-in-training would be studying these manoeuvres, the same way he and his fellow Angels had pored over accounts of ancient attacks and counter-attacks between Angels and demons on the storied battlefields of old.

The Angels looked anxiously to where the demons had temporarily retreated to. Now that they had the numbers, the Angels wanted to attack. Jackson stepped away from his spot at the front of the pack and approached his stepfather.

"Where is everyone else?" he asked Mark. "Are they safe?"

"The sanctuary has been abandoned. The non-warriors have left for the Northeast. Your mother and Chloe included," Mark Godspeed said. Jackson breathed a sigh of relief. "There are some from the sanctuary who are still loyal to the Council. There were some . . . struggles."

"Detective Sylvester thinks there is a head demon. That if we find it and kill it, we can stop this madness," Jackson said. "And I believe him. We've been trying to flush it out, but so far – nothing. Sylvester thinks we might be able to tell where the directions are coming from based on the patterns of the attacks. But we haven't heard anything from the resistance in a long time."

Mark looked at his stepson. "Then we need to hold them as long as we can. Give them more time."

Suddenly a demon-bomb soared past overhead and smashed into a building. The Dark Ones had regathered and were on the attack again.

Jackson pulled his sword out and turned to his Battle Angels.

"Angels! We are fighting in full strength!" Jacks shouted. Pride and strength poured into his body as he raised his sword and was met with cheers. "They have taken many of us, but now we are stronger! Let's give these Dark Ones everything we've got!"

It didn't take any more convincing. As soon as Jacks gave the signal, streams of Battle Angels began pouring towards the Dark

Ones, who were now advancing. Battle yells erupted from their demon throats, but the Angels answered with their own cries.

The battle had started anew.

They were coming, more than ever. The Angels had been reinforced by the entire battalion of Battle Angels, but compared with the demons, which were getting replenished from a seemingly endless supply of evil emerging from the ocean, they were still outnumbered.

"Mark! Take some around to the other side!" Jacks cried out as he saw a line of demons moving along the rooftops and streets to the west. Mark formed a loose group of Battle Angels, and they tore off towards the enemy, swords ready.

Reassured by Mark's action, Jackson and his warriors turned and faced their foes again. The demons were moving hard, some of them even avoiding the Angel air patrols by breaking into buildings and smashing through room after room only to ambush Angels from a window above.

Jackson was dispatching one of these very demons when he heard a shout. A young Battle Angel fresh from the sanctuary cried out as a demon crushed his shoulder in his claw, holding him firmly. Jacks was too far away to help.

Suddenly a human emerged from a doorway with an AK-47 and sprayed the demon with bullets before running back again for cover. Jackson tried to get there in time to save the wounded Angel, but it was too late. The demon recovered and reached for the Immortal's legs, then ripped him in two like a rag doll. His Divine Sword clanged to the ground as he took in his last breath.

Then, as if it had been nothing, the demon was up and flying away after the brave human. The demon's blow knocked the human down and did its bloody work before Jackson saw the beast fly off again.

Jackson picked up the Divine Sword from his fallen fellow Angel and looked down at the man with the AK-47. These two brave souls just sacrificed everything in this battle.

He stared forward into the ever-growing mass of demons, his blue eyes sharpening. The Dark Ones looked back at Jackson. If it's possible for demons to feel fear, then that is what they felt at this moment.

"Jacks!" Mitch called, surely having seen the look in his friend's eyes. But Jacks paid no attention.

Jackson Godspeed charged into the carnage with a sword in each hand, hewing death and destruction among the demons as he expertly swung the blades back and forth.

The Dark Angels screeched and the Divine Swords pulsed with pure white light with each demon life they took, leaving a trail of severed, smouldering black limbs and the lifeless remains of slaughtered demons.

CHAPTER 27

Maddy watched the battle unfold below as she flew above the city. Jets screamed by, rockets exploded, and down on the ground the demons were waging a devastating battle against Angels and humans. All she saw was a panorama of destruction, and she just hoped she would not be too late, when the time came.

Maddy's mind flitted guiltily back to the aircraft carrier, to the moments when she was still in her cabin, before she slipped away. Just before she and Tom were supposed to leave for safety in the helicopter, to join President Linden and form a resistance in the East.

She'd had no intention of joining Tom in the helicopter. What he didn't know, what no one knew, was that right after Jacks had left her, Maddy had been overwhelmed by another vision. She didn't get many details – the vision had been delivered and then destroyed in her mind like a stealth bomb. But she did see one solitary detail that had been immediately branded on her brain as if with a hot poker.

The one clear thing she saw was that Jackson Godspeed was going to die.

And she could not let that happen.

Maddy had picked up the Divine Sword from the corner of her cabin and examined it once again. Again, she could almost hear it talking to her, whispering.

The intricate engraving around the gilded hilt told an ancient story in ancient Angel symbols she could not read. It was the story of her family, the Godrights. She hoped that, one day, she would be able to read the story. But she of all people knew that survival was not guaranteed.

At that moment, when she was pondering her ancestors and her legacy, she had her vision.

Her ring and the Divine Sword grew luminous as she held the weapon in her hand. The sword was heavy, but Jackson had assured her it would feel light and nimble if she ever needed to use it.

Maddy guessed she would find out soon enough.

Suddenly she knew what she needed to do.

Maddy didn't know what she'd be facing, where she'd be going. She just knew she had to go. She had to save Jacks. Merely a fragment of a fragment of a vision had entered her mind, but it had overwhelmed her with the force of a tsunami. It had been strong enough to stem the swelling tide of guilt she was already feeling about Tom, the one she would be leaving up on the flight deck.

Maddy sheathed the sword and roped the sturdy leather sling over her shoulder, tightening it diagonally across her chest like a sash. The sword rested firmly against her back, and all she had to do was reach across in one quick motion to pull it out and fight. She practised drawing the weapon a few times, but it felt clumsy. She tried a few more times, and it was a bit smoother. It'd have to do – she didn't have time to become an expert.

Then Maddy pulled out a sheet of paper and a pen.

Tom:
I don't know how to begin . . .

Maddy stared at the paper, but the words didn't come. She crumpled up the letter and tossed in the wastebasket. There was nothing to say, no way for her to explain to him why she needed to do what she was about to do. She pulled out a fresh sheet of paper and wrote her two-word note to him. That was all she could write, and it ripped her heart in two. But she was compelled by something almost beyond her control. She had to save Jackson, even if it meant losing her own life and breaking Tom's heart.

She folded the note and left it where an officer would find it and bring it to Tom. She knew he wouldn't understand.

Her only hope was that maybe one day he could.

She slowly opened her cabin door and looked down the corridors. Everyone was running around, preparing for this final battle.

No one had noticed her slip away. Her silhouette had been barely visible as she flew, skimming the waves towards Angel City and her destiny waiting beyond.

Maddy was still having difficulty focusing on a single frequency – even one she knew as well as Jackson's. The panic, terror, and chaos of Angel City was overpowering her ability to control her gift, so she had to make do with brief moments and those slivers of time when she could feel Jackson's presence, his location, even his mood.

And she knew he was in danger – mortal danger. More than he could possibly know.

As she flew near the heart of the battle, Maddy could tell she was getting closer to Jacks. But it was as if she were walking blind in the dark, hearing only muffled, far-off voices call out every few minutes, and then stumbling in that direction until she heard the call again, this time coming from a different direction. It was frustrating, but she had no choice. The alternative was to just give up. And that was no alternative at all.

Maddy peered into the distance, towards the heart of Angel City, where she'd spent her entire life. And where her uncle Kevin still was. Still safe. The demon attacks hadn't made it that far.

Yet.

And if she had anything to say about it, she wasn't going to let them. And that meant saving Jacks first.

Suddenly, Maddy heard a heart-stopping scream. It was like nothing she'd ever heard before in her life – high-pitched, but deep and booming like a roar. A proclamation of death. And it was headed directly towards her.

In her peripheral vision, Maddy saw *it*: black and terrible, its shape shimmering with dark flames, its wings and horns melding together in a blur as it bore down on her. A Dark Angel. Its scream was a war cry.

Before she even had time to think, Maddy set her wings and banked straight down, soaring towards the Angel City rooftops. The demon followed, its eyes burning iridescent and unblinking in its dark form. Maddy put on as much speed as she could, then veered sharply right.

The Dark Angel screamed again as it followed her. The smoky wind of the burning Angel City whipped against Maddy's face. Her famous wings strained as she flew as fast as she could. But looking back for just a second, she could sense the demon was getting closer by the second. Maddy's heart pounded faster and faster in her chest, adrenaline spreading all through her body.

She dipped down farther, below the rooflines, ducking under power lines and shooting down alleys. And yet the demon stayed on her. There was going to be no outrunning him.

She reached back to feel for her sword.

As she grabbed the hilt and pulled up, the force of gravity was incredible, like the slow climb after a huge drop on her favourite roller coaster, except about five times more intense. Every muscle in her body strained to hold her weapon as she climbed . . . climbed . . . climbed.

Below her in the dark air, she saw the demon overshoot her. He was trying to recover, flapping his shimmering, scaly, massive wings to follow her up. She would only have a few seconds. . .

She reached the peak of her climb. For a moment Maddy was entirely weightless – her body, clothes, and hair hanging in mid-air. Then she began pitching backward, and she let gravity pull her down again. She simultaneously began shooting back like a loop-de-loop, while reaching behind her and pulling the sword from its sheath.

Jackson had been right! The once-cumbersome sword suddenly felt easy and nimble in her hand, now that she needed it.

As she got the Dark Angel in front of her in her sights, Maddy let out her own battle cry. It may not have been as terrifying as the demon's, but it made her feel better.

With her back-breaking climb, she had managed to loop back

on the Dark Angel. Furious, the demon realized what had happened and screamed as it tried to turn around in mid-air. It sensed the sword, but it was too late. Maddy's blade and Divine Ring grew brighter and brighter as she sped towards the demon. She raised the sword and swung it down with all her might, catching the demon's right arm and wing.

A flash of light shot across the black-vermillion sky as the blade connected. The demon howled, leaving Maddy's ears ringing as she flew past, drawing the sword close to her body again. The Dark Angel began tumbling downward, but then managed to slow its descent. She had winged it, and it was now far, far below her. The creature dropped farther and farther down into the dark streets until it disappeared completely. She heard a crunching smash below her as it landed on the top of a parked car.

Panting from the chase, Maddy stopped and circled in the air, looking at the spot below where the Dark Angel had disappeared. The sword suddenly felt incredibly heavy again, and she grunted as she shifted her grip on it. She couldn't believe she had done it! All those agility drills during Guardian training had definitely paid off. If she ever saw him again, she'd have to thank her teacher, Professor Trueway. And Tom, of course. With a pang, she thought again of Tom, whom she'd abandoned on the aircraft carrier. She had broken her promise. But then again, she knew in her heart that she'd simply had to. She owed it to Jackson.

Maddy chased these thoughts from her mind; she had a half-dead demon to think about. Flapping her wings to hover, she peered down from her perch but could see nothing among the buildings below.

Was it dead? Would she have to go down and find out? It seemed to Maddy that it would take more than just a few blows to the body to kill a demon. And wouldn't a wounded Dark Angel be even more furious and dangerous than a healthy one?

Under normal circumstances – or, at least, as "normal" as circumstances can get in the midst of an apocalyptic demon battle – she'd certainly go down and check it out. But she had more important things to think about now.

Maddy began rising again, flying in the direction where, before the demon had interrupted her, she'd last been able to sense Jacks's frequency. All around her in the distance, Angels and humans were waging battles. Were the demons winning? She couldn't tell, and part of her didn't want to know. She just kept rising, her wings glowing purple in the hazy, dark sky.

Suddenly, unbidden, a flood of relief washed across her as she began to realize that she had just not only *survived* a demon attack, but had also *taken out a Dark Angel*. Maddy could barely believe it. She felt that sensation of lightness and near-giddiness that comes when you survive a traumatic event. She almost felt like laughing. *She had faced off against a Dark Angel and had won.*

Relishing these thoughts in the sky high above the smoke and chaos, she drew in a deep breath of crisp air. It felt fresh – she felt alive. It was a grateful breath and she was thankful for every second of it.

Then, like a flash, it came upon her. She saw Jackson's frequency. Immediately her mind clouded over with indistinct waves of abstract images and feelings. The vision she was drawing from Jacks was unclear.

And she felt pain.

He needed her. And now she knew where he was going to end up. His final destination. She'd seen it, for a split second. Even if she couldn't believe it. It was worse than suicide.

Veering left, she set her course towards the Angel City Hills. Her wings pumped powerfully as she tried to gain speed.

Then, in the distance, although it seemed impossible at first, like some trick of the imagination, she saw it. From her soaring vantage point, she watched a fleet emerging from the clouds, flying towards the heart of the battle. It was unbelievable. *The Angels! The rest of the Angels were here!*

Maybe they could lead her to Jacks before it was too—

Maddy didn't even realize what had happened until the blow had struck her. A ferocious demon claw swatted at her from the side, crushing her right wing with immense force. She gasped in surprise and pain. The demon had just materialized out of the darkness, like a phantom. A hissing, smouldering nightmare.

Screaming in agony and seared by the touch of dark fire, Maddy crumpled, her body reduced to a lump of pain. She tumbled downward, her right wing useless. Downward and downward she fell, into the pitch-blackness below.

Until all was finally black.

CHAPTER 28

Laptops were packed up, documents shoved into bags, hard drives stacked into boxes. It was time for the resistance to move. If there was still any time at all.

A loud explosion tore through the streets outside. The entire office rumbled, some dust falling from the ceiling tiles.

Detective Sylvester was dumping out the dregs of his coffee into a wastebasket and shredding documents. Pinned on the wall beside him was the enormous map of the Angel City basin. The Angels were broadcasting information through a radio while a woman listened and plotted out the demon attacks, wave by wave, with multicolour pushpins. They were trying to find a pattern. Anything to give them the upper hand to find the head demon and stop the war.

Susan came up to Sylvester, a box in her hands. She was ready to go. "I know it may not seem like it right now," she said as she looked around at the room of people getting ready to flee, "but this is a victory. The Angels came."

"A victory, sure, but it might be short-lived," Sylvester said. "We don't know if even the entire Battle Angel battalion can hold them long enough for me to figure out how to get at the leader. And on top of everything, our office is right in the line of fire, and now we have to move again." The detective gestured to the chaos around them as two resistance members started taking down the pin-riddled maps.

"That comes down last!" the detective said.

The two staffers nodded silently and backed away.

"Sylvester, listen to me. They finally came," Susan said.

Sylvester nodded. "Jackson was the key the whole time. I should have known to focus on him from the start."

"You know what they say about hindsight," Susan said.

"That it's twenty-twenty?"

"Something like that."

He allowed himself a slight smile at Susan.

"Louis and our other sources say that almost all the Angels have turned," Sylvester said. "If this is true, then that's huge. That's a crucial feather in our cap. But, even so, don't think it will just be over like that. There are still many factions. Gabriel and the Council won't stand down quietly. This is just the beginning. But at least the tide has shifted."

"You don't have to tell me about Angel politics," Susan said, winking. "I'm an Archangel, remember? Listen, though. Silver linings are pretty hard to come by these days. Can't you just enjoy this for a second?"

Another loud explosion shook the building. Sylvester smiled grimly. "For you, Susan, I'll try my best."

"Archangel Archson! David!" Bill Garcia shouted. The two turned quickly to the sergeant at the door, where people were rushing around, shuttling things out into the convoy of cars.

Garcia was helping someone in. The man was walking slowly, clearly old or injured and in need of Garcia's assistance. Sylvester saw that he had a jacket thrown over his back, and with dread, he noticed that a tiny trail of droplets followed the huddled figured as he entered the room. Droplets of blood.

The man looked up.

It was like peering into the face of a ghost. Susan gasped. "Louis!"

Detective Sylvester rushed a chair over so Louis Kreuz could sit down. His face was pale and unshaven; he was a haggard shadow of his former natty self.

"You're alive, thank God," Sylvester said.

"You're hurt," Susan said, stepping up close to Louis.

"They got me before I could get out, after the Godspeed kid warned me," Kreuz said. "I was able to escape during the confusion when the Battle Angels deserted, thanks mostly to the sympathetic guard assigned to watch me. The other guard, not exactly sympathetic." The anguish written all over Louis's face showed that he had a much larger, more violent story to tell. Sylvester removed the coat that had been draped over Louis' shoulder.

Louis's upper back was a bloodied, bandaged mess, and lower down there was another, even deeper wound. Susan cried out before she could stifle it.

They had taken his wings.

"Oh, Louis . . ." she said, tears flowing.

"This? It's just a scratch," Kreuz said, breathing deeply through the pain. He coughed, and the effort and force of it caused him to double over. His face was rapidly losing colour and had turned almost grey.

"We need to get you to a doctor," Susan said.

Louis just looked at them and shook his head. He pressed his hand against the wound – a gory mess, the bandage not stopping the blood. "I'm a goner. I know it. You know it," Kreuz said.

"Don't say that, Louis. You don't know that's true," Susan said, tears still welling up in her eyes even though she was trying to maintain her Archangel calm.

With his fading strength, Louis pressed his hand to Susan's arm. "My ticket's been punched, Sue."

Looking into his eyes, Susan didn't want to believe it. But Louis still just silently nodded. Kreuz coughed again, and Sylvester had to help him back up to sitting. He was fading fast.

"I know this isn't the best time," Kreuz said with a slight, pained smile, "but right now we got some more pressing matters. The demons."

The boom of another explosion punctuated his words.

"What do you mean?" Sylvester said.

"We can stop those bastards," Kreuz said, looking them squarely, resolutely, in the eyes. "And I know how."

Sylvester and Susan waited while Kreuz slipped into another coughing fit. When he was finished, he looked back up at them, his normally jovial and ruddy face now wan and deathly.

"I know how to get their leader."

Louis died just shortly after giving the resistance the most important information it would receive in the course of this tumultuous battle for humanity. It was information that could turn the tides, and Kreuz had sacrificed his life to deliver it. Sylvester just hoped it wasn't too late.

The loud battle outside raged incessantly, just blocks from the resistance office. Soon the office would be reduced to rubble, and the group's time to move was running out. The radio lines had gone dead. There was no longer any way to communicate. Chaos reigned outside, and those who'd stayed behind or who were left without shelters were streaming in panic in the streets as far as they could go before hitting the imposing Hills. The demons pressed farther and farther into the city, but the Angel and human forces weren't making it easy for them. Still, the Dark Ones kept advancing. West Angel City, with its boutique hotels and exclusive restaurants, had been flattened, and now the demons were only a mile from the heart of Angel City, the Walk of Angels. Before long the battle would be pitched on that famous street.

Detective Sylvester drew his revolver and checked to make sure it was loaded. It was. He opened the locked drawer in his temporary desk, retrieved a cardboard box full of extra ammunition, and dumped it in the side pocket of his old overcoat. The rest of the office had already been packed up, and everyone was ready to move somewhere safer.

Susan approached Sylvester, her eyes red from weeping over Louis. She had known Louis Kreuz for centuries, had worked with him in the secret resistance for many years. She'd trusted him with her life, and he had trusted her with his. And now he had paid the ultimate price.

"David," Susan said softly, "promise me you'll be careful."

"Of course," he said, not meeting her eyes.

"I mean, for me." This made him look up. There was something left unspoken, something tender in her eyes that took Sylvester by surprise. "I – can't lose you," she said.

The odds were long. But Sylvester just knew he had to do something, that he would have to be the one to put Louis's intel to good use. He'd been tracking this theory, had put his heart and soul into it, and they were so close. Communications were down, and no one else knew the truth. He would have to be the one.

Sylvester quietly nodded.

"I promise, Susan," he said. "But I have to do this myself. The phones are down and the radios are jammed. We can only send messengers and hope they can find Jacks and bring reinforcements. Get the others as soon as you can, then wait for my signal. If you don't hear from me, you'll know what to do."

"I'll be waiting for you," Susan said.

Susan reached for him and placed her lips on his, and Sylvester felt a shock run through his body. The detective and the beautiful Archangel both closed their eyes, letting themselves get lost in this brief, heavenly moment. It was a moment that they had perhaps waited too long to seize.

Finally Sylvester woke from the spell and forced himself to pull back. Gazing at Susan, he placed a hand to her forehead and brushed her hair behind her left ear, something he hadn't done to a woman for years. But with Susan, it still felt like second nature.

"I'll see you soon," Susan said, smiling.

"See you soon, Archangel Archson," Sylvester said.

It was time to go.

Time to take down the head demon and honour Louis's legacy.

Sylvester turned back to Susan to indulge in one last, long gaze before he opened the door to the outside. The roar of battle overtook any other words they might have said.

CHAPTER 29

Only darkness remained. Darkness throbbing on and on, like an ache that will never end.

Maddy tried to figure out where she was, what had happened, but everything was jumbled and foggy. A silent stream of images flowed through her mind. Tom lying in a hospital bed. Jackson standing in a Battle Angel suit. The golden hilt of a sword. Kevin shouting at her from the porch as demons speared the darkening sky above. An aircraft carrier. She couldn't open her eyes. And still, the darkness throbbed.

Slowly, one eye fluttered open. Then the other. The coal-black darkness bled into a slightly diluted hue, but she could still see nothing. Her eyes tried to focus on something, but it was an impossible task.

Maddy's head was pounding. Every cell in her body screamed in agony as she tried to lift her head just one millimetre before setting it down again. But all of this was nothing when compared with the excruciating pain in her right wing.

One by one, the memories began flitting back. Leaving the carrier to follow Jackson. Chasing and fighting with the Dark Angel. The relief at having survived. Then the vision of Jackson needing her, cut short by the awful claws of another demon she hadn't even been aware of until it was too late. The overwhelming pain as it struck her. And then the darkness as she fell.

Still immobilized, Maddy tried again to adjust to the lack of light and get her bearings. She could tell that she had landed on top of a pile of rubble near a narrow street between two buildings. The rubble must have been a building just hours ago. No one seemed to be around; everyone else must have fled the destruction. Or suffered an even worse fate than Maddy had.

Tears streamed down Maddy's face as she propped herself up slowly, painfully, on one elbow, then the other. She sat up like that for a few moments as she waited quietly for the sharp pain to cool down to radiating ache. Then, with a shock, Maddy realized she hadn't heard a single noise since waking up. She was deaf. It didn't take long for the fear to settle in as she realized exactly how in dire straits she was. Looking out from the rubble, she saw a golden retriever barking hysterically on the street, its mouth opening and closing as it yelped. But Maddy couldn't hear any of it. The dog wore a collar and was dragging around the shreds of a blue leash.

Maddy sat still and watched the dog, thinking about its owners. She wondered if the leash was frayed because the dog had gnawed through it to get free from wherever it was tied . . . or from whatever poor hand had been holding it. Funny, Maddy thought. The survival instinct is popping up in even the most domesticated of America's pets. Then, slowly, the slightest bit of hearing came back. Maddy felt a bit like she was underwater, trying to listen to someone talking on land. The dog was so close, but the barking sounded distant. Feebly, she snapped her fingers, straining to hear the tiniest of sounds. Little by little, the sounds around her grew louder, until she could hear jets flying far, far overhead. Then an explosion somewhere not too far away, confirming the battle was still raging.

And the dog kept barking and barking at Maddy. Then, suddenly, its hackles were raised and the fur stood up on the back of its neck. Maddy heard something behind her.

In horror, Maddy realized what the golden retriever truly was barking at. And it definitely wasn't her.

Craning her neck in pain, Maddy saw it: a hideous Dark Angel. Most likely the one who had attacked her. It had come to finish the job.

The demon was enormous, each of its arms as big as a Corvette, its spined wings spread ominously behind it. Twisted horns ran along its shoulders and arms, and all the way down its back. Its shape continued to shift, black flames coursing around its enormous limbs, its scales shimmering as it moved. The only things that remained constant were its terrible eyes. They glowed with hatred, as if they'd come straight from hell. And then . . . did it smile?

With a shot of blood-chilling terror, Maddy realized that this was the demon from her nightmares. This was the Dark Angel who, in her dreams, had transformed from a normal demon into something bigger and more powerful. Something indescribably worse.

It took a step towards her.

Panic coursed through Maddy's pain-wracked frame. She attempted to stand, but her body wouldn't listen to her. Stabbing pain stuck into her legs as she tried to lift herself up by pushing down with her palms, and she collapsed down on to the rubble once again. Her left wing was still in good shape, but her crushed right wing just flopped down.

Maddy could hear the demon's footsteps now, crunching as it walked along. And she could feel its oppressive heat. She knew she had to do something.

She raised herself up off the rubble as much as she could. Her head, her head . . . Everything hurt so badly.

Panting, Maddy reached out her arms and began miserably dragging herself forward, inches at a time.

Tears began to stream down her cheeks.

The dog, previously frozen to its spot in terror, finally snapped out of its barking frenzy and ran away, tail between its legs, not looking back.

Groaning, Maddy pulled herself another six inches with her arms. The footsteps grew louder, and the heat was getting stronger now. She didn't want to look back. She couldn't. She just needed to get to the edge of the pile. Just two more feet.

With all the effort she could muster, Maddy grabbed onto a broken two-by-four board protruding from the edge of the rubble pile. Using the board as leverage, she hurled herself over the edge, with no idea what was below. Dropping at least ten feet, she landed on a mound of drywall and broken roof tiles. She cried out in agony as her battered body crash-landed and the wind was knocked out of her. She began rolling down the slight slope of the pile before her body came to a stop against a half-smashed concrete pillar.

Every breath was painful. As she struggled to pull herself up, she heard it. A deep, raspy baritone.

Was the demon . . . laughing?

Maddy looked up and saw it just standing there, watching her.

Suddenly it jumped down from the top of the rubble and landed just below, sending a tremendous rumble through the pile. With slow, confident steps, it started walking towards Maddy again.

Frantic, Maddy used every bit of willpower she had to get up on her knees and scurry a few feet forward and around the concrete pillar, then tumble down the rest of the rubble pile to the street below. Her head smacked against the asphalt and her bad wing rolled painfully under her as she came to a stop.

But now, try as she might, she couldn't get up. She could feel the blood on her head, sticky and warm as it dripped down across her eyes. Somehow she hadn't really noticed it before.

The demon took its time coming down to the street, apparently relishing in this experience. Then, with a deafening roar, it pounced and landed right in front of Maddy, missing her by less than an inch.

Hyperventilating, Maddy used the last of her strength to reach behind her for her sword. Of course! But it wasn't there. Both the sling and the sword must have been ripped off her body when she fell.

Now Maddy truly began to lose hope. She pulled herself along her side on the asphalt, which was scattered everywhere with dangerous debris. She dragged herself through the harsh surface, her fingernails growing bloody as she desperately tried to escape. The demon's heat had become nearly unbearable, as searing and piping hot as steam.

Then Maddy saw it, gleaming like a beacon. Her Divine Sword.

It was only about fifteen feet away, resting on some crumbled concrete as if waiting for her. Her Divine Ring sparkled brilliantly. With hope once again rising in her chest, she feebly lunged for the sword, only getting herself a foot or two closer. The demon moved forward quickly, confidently. Almost gently, but certainly firm, it put its terrible clawed foot down on her arm. Just enough to hold her in place. Maddy's mouth curled open. At first no sound would emerge, but then a wild scream escaped her throat as the demon's heat blistered the skin on her arm.

Like a revelation before dying, Maddy realized why she had dreamt of this demon so often. She had been dreaming of her own death, the death she never could have predicted for herself. It seemed so obvious now as the darkness closed in.

In her final seconds, Maddy's mind once again looked back over everything that had happened since that fateful night at her uncle's diner. An Angel in suit pants and a hoodie walking into Kevin's and changing her life for ever. Jackson winning her over. Saving Jacks on the library tower. And then her choosing to become a Guardian instead of going to college. She thought of the attendant fame and fortune and glamorous events, of how she'd gotten caught up in it all. She thought of everything. The kaleidoscope of memories flitted before her eyes in splashes of brief, vivid moments.

Until, finally, her memory settled itself on one image: her parents.

She'd finally get to see them.

As her brain flickered towards unconsciousness, she could have sworn the demon was leaning down close to her, its terrible mouth full of blackened, twisted teeth, to whisper in her ear:

"Maddy . . ."

It knew her name. Just like it had in the dream.

The Dark Angel pulled its putrid maw away from her face and raised its thorny arm for the fatal blow. Maddy closed her eyes and waited for the inevitable. It was useless to try to fight back. The heat grew stronger and stronger. She tried to move her face away from the onslaught but could only turn one cheek. Her arm was already blistered and burning, and now steam began rising from her exposed skin. Maddy gasped in agony, her breathing labored and her lungs burning with pain.

Now her only solace was that death would come soon.

The darkness was just about closing in on her when suddenly Maddy was aware of a distant popping sound. Repetitive. She came to slightly. As her eyes fluttered open, she realized it was gunfire.

Pop-pop-pop-pop-pop.

The demon moved back one step and began swatting at itself, as if it were being bitten by flies, before turning around to face whoever was attacking it.

Pop-pop-pop-pop-pop.

The Dark Angel roared so loudly that Maddy was deafened for a moment once again.

"Hey! Hey! *Hey!*" a voice yelled to the demon. "Over here! Over here! Come on, you dumbass!"

Pop-pop-pop-pop-pop.

That voice . . . Maddy recognized it. . .

Tom.

Somehow he had found her.

She pulled herself up slightly and saw him standing there,

wearing his olive-green flight suit and a bandage on his head. He had an M-16 in one hand and a pistol in the other. They locked eyes instantly, and for a flash they shared a look of understanding. They both knew what he was about to do, and Maddy's heart crumpled just as soon as it had soared. She shook her head.

In response, Tom trained his M-16 on the demon and began firing again. Squealing, the demon began moving away from Maddy, towards its attacker down the dark street. Its unthinkable face twisted into a snarl, black teeth glinting in the red light of a burning pile of wreckage on the concrete below.

"That's it, you ugly SOB, follow me," Tom shouted as he ran backward down the street, trying to draw the demon farther away from Maddy. He knew he couldn't kill a demon. But he could distract it. Maybe long enough to save her. "Run, Maddy!" he yelled.

Maddy was frozen to the spot, watching him with terrified eyes. How could she just *leave*?

"Go, Maddy! *Go!*" Tom unleashed a round of ammunition into the demon again and continued running down the street.

It was as if Tom had somehow willed new energy into her body, and she was able to stand up on one leg, then the other. Tom was farther off now, too far for her to help in her injured state. She felt her crushed wing throbbing against her back, and it made her feel beyond helpless. She should be the one saving *him*. Her eyes welled up at the thought of the sacrifice he was making. She took a few hobbling steps away, then stopped and turned to look over her shoulder.

Tom was running as fast as he could, his guns held out and at the ready. He ran forward and fired backward, shooting wildly at the demon as he fled from it. But the Dark Angel was closing in, loping closer and closer with every thundering footstep.

"*Tom!*" she shouted.

"Don't stop!" he screamed.

At the intersection of the street, underneath a shredded stoplight, another demon materialized, blocking Tom's way. It was a regular Dark Angel and smaller than the other one, but at ten feet tall, this didn't reassure Maddy one bit. Tom turned and fired at the second demon. The beast shuddered under the assault, but the bullets only slowed it momentarily. Already recovered, it continued advancing on Tom, who now dropped the empty machine gun and began emptying the clip of his Glock nine-millimetre.

Then, out of nowhere, like a left hook to her jaw, Maddy watched from a distance as a claw plunged straight into Tom's back and emerged through his chest. The enormous Dark Angel from Maddy's nightmares had caught up to him. She stopped in her tracks and cried out as Tom dropped to his knees slowly. Blood dripped from his mouth as he looked down, strangely peaceful, at the claw that had impaled his body. Flames started to rise up around him, but it didn't look as if he could feel any pain. The second demon was circling the scene now, and Tom's gun fell to the ground with a clatter. The demons hissed with pleasure.

Coughing up sprays of blood, Tom reached into his side pocket and produced his knife. With a decisive motion, he plunged the glinting blade into the demon claw protruding from his chest. He twisted the knife with the last of his strength.

The demon howled and ripped his claw out of Tom's chest.

Tom smiled. He had saved Maddy. That was all that mattered to him.

The claw had been the only thing holding Tom up, and when it was gone, he took his final breath and tumbled over on to the pile of dusty rubble at his feet. He had done his duty.

Maddy witnessed it all from afar, rendered speechless with grief and shock.

"No!" she wailed, tears blurring her vision. The demons circled the pilot, the black flames off their bodies rippling in the distance. They still hadn't turned their attention back to Maddy.

Suddenly she remembered Tom's last words: *Don't stop.*

With every shred of strength she had, she fled from the grisly scene, looking for anywhere to hide. Her Divine Sword still lay near the rubble, unclaimed; she didn't have the strength to pick it up anyway. She just needed to *go*. Blood pumped frantically through her veins as she hobbled. Then she took a left down a service alley behind a row of stores. She looking back behind her, down the smoky passageway half-lit by the fires in Angel City reflecting off the clouds, and she saw no demons on her trail. She came upon an old metal door that looked like it might lead to some sort of storage room or basement. She tried the metal handle. Locked.

Hrnnnh. She lowered her shoulder and tried to smash against it, but the only effect it had was a little bounce. Pain shot through her body. *Hrnnnh.* Crying out in pain and grief, she tried again. *Hrnnnh.* Nothing.

One more time with everything she had. She squared herself and set her jaw, and went for it with all her might. The door burst open and she tumbled into the pitch-dark room, which looked to Maddy like a janitorial closet. Panting, she frantically pushed the door closed and somehow managed to get it to stay shut. It wouldn't keep the demons out, but at least they wouldn't be able to see her from outside.

It was pitch-black inside the small room, but she could sense she was alone. Maddy slumped down against the wall next to a mop and bucket. She tried to retract her injured wing, but she didn't have the energy. She was beyond exhausted, spent. She decided to let her grief run out of her with big, gasping sobs. Tom was dead. He had saved her. And now he was dead.

The tears wouldn't stop flowing.

Tom is dead. Tom is dead. Tom is dead.

And then the darkness came again.

CHAPTER 30

A rocket screamed down and exploded in the street two blocks away, rattling the rooftop Jackson walked on. He didn't even flinch as he scanned the sky for Battle Angel reinforcements. He didn't know how many hours of pitched battle in the skies and streets of Angel City had passed. With the demon invasion came darkness that had shrouded the sun and turned the day into a permanent twilight. Had it already been a full day? Time seemed to stretch and compress before Jacks in the fog and exhaustion of this war that none of his studies could have ever prepared him for.

Mitch was there by his side, assessing the situation. Both Angels looked battle-worn, their armour tarnished, marred by more than a few stains of demon blood.

"They're coming so fast, faster than we can kill them," Mitch said. "How can we hold them? They're wearing us down."

"I don't know," Jacks said. "But we have to. We have to get to the leader, Mitch. It's our only hope."

"Well let's hope the detective gives us something soon," Mitch said. "We can't hold them for ever."

Jackson looked up and saw a small group of Battle Angels returning from the west. Archangel Godspeed was leading them. Their eyes were dead-set and determined.

"Mark!" Jacks shouted, glad to see his stepfather all right.

Suddenly, off to Mark's left, they saw a line of Dark Angels flying just above the horizon, trying to speed around the Angel defences. Jackson pumped his wings – once, twice – but Mitch put his hand on his shoulder.

"Mark and I got this," he said. "Right, Mark?" he shouted up to the Archangel, who was flying just above. He nodded at Mitch.

"You, you, and you – follow me!" Mark yelled over the din of the battle to a cluster of Angels flying past. Mitch smiled at Jacks as he launched off the roof to join Mark in their pursuit of the demons. Jackson watched them disappear into the dark sky, his heart tugging as the image of Mark and his best friend faded from his sight into the storm of the demon assault.

"Jacks! Jacks!" a voice screamed suddenly. Jacks felt the whoosh of an Angel rushing up past his battle aides. "I found you!" He was a Guardian whom Jackson had met only a handful of times. Jackson thought his name was Trevor. "I finally found you."

Demons clotted in the streets below, advancing faster and faster.

"What is it?" Jacks said a bit impatiently.

"Louis Kreuz—"

The name grabbed Jackson's attention. "Did he make it out?"

"The ADC agents took him, Jacks. He escaped today . . . but not before they took his wings. He was injured pretty badly. . . It was worse than just his wings." Trevor's brow darkened. "He had a message for you. He wanted me to give it to you personally."

"A message?" Jacks's pulse quickened.

"Well, I really don't understand it," the Guardian said. "It doesn't make any sense."

"What is it? What's the message?" Jacks asked. He had to stop himself from grabbing the Angel by his collar.

"It's only one word," Trevor said. "Well, a name, actually."

Jacks stared at the messenger, the anticipation nearly killing him. He knew Kreuz's message could mean the difference between victory and complete, utter defeat.

"The message is: *Gabriel*," Trevor said.

The name was like a bolt of lightning searing into Jackson's body and soul.

Suddenly it all made sense.

"Jacks, are you all right?" Trevor asked, surely a little disturbed at the effect his message had had on the Angels' battle leader.

"Yeah. Yes, I'm fine, I'm fine. . . Thank you for bringing me this message," Jackson said, trying to recover so the Guardian would leave him alone. "Just, please, keep it to yourself." Trevor nodded and backed off, much to Jacks's relief.

Jacks looked up to the Angel City Hills, his mind's eye burrowing into the evil truth that was deep beneath them.

Of course. Of course. *Of course*.

It was Gabriel. Gabriel was controlling them.

He was the head demon.

CHAPTER 31

This time when Maddy opened her eyes, there was no reprieve from the darkness. She felt woozy, but with some effort, she recalled that she had escaped to the service room off the street she'd run down. Then, in another instant, she recalled the fatal, terrible fact that pounded in her brain with every beat of her heart: Tom had died saving her. Misery welled within her, but she tried to quell it as much as she could. Though she would never get the chance to sacrifice herself to save Tom, which she would have done in a heartbeat, there still was someone she could help. It might not be too late. Maddy could still hear the muffled sound of explosions outside, confirming that the battle for Angel City had continued to rage for however long she'd been passed out.

Moving blindly still, Maddy pulled herself to the wall and sat up straight, banging her burned arm into a mop and bucket that went clattering across the smooth concrete floor. The pain in her right wing was excruciating, unreal, and Maddy nearly swooned under the pressure. Taking sharp breaths between her teeth, she forced herself to focus on staying conscious.

Before she went outside, she knew she needed to retract the injured wing, which hung limp and useless, flopping around and causing agony with every move. Maddy sat down and braced herself by leaning forward.

She focused as hard as she could, pushing through the unbelievable pain to try to get her wings to retract. But only the left one did, while the right wing just hung there lamely, emanating none of the luminescence it once had. Maddy cried in pain. "Come on, come on . . ." she whispered through gritted teeth and tears.

She gave it one more shot. . .

"Gaaaaaaaaaaaaaaah!" she screamed, surely loud enough for any human, Angel, or demon outside to hear. But perhaps it helped, because the wing, making a strange, belabored sound, was finally able to retract. Maddy crumpled to the ground and lay there until her breathing calmed down. Then she sat up once again, this time resolute and feeling renewed.

After waiting what seemed like an eternity for the slightest sound or evidence of danger, Maddy slowly pulled the creaky door open. She saw no one. A thick smoke had settled across the city, filling the street, giving it an ominous air. She looked back and forth past the other buildings, but there was no sign of any Dark Angels. Or anyone else, for that matter.

The sky was still dark, but that didn't tell her anything: whenever the demons attacked, the sun disappeared beneath a shroud of black clouds laced with vermillion highlights. Day and night passed identically underneath this darkness.

She could hear the roar of jet sorties flying above and explosions not too far off. The sounds of the military gave her fresh agony, as the thought of Tom's death entered her mind.

Looking down, Maddy assessed the damage to her arm from the demon's white-hot touch. And it was bad. Her jacket had caught fire during the struggle and the lining had been burned through underneath, exposing a layer of red, blistered skin. Maddy had to look away from the grotesque sight of her own injury. She wasn't sure what degree burn it was, but she knew it wasn't good.

Maddy started down the street as well as she could in her state. She passed the place where Tom had given his life, happy to move away from where the demons had been. But then something – some unavoidable, potentially suicidal impulse – told her to go back. Back to where it had happened. She needed her sword. But . . . why? Why was her body telling her this? It's not as if she was in any condition to fight a demon. If she had to face another Dark Angel, she would surely be killed, sword or not. Nevertheless, deep inside, she felt she needed it still.

With incredible caution, she entered a neighbouring building that had been abandoned and crept quietly to the third floor to look out one of the broken windows at the scene below.

Everything seemed quiet. A few tendrils of smoke from flaming wreckage drifted diagonally as the wind puffed. The demons had left, apparently. Down on the street, she saw her Divine Sword, its hilt almost seeming to grow in luster as she looked at it. Suddenly her face was slightly lit by a dim glow from her Divine Ring. Maddy scanned the scene until she was sure she would be safe.

And then, down the street, she spotted it: a dark shape sprawled on the ground near the intersection.

Tom's body.

Maddy's blood went cold as she looked at the unmoving figure stretched out on the lonely asphalt. She girded her spirit and forced herself to go on.

She made her way down the stairs to the abandoned street filled with detritus from the battle. She approached her sword, then kept on walking. She'd get it after.

Maddy approached Tom slowly. Behind his body, in the middle of the intersection, the stoplight still dangled there, one side of the cable snapped off from the pole across the street. Its bottom-right corner scraped back and forth on the asphalt as the wind blew it to and fro.

A putrid, sulphurous smell inundated the area, reeking of demons, but at least the heat and humidity of their dark presence had dissipated. A jolt of pain flashed through Maddy's burned arm.

Maddy studied Tom before approaching. He looked peaceful. Above the shoulders he looked more or less like himself, save for the stream of blood that had run down the side of his mouth. But starting from his chest down to his belly button, it was all gore. Maddy thought she could feel her heart literally breaking as she looked down at the pilot who had saved her life. Stepping forward, she took off the remnants of her navy jacket and covered the fatal wound.

"Tom, I'm so sorry. So, so sorry," she whispered, wiping her tears with her good arm. Putting her hand underneath Tom's still-bandaged head and her fingers in his hair, she leaned down. She pressed her weeping face to the small indentation in between his Adam's apple and his clavicle, just above where the demon had done his damage. But Tom did not respond, of course. She could feel that his skin had already started going cold to the touch.

Maddy tried to pull herself together. What could she do to make this even a little bit right? She could at least give his body shelter. She lifted her head and wiped the blurring tears away. Then, as gently as she could, she wedged herself under Tom's right armpit and began pulling him out of the street, inch by inch, the heels of his boots dragging and scuffing the pavement along the way. It took everything she had just to move him a few inches at a time. But soon, panting, she had him near the half-shattered remains of a door to a house that was still standing on the corner.

With great effort she pulled him over the threshold and into what looked like some kind of office foyer. She laid him straight out on his back and placed his arms flat against his sides so he looked comfortable. Maddy then shifted her jacket up so the garment covered not only his wound, but his face, as well. She whispered a small prayer. Taking a few steps back she looked at his body, which finally looked serene.

"I'm sorry, Tom," Maddy said over the body. "This is the best I could do. I would stay here longer, all day and all night if I could. But there's something I have to do still."

With a solemn and heavy heart, Maddy gave Tom one last, final look, and turned to walk back to the fated spot.

Her sword was still waiting for her on the deserted street. Reaching down for the weapon, Maddy found the hair on the back of her neck turned stiff as steel wires.

Something was behind her. She froze. She took one breath, then another.

In a smooth motion, Maddy attempted to reach down, unhook the leather latch, pull the sword out of the sheath, and spin around on whatever demon was approaching. A shout escaped her lips. The sword flailed as she spun, grunting, as she lost her strength to bring the weapon around effectively.

She braced herself to face her fate, but instead of a Dark Angel, she saw the dog that had been there barking at the demon earlier. It cowered as it saw Maddy raising the sword, and Maddy was filled with guilt for scaring the poor, terrorized animal. She lowered the sword and put her hand out.

"It's OK, girl," she said. "No demons here."

Reaching into her pocket, Maddy found a packet of facial tissues and a granola bar. She opened the package and split the bar with the dog, who ate it gratefully, then came up to Maddy and sat next to her. Maddy sat down and petted her while she ate her half of the bar.

Suddenly, a fighter jet screamed overhead, skimming the rooftops. It was so loud Maddy was deafened for a moment. The dog fled into a nearby building. The roar of the engine rattled whatever windows were left on the street. Then Maddy saw what the jet was pursuing: a demon, maybe ten blocks away, that had emerged above the rooftops. Though the demon was somewhat far off, Maddy still ducked for cover behind an intact SUV. Also in the distance, Maddy saw the glow of another flying figure – probably a Guardian and her Divine Sword. It was trailing the Dark Angel, which seemed to be getting farther away. Meanwhile, the jet banked left and launched two missiles above the buildings, which exploded in a tremendous fireball against the demon. The demon tumbled, temporarily stunned but not killed by the explosion. It bought enough time, however; just seconds later, Maddy saw the Angel move in. A flash spilled across the horizon as the demon was killed. Maddy watched helplessly as the Angel and jet both flew off in the opposite direction. She wished she had some way to signal them. But, after a second thought, she realized that this was best as a solo mission.

Suicide missions always are.

Maddy kept up her furtive pace down the Angel City street until she found what she was looking for. A pharmacy. The front of the store advertised a special on diabetes kits and a "Special Saturday Coupon Saver" on bottled water. She walked up to the front door and drew her weapon from behind her back. Covering her face and turning away, Maddy rammed the butt of the Divine Sword against the plate-glass window. The pane shattered into thousands of glittering fragments that tinkled to the ground. A backup alarm, probably running on emergency battery life, started weakly ringing and flashing green inside the store. Maddy used the sword to clear away the jagged pieces still sticking out from the metal doorframe and walked into the pharmacy through the makeshift entrance.

She walked down the aisles of the darkened, abandoned store, looking for bandages. She found them in what she assumed was the first aid aisle, then scanned the shelves opposite it until she found some medicated burn cream. With a sigh of relief, she then found that the door to the prescription-filling area had been left open. In the pharmacist's area, a stale doughnut and a half-full cup of coffee with red lipstick on the paper rim sat on the counter next to a workstation. A skim of mould floated on the top of the coffee, which had been sitting there for who knows how long. Maddy scanned the shelves of innumerable drugs. Azithromycin, Prevacid, Fluoxetine. How would she be able to figure out which one was the right painkiller or even what dosage to take? Sighing, she walked back out to the main store area, empty-handed. Back in the over-the-counter section, she found a bottle of ibuprofen and swallowed a few of the brown, sugar-coated caplets. It'd have to do. She couldn't afford to be groggy or take something totally wrong on a blind assumption.

Maddy found the bathroom. It was dark inside, but a green glimmer from the backup alarm lit her face up in the mirror in blinks of light and dark. Back and forth. The green light made everything seem even more ghoulish than it already was.

Turning on the tap and squeezing out some soap, she washed the hand on her good arm. She was trying to recall all the instructions she'd learned during first aid training in her high school health class. What had they said about treating burns? She couldn't remember clearly. But she was pretty sure that, no matter what they'd taught her, they hadn't prepared her for a burn *this* big.

Gritting her teeth in anticipation of pain, Maddy turned to her burned arm, which she had pretty much avoided even looking at since she woke up in the dark room. It was black and raw. Delicately, Maddy reached with her fingers to pull out a piece of her burned shirt, which had melted into her skin.

The instant her finger tugged on the charred, loose scrap of cloth, Maddy screamed in pain and buckled forward. She almost collapsed on to the white tile floor; only a last-minute grab of the sink had held her up. Tears of pain dampened her cheeks. *Well, that's not going to work*, she thought. She'd have to make do. If by some miracle she survived and was able to see a doctor, they'd just have to deal with pesky details like clothing melted into skin later.

Maddy washed her good hand again, then put the tube of burn cream between her teeth to keep it steady while she unscrewed the lid. She squeezed the tube, and some of the goop came out. Taking in a deep breath and holding it, she slowly and carefully began to apply the medicated cream along the burn area. Beads of sweat formed on her forehead, her clamminess made even more ghastly by the flashing green light. At last she finished and let out a huge breath, sobbing. *OK. One last thing*. Using her teeth, she ripped open the package of large bandages. She delicately layered them over the burn area, careful not to leave any part uncovered. It was excruciating. But after she finished, as painful as the process might have been, at least the arm started to feel slightly better. At the very least it was covered. She pocketed the rest of the bottle of ibuprofen and left the store the same way she came in. Her feet crunched down on broken glass as she stepped out. She could hear the alarm still sounding as she made her way down the road, which was lined with burned parked cars. No matter; no one would be coming to see about the alarm for a long time.

Maddy walked for a long while, keeping the main action of the battle to her side. At last, she looked ahead and saw that she was just near the foot of the Angel City Hills. A pang of worry struck her as she realized that, not so far off to the east, was Uncle Kevin in the emergency shelter. The battle lines were pushing just up to that neighbourhood, and all she could do was hope that there was some way to stop the demons before they broke down the shelter walls.

Maddy looked to the Hills. Her gaze moved higher and higher, up into the dark trees, which reflected the glare of flames across Angel City. Somewhere up there was the entry. It was drawing her. She had no doubt she'd find it. She just hoped she didn't have to knock.

She began to climb.

CHAPTER 32

The elevator door opened to reveal an abandoned sanctuary. Slowly walking forward, Jacks found himself alone in the main passage. Nobody was home.

Down at the end of the hallway, someone – or something – scurried across an intersecting hallway, then disappeared.

The lights were dimmed, running on emergency power, lending the deserted sanctuary an even stranger feeling as Jacks explored the marble passages. Of all the places he imagined he would end up on the day of the ultimate battle for Angel City, this was not one of them.

Soon Jacks reached the main hub, where abandoned shops and restaurants stood as if keeping watch over the centre fountain.

It looked as if some kind of struggle had taken place here. A café table next to the fountain had been overturned; empty plastic cups littered the area, their iced skinny mochas spilled on to the normally well-polished floor. Several of the darkened stores had suffered broken windows.

Jacks moved slowly, carefully, through the familiar passages, seeing no one. His solitary footsteps echoed down the tunnels.

He was about to pass Emily's rooms. He became quieter and quieter as he approached, until he heard a strange sound coming from her quarters. With hushed breath, he stepped closer and closer, until he finally reached the threshold.

False alarm. The door was wide open, and the TV had been left on to blare its buzzing static throughout the halls. Strangely, though, a Louis Vuitton suitcase with designer clothes poking out of the top sat on the couch just next to the TV. Emily must have left in a hurry. But why?

Then something caught Jacks's eye, and he looked down to the floor. There were a few drops of blood.

What had happened here?

The Battle Angel made his way closer and closer to the outer ring of the sanctuary. The lights became fewer, and an ominous air grew as he approached the passages to the Council chambers. He had no idea what to expect, or whether he could even get in, but he was sure it would not be simple.

A distinct uneasiness hung thick in the corridors as lights flickered in and out. The place was entirely deserted. And it felt as if the source of unrest was coming from within the sanctuary, and not from the demon assault without.

Suddenly, Jackson was without a doubt that Gabriel knew he was coming.

He was nearing the solarium, where he'd spent so much time with Gabriel. Listening to him talk. Believing his words. Trusting in his justifications.

Jacks could see now what Gabriel had wanted from him. He needed a powerful and loyal Angel to stay by his side when the inevitable conflicts arose in the Angel community. The Council was unimpeachable, but after the humans were defeated, Jacks was certain that being in league with the demons would not sit well with all the Angels. There would have been problems.

Gabriel could have used someone like Jacks to "smooth over" those problems. And the True Immortal had wanted him to start by getting rid of Kreuz and Sylvester. Kreuz had not only known too much, but he'd also been sharing it with those opposed to Gabriel and the Council. He had needed to be dealt with before it was too late.

But luckily, fate had intervened. Gabriel had overestimated his ability to influence Jackson. He hadn't counted on the powerful influence Maddy's absence had proved to be for Jackson.

Jackson's mind raced with these thoughts as he walked along the entry to the indoor garden. The large glass door was ajar, although the inside lay dark and slumbering. Jackson took a few steps forward.

"Don't come any closer," a stern voice said.

A gun barrel sparkled in the darkness. Jacks froze.

Then he saw the silver frames of a pair of familiar glasses reflecting the little light that was coming from down the hall.

"Detective Sylvester?"

"Jackson?"

The detective stepped into the light, letting out a large breath. "What are you doing here?"

"I could ask you the same question," Jackson said.

"I'm sorry, I thought I had the place to myself. You gave me a little scare," Sylvester admitted.

"Wait. What were you hoping to do by coming here?" Jacks

looked dubiously at the service revolver, now back in its holster, that the detective had just pulled on him.

"To be honest, I hadn't really thought that far. I was going to think of something. I couldn't get in touch with any of the others. Radios, cell phones, landlines – everything is down. It's chaos out there," Sylvester said. "I wasn't about to bring Susan along with me. I told her I knew how to get you here. If I'd told the truth, she would have never let me come alone."

"Turns out it was closer to the truth than you'd thought. I'm here now," Jacks said. "Louis was able to get me a message. *Gabriel*. That was it. But it was enough. Louis is no fool. But how did he figure it out?"

"Apparently Cassius Holywaine flipped at the last minute. Engineered Louis's escape."

"Cassius from the Council of Twelve?" Jacks asked.

"He had an attack of conscience," Sylvester said. "He told Louis that Gabriel was behind all of this and broke Louis out. Louis made it. Cassius wasn't so lucky." The detective shook his head. "It was so obvious and I was blind to it," Sylvester said. "Hiding in plain sight. Whatever pieties Gabriel may show in public, he's never been a friend to humanity. Rather than work for them, why not just create a world without humans and take everything for himself?"

"Yeah, without humans, but *with* demons," Jacks said. "What I don't understand is, why the Dark Ones? What did Gabriel think was going to happen after the demons destroyed everything and made Earth their home?"

"Demons were once Angels – remember that," Sylvester said. "Fallen Angels."

"But they chose the dark path themselves," Jackson said.

"Yes, and that's the same path Gabriel is choosing for all the Angels," Sylvester said. "Gabriel doesn't see much difference between Angels and Demons, since both are no longer connected to Home. He sees the difference only as a matter of degree. Gabriel knows that Angels and Demons were becoming more alike than anyone would want to admit. Just look at what Protection for Pay has done to the Guardians."

"And if he can control the demons now, he'll be able to control them afterward," Jacks said grimly. "He'll have a Dark Army to ensure that no one else can challenge him on Earth – for ever."

"It's not too late, though, Jacks. You're here now," Sylvester said. A distant rumble from outside sounded through the tunnel. "What's going out there?"

"It's not good," Jackson said. "Even with the full Angel battalion . . . the demons just don't stop."

"Your stepfather . . . ?" Sylvester tentatively asked. He knew not all the Angels had turned against the Council.

"Mark's out there right now," Jacks said. "Fighting."

Sylvester and Jackson had reached a far corner of the sanctuary when all of a sudden a voice spoke up.

"Stop right there, Jackson." It was an ADC agent. He held a Divine Sword in his hand and stood in front of a solid, closed doorway. He looked formidable on the outside, but instantly Jacks could tell he was terrified. Sylvester drew his revolver, but Jacks waved him off.

Jacks put his hands up to show he meant no harm. "Hey. I'm not here to hurt you. You know that what's going on is wrong. You need to step aside and let justice take place."

The guard lifted his sword, but it wavered in his uncertain grasp. "I don't know what you're talking about," the Angel guard said from behind his black armour, his voice quavering.

"There's still time to join the others," Jacks said. "Gabriel weaves a spell with his words. I probably know that better than any of us. But I found out the truth. You don't have to let him rule your destiny."

"You won't be able to beat him," the agent said, beads of sweat breaking out on his forehead. Jacks suddenly realized something was wrong. Very wrong. Something worse than what he was already anticipating.

A foul odour drifted in from the other side of the door.

"What's in there?" Jacks asked.

"I d-don't know," the guard stammered. "And I'm not going to find out. He only told me that if I failed, there will still be another."

"Another?" Sylvester said.

The guard motioned behind the door, practically shivering at this point.

"It's not too late," Jackson said. "You can join the others. Just lower your sword and let us pass. We won't hurt you."

"How do I know I can trust you?" the guard said, his eyes nervously darting between Jacks and the detective.

"You just have to," Jackson said. "Let us through, or we'll go through you. Your choice."

The guard mulled his options one more time, sweat glistening on his face beneath the black armour.

"Last chance," Jackson said. The Guardian began reaching for his Divine Sword, which lay slung across his back.

At last, the guard slowly leaned over and lowered his weapon. He then began fleeing away from the door, past Sylvester and Jacks, and down the passageway.

Whatever was behind the door must have been what cleared everyone else out of the sanctuary.

The guard's retreating footsteps echoed away. It was deathly quiet now. So quiet that Sylvester and Jackson could hear each other's heartbeats. They held their breath and listened at the door for any telltale sign. But they could hear nothing. Still, they knew there was something beyond the door in the passage leading to the great atrium.

The door itself was sweating condensation because of a great heat on the other side. Jackson moved his hand just six inches away from the door, and he could feel the heat radiating off the mahogany wood. He slowly reached down – the brass handle was scalding hot.

Sylvester rummaged in one of his overcoat pockets and produced an old handkerchief.

There was no other way in. Whatever lay beyond these doors would have to be faced.

One of Sylvester's hands started shaking uncontrollably. His vision started to narrow with blackness as the anxiety came on. The great shame of his nerves. He was not afraid for himself; he was afraid of failing others. Of failing so many others at this point. Millions. *It would be a greater failure than he could ever imagine*. He had to face it; he had to fight it. He looked the fear in the face. . .

"Are you all right?" Jacks said.

"Yes," Sylvester said, taking a deep breath in. The anxious blackness around his vision started to flicker away. It was time.

Jacks nodded at him. Sylvester opened the door silently, an inch at a time. The heat grew more intense as the door opened wider, and the darkness remained just as deep.

Jackson stepped across the threshold.

An enormous shadow moved in the dark, then shot up right towards him. It was as if Jacks had been struck by a locomotive. The demon had smashed into him before he'd even seen it. Jackson crashed against the door, splintering the formidable wood.

"Jackson!" Sylvester pushed through the door. And stopped dead in his tracks. Next to him, Jacks was attempting to clamber to his feet, the wind knocked out of him from the surprise blow. They were both frozen in wonder and disgust at the monstrous demon in front of them.

It was the largest demon they had ever seen, bigger than they could have ever imagined. It was at least twenty feet high, and almost as wide across, its hulking mass curled over so it wouldn't break through the ceiling. There was absolutely no way of getting around it. It stretched out its scaly wings and beat them against the walls. A dark flame burned at the very centre of its mass, fueling the engine of evil. The worst were its heads: Jackson and Sylvester could not even count all of them, but it seemed as if there might be eight of them. Spewing out of the main, horn-lined body, each head was even more terrible than the next.

The acrid smell of demon smoke was choking the hallway, and the heat was almost unbearable.

The *thing* then roared, each head's throat screaming at once to create a symphony of evil.

Jackson did not wait long. Springing forward, he swung his Divine Sword overhead, and separated one of the heads from its neck. The slithering stump of a neck spewed thick black blood as the head rolled to a corner. The demon squealed and brought everything it had at Jackson, snapping at his legs, arms, and chest with its many heads.

Swinging the blade back and forth, Jacks did his best to block the attacks, but there were so many at once. Black teeth bit at him, ripping into his body armour. A little while longer and they would tear through.

Mustering all his strength, Jackson jumped up. His wings burst forth, and he managed to spear one of the demon's heads right in the mouth as it tried to follow him. He could feel its final screams travel down the blade before he pulled it out. And yet, still, the demon was not slowing down in the least. The thing was actually becoming more vicious.

"The main one, Jacks!" Sylvester yelled, pointing to the largest of the heads, which had a particularly menacing set of black-red eyes and a cavernous mouth like the jaws of hell themselves. "It's the only way."

Jackson nodded, fiercely trying to slice his way in. But the demon was not dumb. It knew how to guard itself. Jack was still far from being able to strike when three of the heads went for his legs at once. Grunting, Jackson was knocked down to his knees, and another head slammed him down on to his chest from behind. The remaining heads were poised to make the fatal blow, saliva dripping from their terrible maws.

BANG. BANG. BANG. BANG. BANG. BANG.

Smoke wisped out of the barrel of Sylvester's revolver. He had emptied all the rounds of ammunition, aiming right at the eyes of the demon's main head.

The demon squealed, thrashing, as its heads coiled back in to tend to the injury. Still, the bullets would feel like a fleck of dust stuck in its eye – irritating but nowhere near fatal. But it could be enough to slow it down.

"Now, Jacks!" Sylvester shouted, struggling to reload his gun. The demon lunged towards Sylvester with one of its heads. The detective put up his arm to protect himself, and it was bent back at an unholy angle as he was smashed down to the floor, and then against the wall. Sylvester slumped to the ground, not moving.

"No!"

Jackson had been able to get to his feet. He would only have a moment. The demon was still partially blinded and distracted by Sylvester's gunshots. But the other heads were still going to keep Jackson at arm's length.

Jacks reached back and launched the Divine Sword like a javelin harder than he had ever thrown anything in his life.

His aim was true. And perhaps something forged in the weapon itself kept its course straight. The sword struck the demon's left eye, plunging in all the way to its hilt. Fountains of black blood came pouring out as the demon shrieked and dropped to its knees. Suddenly, the entire tunnel was filled with the brightest light. Every single speck of dust – and every centimetre of the demon – was now clearly visible in the light. The blinding illumination flashed off the blade of the Divine Sword and then was gone.

Gasping, Jacks dropped down to his knee, catching his breath. The demon's final death quivers filled the tunnel with rumbling. But Jackson knew it was dead. The sword had told him that.

After a few moments, Jackson was able to stand up. He moved quickly over to where Sylvester lay, crumpled against the wall. He feared the worst.

But Jacks was relieved to find that, though he was unconscious, Sylvester was still breathing.

"Detective Sylvester!" Jacks said. He lightly slapped him on the cheek, to no effect. Jacks picked up the revolver off the floor and put it in the detective's overcoat. He then pulled him up to sitting. It'd have to do for now.

Jacks approached the steaming demon carcass. Its bulk almost filled the whole hallway. Carefully, he began climbing the heap. Its scaly skin was now hardening, although it was still scalding hot. The soles of Jackson's boots steamed as he walked on the skin.

The demon's lifeless main head was facing him, its eye sockets totally empty.

"You have something of mine."

With a satisfying tug, he pulled the Divine Sword out of the demon's skull and wiped it clean against the hardening scales of its wings. Taking one last look at the unconscious Sylvester, he climbed down on the other side of the deceased Dark Angel and looked forward, down the dim passageway.

At the end of it was the main hall, where he had spent much time with Gabriel. The inconstant light from torches or candles was burning there in the distance, pointing the way towards the chambers – where Gabriel would likely be waiting.

Jackson walked down the dark hallway towards the atrium, more determined than ever. He ran his forearm across his face to wipe away the sweat that had accumulated during his struggle with the demon. He couldn't be sure he was ready for Gabriel, especially after all he'd been through. But he might never be ready, so now was as good a time as any.

Two torches burned along the wall. From far above, at the tallest point of the arched main hall, a ghostly red glow shone through the skylights. Angel City was burning. The dim red light illuminated the sandstone frieze that had been recovered from an ancient Angel ziggurat, which told the story of the Angels defeating the Dark Angels during the great Demon Struggles of long, long ago. Jackson wondered how many thousands of years had passed since then. And now they were back here again.

To the right of the atrium lay the Council chambers, its doors wide open. Here was the huge, chapel-like space where Gabriel had made all the decisions with the Council. It was the place where he had decided to doom Angel City.

Jackson saw flames flickering from within. With slow, precise footsteps, he approached the open door. The torchlight cast his long shadow across the chamber's threshold.

Although Jackson couldn't see anyone yet, the voice he heard was unmistakable.

"I've been waiting for you, Jackson," Gabriel said. "By all means, please come in."

CHAPTER 33

Holding his Divine Sword up at the ready, Jackson took a cautious step inside. It was deathly quiet; the only things he could hear were the muffled sounds of battle clamouring in from outside. Each step he took echoed in the large open chamber.

Lit candles flickered along each side of the row of Grecian columns topped by Corinthian capitals. A slight draught made the flames waver, casting orange-tinted shadows that danced along the arched ceiling.

Gabriel sat, alone, at the head of the large Council table.

"I must admit, some part of me is quite happy to see you, Jackson. I'm impressed you made it this far. We trained you well."

Of all the Council members, only Gabriel remained. An ageless king upon an ageless throne.

His shock of white hair glinted more brightly as ever. Shadows danced in and out of his face.

Jackson carefully continued walking in, making sure to keep the Divine Sword between him and the True Immortal. Gabriel seemed quite untroubled.

"I'm afraid that whatever victory you have had here will be a short-lived one, Jackson," said Gabriel. "And only what some might call a moral one. The demons will not fall today. I've made sure of it."

"How could you?" Jacks asked. He looked at the ancient True Immortal before him, the Angel who had been symbol of all that was righteous and pure since his childhood.

Gabriel just shook his head. "After all we've been through, all our talks, I thought we had an understanding. That you had moved beyond weak, immature sentimentality to a bigger, more important revelation. I thought you understood what is necessary for the Angels to thrive. I overestimated your capacity for understanding such complex, eternal matters. My heart grows heavy thinking of how you betrayed me. Betrayed us. Betrayed the Angels."

Jackson was incredulous. "You're the one who has betrayed."

"Jackson. You didn't really think we'd let *humans*, the weakest creatures of all, run this planet, did you?" Gabriel said. "All Immortals are of the same family, Jackson. Whether of the light or of the darkness. And now is our moment to stand together and take hold of our common destiny. For too long we perfect Immortals have dealt with humanity's defects and weaknesses. No longer. Today, we take our birthright. I'm just disappointed you won't be joining us, Jackson. I really had high hopes for you. I see now that my judgement was wrong."

Gabriel's face showed genuine regret. He was thoroughly convinced of the rightness of his actions.

"But my biggest regret is allowing you to grow as strong as you did," Gabriel went on. "I should never have let you become influential enough to draw the other Immortals to you. The law of the Angels will land harshly upon all those you persuaded to leave."

"Everyone has joined," Jacks said.

"Yes, well. The punishment will surely take a long time," said Gabriel. "But eventually, they will be let back in. And they *will* come back, don't you worry. Once they see how miserably you've failed. How you've led them astray trying to deprive them of their destinies. They will come to curse the Godspeed name.

"I'm sure it's difficult for you to understand how much damage you've done in so short a time. But I'd like you to at least try," Gabriel said. "It will take us very long to fix the wreckage that you've caused. We'll have to rebuild our loyalties, bring everyone back into the fold. It will likely take years, even decades. But fix it we will. Trust me, Jackson. With humanity no longer bothering us, we will have all the time in the world. Angels will become utterly ascendant, the way it always should have been."

"Do you really think the demons will just stop once they're done with the humans?" Jacks said. "You think you can trust a Dark Angel? They'll turn to the Angels next."

Gabriel smirked. "I've known them a long time, Jackson. I know their secrets. All of them. I know how to deal with them. They wouldn't dare cross me." He paused. "They . . . fear me.

"The lower orders of the Earth will be fully given over to the Dark Angels. Humans are their natural playthings," Gabriel said. "And we Angels will take our rightful place as the fully acknowledged pre-eminent beings in the world. We'll no longer have to worry about petty mortal annoyances. We'll be able to fix our thoughts always on the perfect, Angelic nature from which we come."

Jacks stepped forward, his Divine Sword leading the way. "Call them off. The demons. It's over. The Angels aren't following you any more. You're alone in this."

Gabriel laughed at this. "They'll do as they're told once this is all over. Just like they always have. But you're too young to know that," Gabriel said.

Suddenly Gabriel stood up. He almost seemed larger than life. "Believe me when I say this, Jackson. It gives me no joy to think that I will have had to kill two members of the Godspeed line."

"*What?*" Jacks said. What did he mean, *two*? He didn't fully understand, but blood began rushing into his head and limbs, as if his body knew what was happening before his mind could make sense of it.

"Your father, Jacks," Gabriel said. "We could not allow him to live."

"But his killers were brought to trial. . ." Adrenaline and shock shook Jackson to the very core. His knees wavered and nearly buckled as the weight of revelation was forced upon him.

"I *am* the Angels, Jackson. Nothing happens without my knowledge." Gabriel's expression was grave, but then it twisted into an almost sadistic grimace. "And I did that particular job myself."

Gabriel killed my father. Jackson had sat for how many hours with Gabriel, a sworn True Immortal, founder of the Council of Twelve. He'd been the embodiment of everything a leader should be, the very Angel who had brought the others out of hiding and into the open. Gabriel had even told him how exemplary a Guardian Jackson's father had been. And all that time, he'd just been pouring words into Jackson's ears, completely unfazed by the fact that he'd murdered the father of the Angel sitting next to him. How many times had Gabriel put a comforting, fatherly hand on Jackson's shoulder? If only Jackson had known it had been the hand of death.

Jackson lifted his head and looked at the killer in front of him. His lip curled in rage.

The True Immortal examined Jacks coldly. "It's no use, Jackson. I made you. And now I will break you."

Through clenched teeth, Jacks drew in a deep breath and then let out a terrible cry as he rushed towards Gabriel.

Gabriel simply kept on smiling. Then, suddenly, his wings burst through his golden robes and he flew up from the floor. Jacks met him in mid-air, and they collided with a tremendous crash that shook the columns.

They flew around the marble columns, causing them to smash back and forth into one another. Broken stone and chunks of marble crumbled to the floor with each of their collisions. Bits of debris slowed, froze, and then sped up again as they fell to the ground – the two Angels were using and blocking each other's time freezes to get an advantage over the other.

Suddenly Gabriel launched forward and hurled Jacks all the way out into the main hall. He crashed into the far wall above the frieze, which showed the Council leading the Angels to the Awakening. Jackson crumpled and slid thirty feet down to the ground, landing hard.

Shaken by the fall, Jackson looked up and saw a dark shape moving at him fast. It was Gabriel, flying directly towards him. With rapid speed, Jacks pulled his Divine Sword from its sheath. But before he could bring it around, Gabriel powerfully pinned the young Angel's arm down with his foot and then kicked the sword to the side, leaving Jacks defenceless.

Jacks thought fast and swept his legs under Gabriel, who flew up to avoid the attack. But it was enough time for Jackson to clamber to his feet. With a powerful thrust of his wings he met again with the True Immortal in mid-air, colliding into him, hard. Spinning and spinning, the Angels whirled up near the top of the chamber. Their wings became tangled as their hands reached for the other's throats and arms and wrists. And then, like a stone dropped from a great height, they fell, still grappling with each other, smashing down into the storied marble floor so hard that a large crack split down the length of the atrium.

Jacks was stunned by the impact, and he'd barely had a chance to get to his feet before Gabriel was on him again. The True Immortal swung his fist straight into Jackson's stomach, then kneed him in the face as he doubled over.

Groaning and spitting out blood, Jacks attempted to pull himself up.

"I told you, it's useless," Gabriel said. "What chance does a Godspeed stand against a True Immortal? None, I'm afraid."

Gabriel reached into his robe and pulled out a gilded dagger, which glistened with the symbol of the Council. He raised the blade above Jackson's head.

CHAPTER 34

Every step was agony for Maddy as she wheezed her way through the passageways beyond the sanctuary. Maybe she'd just been in shock before and hadn't noticed it, but now it felt as if at least one of her ribs had been broken. Every breath, every step forward, hurt. That ibuprofen most definitely wasn't cutting it.

She was beaten up and bandaged, with a severely mauled wing. But it didn't matter. She knew in her heart that time was running out. For Jackson, and for all of them.

Focusing on Jackson's frequency, she could glean just one image. Gabriel's face. What did it mean? Her only choice was to follow her instincts.

Even if the allied Angels and humans could somehow vanquish the demons, there was no way Jackson would survive a battle against a True Immortal, one of the Twelve. And certainly not against Gabriel, the engineer of the NAS and the powerful leader of the Angels since their first day moving out of the shadows. He was the symbol of Protection for Pay, and, moreover, of the entire Angel world.

Going after Gabriel was suicide.

Maddy could only hope that her vision was trying to tell her something else, that Gabriel was just a red herring.

As these grim thoughts passed through Maddy's head, she

came upon a heavy wooden door connecting two passages. It was partially open. A heavy, humid heat lay in the air, telling her only one thing: demon. Carefully, she stepped forward, her senses sharpening as she advanced. But then, across the threshold, she saw an enormous black mass, practically as big as a small mountain. It wasn't moving, reassuring Maddy it was OK to continue on.

She looked in wonder at the goliath demon corpse that lay in a heap in the hallway. Then, in the corner of her eye, she noticed another figure, slumped off to the side.

And it was breathing.

She rushed over to find Detective Sylvester, injured and leaning against the wall. He was unconscious. She tried to wake him, but his only response was a mumbled groan of pain. His arm was curled strangely, unnaturally, at his side. But his breathing seemed normal, and as far as Maddy could tell, it looked like he would be all right.

"Detective, detective," she whispered, trying again to rouse him.

Moaning, Sylvester slowly drew to consciousness. His eyes opened wide in surprise as he recognized Maddy.

"Detective! Thank God you're all right. What happened?" Maddy asked, practically breathless.

"Jacks . . ." Sylvester muttered. His eyes started fluttering closed again.

"What?" Maddy said. She had no way of determining what had happened here. All she knew was that the demon had failed, and Sylvester was alive. She also knew that it couldn't have been the detective's pistol that had cut off the demon's head. It must have been

Jackson. But she had no idea where he was, or what state he was in. He could be injured . . . or worse.

"Stay here, Detective Sylvester," she said. "I'll come back for you." *If I can*, she thought, but she didn't say that aloud.

Just down the dark passageway she could see the faint glimmer of torchlight. There was but one way for her to go. And that was forward.

Just when she had thought she had already scraped out every last milligram of willpower, Maddy discovered some newfound strength. She took another look at Sylvester to make sure he was still breathing on his own, then held her breath so she wouldn't smell the horrible demon as she scaled over the massive corpse.

She stopped short for a moment. A voice echoed down the passage. Through the distortion Maddy could tell it was Jackson's voice, crying out in agony.

Oh no.

What if she was too late? The premonition of Jackson's lifeless face flashed across her mind. Gritting her teeth, she forced down the thought and ran as fast as she could, tears of pain welling up uncontrollably as she entered the main hall. She passed the dark, silent marble sentinels that watched over the final passage to the main hall and Council chambers.

Maddy crossed the threshold into the atrium. There she saw two things. First, Gabriel, standing with a dagger poised for murder. His eyes were sharp and terrifying, and imbued with a demonic power. The second thing she saw was Jackson, lying helplessly beneath him. His face was battered, his battle armour torn.

She had less than a moment to react.

"Jacks!"

Maddy reached down and hurled her Divine Sword towards Jackson with all her strength, just as she froze time for everything except herself, Jackson and the blade. The veins on Gabriel's forehead bulged as he slowed under Maddy's time freeze, attempting to counter it by slowing the time around the sword. The weapon skittered in slow motion across the marble floor as both Maddy and Gabriel strained under the pressure of battling each other's time freezes. At last the blade took one final clatter and slid to Jackson's feet. Gasping, Maddy let go of her time freeze just as Gabriel lost control of the Divine Sword.

In one fluid movement, Jacks leaned down and picked up the sword to defend himself from Gabriel's next blow. A flash of light exploded across the room as he picked it up and blocked Gabriel's strike.

Gabriel screamed and recoiled from the sword as if it were a hot flame, his eyes flashing red for a moment. Was it possible that he was not only controlling the demons, but that he had actually *become* a Dark One himself? Taking a few steps back, he recovered, covering his face with one cloaked arm and then pumping his wings to drop back.

Jacks took a tentative step forward. Then another. He thrust the sword at Gabriel, who rose a few feet off the ground, but the True Immortal dodged each stab. Gabriel was ancient but nimble. Reaching back and flying forward, Jacks swung the sword in a large arc with all his strength. Launching himself up with his wings, Gabriel caught Jackson's arm and bent it backward, pushing the sword away. They both grunted under the pressure as they pressed against each other until they dropped to the ground. A slight smile emerged on Gabriel's face as he bent Jackson's arm farther back. In just a few moments, Gabriel would be on top of him.

Jacks needed to make a move.

Suddenly Jacks let his sword fall to the ground and grabbed hold of Gabriel's wings. Before he knew it, he was leveraging his weight against the True Immortal's chest and using all his force to pull and tear at Gabriel's wings. Jackson's own cybernetic wings pressed against the ground as he fought, giving him even more strength. Spittle and foam flitted out from Gabriel's clenched teeth as he tried to free himself and his wings from Jacks's vice-like grip.

Then, *one*, *two* – the sounds were distinct, like enormous branches breaking and echoing in the halls. Jackson had broken Gabriel's wings, the bones snapping under the immense pressure. Jacks roared as he broke them, while Gabriel screamed.

Overwhelming pulses of blinding light and waves of force suddenly burst forth from the True Immortal, knocking first Jackson, then Maddy down on their feet, then rumbling out all across the compound with the force of an earthquake. Everything turned bright white in front of Maddy, and she stumbled forward, reaching blindly. Slowly, as the rumbling lessened, she began to regain her sight. Still blinded, Jacks had managed to pick up her Divine Sword and was now stumbling backward, away from Gabriel, who lay on his back. Crumpled underneath him on the ornate marble floor were his broken wings. Jacks sliced at the air in front of him, unsure of what happened. Gabriel was quiet and still, his chest moving up and down only slightly.

"Jacks!" Maddy cried. "It's clear!"

She rushed to him and put her hand on his arm, letting him know he no longer had to defend himself with the sword.

"It's over."

Gasping, Jacks fell to the ground, taking Maddy with him. His sight was slowly restored, and he eyed Gabriel's shape just ten feet away. Gabriel's breaths came out in rasps, his chest rising and falling.

Maddy and Jacks edged up to him carefully.

Gabriel's eyes were open, but it was clear he could not move his head. His eyes flitted around helplessly, as if asking Jacks and Maddy for help. Jacks still held the Divine Sword, keeping it ready to attack, just in case this was some kind of trick. But soon he realized that it wasn't. Maddy reached for Jacks's arm.

The True Immortal's frame began to shake slightly.

"What's happening?" Maddy asked, her eyes opening wide.

"I think he's . . . aging."

The eternally youthful Gabriel slowly began to age before their very eyes. The skin on his face greyed and faded into wrinkles, and his hair lost its luster until it started to fall away and dissolve into nothingness. Liver spots bloomed on his face and arms, the wrinkles spreading everywhere now. His broken wings became yellowed and bony, until the sharp feathers evaporated into a fine dust. He was growing older with every second. His eyes rolled around in their sockets in agony; his mouth fell open, but no sound came out.

Maddy shrieked and jumped back as his skin began to sink in against his bones, every ounce of fat and muscle shrinking and dissolving until all of it was gone. The skin itself began to melt

289

away, leaving only a mess of dissolved blood vessels and bones, which then, too, dried into dust. The eyes were the last to go. Like overripe fruit, they rotted and turned in upon themselves before dissolving into nothingness like the rest of him.

Turning away, Maddy felt like she was going to be sick. But Jackson didn't take his eyes off the grisly spectacle. The face of death for the one who had brought the Angels to corruption and the brink of destruction. Who had killed his father.

Now nothing was left of Gabriel but a pile of dust underneath a ceremonial Angelic cloth. A breath of chilling air blew in from the sanctuary halls, and the dusty remains blew into the air, disappearing, until there was no more trace of Gabriel, leader of the Council of Twelve, True Immortal, founder of the NAS and Protection for Pay, engineer of the Great Awakening – and wholly corrupted collaborator with the Dark Angels.

"But . . . I thought he was a True Immortal," Maddy said.

Before Jacks could take a stab at the answer, a voice called out from behind them.

"He must have broken that bond when he went into league with the demons."

It was Sylvester.

"Detective!" Jacks said. "You woke up! Are you OK?"

"I'll live." The detective held his broken arm with his good hand. "That was probably the only real sleep I've gotten in the past couple of weeks." He looked at Jacks and Maddy with concern. Jackson's face had been more than bloodied in the battle, and Maddy's amateur bandage job was coming apart at the seams.

"Don't worry. This looks worse than it is," Jacks said.

The detective gazed down with a mixture of wonderment and pity at the robe that had, until just moments ago, graced Gabriel's powerful frame. They were now little better than rags.

The three stumbled out of what was left of the Council chambers. Crumbled marble, broken glass, splintered columns and collapsed beams littered the sanctuary halls, evidence of the quake. The sanctuary was ruined, and from this point forward would be known as the lost underground city of the Angels.

Emergency power flickered in the corridors, lighting all the dust swirling in the air. Along a corridor, the wall of televisions was nothing but flickering static behind them.

After encountering a number of blocked passages, Jacks, Maddy, and the detective at last made it to the main elevator to the surface. The doors appeared to be undamaged, but Jacks still looked dubiously at the call button. He pressed it, but the elevator didn't respond.

"We're going to have to climb up."

They found the emergency stairwell and started making their exhausted climb up to the surface. What they would encounter up there, they had no idea.

After they had been climbing for a few minutes, they found that the quake caused by Gabriel's death had caused a portion of the stairwell to collapse. Their path wasn't fully blocked, thankfully, and they began pulling some of the rubble down in big chunks. And then they kept climbing.

At last they reached the exit. Maddy held her breath as Jackson opened the door to reveal the vast ruins of the once-grand glass cube structure. A warm breeze ran up the hill as the three of them walked through the wreckage to the ridge that looked over the city, not one of them wasting the energy to look back. Maddy greedily gulped at the fresh air, thankful to be free of the stifling stairwell.

Dawn peeked out from the horizon, finally breaking through the cover of blood-red and black clouds. Welcome bands of orange and purple streamed across the sky as the smog began to dissipate.

Jackson tentatively eyed the sky above, still prepared to do battle with any remaining Dark Angels. But there were none.

"Look!" Maddy cried, pointing towards the ocean.

Gabriel's demise had caused the demons to lose their impetus. The Dark Angels were fleeing, their Dark Master now dead. Jacks, Maddy, and Sylvester watched as bands of furious Battle Angels drove the demons back into the ocean, this time for good. Flashes of light burnished on the horizon, each one marking the demise of a Dark One.

Tears of joy streamed down Maddy's face. She leaned on Jackson as they looked down from the hill upon the city, gleaming with the day's first light.

A new dawn had broken over Angel City. The warm golden light revealed a city rife with smoke, destroyed buildings, a populace in hiding, and so many dead soldiers, citizens and Angels. But this was not a broken city. Angel City had survived. As Jackson, Maddy, and Sylvester looked out on the destruction, it was clear that it would be different from now on – far different than anyone could have ever imagined.

But the Immortal City had proved itself immortal. It was a new day.

CHAPTER 35

M addy, Jacks and Sylvester had stepped out of the Council chambers and into the sunlight of a new world. A different Angel City.

"Jacks . . ." Maddy said, overwhelmed by all that had happened. She held on to his arm as she looked out across the Angel City basin. "They're gone, Jacks. It's all over."

"I feel like I'm dreaming," Jacks said. In the distance Angels were returning from the final mission of the battle, flying to the appointed meeting spot at the base of the Hills. "But then I look at you, and I know it's real."

A few steps away from them, Detective Sylvester was saying a prayer of thanksgiving under his breath. Lifting his glasses, he dabbed at his eyes, which were tearing up.

"Sylvester . . ." Jackson said. "What you did . . . Thank you. You saved my life."

"Just doing my duty," the detective said, choking back emotion. "I suppose that's why I ended up here." He looked at Maddy and Jacks. "Why we all ended up here."

Suddenly a thought bolted through Maddy's mind.

Kevin.

In a panic Maddy looked east towards the Angel City neighbourhood harbouring the shelter. From this distance the area looked fairly unscathed. Maddy breathed out a sigh of relief.

They began making their way down the hill to where the others were waiting. Just before the sanctuary was completely out of sight, Jacks looked up at the ruins of the glass cube.

"The world will know of both the heroism and evil of the Angels today. We won't hide any longer. No more lies."

They reached the meeting spot near the foot of Runyon Canyon, which, ironically, had previously been a hot Angel sighting spot for tourists and paparazzi. Today, the day the Angels were out in droves – the day they had *won* – there was not a camera or tourist in sight.

Angels were landing all around, many with injuries. Battle commanders were barking orders and screaming at Angel nurses to start triaging patients. Still, the light from the morning sun was streaming across the scene, and in this moment of victory, despite all the sacrifices and casualties, there seemed to be a lightness and hope that Maddy had forgotten could exist.

A hush came over the temporary camp as the Angels realized who had just arrived. They watched in awe as Jackson Godspeed, with limping Maddy Montgomery and Detective Sylvester, emerged from the top of the Hills.

"Gabriel is gone," Jackson announced. "He was the one who brought the demons. He was a traitor to the Angels and humans alike. And in his death the demons lost their courage and their way. Gabriel has fallen. And from this point forward, no longer under his corrupt hand, Angels will be fallen no longer."

The crowd regarded their leader with silent pride.

One of the Battle Angels came forward. He looked at Jackson

with sadness on his face. Maddy's stomach tightened, nervous about what he had to say.

"Jackson . . . we lost Archangel Godspeed."

"Mark?" Jacks's voice faltered.

Jackson dropped to one knee, holding his head in his left hand in grief. He took in deep, gasping breaths. Time seemed to slow down around Jackson, and the whole world felt like it was underwater. Maddy was speechless.

"Mitch was with him," the Battle Angel continued. A deadly silence hung in the air, a terrible cloud of expectation. Maddy had to stop herself from turning away, afraid to hear Mitch's fate.

"He was badly hurt holding off the demons. But he's going to make it."

Maddy exhaled, and Jacks nodded.

"I'm glad," Jackson managed to choke out. "Both of them . . . would have been too much."

"Your stepfather didn't die in vain," the Angel said. "A pack of demons was moving towards an emergency shelter full of citizens. It was as if the Dark Ones knew they were about to go down, and were trying to murder as many as they could before we sent them back to hell. Mark and Mitch managed to hold off ten Dark Ones before they fell. But it was enough time for a civilian militia to evacuate the shelter. Mark's a hero."

Still kneeling, Jacks nodded, pressing his fist against his mouth as he tried to process the waves emotion crashing over him. This was a moment he would remember for ever, the moment he heard his stepfather – his dad, really – was no longer.

Jackson continued buckling under the news as he remembered

what he'd just learned: that his own father had been murdered by Gabriel. He grieved for both of them, father and stepfather, both victims of Gabriel's treachery. They had sacrificed their lives for the lives of others.

"I'll never forget him," Jackson murmured as he struggled with the tears, his throat as he realized he'd never see Mark again.

The freedom fighters in front of him, Angel and human alike, became quiet and circled around Jackson. They looked at him with pity and compassion – and reverence. News had already spread about what he had done. He had vanquished Gabriel, the ultimate traitor and leader of the demon army. Jackson Godspeed slowly stood up and met the eyes of his fellow fighters, those who had withstood the demon attack alongside him. They had put everything on the line to halt the onslaught; they were Angel and mankind's first defence against annihilation.

"All of you who fought here today are heroes," said Jackson. "Don't ever forget that. I'm proud to have been with you. We're going to have time – too much time – to be sad about our losses. But right now, before we even think about our path to healing, let's take a moment of silence in honour of those slain."

Maddy bowed her head in memory along with the rest of the crowd. Her first thought was of Tom, then Mark, and then of what Jacks must be feeling right now, as well. Hot tears ran down her face, dripping into the dirt below.

After a full minute, Jackson lifted his head and looked at everyone. His eyes were rimmed with tears.

"Thank you," he said.

*

Farther down the hill, Maddy found a US military tent. She walked in to a soldier's salute.

"Lieutenant Commander," the soldier said.

"Private," said Maddy. "Any chance you've got a working radio around here?"

"Yes, ma'am." He rifled through a desk drawer, pulled out a radio, and handed it to her.

She pressed the button to activate the mic. "Can you hear me?" she spoke into it.

"Roger. Go ahead," the radio crackled.

"This is Madison Montgomery Godright. Two blocks east of La Brea, just south of Sunset, there is a doorway at number two-forty-three and a half Formosa. Inside you'll find a body. The deceased is First Lieutenant Thomas Cooper of the U.S. Navy. He died a hero. . ."

Inside the temporary Angel medical tent setup, Maddy screamed and struggled despite all efforts not to. An Angel doctor was peeling the makeshift bandages off her arm, pulling lots of destroyed skin off with them. Maddy's consciousness began fading in and out, the pain so great that she lashed out at the doctor.

"Nurse!"

A nurse held her down and Maddy felt a prick – she'd been injected with something. Soon a warm fogginess spread throughout her body, and her arm didn't feel quite as bad.

"This is a bad burn you've got here, Miss Godright," the doctor said. "But it's not as bad as it could be. We Angels have actually discovered a next-generation burn treatment that will help you look as good as new. The FDA has not yet approved it for human use, but it will be fine for you. It'll leave a scar, that's for sure. There's no way around that. But it won't be disfiguring. For now we will re-dress the burn and then begin treatment as soon as possible."

Maddy nodded.

"Can I see the wing?" the doctor asked.

In an effort to avoid dealing with two excruciating pains at once, Maddy had only told the doctor about her burn. But he'd figured it out on his own. She began to sweat as she thought about the pain that had overcome her when she had retracted it in the storage room.

"Do I have to?" Maddy asked.

"I'm afraid so. It's the only way for me to diagnose it and treat you."

The doctor and nurse stepped away to give Maddy enough room to spread her famous wings.

Maddy could feel her Immortal Marks tingling, and then her right side began to hurt, badly. It felt a little bit like the first time her wings came out that first night, in the bathroom. Her breaths were coming fast and hard. Suddenly, her left wing ripped out with a *whoosh*, but the right wing wouldn't follow. As expected, the pain was excruciating, even with the shot the nurse had given her.

Maddy yelled in pain. Just as she was starting to tumble off the examination table, the right wing emerged. The force of it caused Maddy to fall to the floor, knocking over her IV on the way. The doctor and nurse helped her to her feet. Her injured wing hadn't straightened like it was supposed to.

Trying to deal with the pain as the doctor attempted to straighten it out, her entire body became covered in a sheen of sweat.

"Yes, yes, mm-hmm . . . three, four, two lateral movement," he said to the nurse, who was taking notes. He kept relaying numbers that Maddy couldn't understand. Finally he stopped reciting and looked at Maddy. His face was unreadable.

"As for the wing . . ."

"What? What do all those numbers mean?" she asked.

"It just means it's very badly sprained and bruised. You won't fly for a couple of months, at least," he said. "It's not broken, however. You're lucky. You should see some of the wing injuries we're dealing with in here. Some of these Guardians will never fly again. Tragic."

Maddy thought of Jackson when he couldn't fly and how he had to struggle with his very identity. The depression, his slow decline. With all the recent developments in Angel medical technology, she hoped there wouldn't be too many Angels who were permanently disabled. Otherwise there might be a whole generation of Guardians sentenced to live underneath the shadow of this demon battle.

The door was locked, and she'd lost her keys somewhere along the way. Maddy had to knock.

She was met by her uncle, who had deep, dark bags under his eyes. His face was creased with worry and sleep deprivation.

"Maddy! Thank God!" He rushed to her and then paused when he saw her bandaged arm. "What happened? Are you OK?"

"I'm fine. It hurts. My arm is burned and I'll probably always have a scar. But I'm luckier than some." Maddy's voice faltered.

"What is it?" Kevin asked, a look of anticipated dread falling upon his face as he looked at his niece.

"Tom . . . Tom's dead, Uncle Kevin," she managed.

"What?" Kevin said, unable to contain his shock.

"He's gone. I made a choice to protect Jacks, and then Tom had to die protecting me." Maddy began crying silently. She knew this must be affecting her uncle: he and Tom had developed a close bond. No matter how hard she tried, every thought brought her back to Tom's sacrifice.

Kevin searched for the right words. "This was a war, Maddy. You're not responsible for what happened in a war."

"But I'm the one who's supposed to be a Guardian," Maddy responded. "And I couldn't save him. I couldn't even save myself."

Kevin put his hand on her shoulder. Maddy leaned in and let him hug her. He was careful not to press against her burned arm.

"It's not your fault," Kevin said. "It's the fault of Gabriel, of the demons, the Council. It's the fault of the whole system, which had become rotten to its core. Your father knew this twenty years ago, which is why he started fighting against the NAS."

"I couldn't not go after Jacks," Maddy said. "I felt it so deep."

Kevin looked down at her with gentle eyes. "Tom felt the same way about you."

Maddy shed a few silent tears. "Why is everything always so complicated?"

Kevin just squeezed her tighter.

Maddy felt emptied out. And so tired. So, so tired.

"Will I ever be able to forget?" she asked.

"You will never forget," Kevin said. "But you will be able to live. And that's what those who have fallen would have wanted. That's what my sister, your mother, would have wanted. And your father. And now, Tom."

CHAPTER 36

Donations were streaming in from a grateful world to Angel City, which had served as the bulwark against the demon onslaught for the rest of the Earth. A horrified globe had watched the destruction unfold, and knew that if the Immortal City hadn't made a stand, they would have been next.

Now supplies, money and volunteers were streaming in to help pick up the pieces and rebuild a new Angel City. Instead of looking at it as a tragedy, many were trying to see it as an opportunity to look ahead to a brighter future.

That, and to think about what role the Immortals were going to have in it. That was the question on everyone's minds.

Maddy did not have time for such questions, however. Not yet, at least. Four days after the end of the battle, she moved along what remained of the Walk of Angels. The famous street had been transformed into an open-air square for citizens to pay tribute to the Angels and humans who had sacrificed their lives in the battle against the demons. People brought flowers, left poems and placed framed photos of those who'd been lost.

The warm sun spilled across the street, a welcome reminder that not all had been transformed. Maddy walked silently towards an open spot along the makeshift memorial.

Despite her large sunglasses, someone in the crowd recognized her.

"It's Maddy!" a voice cried out.

Cameras began whirring, and people started shouting. Just like in the old days, when paparazzi and hordes of devoted fans would swarm around exclusive events. But as Maddy made her way to the memorial fence, the crowd grew quiet and respectfully parted to let her through. She carried a brown shopping bag under one arm and a bouquet of flowers in her other hand.

The crowd remained hushed. A news camera was trained on her, quietly capturing the moment. They knew the instrumental role she had played in defeating the demons, and even though everyone was eager to hear what she had to say about the aftermath, they knew better than to bother her during such an emotional time.

Maddy opened the paper bag, pulled out a framed photo, and placed it along the fence. It was of Tom, standing by an F-18 fighter jet, grinning. The photo had been taken right after his graduation from flight school, and he looked completely at home. The label on the frame read: 1ST LIEUTENANT THOMAS A. COOPER, UNITED STATES NAVY.

The reason for Maddy's dark glasses became apparent, as her eyes began to well up with tears, thinking about what Tom had done for her. He had let her save Jackson and, ultimately, the city.

Next Maddy arranged the flowers, placing them in a vase that had also been in the bag. She paused for a minute, studying the photo before her, then turned to face the large crowd.

She took in each and every face of those who had also lost someone. These were faces that needed hope.

"I'd like to say something about Tom Cooper. Tom represented what was best in us as humans. He was loyal and loving, imperfect and maddening. He had heart. He was courageous. He was a true hero, in the face of tall odds. He saved my life, and died doing it. I know what it's like to want to save someone you love. I know the feeling that led him to want to sacrifice his life.

"Many of you have also lost people you loved during this battle for Angel City. You may be wondering, *Why him? Why her?* There are no answers. Just know that they did not die in vain. Here we made a stand against the darkness. Here, in Angel City, the darkness was vanquished.

"Tom had faced death once before while defending this city, this country, this *world*. His plane crashed during the second wave of attacks and it was only through chance that an Angel found him floating in the waves." Maddy's voice broke for a moment, and she wiped tears away from under the sunglasses. "Even after he'd been badly injured, Tom still risked his life and gave his all. He saved me and, in the process, saved us all. And for that, we should be grateful. I know I will never be able to repay him for everything he's taught me, or for what he did for me."

Leaning down, Maddy reached into the brown paper bag for the last item she had brought with her.

She lay Tom's leather jacket – the one he'd always worn to fly, and the one he'd worn when he first kissed Maddy – on the memorial.

"Tom, we'll never forget you."

The Walk of Angels was now a place for open displays of grief, a place for respect, and a place for reflection. Instead of paparazzi and designer boutiques, the pavement was lined with tributes, poems and photos of those lost in the battle with the demon army. With cell phones and Internet still mostly down, it was also a place for families and loved ones who had been separated in the demon attack to try to find each other again. On a chain-link fence to the side of the temporary memorial for those who had died were pasted hundreds of notices looking for the missing.

Those military and civilian militia members wounded in the battle also moved in the crowds, paying solemn honour to those who had fought shoulder-to-shoulder with them on the front lines. Displayed above them was a large photograph of Archangel Mark Godspeed. In the portrait, Jackson's stepfather stood in the head offices of the NAS, wearing his tailored Italian suit, one hand in the pocket of his trousers, the button on his jacket undone. This was the way Jacks would always remember him. To the left of the portrait was a smaller photo of Mark with his family, Kris, Chloe and Jacks.

And pinned nearby was a large photo of Lieutenant Tom Cooper, US Navy.

CHAPTER 37

Maddy slipped past the security guard quietly. She knew he'd let her in if he saw who she was, but she just didn't want to deal with being recognized right now. She didn't want to explain why she was there at 1:45 in the morning, especially when she didn't really know herself. Another night wide awake. She'd put on her hoodie and jeans and crept out of the house, careful not to wake Kevin, who was safe and snoring down the hall. Maddy got in her car, but she hadn't had a destination in mind. But something had drawn her to the temple, and this was where she found herself now.

She stood in front of the ruined arches of the Temple of Angels, here and there a spot in the wreckage still smouldering, a full week after the battle. For years the temple had been the focus of the most glamorous and prestigious Angel events, a thousand camera shutters clicking every second as the perfect Immortals exited their limousines to walk the red carpet. Maddy stepped carefully among the rubble that used to make up the grand entrance, where all the on-carpet interviews were done – where, every year, Tara interrogated every beautiful Angel about "who" she was wearing. Now it was just a heap of marble and stone. A crow jumped around the top of the debris, poking its beak into the stones. It cawed at Maddy as she approached.

"Shoo." She waved at it and it flapped away into the night.

Walking farther inside, Maddy's eyes scanned up to the skeletal flying buttresses, the only standing remains of the collapsed half of the temple. The back half of the temple remained somewhat standing, with the roof sagging and broken in parts, but still proudly hanging on. Partially broken panes of stained-glass windows looked up to the stars. This used to be the site of all the pomp and circumstance of the Angels, Maddy thought, the focal point every year for the world to observe everything Angel. Would it ever stand again?

Maddy heard a noise and jolted upright.

"Hello?" she said cautiously.

A face emerged from the shadows. She would have recognized the pale blue eyes and full cheekbones anywhere.

It was Jackson.

"Jacks? What are you doing here?" she said in shock.

"I could ask the same of you," he said, walking out of the shadows and into the moonlight spilling into the mostly collapsed church.

"I couldn't sleep," said Maddy.

"Me neither," Jacks said. He looked at her with those eyes. "How'd you get in?"

"Snuck in. You?"

"Slipped the guard a hundred," Jackson said.

"What were you doing hiding out over there?" she said, pointing to the shadows behind the pillar.

"We're not supposed to be here, you know," he said. "I heard someone, and I wanted to see who it was. And turns out it was Maddy Montgomery."

"Turns out," she said.

"Everything . . . OK?" he said.

"I don't know," Maddy said. "What about you?"

"I don't know, either."

A meaningful silence settled between them, and they began walking together through the ruins. They came to the famous entrance where Guardians were led just before Commissioning. The stone arch had collapsed, but the monument at its centre was still intact, though it now lay on its side, partially buried in the wreckage. Most of the big block lettering etched into the stone was still legible.

"I read that oath right before my Commissioning," Jacks said to Maddy. "'Do Your Duty.' Those words flashed through my head right before I left to save you outside Ethan's party. And I wasn't thinking about my duty to the Angels. I knew I was being called for some higher duty. It seems so long ago now."

"You've done your duty, Jacks," Maddy said. "We all have." Her voice quavered as she spoke.

Jacks put his arm around Maddy to comfort her as they sat down on the edge of a slab of marble that had toppled down and cracked into three giant pieces. "I haven't had a chance to . . ." His voice trailed off. He didn't know what to say. But he did know that, when it came to Maddy, he didn't really need to say anything.

In this predawn winter hour, Maddy's body felt cool under his arm. "You're cold," he said. "Here, have my jacket."

"That's OK. I don't want you to be cold, Jacks. I'm fine. . ." she said unconvincingly.

"Yeah, right. You're shivering, Mads," he said. "Just take it." He wrapped the jacket over her shoulders.

"Thanks," she said, smiling slightly.

They sat there in silence for a while, just being.

Until Jackson broke the silence.

"Remember our first date?"

"At the diner?"

"That didn't count," Jackson said. "Our first *date*, not when we first met."

"You mean up at the viewpoint."

"And then flying," Jacks said. "You were so suspicious."

A wisp of a smile came across Maddy's face. "With good reason."

"I was just trying to be nice," Jacks said.

"You were trying to show off."

"Well, it worked, didn't it?"

"I guess you're right," Maddy said. "Maybe."

"You have to admit you liked it."

"The Ferrari was a bit much." A thoughtful, dreamy expression overtook Maddy's face. "We flew over Angel City. My first time. The city was so beautiful." She looked out at the ruins around her. "That's how I want to remember it. Not like this. Not . . . broken."

"It can be rebuilt," Jacks said.

Maddy nodded but kept her gaze fixed on the destruction.

"Let's go back inside, where it's warmer," Jacks said. They made their way back into the section of the temple that was still partially covered. The half-wall blocked out the cool breeze, and it was almost cozy.

"Kris and Chloe . . ." Maddy said, thinking of Jackson's mother and sister, who were suffering the loss of Mark Godspeed, too. "How are they?"

"In shock. We all are. Everyone's lost someone. No Angel family is untouched. Gabriel's evil has run deep." Jackson's voice was breaking up as he spoke of his stepfather. "I know he and I had some differences in the past. But even if he wasn't my real father, he was always my dad."

Maddy put her hand on his shoulder.

"Jacks, what you did . . ." she said. "The deal you must have made with Linden to get me and Tom to safety . . . I don't know what to say."

"I wanted you to be safe. And . . . not alone," Jacks replied. "I never thought we'd survive the demons."

Jackson moved closer to Maddy.

"You loved him, didn't you?" he said.

She hesitated, looking at him.

"Yes," said Maddy. "I did."

She turned away. Jackson reached out to touch her shoulder, triggering her to turn back around to face him.

"I've loved you," Jackson said. "I never stopped loving you."

All of a sudden, Maddy was overwhelmed by a rush of tenderness. Every emotion she'd ever felt for Jackson hit her all at once.

"Jacks . . ."

But before she could get the words out, Jacks was kissing her. She reached her arm around his waist and pulled him in closer. Opening her mouth, she embraced the kiss, their lips and mouths becoming one.

The human-Angel war, the demon sinkhole, their fight on the carrier, the siege, the loss of Tom, Angel City brought to its knees – it all collapsed in on itself at this moment.

None of it mattered right now. She just needed him. And he needed her.

Together they breathed deeply as they kissed, their bodies pressed close – a perfect fit, as if melded together.

Maddy took one small, slow step back, then another, and drew the Angel towards her. As they continued to kiss, Jackson pulled his jacket off her, one arm at a time. Her body no longer felt cold.

He softly laid the jacket on the ground behind her and then slowly lowered Maddy down on to it. She reached up and pulled him down to her, rolling his shirt off as she did.

And she realized this was how it was going to happen. Of course. It was perfect.

Jacks pulled at Maddy's shirt, and she let him take it off. Then, shivering from excitement rather than cold, she wrapped her arms around his bare torso and let every muscle, bone, ridge and valley of his chest press against her. She wanted to feel him as close against her as she could so she could feel the warmth of their bodies co-mingling in the early-morning air.

Jacks pulled back slightly and looked at Maddy, his face silhouetted by the waning moonlight. With a *whoosh* his wings emerged. Maddy ran her hands upon the strange new wings, which bristled and felt hot under her touch. The sensation was both familiar and strange – part old, part new.

"Is everything all right?" Jacks asked.

"Yes," she breathed, and they kissed again.

Finally they broke apart, catching their breath. Jackson's gaze glimmered towards her.

"Do you want to?" he asked after what seemed like an eternity.

Maddy nodded, biting her lower lip. "Do you want to?"

"Yes," Jacks said.

Maddy curled up into a shadow, slightly embarrassed.

"I'm feeling shy," she said.

Leaning forward, Jacks placed a hand on her cheek and kissed her forehead. "Maddy, you are beautiful."

She smiled and pulled his face close to hers.

Maddy looked into Jackson's blue eyes. She felt his weight upon her and embraced it, and she pressed her lips, hard, against his.

She cried out, and it echoed through the remains of the temple.

"Are you all right?" Jackson's worried voice said.

"Yes," Maddy breathed, overwhelmed with sensation, emotion – everything. She placed her hand around his waist and pulled him closer. "Everything's all right."

She was trembling. She couldn't stop; waves of energy were crashing over her body.

"Was that . . . OK?"

"Yes," Maddy said, running her hand through her hair.

Jackson placed his hand on Maddy's cheek and gazed into her eyes. "I've dreamed about this, Maddy, being this close to you. But this was better than anything I ever dreamed."

Maddy nodded, biting her bottom lip slightly. She felt the

warmth of his body next to hers, his skin so warm, and she pulled him even closer. "Come closer, Jacks," she breathed in his ear. "Come as close as you can."

After some time, Maddy dozed off in Jackson's arms, her head resting on his chest. She had no dreams, or nightmares. Her sleep was quiet and deep, and when she woke she saw some tendrils of pink dawn peering through what was left of the once-glorious stained-glass windows. Jacks was awake next to her, his arms still wrapped warmly around her. His eyes were focused on the remnants of the windows, which now told a shattered and fragmented history of the Angels.

"Hey . . ." she whispered.

"Hey," he said back quietly. He touched his lips lightly to her forehead. "Did you get some sleep?"

She nodded.

Jacks turned his gaze to the rising light. "We should get going before it gets too light."

"OK."

Wrapping his jacket around her, Maddy slipped back into her clothes. Jacks turned around and did the same, although Maddy couldn't help but sneak a look and smile.

Outside they made their way through the rubble to where they could sneak out under the fence unbothered and unseen. The pink-purple glow of the dawn bathed the scene in a dream-like light. But when Jacks reached out for Maddy and squeezed her hand, Maddy knew he was real.

Maddy felt she should say something, anything, to let him

know what she was feeling. The night – *their* night, Maddy and Jackson's first time – couldn't just *end* like this.

"Jacks, I—"

He looked at her expectantly.

"Never mind. . . It's nothing, actually. I just want to remember it like this. *Us* like this," she said. "The other part can come later."

Jacks nodded and smiled. "Of course, Maddy. Whatever you want."

CHAPTER 38

T he spectators along the street were silent as President Linden, Maddy, and Jacks took their sad tour past the destruction
along Angel Boulevard. The charred remains of palm trees loomed
over the broken sidewalk that had once been the polished Walk
of Angels, with its Angel Stars and throngs of tourists and their
incessantly snapping cameras. The tatters of the Angel billboards
presided over them all, smoke-blackened reminders of a different
place and a different time.

This was a solemn procession of the United States government
and a full delegation from the GAC, along with Maddy and Jacks,
who had become the most public symbols of the heroic resistance
against the demons. A small group of selected reporters had been
allowed to come along to cover the occasion. Jacks wore a dark
suit that fit him like a glove, and Maddy was in a chic yet simple
black dress. It was one of the few items she'd taken from the giant
wardrobe in her apartment. She'd recently learned that the luxury
building had been caught in the crossfire and was little more than
expensive debris now. Her extensive wardrobe had also been a
casualty, but Maddy found she still preferred her usual jeans and
hoodie combo anyway.

Jacks and Maddy exchanged secret nervous glances. This
was the first time they had seen each other since the morning

before, when they'd left the temple after their momentous night together. That whole experience had seemed so unreal to Maddy. It had ended in an otherworldly dawn glow, and now that they were out in broad daylight, it was hard to say where they stood. All Maddy knew was that Jacks had called her before the procession and said he had something to tell her, in person. His voice had sounded slightly strange. Not *bad* strange, but still strange. She was simmering with curiosity, but it would have to wait until after their public appearance.

And Maddy herself didn't know where she stood. There were so many conflicting emotions and sensations running through her, causing her to feel both exalted and totally exhausted. It was enough just to lose her virginity, but now, after all that had happened, while she also grieved for Tom . . . She almost wished she felt *guilty* about it. She had no idea what the future held, but that night at the temple with Jackson had felt so natural, so right. She wondered if Jackson felt the same way.

The entourage reached the makeshift memorial. Footage of Maddy's appearance there just a few days before had spread around the world, with many taking strength and courage from her words. She was becoming a symbol of renewed strength after tragedy.

Linden paused at the memorial, a somber look on his face as he and his group took in the almost overwhelming display of grief and respect. The entire nation, and even the whole world over, was now looking to him for hope and strength. He had transformed from a fringe candidate to leader of the free world in such a short time. Many of his enemies and detractors were waiting for him to falter, but he had not so far. He had shown himself to be strong, even when faced with near-impossible decisions. Linden had followed his own moral compass. And the people were now grateful to him.

The president now focused on the picture of Tom that Maddy had left at the memorial. Then he looked up and cleared his throat as he turned to the cameras.

"I'm told a brave young man named Thomas Cooper, an ace navy pilot, died in Angel City. He didn't perish in his jet, but rather fighting on the street. For something – and someone – he loved." Maddy could feel her hands growing clammy, her face losing colour. A lump grew in her throat, but she had promised herself to hold it together, at least until the cameras stopped rolling. Linden continued. "His story is one of hundreds that will be told over the coming generations. Let us not forget them, ever.

"And as for the Angels, much blood was spilled as they came to aid humanity in our greatest hour of need. Archangel Mark Godspeed was one of many who sacrificed all." Linden looked behind his shoulder to the memorial that had been built up around Mark's photo.

He motioned next to the memorial for Louis Kreuz. There was a black-and-white 1930s-era photo of Louis at the height of the days of the Guardian Training System, when he had unparalleled power. Of course, he was in his trademark pose, with a cigar stuck in his mouth.

"Then there was the heroic Louis Kreuz," Linden said, "who sacrificed everything to bring vital information to those fighting the demons. This information ultimately led us to defeat the army. Louis was a larger-than-life character who was synonymous with Old Angel City. We will always be in Mr Kreuz's debt."

A surge of emotion came over Maddy as she thought about her past with Kreuz, how he had at first been so rude and brusque with her when she started Guardian training, but then had later revealed himself to be a great ally. Louis had been trying to protect her the whole time.

"And now, I must say it is a humbling honour for me to be standing here with two battle heroes. It was our darkest hour, and Jackson Godspeed was able to rally support within the Angel community, support without which I would not be standing here today, speaking to you." Linden turned to Jacks. "Jackson, on behalf of the Global Angel Commission, and indeed on behalf of all humans around the world: thank you. And I want to state again how much we feel for your and your family's loss. Your stepfather was a great hero."

Linden reached forward and shook Jackson's hand. Cameras snapped and whirred, but Jackson noticed that they weren't shouting and hollering, like the paparazzi would have. They were solemnly documenting the occasion.

Now Linden turned to Maddy.

"And Madison Montgomery Godright—"

The president was interrupted by several shouts from the crowd.

"Maddy!"

"Maddy!"

But this sounded different from the insane crowds of "Maddicts," the droves of Angel devotees ready to give anything, go anywhere, for a glimpse of their favourite, perfect Immortal.

No, these voices sounded out like a cry of shared pain, a cry for help and guidance in these dark times.

Linden continued. "As a half-Angel, Madison was in a unique position to help bring our combined forces together. Even before the demons invaded, Madison had already proved her unique heroism by exposing the corruption of the Protection for Pay system. Inducted into the US Navy as Lieutenant Commander Godright, she was able to give us the strategic edge we needed to stay one step ahead of those monsters."

Maddy's face began to burn with shame as she recalled how she had abandoned her post during the epic final battle. But Jackson had needed her, and it'd turned out to be her destiny.

"And I know she, too, is grieving in this time, especially for her close friend Lieutenant Thomas Cooper. Let our thoughts and prayers be with all of those who have lost loved ones in this unprecedented attack on humanity."

Jackson's eyes flicked over to Maddy as Linden mentioned Tom. He saw that her face went pale for a moment, but the colour soon returned. Still, she didn't meet Jacks's gaze.

"Madison has proved herself to be a great ambassador for both our people and the Angels, and the speech she made right here only four days ago has captured the attention of the globe. It is my pleasure to announce that I will be offering her the position of special counsel to rebuild Angel City."

Applause rolled through the crowd and Maddy nodded in appreciation, but inside she was thrown off guard, rolling with near-panic, wondering whether she was even qualified to hold such a position.

Maddy exchanged a quick look with Jackson; she hadn't been notified of *this*. Jacks gave her a gentle smile. *"You're going to do great*," he mouthed to her, just like he had before her first TV appearance after receiving her wings.

President Linden looked out again at the assembled crowd as the journalists and camera crews recorded every moment.

"Now that Gabriel has been destroyed and the rest of the Council has been disbanded and stripped of their control, we can be assured of a new, prosperous era in human-Angel relations.

We are about to enter a new age of cooperation between Immortals and humanity. Therefore, as a show of good faith, I am announcing the immediate repeal of the Immortals Bill, subject to further review. This is not a reward to the Angels for intervening in the demon attack, although we will always be grateful. But we believe under the extraordinary leadership of young Jackson Godspeed, the Angels will find a new direction. A new purpose. And a renewed ability to let people believe in them. We already saw that in the Battle of Angel City, and we can be assured that we will continue to see that in the future."

Linden motioned to Jackson.

"We will be honoured to work side by side with the Angels to renew and rebuild this city into something even greater than it was before. We will be allies, and never enemies."

Applause once again rolled through the crowd, and a few cheers broke out. Linden turned to Jackson to shake his hand, but Jacks signalled him off and stepped forward instead.

"I'm sorry, everyone. And thank you, President Linden, for all that you've just said. But we can't do that," Jackson said.

Linden's face froze into a veneer of shock and confusion. Puzzled murmurs ran through the crowd. The cameras recorded everything, beaming it around the world. Maddy was stunned and didn't know what to think of Jackson's words. What was he doing?

"I mean no disrespect, sir. The Angels support you and your cause. Trust that we fully appreciate everything you are doing and stand for," Jackson said. "I just don't want to make any promises we won't be able to keep." Jacks cleared his throat and regarded the shocked masses with confidence. "It will all be clear soon."

Still in shock, Maddy leaned in close to Jacks and whispered in his ear.

"Jacks, what is *going on*?"

Under his breath, Jacks answered, "That's what I needed to talk to you about. I'll explain soon enough. Just not here." He turned to Maddy. "And you need to get ready to make a decision."

CHAPTER 39

B efore Maddy had a chance to ask any more questions, Jacks was making as polite an exit as he could. He left a shocked President Linden to deal with the crowd and whisked Maddy to one of the waiting black sedans that had brought them to the event. Jackson told the driver to go to Kevin's Diner, then sank into the leather seat beside Maddy.

"I didn't want to bring it up like that," said Jacks. "But I couldn't just play along with Linden. It wouldn't have been right."

Maddy just stared at him, speechless and confused. After all that had happened, was Jackson now saying that the Angels wouldn't be cooperating with Linden and humanity?

"Jacks, what's happening? What did you mean back there?"

He flashed a weak version of his trademark smile, then turned to look out the window, a strange expression casting over his face. "How long has it been? And you still can't just trust me?" he said.

Maddy didn't know what to say. It wasn't that she didn't trust him. It was just that too much was changing too fast, and she didn't know how to process it.

They spent the rest of the ride in silence. Maddy stared out the window. They reached the restaurant within a few minutes, and they got out of the car and stepped into the empty parking lot.

She hadn't even bothered to ask why Jacks told the driver to take them there. That was the least of the mysteries facing her today. The diner had remained closed to the general public in these days after the demon attacks. Not because it had been damaged, but because Kevin had volunteered to sponsor a relief kitchen to feed those displaced by the destruction. They had an enormous setup in the Angel City High School cafeteria, where he was whipping up his trademark omelettes, hamburgers, and milk shakes with a team of five cooks working under him. The displaced were stretched out on cots in classrooms, hallways, and the gymnasium, and though it certainly didn't feel like home to them, Kevin's cooking was slowly helping them regain their health and happiness.

So Maddy and Jacks had the diner to themselves. Maddy opened the door to the darkened space and flipped on the overhead lights. They settled into one of the worn, cracked booths she knew so well.

Maddy sat silently, then looked warily, expectantly, at Jacks.

"Maybe we should have a cup of coffee," Jacks said.

Maddy stood up to put a pot on, but Jackson put his hand on her shoulder to stop her. "I'll do it. I'm not just some helpless Angel, you know," he said with a wink. He stood up and went to the kitchen. "How hard can it be?"

She heard a lot of clinking and clanking from the kitchen that didn't bode well. With a slight roll of her eyes, Maddy smiled weakly. Just then she realized that the last time Jacks had been in the diner was the fateful afternoon she had saved not only her Protection, Jeffrey Rosenberg, but also Lauren, his assistant. That was what had started the big crisis with Linden and the Immortals Bill. Tom had been there and then Jacks had come in. . . . There he was again. Tom. Maddy's mind kept returning to him, no matter how hard she tried to put his memory to peace in her heart. She just kept replaying the dismal scene on the smoky street, when he'd told her "*Don't stop.*"

Jacks emerged from the kitchen a few minutes later, holding two steaming cups in his hands. He handed one to Maddy. Whatever was in them at least *looked* like coffee, and Maddy took a cautious sip. Not bad. Definitely not as good as her uncle's, but for a first-timer, not bad.

Jacks cleared his throat again. Maddy eyed him more than a little expectantly.

"I'm really sorry about what happened, Maddy," said Jacks. "I really did want this to be different. I didn't know Linden would do what he did today."

It took all of Maddy's willpower to stay patient, and she was feeling more than a little exasperated. "Will. You. Please. Tell. Me. What's. Happening."

Jackson looked at her, coffee cup between his hands.

"Maddy . . . considering everything that's happened . . . with Gabriel's turn to evil and the corruption of the Council . . . the NAS and Protection for Pay causing the Angels to lose sight of what's important . . . and now with the demon attack in our wake . . . It's clear."

"*What's* clear?" asked Maddy.

"We must leave," Jacks said.

What? This was not what Maddy had been expecting.

"*Leave?* To go where? What do you mean?"

"The Angels' time among the humans is done," said Jackson. "We must return to the way things used to be. We have to go."

"What?" Maddy said, shocked. A burst of butterflies began fluttering everywhere in her stomach.

"There is one who is higher than us all," Jacks said.

"You mean . . . God?" Maddy asked.

Jacks smiled. "He has many names, Maddy. And it is time to go Home to him."

Maddy was silent. Stunned.

The Angels were leaving?

"Home?" Maddy said, still in shock. "Can you even do that?" She had heard rumblings of this place during her time with the Angels. It was where the Angels had come from. But the way people talked about it – or, really, *didn't* talk about it – it had just seemed like a nebulous, old-fashioned rumour among the flashy cars, paycheques, and parties of the Immortal City.

"I can't describe to you how I know we should go," Jackson said. "But I just know that this is the right thing to do right now."

Jackson's gaze drifted out the window at the city. His brow darkened.

"Mark and all the other Guardians who were killed . . . and even Tom – will they have just died in vain?" Jacks looked up at Maddy. "Our heroes can't have died just so we can go back to the way things were. Maddy, you're always talking about change. About getting out of here to do something bigger and more important. And now the time for all that has come."

The sun began to set outside, revealing a brilliant Immortal

325

City awash in the orange light of sundown. Beams of rich, reddened light streamed in through the diner windows.

"This is what my father, my birth father, would have wanted. And I think it's what Mark would've wanted, too, if he'd lived to see the end of the battle. It's what the Angels are now supposed to do. Gabriel was the one who led us out of hiding and into the public eye, and he turned out to be a traitor, leading us away from our destiny for the sake of his own greed."

Jackson pierced straight into Maddy's soul with his pale blue eyes. "We're going Home," he said.

It suddenly made sense to Maddy. Of course they were going to leave.

Yet she was still speechless as she tried to sort out all the conflicting emotions and questions that flowed through her body and mind. Jackson was . . . leaving? Along with all the other Angels? And with a bolt of shock she realized – wasn't she an Angel, too? What was Jackson trying to tell her . . . ?

"I've asked you to make these kinds of decisions before," Jackson said. "But this one's the most important, Mads. Once you'd made your choice, there's no going back." Time stopped for Maddy as she waited for what he was going to say next. "Will you come with us Home as one of the Immortals, or stay here on Earth?"

Maddy was overwhelmed. What did it even mean, going Home? She stammered, "I-I—"

"I don't need an answer this instant," Jacks said. "I wouldn't expect one. I can only imagine what you're feeling now, which is why I didn't want to have to spring it on you like this. But think very carefully about it, Maddy." He reached out and touched her hand. A flow of what felt like pure energy shocked between their fingertips, just like when they'd first met, just a few booths away. "I want to make sure you do what's best for you. But you do know what I hope you'll say. . ."

She was stunned. "I have so many questions, Jacks," she said. "About . . . everything. All of this." Their hands remained clasped, his steady and hers trembling.

"I know you weren't raised as an Angel, so the urgency here might not make sense to you," Jacks said. "But just know that Home is where we belong. It's where we can all be True Immortals, and do the most amount of good for the most amount of lives. For Angels and humans alike."

"But how can I make a decision like this?" Maddy asked. "Angel City is the only home I've ever known, Jacks. What would the Angel Home be to me?" Uncertainty ran across her face. "How would I know if I even belong there?"

"Look into yourself, and you'll find the answers," Jackson said. "The knowledge of Home is there already. It lives inside you. You just need to find it. You're an Angel, Maddy, in every sense of the word." Their fingers became intertwined, and a rush of feeling came over her as she thought back to their night together at the temple.

Maddy opened her mouth but closed it before she could speak. Jacks pulled himself closer to her.

"This wasn't my plan all along, Maddy," Jacks said. "I wasn't sure we were going to leave until earlier today. I don't want you to think that what happened between us that night . . ."

"Even if you had known, Jacks . . ." Maddy started. She blushed.

"I'm going to let you go," said Jacks, smiling and squeezing her hand. "You have some thinking to do." He stood up and leaned down to kiss her on the cheek.

And then the perfect Immortal was gone, the door to the diner jingling as he went through it.

Maddy couldn't tell how long she'd stayed in the diner after Jackson left. She became lost in thought, her mind trying to make sense of all that had just happened. She thought about what he was asking. To go away with him. For ever. To somewhere he couldn't even fully explain to her. To the place from which the Angels had come. To Home.

Suddenly, the front door jingled, and Kevin entered the diner, breaking Maddy's daze.

"Hey, Mads," he called, carrying some sacks into the kitchen. "I thought maybe I'd find you over here. I saw the light had been turned on."

Maddy smiled at him but didn't answer.

"I brought back some enchiladas from the shelter, if you're hungry. They're vegetarian."

"No, thanks, Kevin," she managed.

Kevin continued to talk as he walked into the kitchen, upping the volume of his voice so she could still hear him.

"Everyone was talking about your appearance with Linden at the shelter. What in the world is going on? Do you know?" Kevin came out of the kitchen and into the dining area. "Maddy, are you all right?"

"I'm fine, Kevin," Maddy said, trying to put on the best smile she could muster. "Just a little tired after all the excitement. I think I'm going to go back to the house."

What could she say to Kevin? That she had to decide whether or not to leave him and the humans, for ever? Maddy knew she was going to have to make this decision on her own, whether she liked it or not.

"All right, Maddy. Let me know if you need anything," said Kevin. He opened the front door for Maddy and watched her walk out.

Upstairs in her bedroom, Maddy looked out the window towards the hill that held the remnants of the Angel City sign. It had been battered and bruised, and was now barely readable. But one of the first things the relief crews had done was train a temporary spotlight on the sign. The gesture provided a symbol to the people – and the world – that the spirit of Immortal City could not be stifled. The light radiated across the Angel City basin, illuminating an exhausted, but not defeated, city. They might be kicked down, bruised, even shattered – but they had not been defeated.

Looking at the sign, Maddy suddenly knew where she needed to go. She pulled on her hoodie and her favourite jeans. She slipped down the stairs quietly and went out the back door.

Maddy could have walked to this place in her sleep: down from Franklin, then right at Angel Boulevard towards the Walk of Angels. How many times had she made this walk when she was just a student at ACHS, dreaming of college and getting out of Angel City?

Most of the damage had been done farther west, across Highland.

But still, the tourist shops here had yet to open up again, and most were boarded up or had their metal grates drawn down and locked with thick padlocks.

Maddy could see vague shapes moving behind a few grimy, darkened windows. She swiped away the dust on the outside of one of the windows and cupped her hand over the glass to look in.

Inside were all the souvenirs and tchotchkes you'd expect to see at your standard tourist store on Angel Boulevard. Something for every Angel fan in your family. There was the "My Wife Went to Angel City and All I Got Was This Stupid Mug" mug. The classic oversize "I Was Saved in Angel City" T-shirt, Immortal City snowglobes, costume Angel wings. And then she saw it – an action figure.

Of her.

The box read, MADISON GODRIGHT, GUARDIAN FIRST CLASS. WITH RETRACTABLE GLOWING WINGS! *BATTERIES NOT INCLUDED* NEW!!

Her action figure came dressed in a sexy Angel gown – a red-carpet look – but the box advertised that inside there was an "action" outfit that resembled the training suit she'd worn during Guardian school. The doll's wings were out, and they hadn't done a totally bad job of making their purple colour seem slightly translucent. They even looked like they glowed a bit.

Maddy was transfixed by the figure. She had seen an early mock-up of it, but not the finished product, because it came out right when her illegal save caused the huge scandal.

She thought of kids taking her figure home with them after a family vacation, looking to her as some kind of hero.

Maddy slowly backed away from the window. Her hand had made a clear print in the dusty glass. She turned and looked down the abandoned boulevard. There was no traffic; the street was still closed except to police and emergency vehicles. She walked into the empty street, stopping on the double yellow line in the middle at a portion that was cracked, probably from one of the earthquakes that had heralded the demon approach.

She looked both ways down the boulevard and tried to imagine an Angel City without Angels.

The night was quiet, the machines of the recovery effort at rest for the evening.

It was a short walk down the Walk of Angels, past the checkpoint on Highland and the battle monument. Past the Temple of Angels, too. Her pulse quickened as she thought of what had happened there. But that was not why she had come.

Her feet took her to the now-familiar spot of Tom's memorial. His leather jacket still lay there below his picture.

Maddy had always thought it was kind of silly when people talked to tombstones; she remembered from her AP English class that it was called apostrophe when somebody did that in a book or poem – but right now she was going to stop her scoffing. She looked at the picture, the jacket, the flowers, the candles. She found herself, desperately, moved to speak.

"Talk to me, Tom. What should I do? What's the best thing for me? Please tell me. You must have some insight there, where you are. . ."

Just a few yards away she saw a small child with a teenage girl. The child was lighting a candle and weeping before a picture of a couple, most likely their lost parents. Maddy's heart panged for them.

The girl turned and looked at Maddy. Her face looked beautiful lit up by the candle. Tears streamed down her face.

The teen and the child exchanged a few hushed words before cautiously approaching Maddy.

"I'm sorry for bothering you, Maddy. But my brother and I just wanted to say thank you," the girl said. "I'm so sorry about your friend. I saw it on the news. But it means a lot to us that you Angels know what we're going through, too. And that you'll be working with the president to help."

"This is for you," the small boy said. "You can use it for your friend. My mom and dad already have one." He handed Maddy the candle.

"Thank you," Maddy said, flooded with feeling. "Truly." She waved through tears as the boy and his sister walked away down the boulevard.

Maddy arranged to meet Jackson at the sea. Just west of Santa Monica, near the state park, the area hadn't suffered any destruction. Tall, stony bluffs rose up from the sea as the waves rolled in against the rocks, sending fine sea spray up into the air. She wanted to clear her head, outside of Angel City.

She arrived there early, and found that hers was the only car in the parking lot. Wisps of sand swirled along the asphalt in the breeze. Maddy walked to the wooden fence that stood above the waves, and then looked out upon the gorgeous emerald and blue Pacific Ocean.

She heard the thrum of a powerful engine behind her, and then Maddy saw the telltale headlights of Jackson's black Ferrari as it whipped into the parking lot. Some things never changed, she guessed.

He stepped out of the car and walked towards her.

"Hi," Jacks said. He leaned in, and before she knew it they were kissing there, beneath the palisades of stone and above the water. After a moment, Maddy pulled away but still stood close to him. She looked out into the ocean, where the sinkhole once had been. Nothing remained of it now; millions of gallons of ocean had just filled it in. It was as if it had never been there.

"It all seems too real now," Maddy said after a time. "What happened. We'll never be the same."

"I don't want to be the same," Jacks said.

"I wanted to see it today." She motioned out to the ocean. It shimmered under a soft golden halo as the sun began to drop along the horizon. "I wanted to see it in the full light. Not under the influence of them . . ." Her mind shivered as she recalled the image of the demons invading the sky, spreading darkness, violence, death. Spilling like ink across the Immortal City from the ocean and staining everything with their evil as they attacked.

Jacks waited to let her speak. He knew her enough to know she would do so in her own time.

"Jackson, you are wonderful," Maddy said. "You are everything and anything I could expect a man, or Angel, to be. What happened in the Temple of Angels the other night, Jacks, was beautiful," Maddy said. "I can't even describe it. It was one of the most beautiful things to ever happen in my life. To us." She looked at him. "I will treasure it for ever."

Jacks took in a breath, waiting for the *but*.

It didn't come. But he knew what Maddy was about to say.

"You were always stubborn," Jackson said, with the beginnings of a wistful smile on his face. "You do understand what you're giving up if you make the choice I think . . . I *know* . . . you're making?" There was no anger in his voice, but it was clear that the last thing he wanted was to part from Maddy.

Maddy nodded, fully accepting the gravity of her choice. "Yes. I understand. But, Jacks, I can't go with you. I belong here. I have good to do here, in Angel City."

The waves below them rolled in, sea foam boiling up along the rocks and running back out.

"Is it because of . . . him?" Jacks asked quietly.

She looked out at the Pacific Ocean, thinking of Tom. "Maybe, partly. I can't just leave his memory, Jackson. I'll somehow be tied to it for ever. It's a part of me now, just like you are."

Maddy turned away from the glittering sea and looked back towards the Immortal City.

"This city needs me, Jacks. And maybe I need it," said Maddy. "It's funny, I'd always dreamt of leaving. Just wanted to get away. It didn't matter where, just not AC. But now I can't imagine being anywhere else." She looked at Jacks. "I'm from this world. Angel City is *my* home.

"President Linden has given me a chance to do good. To help the rebirth, starting from the ground up. And to help rebuild the people, too." Maddy turned and looked back at Jacks, and then her eyes met the ground at her feet. She looked up again. "They might need me. And I need them."

For once, Jacks didn't try to argue or fight. He just nodded.

"I understand, Maddy."

"You do?" Maddy had expected a different response. But she had forgotten that she wasn't the only one who had changed.

"Yes," Jacks said. A sadness weighed in his heart.

"I love you, Jacks," Maddy said, the same sadness filling her body and soul. "And I'm sorry. But I can't go."

CHAPTER 40

The occasion would be marked in the annals of Angel history as the last televised appearance of an Immortal. Rather than rolling out the normal fanfare – the bleachers of screaming fans, limousines, red-carpet interviews, security personnel, sports cars screeching to a stop in front of ballrooms, black sunglasses, black earpieces, frantic publicists, spotlights knifing into the sky, gifting suites, big forced smiles, fawning Botoxed reporters, surging masses of paparazzi and, above all, the perfect Angels themselves, donning designer dresses and suits, waving to the crowds, endorsing products, plugging their reality TV shows, hiding their drug use – there was simply the calm backdrop of the beautiful green park in the Angel City Hills. Jackson's mother, Kris, and his sister, Chloe, stood beside him, along with dozens of other Angels and Archangels. Archangel Susan Archson was there, standing next to David Sylvester, formerly known as Detective David Sylvester of the ACPD until his formal resignation the day before.

Jackson Godspeed stepped forward. Before he began speaking, he glanced quickly over at Maddy, who stood off to the side, separate from the main group of Angels. Jacks had asked her if she could be there for the occasion.

"I am speaking for Angelkind throughout the world today, with one voice," Jackson boomed through the microphone. "Gabriel and the Council brought the Angels out of hiding after America's Civil War because he didn't have faith in humanity to stop its bloodshed. He'd watched and judged humankind, and ruled that they were condemned to a relentless cycle of war. But he didn't have the right to judge. Or condemn. And from this fatal trespass, the NAS was born. My father fought against this. And I ended up fighting it, too, even though it was almost too late when I finally woke up.

"I'm not an Angel who thinks that we should never have come out of hiding. If you talk to most scholars of the Book of Angels, it was written that we would ultimately come to Earth as Guardians, so that humans could see that we truly exist. But it was never written that we would take part in humanity in the way that we have. Guardianship became twisted beyond its original purpose. And then we reached the crisis.

"But against all the corruption and betrayal, there were many Angels who ultimately stood up as the dark days of the demons came. These Angels are heroes.

"Archangel Mark Godspeed, someone I'm proud to call Dad, was one of those Angels. He sacrificed his life for the true Angel ideal, which, deep down, all of us wanted to follow all along. We knew we should be following it, but we didn't know how. Not until it was almost too late. But it wasn't too late.

"I was able to become a true Guardian. All of us who took part in the Battle of Angel City were. It is the greatest gift that humanity has given us. When Gabriel fell, we were able to really see what we had become after the Awakening, after decades of Protection for Pay. It was like a veil had been ripped from our eyes.

337

And suddenly, our true, original Angelic natures were returned to us. Our nature is one of service and love for humanity. It's not tied to money, greed, or celebrity. Our true nature is selfless. Full of unconditional love.

"I believe that the reason we came and made ourselves visible almost a hundred and fifty years ago was to learn this lesson from you. We were supposed to protect humanity, but humanity ultimately protected us from ourselves.

"And now we have to leave. But please know that we will not be leaving *you*. We will no longer be visible, but that does not mean we will be absent. Miracles will occur, the old-fashioned way. The Angels will be present in the lives of humans, but as invisible helpers only. And not because we are being paid. But because we must help. *Everyone*." His eyes sparkled. "The way it was meant to be."

He looked directly at the camera as his speech came to a close.

"Thank you. I speak for all Angels here today when I say it has been an honour and privilege living among you in the Immortal City. Thank you. And goodbye."

The few photographers allowed at the event quietly took pictures as Jackson took a few steps back into the group of Angels, who were already starting to disperse.

Although President Linden hadn't attended the event, he had publicly stated his disappointment that the Angels would be leaving so soon after coming under the leadership of "someone we can believe in – Jackson Godspeed," but knew that this was best for everyone, both Angels and humans.

A balance could now be restored, one that had existed for millennia but had been overturned during the Great Awakening.

A public outpouring of gratitude for the Angels had spread throughout the world. But there wouldn't be a series of hours-long specials covering every aspect of the Angels' lives as they got ready to go Home. They were leaving, quietly and humbly. The world mourned.

Several Angels approached Jackson after his speech. Now that he was taking them Home, he had become quite in demand among all the other Immortals. He was still getting used to it, but he was handling it well. He looked over at Maddy and gave her a *what can you do?* smile, which told her he'd catch up with her when he was able.

Archangel Archson and David Sylvester emerged from the crowd and approached Maddy.

Susan gave her a big, long hug.

"It's so good to see you," her teacher said. "And I'm glad you could make it for this. To see the Angels before . . . well, you know."

"Of course. I wanted to be here for Jacks. And for all the Angels." Maddy looked around and noticed there were a couple of conspicuous faces missing. "But what about the others?" Maddy asked. "Like *you-know-who*, my old Australian friend?"

Susan explained that not all the Angels were ready and willing to go Home. During the battle, Archangel Churchson and several Guardians, including the redheaded Emily Brightchurch, had absconded from the sanctuary and were still missing.

"They probably don't realize it yet, but they will be called Home," Susan said. "Whether they want to be or not. Judgement will be fair but swift."

Maddy's mind swirled with what that would even mean.

"Detective Sylvester, you're going with them?" Maddy asked.

She hadn't seen him since the final morning of the battle, when he had helped Jackson topple Gabriel.

"Yes, Madison, I am," he said. "And it's just David now. I'm no longer with the force."

"It's where he belongs," Susan said. "With us. No matter what he may have thought about himself for so many years."

Maddy felt conflicted, a bit guilty, when Susan said *where he belongs*.

"I meant nothing by that, Maddy," Susan said. "I think what you're doing is so incredibly brave. Maybe a bit stubborn." Susan smiled a bit and searched Maddy's eyes with hers. "But ultimately right. The humans still need heroes. And you can be their first one in the post-Angel age, as the Immortal City rebuilds."

"The people of Angel City already have a real hero," Maddy said. "They will always remember Jackson Godspeed. For ever."

"They know what you did, too, Maddy," Susan said. "And the things you will do, I'm sure. You are, after all, going to be special counsel."

Maddy blushed at the mention of the title, which was still taking her a bit to get used to.

"Darcy has been calling like crazy," Maddy said. "She wants to book my appearances as 'the Face of the New Immortal City'."

Susan laughed. "Some things will never change, no matter how much the rest of the world does."

"I should probably call her back and tell her she's going to need a new job," Maddy said.

Maddy looked over and saw Jackson across the milling group of Angels.

"Would you two excuse me for a second?" Maddy said.

Jacks was talking to an older Angel, who seemed to have some pressing matter to discuss. It was clear that Jacks was distracted and was looking for a polite way to get out of it.

Maddy stepped up. "Excuse me, I'm so sorry to interrupt." She turned to Jacks. "Jackson, I have an important question."

"I'm sorry, Archangel, but we'll have to continue this conversation later, I have some pressing business with the special counsel," Jacks said.

He took Maddy's arm and led her away.

"Thanks for getting me out of that," Jacks said. "Archangel Holyfield wouldn't stop blabbering."

Maddy smiled. "Special counsel." She shook her head.

They walked off to the sidelines of the crowd, where no one would bother them. They had a view of the park in the Hills just above them.

"Are you ready? To leave?"

Jackson smiled at her. "I think we are."

Maddy noticed how often Jacks said "we" now when talking about himself and the Angels. She wondered how many leaders did that.

"How does it . . . work? Your big departure . . ." Maddy felt again like the clueless waitress, being introduced to all things Angel for the first time. Even basic things that most normal humans already knew. Except this wasn't known to anyone.

Jackson smiled, his eyes glinting.

"It's simple. When the world wakes up tomorrow," Jacks said, "we won't be here. Some things are better left as mysteries, Maddy."

He seemed . . . happy to Maddy. Better than the embittered Jackson, his wing injured and out of the spotlight. Better, too, than the self-centred playboy zipping around the Halo Strip in his Ferrari.

Jackson had found his destiny.

It suited him well.

Beyond the light screen of trees, farther down the hill, Maddy saw the rest of the Angels walking to their waiting cars.

"You should probably get going," Maddy said. Her heart was racing, and she was practically breathless.

Jacks looked down towards the departing Angels. "I probably should."

But neither of them wanted to say it. The final parting words. They lingered for a few more moments.

At last, Maddy spoke.

"Goodbye, Jackson," Maddy said.

"Maddy," Jacks said. "I will always be with you." He put his hand up to her cheek and rubbed away a tear with his thumb.

His famous pale blue eyes sparkled, the way they had when he first started winning her heart, bit by bit. He was still the perfectly handsome Angel who had swept her off her feet, after all, even if he had changed so much during the course of the demon war.

"I have to go now, Maddy," Jackson said. He gave her a bittersweet smile. "No regrets."

"Jacks . . ." But there was nothing left to say.

Jackson leaned down and gently pulled Maddy close to him. He pressed his lips to hers, and she felt the same blissful shock that had jolted through her the first time he touched her hand in the diner. For just that moment, nothing in the world existed except their kiss, their beings fused. Their entire history born into this act. Anything that ever needed to be said, or could be said, was said at that moment, silently, through the kiss.

Jackson pulled back.

"Goodbye, Maddy."

CHAPTER 41

M addy sipped from her cup of tea, steam rolling up and out of the brown mug as she placed it back down on the table and sank into the comfortable booth of Kevin's Diner. Outside, plentiful sunshine poured down on the palm trees, and from where Maddy was sitting, she could almost pretend the Battle of Angel City had never happened. One day, it would all look like this again.

Kevin's Diner was doing brisk business again after its grand reopening. Chatting customers filled the tables and booths, drinking coffee and tucking into plates of blueberry pie and triple-decker club sandwiches.

Maddy watched as the new girl, Sophie, rushed plates of hot food around to the customers. Kevin kept complaining that poor Sophie was hopeless, that she didn't know her ham omelettes from her hamburgers, and that she still couldn't remember what was in a Maddy Special, but Maddy knew that her uncle had a soft spot for the new waitress. He did sometimes proclaim from the back of the kitchen that Maddy could "never be replaced," which was usually followed by a no-strings-attached offer for Maddy to come back and wait tables anytime she wanted. He knew she had a new job, though. She had a city to help rebuild.

Jackson and the Angels had departed. Just as Jacks had promised, when Maddy woke up the next morning, they were gone. There were competing stories around the city, traded in cafés and bars, about how they had left. Some claimed they had seen a blinding white light at dawn that overtook the city. Others claimed that the Angels had wandered out into the desert. And some especially fringe conspiracy theorists insisted that they were on a UFO with Elvis and Steve Jobs. To Maddy the "how" didn't matter. And yet, they – and Jackson – were gone, regardless.

Taking another sip of tea, Maddy looked out at the hill beyond the gleaming window of Kevin's Diner, up to where the Angel City sign used to be.

The Angel City sign hadn't been so fortunate during the demon battle. A demon had crashed through the *A* and the *N*, setting the remaining *G*, *E*, and *L* on fire. They had been charred on the hill above the city. And shrapnel from an exploded bomb had sliced the *I* and *T* in "City" right down the middle.

They'd taken down the destroyed sign, leaving what looked to Maddy like an open wound. It was the sign that signified you were in the great Immortal City. But the Angels were gone. It was no longer "Angel City."

After the crews had taken the sign down, the city officials found themselves asking, "What did this place used to be called again?"

They had to dig out some dusty books from the stacks of the Ventura County Library, but eventually they found the information they were looking for.

The workers were putting up the new letters, one by one. Luckily the two names held the same number of letters, so it wasn't going to be too extensive of a job. The city officials had bigger things to worry about. But the people felt it was important to start fresh, and Maddy agreed with them. The people would never forget the Angels, but they needed to think of themselves now.

The city workers up on the hill had already gotten most of the letters up. They shined bright and clear in the sunshine of a beautiful day: H O L L Y W O

"Hollywood." Maddy tried saying it aloud. It sounded strange. Didn't really have the same ring as "Angel City". But she guessed she could get used to it. She'd have to. They all would.

Her senses became sharpened as she shifted slightly in the vinyl of the booth, the sun reflecting off the plate-glass window of the diner, sending a shaft of light across her hands and the cup of tea in front of her.

Maddy's phone beeped, and she pulled it out of her bag. It was a text from Gwen, the best friend she'd reconnected with after the battle.

The text read: Here are the pics from last night. but something must be wrong with my camera. check it out.

The phone beeped as a few photos came in. They were pictures Gwen had taken when they were just messing around at the diner the night before. There was Uncle Kevin in his apron, smiling. A picture of Gwen that Maddy had taken. And then Maddy saw what Gwen was talking about in her text. In all the pictures of Maddy, there was a strange blue light glowing around her.

Maddy zoomed in on the photos and focused on the glow. It was somehow very familiar. Why wasn't the light around Gwen or Uncle Kevin in the pictures?

Practically in a trance, she quickly opened up Instagram and looked at some other photos of herself that had been taken on different cameras.

In each one, she was haloed by the strange blue tinge.

And then she knew how it was familiar. It was the same colour of Jackson's famous wings.

Maddy looked at the photos of herself and then around the diner for something she knew she would never be able to see with the naked eye. She felt something deep inside her. It was a sensation she'd never experienced before. She could feel a presence. Right there, next to her.

"Jacks," Maddy said, tears spilling from her eyes.

ACKNOWLEDGEMENTS

Immortal City has been such an amazing journey over the last four years. I am so grateful to everyone involved. Those who encouraged, those who opened doors, those who worked side-by-side with me, and most of all, the amazing fans that welcomed Maddy and Jacks into their hearts. The acknowledgements for book 3 are a bit of a curtain call, so I apologize in advance. Thanks to both my amazing editors, Laura and Liz, my agents Claudia and Simon, and my team at PPY, Allen, Brian and Susan. Thanks to my publicist at Penguin, Elyse, the entire team at Razorbill, and the supportive folks at Penguin Young Readers Group. Thanks for the Tweets! Brian, thank you. Thanks to my parents Brad and Janet, my sister Julia and brother-in-law Bill. And Mike, thanks for the tech consulting. Oh, and thanks to little Frankie, who isn't so little anymore. Drew, Desmond, Mike, guys, thank you. Both Mrs Nelson's Toy and Book Shop and Once Upon a Time bookstore have been relentless supporters; thank you guys for always having me in!